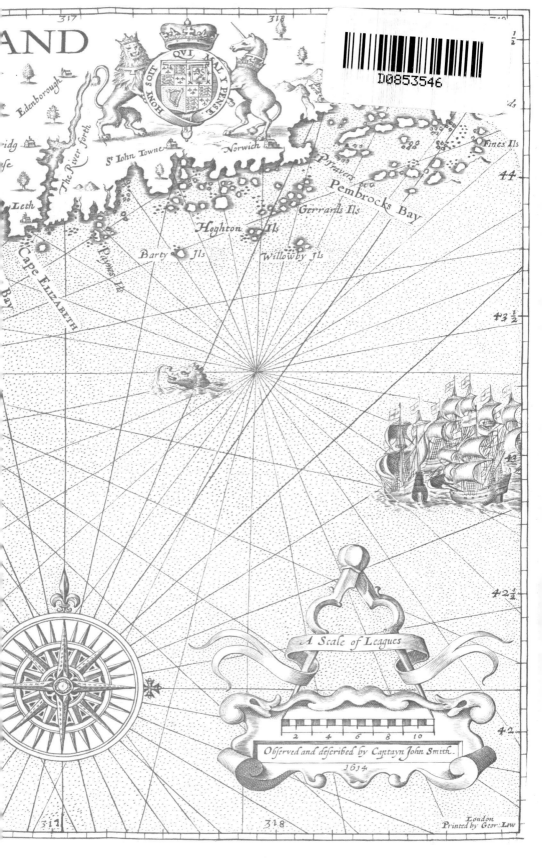

The LEAVES *of* FATE

In the Land of Whispers

BOOK THREE

The LEAVES *of* FATE

a novel by

GEORGE ROBERT MINKOFF

McPherson & Company

For Nancy,
Yet again...again

Published by McPherson & Company
Post Office Box 1126, Kingston, New York 12402
www.mcphersonco.com
Manufactured in the United States of America
DESIGN BY BRUCE R. MCPHERSON. TYPESET IN GARAMOND
FIRST EDITION
1 3 5 7 9 10 8 6 4 2 2011 2012 2013 2014

Library of Congress Cataloging-in-Publication Data

Minkoff, George Robert.
    The leaves of fate : a novel / by George Robert Minkoff. — 1st ed.
      p. cm. — (In the land of whispers; bk. 3)
    Sequel to: The dragons of the storm.
    ISBN 978-0-929701-82-0 (alk. paper)
    1. Smith, John, 1580-1631—Fiction. 2. Virginia—History—Colonial period, ca.
    1600-1775—Fiction. 3. Jamestown (Va.)--History—17th century—Fiction. I. Title.
    PS3613.I64L43 2010
    813'.6—dc22

                                            2010036619

Publication of this book has been made possible,
in part, by a grant from the Literature Program
of the New York State Council on the Arts, a state agency.

Endsheet map: New England, drawn by Simon van der Passe from Smith's 1614 explorations, for
Generall History of Virginia, 1624, by John Smith, courtesy of The New York Public Library.

One hundred copies of the first printing have been specially bound,
numbered, and signed by the author.

How all occasions do inform against me...

HAMLET, ACT 4. SCENE 4

PART ONE

Angels in Their Silent Gather

THE ALCHEMIES OF THE RIVER

Shadows float through me on their wisps of blood. In salted storms, in bleeding clouds their currents swirl. A flesh of vapors dissolves. I hear new words. Constantly now. No longer as fleeting leaves. There are men of new silhouettes. The light drowns. The moon bears a strange glow. The life through me craves in an ancient hunger, as I am born into a new forgetfulness.

Chapter One

LOVE BY TOOTH AND FIRE.

BY WHAT CONSEQUENCE am I foretold! Death now my company, I sat alone. The old mariner stiffened in his decay, worms soon his alchemies. What magics to digest his course? His clock has sprung the winding spring, the phantom pendulum now swings confined in its ghostly orbit. Who guides you now, my mariner? Which demon, ship or seer shall map thy journeys through the air? What haunted wind to bloom a specter's sail? Your rumored boat to heel upon a rumored sea. By what nothing do you blank in this your final passage? Presume the wind, old friend, its motion is the soul. All directions are its gate.

I, the exile, had returned alone to feast my desolations into quest. In the distance, through canticles of air, the birds flew in darkening sheets of pantomime. Blanket me in feathers now — your light wanders in shadows upon the earth. Be at my feet and squabble crumbs. War thimbles on your beaks. Am I that castaway to think in masquerades? For in the woods the tribes might call me son. I, the heir of voices; I am a *werowance*, the voices still sound for me. Oh, Pocahontas, my forest love, what adoptions were in your glance? Should I flee to you? I, alone, now less a danger to your father. Would he rather give me a little food, or a little taste of death? All our plagues are in the choice. What lethals seat in my love's caress? Shall I rise now and seek that bliss in some parting from myself? Into what tombs my rebirth; into what mortuaries am I reborn?

I was about to stand. A darkness at my side, I turned. Above me stood the ruins of a man, his beard half balding on his cheek, his skull against the tight drums of his skin. What skeleton this, that walks its rattles upon my earth? His eyes had sunken into bony caves. His clothes fell in threads down the hollows of his chest. Both of his thumbs were missing. At their lower joints were nubs and shards and splinters of broken bones protruding through the scarlet of raw flesh. He sat at my side, stared into the bay. The sky hissed its gloom through the serpents of its rolling clouds. "You goin' to have a chew?" he said. "Got a barrel…for the proper curin'." At first I did not understand his words. "Not yet fresh gray, tight boned…shame it's an ancient gristle of not much meat," the man repeated, almost annoyed, directing his boot toward the dead mariner.

The day was warm. The man shivered in his strange excitements. He stroked the old mariner's hair, pinched his arm. He smiled, his scurvy gums bleeding down the spaces between his teeth. His mouth smelled of death. "A two-day kill brings its own spice. We could stew a mite with rabbit for the savor."

The wind ran its teeth across my face, hinting at the reek of putrefying flesh. The man spoke. "I got salt. I'll do most the work if I get a bit…none's to waste…worth its weight." Enticing me, he moiled in his own thin laugh. I looked into the claw of his face, the stubble on his cheek, its wreck, the bald spots of his beard. Behind the desperate pulls of leathered skin was an apparent face, so familiar in drift that I searched it for a recognition. "You're John Laydon. You married Anne Burras, Mistress Forrest's servant. I'm Smith. I'm Captain Smith."

The man buried his face in his hands and wept, his tears sliding in drops to the wounds of his missing thumbs. "You never would have done…what Percy done." Around me contagion beckoned.

"Hung me by my thumbs, he did," John Laydon nodding to his own witness, "putting weights on my feet, till my thumbs broke loose my hands. The ground came to me. I ran…they too weak and lazy to follow." The man hysterical in remembrance now. "I ran into the forest, rubbed dirt into the wounds. Mud stops the oozy. I ate birds raw and rats, dug roots. Vermin made in fleshy cakes. Rot sweets the meat." The man giggled, his hands to his mouth, holding to his lips a thought. "Percy…cruel…in jealousies tore me hurt." Laydon laughed. "Me, the apostle, me that made conclusions. Percy could not eat his jealousies so he spiced his angers upon my thumbs. The food was gone, we victualed on the horses, ate the hogs. The savages murdered us in the woods, killed our mares. We cooked our dead horses. War came upon us in its fists. For war better provides the meat. I ate the dead savages, buttered them on my fires cured with salt and bubbled on the heat. No one ate but me in secret, and envious Percy waited his time to strike. All were boned and starved and me still fit. Dead flesh is stale. Fresh ripens for a better fit. All goodness to the blood. It is a slander to say killing those that are to die is murder. It be said love sweet tongues its sweetest meats, then why not heat it with a little fire? My wife blessed me when I struck her dead. By God our flesh now better joined. I cut the child from her womb. To eat oneself is a cannibal and doubly cursed. No heaven on that stew. I gave the child to the river as a royal gift. Percy hung me to confess, but I still live. No more cannibal than saint. I did my right."

There was a silence for a time. All I had sacrificed had come to this. I thought to the pistol at my side. I could kill him, have some peace. I looked to John Laydon. He was mad. Madness cradles a cruel comfort. Behind the mask, the deeper mask cracks in sorrow. Laydon spoke again, his chin thrust forward, his own blood upon his lips. The words then came in secret deaths "I am alive and yet you accuse me with your eyes." John Laydon licked the blood from his lips. "I have fed upon the apple of my own blood. I have healed myself. I have eaten of my own. What foods make your cure, John Smith? Do you not think men would eat their brains, had they the reach?" He looked at me. "Who has not eaten of his own forbidden fruit? Each man thrills that orchard through his spine to the chilled excitements of his brain. What shell the skull that lusts to its own forbidden meat?" Layden smiled to a violence seeping beneath his stare. "All dead but me, and you accuse and look away. I have tasted of salvations, pierced myself in flames and resurrections, and you were not what you supposed. At best, you were ignored. While you lay wounded, Martin and Percy sought vengeance by murder on the savages and were you told? Were you? You filled your books with halves, and you confess to what? Another book. How cracks your hollow wafer now?"

Laydon, a smile upon his blood-rouged lips, parceled his tale. Martin, flexed in anger, marched his men by stumble overland. "Sneaked they did," by Laydon's account. At Nansemond, they sent two messengers to the savages with greetings and words that they wished to buy a small island off the main, offering copper and hatchets to pleasure any trade. The messengers not having returned, the company waited. "Martin, eaten on a coward's panic, he was, sent men to seize the island by force. On their way, seeing some savage in a canoe, the soup not salted yet, we asked after the missing two. The savage fled, saying they were dead, their heads cut off, their brains beaten out and scraped from their skulls with mussel shells. The savages made an oyster's bloody porridge, it is said." Laydon now danced the story as he sat, swaying back and forth. What license madness brings when we loosen the chains of all restraints.

The company now anointed itself right and wholly just. Martin and Percy came upon the savages with war, burning their village, stealing the pearls and copper bracelets from the mummied corpses of their long-dead kings. They destroyed their tombs and threw their ancient bodies in the fire. Smoke to dust and smoke, all their ancient death now gone. The walled village they kept as their fort, reinforcing the *palisado* with fresh logs.

Percy returning to Jamestown, reporting all was well, but for some small assaults. Martin following in a few days with talk of war. Seventeen starving fled in a stolen boat to Kecoughtan, pretending to come in trade. All were murdered. Lieutenant Sicklemore and those who remained at Nansemond were found dead, their mouths stuffed with trading beads, their bodies butchered in contempt. "All this while Martin and Archer and Ratcliffe still conspired for your death, and you and your mariner gone."

Percy, made president, sent Ratcliffe to build a fort at Point Comfort. Soon after, Captain West abandoned the settlement at the falls and returned, his men mostly dead or dying of starvation and fevers. Captain Daniel Tucker was appointed to calculate and divide the stores, which amounted to half a cup of meal a day a man. These starvation victuals to last three months, the company made last four. This disaster down their throats, there being no hope of resupply from England before the spring. It was now November. Percy requested Captain Ratcliffe to sail to a meeting with Powhatan at Werowocomoco and have commerce with him and trade for corn. Ratcliffe ventured some fifty in a pinnace, accompanied by a boy and a girl Percy believed to be Powhatan's son and daughter, "although I thought they were but common savages. They being sent as hostages to keep Powhatan at peace, Ratcliffe having his thoughts on the girl for other matters." Laydon licked his crusted lips.

Powhatan received Ratcliffe and his men with all the grand gestures of a peace. And so the savages fight their wars by stealth, their armor wrapped in corn and furs. Ratcliffe, to show himself great, released his hostages. Captain Fettiplace and his few, Laydon among them, were to stay with the pinnace, while Ratcliffe and thirty-six walked through the cool, resisting waters to the shore. Into the village Ratcliffe and his company swept in thoughts of hunger and its greeds, running to the savage huts, tearing at the furs hanging in the doorways, searching for food. Their weapons forgotten or left or stolen. Screams soon in muffled conquests. Ratcliffe, realizing too late his danger, called his men to stand as one. The few still living answered, stumbling to his side, unarmed.

"Taste blood and awaken, eat the drips upon the claws of war and savor then the eggs of slaughter." Laydon's eyes now wild. "Ratcliffe was taken alive as prisoner, bound naked to a tree, a great fire lit before him. The women of the tribe carved away his skin with mussel shells, scraping the slabs of meat to the bone, white, and glazed blood beneath the butchery. Ratcliffe still living, they threw his pieces into the fire before his eyes. Then, tied to a tree, bleeding in fountains, the savages burned him as a torch, the flames rising all around as his cloak."

He who once said that God was flesh had died a death befitting of himself, I mused.

"Only one escaped to the pinnace. There, with William Fettiplace, they held back the assaults of the savages, returning then to Jamestown with the bitter news. No victuals brought back. We could have had trade for Ratcliffe's shoes. That sweet leather is not so base.

"Although defeated, our chance at vengeance kept its dish for another time. So weak we were, our angers lazy. Our stomachs pained, our thoughts upon ourselves and our own relief. Pain and pleasure are the only eye the Cyclops hunger knows."

John Laydon giggled in a passing smirk to death. His skin so tight to his bones, it seemed a frozen stone sculptured to his face. Again his tale he spoke. "We all moved through a haze of madness. Those we thought healthy by daylight died by night. Death so common, the living seemed the fraud. My wife giving her life to me. Her salted bits of meat her gift, her love, salted in its wooden barrel. Men turn beast and wild when they starve. Percy then mad. I danced on the end of ropes by my broken thumbs for his cruelty. I fled into the woods, stole the dead at night. By day men cried and denied their God, driven mad by suffering. They ran to the savages but I was always true and kept the Sabbath in the woods.

"The weather warmed. Of the five hundred only some sixty now breathed at Jamestown. The company so weak and lazy I could in daylight steal to the open gates and hear the news. Captain Tucker was building a large boat with his own hands, and with some little help from the colony.

"No one had been to Point Comfort for months. Such was the trial of our indulgence, no communication from that fort and none we sent. Men sat and died while I labored greasy fingers at my feasts. Percy went to organize an expedition against the savages who had murdered ours on the Nansemond River. It was guessed that the silence from Point Comfort meant they too were starving, or had butchered each other over crumbs. But on arriving, Percy found a healthy colony, well fed, with foods in such plenties they fed their dogs with the victuals from their stores. They lived on oysters and fish and what fowl they could shoot. Percy, seeing men fat, raged, calling down treason on their heads, to let Jamestown starve while they had sufficient for tenfold their number.

"Men wallowed in fat, their belts tied hard against their girth, which oozed in sacks to the cover of their waists. Percy would have had all their heads, but ate his fill, promising to bring half of Jamestown to Point Comfort by next tide.

"As plans were made for his departure, two sails in soiled gray grimed the scene, patched in weathered tatters. Two boats, open pinnaces. Foolish men, fearing a Spanish fleet, took to their weapons. The boats approached, white wake, the bow pushed waters. A lover's slight of hand, the water parting as an open slice, a voice from its deck came, saying, 'The lost have returned.' It was Sir Thomas Gates, Sir George Somers, Captain Newport and their company, presumed drowned in the hurricane's wild flung swells. After ten months of shipwreck in Bermuda, they had built two boats and made the Chesapeake. A hundred new colonists to the feast. By next tide they came to Jamestown. I climbed a tree to better vantage Gates's face at the sight of our ruin. Everywhere the smell of death, a hollow wreck, the town's wooden boards drummed to hanging fragments.

"Men knelt and prayed. Bread was baked. Now a little food. I watched from the corners and heard the words: the colony was to be abandoned. Stores put aside and packed on the boats. They would sail for England.

"Jamestown was to be burned, but at the last the fort was reprieved. 'Let it be a sanctuary for any goodly men as we who chance this way in need,' said Gates. And so by wind they left, not hours before you arrived."

Broken in speech, I looked at John Laydon. The vistas of my world had come to this. But trumpets sometimes call their fanfares into sight, their sound too whispered to raise the ear. The soft curve of the horizon now transfixed in sails. A fleet of ships bearing where I stood. My eyes teared, my mouth tasting rescue. Bloom your fabrics, resurrect the tatters of my dream. John Laydon stood, stepping back from the water's edge toward the ruined fort and the forest. The ships making toward the shore, Laydon moved further into the cape of his own darkness, walking toward the fort, repelled by the rescue that was not his. He disappeared, running toward the forest as if fleeing into his own ghost. I never saw him again. Whether he died by savages or starvation, or if he still lives, the question marked! For what his self-made tale? Laydon now orphaned to the air, a path to wayward memories, a course to words.

Trumpets called from the ships to the empty fort, flags waving, banners of noble houses—the crests, the heraldries of England had come to this beach, and I, dressed in deerskin clothes, stood by a corpse, my only herald, the only armor for my cause. I waited. Hundreds to the deck, new colonists and three pinnaces with the survivors of Jamestown. The world is a slip to befuddle the wise. Lord De la Warr's fleet had met the pinnace of Gates and Somers and Newport in the Chesapeake Bay before they ever made the open sea. So simple the conspiracies of fate, and to such wide effect. He brought them back.

The ships tethered to the beach, ropes tied to the trees, our simple dock. Wooden planks laid down so his lordship could walk unsoiled upon the land. How many flags to address the wind? Trumpets lacing calls in proud announcements. Swords and polished brass, silks shining like armor fabric. His marshals by his side, Lord De la Warr walked to the beach and knelt, praying among the splendor of his flags. Those flags rising above him in the spires of their heraldries, their eagles turned on vaulted wings, and cherubs sang pink through wind-puffed cheeks.

LORD DE LA WARR STOOD AND WALKED TO ME. BY HIS SIDE, PERCY and Captain Argall, whom I had not seen since August last when his ships came by a shorter northern route to the Chesapeake. Argall still seemed to me my twin, same beard and face, but better dressed and of somewhat larger size. He nodded to me a distant welcome. Lord De la Warr, inspired of his station, calm, feeling all eyes upon him, he looked at me a look of vague surprise.

Angels in Their Silent Gather 15

"Heathen or gentleman?" he asked.

"Captain Smith," replied Lord Percy.

"Ah, yes." Lord De la Warr motioned with this hand, the procession to continue and I to follow, included in the group. Percy cleared his throat to gain some attention of his lordship, who in stately disregard walked on toward the fort. The two hundred colonists in a wandering mass gathered behind the banners of the parade. They stepped over the mariner in his seated death. As we walked, his lordship asked, "And who's your friend, the dead one on the beach?"

"Jonas Profit, an old mariner, loyal to our cause, rounded the world with Drake," I said.

"Oh, didn't everyone?" smiled his lordship. "Seafarers have always made an easy entertainment of the truth."

THROUGH THE BROKEN GATES OF THE FORT, ITS SPRUNG HINGES, ITS rude wrecked planks cast aside, we in fetid squabble pushed along the narrow streets, the thatched roofs of collapsed dwellings, sunken into an empty dark. The road strewn with fresh debris, a vacancy confettied by neglect. At the church, a hovel now, water ran along the trough of the slaughtered roof, walls pitched inwards, staggering on their rotten pins. Before the place his lordship faced the crowd. Pastor Buck, our new minister, gave a sermon, thanking the lord on this tenth day of June, 1610, his eyes upon his employer, Sir Thomas Gates. All those sentiments to efface the dread. Anthony Scott, cousin to Samuel Argall, read Lord De la Warr's commission from the king, and the new charter also voiced. The colony now no longer the king's, but a private enterprise, separate from his sovereign rule, but governed at his bequest by others made regent through his divine authority. The new governor having all power to make and change laws, directions, instructions, forms and ceremonies of government; appoint any and all to the offices he created; to abrogate, revoke or change whatever was necessary within the precincts of the colony and even unto the surrounding seas. He was by the king's own signature made an almost sovereign under English law, only limited by the precedents of that law, the king and English common practice. *But England's a long way off*, I thought. Around his lordship, his banners waved their separate frames, their faces in colored toss and furrowed snaps roll upon the breeze. Now this desolation's all emblazoned in stands of colored tints. Music fanfared in drums and rhapsodies of blind asides. His consorts rounded in their silks cheered as Lord De la Warr stepped forth to speak.

"All that are destruction and miseries in this place have come by vanity. All who have idled are its cause, and all who have put station before the future of this enterprise." So he spoke, his hands in gold-laced cuffs, gold braided, in shining reds. A lesser king, made by his sovereign a king, a crease upon the paper fold of state to what tear of nation I did not know. After the speech, I was brought back through the town to the Governor's ship, named after himself, the *De la Warr*. I surmised myself being held to some judgment...justice here always writ on the gallows of a fickle mood. On the beach I did not see the body of the mariner. It was taken to some barren hill and buried, I was later told. In mysteries we live our lives, to die into mysteries, our bodies cast into mysteries. All that we are, forgotten upon the turning of a spade of dirt.

By the Jamestown walls near the river, men were lifting black lacquered cannons, strung with dirt and vines and ooze from the pit into which they were thrown when Gates and Somers and Newport abandoned the place. "Well hid, this heavy booty," laughed one of the diggers as I passed. The cannons set upon their carriages again. Men staggered under their weight. Around me a world seemed to awaken to its grave.

I was led to De la Warr's cabin. There I was told to sit. Thin rays of light broke through the windows in frozen shafts. The colors of the room held to the nervous shadows, their darkness insinuating opulence. Shortly, De la Warr entered, followed by Newport, Percy, Argall, Martin and the recorder for the colony, a William Strachey. They did not talk. Newport nodded in my direction. Martin smiled a smile of some sinister delight. De la Warr spoke—his age, but a few more years than mine, hanging in tallow skin down the flats of his face. His eyes, blue in surface of a watery fire, told the tale of a refined madness. "Captain Smith, there are many serious charges brought against you here, contained in this letter, a copy of which Captain Martin has given me, and testified to by Captain Newport"—De la Warr smiled in Newport's direction—"soon to be my vice-admiral Newport. These charges include crimes committed when you were president and after. The most serious is fleeing to the savages before a proper justice could be brought against you, inciting the savages to war and barring them by force from trading with the colony, so leading to the death of five hundred and forty Englishmen during the time of starvation. How say you?" De la Warr leaned back into his chair, trying to dust an indifferent crumb from the lace of his sleeve with a whisk of his hand.

"These are slanders. I fed this colony when gentlemen and their servants idled. I explored this bay, drew maps, when others played. I left Jamestown, true, but with the king's own commission to find his abandoned subjects from Roanoke, discover Raleigh's lost. And so I made my expedition, even wounded. Even treacheries against me, I have held to the purpose of this enterprise."

Lord De la Warr nodded to his own silence, looking to the others. The breath of this enterprise holding its judgment upon me. Captain Newport spoke to the truth of the accusations, "though there is some overstatement here." Their venom spent, Martin and Percy succumbed to an exhausted quiet, Percy, uncomfortable in his seat, adding a kind word about the difficulties of the presidency. Then Samuel Argall rose to speak. "I have had some witness of the man here accused, and I believe all these charges false," he said. He looked to me as a mirror into a second self. To hear me plead for me by a second voice. What glory found to glory. Then William Strachey, whom I had never met, spoke. "My lord, by all the reports and letters here gathered, both by written word and tongued discourse, idle, lazy men and fouled plans brought this colony to its corpse. To blame the innocent is to birth another folly. In your speech today, my lord, you named the cause with its own name…be in that guilt enough for all to share." Cool, the reasoned Strachey to his seat again. Lord De la Warr licking his teeth, as if to sharpen every fang. Then his lordship spoke. "The cause of these accusations may have been informed by some misjudgments. The balance is not upon the tongue but in the substance. I will take some advisements and some council. Till then Captain Smith is to be imprisoned in my ship's hold. So it is ordered; so let it be."

As Lord De la Warr stood, the others stood. Hands upon me then, I into darkness. Words whispered to me by Argall I did not hear. Strachey to his lordship's side. The others assured, relaxed into vengeance.

Chapter Two

WAS TAKEN DOWN the ship's stairs to a small cabin below the waterline, given a candle, the door locked behind me. The waters of the river rushed in drum and whispers past the hull. The muffles of the water's thorn, its slide in hiss. I sat into the single round of light and thought. I laid my drowning head upon my pain. I thought of my love. What baptisms now would my passions make? I called for some paper and some ink to write a bold narrative of my cause, a confession of myself. The water cool against the hull, and I in the belly of darkness. All that we are, are passions marshaled in an emptiness, our words linked in cacophonies, our dictionaries melodies to ourselves.

I thought upon the mariner again, his last crust upon a silent beach, his gray flesh. The earth digesting of its own. Silence is a voice of sorts. Pale in a shade of distracted green, the river in its distance, its horizons slightly curved as an upturned eye. Only its voice has chained the wind, and I to gulp upon its echoes.

And what do I become by ear? What do I hear? What do the river's whispers know? John Dee had his visions too, angels speaking from a crystal ball. But Dee could not see those living ghosts within his looking glass. Not even he, the witness derelict. Those angels as a guide for another's willful sport, so the story goes. And you, old Jonas, always exiled to a shadow's dance. Your plot ever pinned to the deeper play.

Old Jonas, your stories feed upon secrets. Most of our history is the memory to hide a lie. Elizabeth's court not so Christian as one would think, and Drake not so different in his theologies from Old Bess. "It explains her forbearance," said the mariner, "a smile to those bound to the surface farce. Cosmetics are rainbows powdered but to disaffect. And where do I begin the most dangerous of all my revelations?" Old Jonas, his agitations lingering. "Even Pope Alexander VI chained his Vatican to a personal heresy. He who threw down his scepter to divide the world, half to Portugal and half to Spain, ensuring a Catholic peace among the Catholic nations. But in the underneath, where rules the power from below, there contests the fire. Conformities always hunger for the heat that melts their chains. And Alexander had his private rooms painted in homage to a heathen idol."

Not days ago we sat the James, a moonlight chill, I listening to a voice and a whisper. The river liquid in its soliloquies, its monologue spoken beneath the common ear, words orphaned in the quiet. Said in silence, my three wounds and I can hear the waters articulate. It tongues the hush, its dictionaries pronounced only a portrait of itself. I, too, the child led by no one's hand. The touch of emptiness upon my skin. My father now a wilderness. Sequestered swells the river's voice, a father to my ear. My father lies before me in its sweep. A loneliness has birthed an exile as its son. To me I am a desolation. My chronicles as a river, a ruin and a corpse. The mariner salutes me in his pallid decay. Slumber and awaken, then to sleep the forever sleep. And where to begin, the last amusement in its final kiss.

Jonas, old friend, we conspire to the needs of our ancient longings. John Dee, you, the forgotten, who wills the secrets into histories. That day Queen Elizabeth rode in her carriage festooned in the celebrities of her rank, an entourage horsed in golden cloth. But Dee her philosopher, and you old Jonas the watchful confidante, together the three to walk the solitaries of their talk. Alone on the quiet beach, the mute waters of the Thames, a rush of sunlight in its painted heat upon the moving wash.

"A girl that was a queen," Jonas recalled, "a woman ruler without a consort. The first in all our history. Dee calculated the day of her coronation, but that time had slipped. It was the summer of 1560 and the queen, in a private quest, played that moment as she solemnized a little laugh, a frown to frame a thought. 'Nostradamus,' she said, 'we played his stars against the planets of his foolishness. My skirts have more wisdom than his pen.' The queen, her smiles to blight the threat. Nostradamus had predicted Elizabeth's reign as queen alone would be a calamity. Calvin in Switzerland predicted the same. It was Dee who calculated the proper day to counter all their astrologies.

"'Your Majesty,' soft is Dee's voice, 'Nostradamus, my wayward friend, educated and doctor, and so an outcast, hunted, slandered as a conjuror. His prophesies are but a joke to spoon a sugared ignorance to a silly mob. He takes them not seriously. He played his sport in errors, and perhaps to gain a politic, a favor at the French court.'

"'His favors could have cost me dear,' Elizabeth enjoying her own wit.

"'Don't all favors?' said Dee.

"With a flirtatious turn of her hair and skirts, her hand gestured as if to command the air. 'I am of other minds. Shall I play my wrist with divinities?' The queen clothed her joke girlish to hide its candor.

"'Your Majesty,' softly the question summons a small surprise. Dee in thought.

"'Well, my philosopher, a queen divinely ordained. How do my stars account, my planets in all their astrologies? What secret rays, what emanations from the heavens congress in my royal self? What magic in this flesh? Is it certain by the touch of my hand that I can heal? Is it true?'

"'Man and God, the language of the heavens,' Dee spoke, 'It is, as we have said, it is known by all the stars, the planets, the sun and moon glow in hidden mysteries emitting rays, some seen, some as invisibilities. The magnet's rays as such conceals its power. But each of earth—its metals, liquids, flesh—attract and concentrate those rays sympathetic to its own nature. As a crystal ball may consecrate those divine rays, so angels can be called and seen within the clarity of its stone. Your Majesty, your person heals, for it is the nature you compel by the gifts in your fingertips.'

"'And what gifts to you, good alchemist, besides a not-so-subtle conjuring of flattery?'

"Dee ignored the taunt. His mind had that eye to concentrate itself in thought. 'When immortal Adam fell, his divinity shattered into a shower of fiery sparks. One to each his children, and so to all of us. We some part divine. Man with God. God with man. Man the creator, only slightly less than God. As great Aristotle said, influence and attractions come by similarities. We are in God, for God is in us.'

"The queen beckoned to her page. A simple chair was brought. Sighing, the queen sat. 'When the news came that I would be queen, I received the message sitting on the grass under a tree reading Plato in Greek. Now that I am told I am of God, a chair would seem appropriate." The queen arranged herself in comfort. "Divine! Wouldn't the Pope be annoyed, not to mention the Spanish. And so, dear philosopher, how do the French wear their divinities?'

"'Rather nervously.'

"'Yes, shouldn't we all?' The queen's levity a fortress to protect her eager mind. 'And good Jonas," the queen continued, "I await your promised commentary.'

"'My apology, Your Majesty. The text is most ancient, written before the time of Moses, the names of herbs and stones archaic to our ear. Translated from hieroglyphics perhaps into Greek in ages long ago. Saint Augustine knowing of the work, but disapproving. Cosimo de'Medici buying its manuscript from a Macedonian monk in 1464, having his scholar Ficino put aside his Latin edition of Plato to translate the book of Hermes the Thrice-Great. He who predicted a thousand years before the coming of our lord, and gave his wisdom to the Egyptians. It complements the teachings of the Jews—secrets therein to have again our heaven. All this known, but through so many languages, that words, and sometimes meanings are lost. Be at peace, it will come. I build a ship of shattered wood.'

"'I wish to sail before I am drowned by hope,' the queen prodded Jonas, the moment blushed and stammered. 'The cards always follow the hand that owns the deck.'

"Dee interrupted, 'Jonas shows his love for you in his caution.'

"'A cautious love calls to me as a coward's bravery.' Elizabeth, the queen, royal in her turns of will.

"John Dee, never abrupt to plead his case, held to the secrets of his history. He who had been arrested during Queen Mary's murdering time, was known to those sent to the stake. Friends burnt alive, bladders of gunpowder around their necks to ease their suffering by blowing off their heads. Sometimes the powder did not ignite, forty-five minutes of a screaming death. Edmund Bonner, Bishop of London, Mary's chief inquisitor, held Dee prisoner in St. Paul's. A pile of coals for Dee's bed, a storage room as his jail. But Dee's theologies were a brazen worship to an all-inclusive church. Narrow in his fanatic hates, Bonner's interview, his viper's questions charmed at Dee. The supremacy of the Pope, the transubstantiation of wine and wafers, all the inquisitor's barbs—its joust was but a tournament with mush. Dee claimed agreement of every parry. A little always to debate, Dee the shadow, danced the light, he in his secret mission to protect Elizabeth, half-sister to the queen, next in the royal line. Protestant and Catholic in England then a tangle in a festering brew, not so easy to tell who was what. Dee's theology now to smile a protection, spy the inquisition, protect the future queen.

"And so in silence do we serve. John Dee now spoke into the eyes of the young queen. 'The book of Hermes that Ficino translated has much to say of these rays and how an image—whether a talisman worn around the neck, a sculpture or a painted image, a brew of herbs, a plant, or metals, either gold or silver or some association of the two—may gather those rays' invisible forces by their magical sympathies. Like attracts like. But to misstep the relationships with the wrong image, material or brew, could do perhaps a harm.'

"'Are your theologies profound enough, good philosopher?' the queen said. 'In Europe we add by fractions to the math of a religious war. All that is corresponds, what of earth is seen in the stars? Our astrologies herald. Our planets proclaim. Now you say in their light they potentate.'

"'No, the stars do not in total rule, we rule ourselves. Freedom is the power to serve our God and recreate his Eden.'

"The queen smiled to the cynic of her memories. 'Mostly I believe God is over-served by those he can't abide. An unwanted worshiper is the worst bad guest.'

"'Here—in the words that worship serves,' Dee the teacher, turning in his mind the pages of Hermes' book. 'God from nothing created all. We cannot. But Hermes wrote in his *Corpus Hermeticum*, that text which is the threshold that secrets revelations, Great Hermes has told man himself can create gods. Not the one God, for only He can create from the void; but as the ancients did, using the proper metals, plants and sculpture or painted image, collect those secret emanations from the stars in such a gather it empowers the idols as a lesser deity. Man's divinity prolifics a wisdom to the births of gods. Not evil demons, but some portion of the one, the good. Such is the knowledge frequent to our knowing hands.'

"The queen to some amusement said, 'On such magics you play yourself heretic and not a stake to be found, and such a pleasant summer day.' The queen whispered, 'Be careful for those who account you conjuror, they wish you ill and would delight to have you pilloried on such an idyll.' More to the mood in its passing moment, the queen continued, 'There are many in my court whose theologies drift not far from yours.' Her finger to her lips, the queen whistled her breath to silence, then a pat upon Dee's shoulder. 'And most were students in this house, my dear philosopher.' The queen began to stand, the jewels on her dress sparkling heaven. 'Be more at court. There the Privy Council and I can protect you best.' Dee offered the queen his arm, which she graced with friendship as she rose. 'Your old students still miss you, although I know they visit you on purposes that come to my ear on strange accounts.'

"'Your Majesty, on the subject we have discussed of late,' Dee pleading to sew patches on a threadbare promise.

"'I am most familiar with the wrappings, the package and your case, dear philosopher,' sighed the queen. 'Travail to your family born by your loyalties to me. I grieve for your father Roland's arrest because of his service to my father, King Henry, and the child, King Edward, my brother by half. Your father made pauper by Mary, you yourself deprived of the rectory at Upton, all income lost. But surely Leicester's generous gift, the rectory at Leadenham is some reprieve.'

"'Eighty pounds a year, and this my mother's home, and at her death it is mine.'

"'But, so close to court and Walsingham and Leicester. Power contagions. Sit close enough to inspire the disease.'

"'My ambitions wash of a different balm. An income to have an English library as great as those on the continental shelves. A place to work. The deanery at Gloucester soon to be vacant, sufficient in its income. A place to have some contemplations on the laws of nature that are within our grasp. The geometries of God, the math of Eden, the first language of heaven, with all knowledge would I anoint this kingdom and this earth a paradise of wisdom and religious peace.'

"'Dear philosopher, I would be your scholar, as you would teach. But the rumors of your work conjure demons in the commons of the street. Be at court to plead a pleasant familiarity, then you may charm by a ready society a deanery.'

"'Your Majesty,' Dee bowing to the words but not to their purpose.

"The queen never so intoxicated with her own advice, knowing a smile to oneself is a congratulatory tomb. 'You have friends you made rich, eager for another golden meal. When you calculated the navigations by star, planet and sun for Chancellor and Lord Hugh Willoughby.'"

"Lord Willoughby, but what…" I startled.

The old mariner raised his hand to usher silence. "Let the tale speak. Your questions will be served. 'In 1555,' said the queen, 'when Chancellor found the Arctic bay and the Russian sled. Then to Moscow, where Ivan, the Czar named The Terrible, gave licenses and monopolies to the English company to trade in all Russia. Wealth came by your friendship, and they at court wanting more. Play the court's game to your sweet good.'"

The old mariner, in his death so soon, its thick into his blood. Urgent the final days, the river ever in its only course. "And you, young Smith, do you have a child's memory of that tale? Perhaps long ago in your infant play, three shadows speaking as if a dream. Something crawls, a darkness hints, shadows speak. Not all gifts come by wound. Think on it. Remember the ghosts, they are a key, Your Lord Willoughby's father died on that northern adventure. His ship separated from Chancellor's, lost into the snows of the Arctic white, anchored in a blizzard, held in a cove by ice, the north coming to its winter night. All desperate in the belief they could hold half the year in the comfort of the ship. Food by fish and deer. Warmth by fire. But they misjudged and froze. All died. And so young Smith, Lord Willoughby, the father's son, saw in you the continuation of our family, and so your history is begun, in secrets come all our childhoods. The bag of gold Drake gave into Willoughby's hand for you, the shadow now the silhouette, and through it the glowing shade of your face." The old mariner, his whispers now the voice of an iron sound. "You, the inheritor to fulfill the adventure's dream."

"I am haunted," I replied, "by an old chill, a wandering sadness not my own. A ghost, a lace of woven smoke, hoarfrost white, a thousand winters in its voice, came to me one night. I then six years old, beckoned by its intent, frozen in its eyeless stare. 'The ring,' said the ghost, 'the regent of our blood, hidden in a cupboard's drawer, where frantic gargoyles merry in a sculptured fête. Tell my son it is a gift to all our line, and all our sons to eternity.'"

The old mariner's head nodding into a passing smile. "And..."

"The prod, but an infant's imagination. My father asking 'Why your tears?' Reluctantly, I told the haunting in my stammers. He, not so simple as to give a reassuring hug, dragged me before Lord Willoughby, where I confessed my ghost to his lordship's scowl. He stood. 'I thought it stolen,' he said, guiding us into his library and a cupboard. Its doors violently opened, papers thrown to the floor, parchments with great wax seals. *Emboss my life in the blood of wax,*

I thought, in my chill not quite. Willoughby's hand now searching in the plundered dark.

"'Yes, there is a latch. And now...' Willoughby's hand withdrew into the light. In its grasp a great golden ring, bejeweled in rainbow facets. 'This ring is legend, given to the first Willoughby by Arthur, the king himself. So it is said for generations in our house. Thought lost, now found.' Willoughby lifted me in his hands, kissed my eyes. 'More sight in these two than in thousands.' He asked more of the ghost, how it looked, spoke, what command was in its voice.

"'The ghost in tattered clothes, moved in a breeze I could not feel. It spoke strange words, "The white evening of the snow, the fog. By what cosmetic do you paint away the sun?" said the ghost. "The ship now lost. The arctic sea calm after the exhaustions of a storm, our rigging iced, a crystal ship sparkles upon the dungeons of a darkening sky. So far you are, my son, from the protections of my arms, and I in search of our nation's desires. And so I have come to clothe myself in frost, seeking the Northeast Passage to China, across the pole, through the Northern Sea."

"'Our maps confound, the cold wind rises, the gale swirls the mist through ice. Pray me to sleep. The waves upon the ship, their crowns clear as thunder in the air. Hail stings the eye.' I told it all in many repetitions. Questions asked. Finally, 'A reward for our child of ghosts,' said Willoughby. Three gold coins to my eager hands, and a buttered cake. Some smiles by his worship to my father. Those words not recalled."

"You, my almost son, have more than rivers in your blood," said the mariner.

Words whisper on hidden lips. My ears sentinels to what mystery? And now visions, my eyes to what account? I questioned my thoughts. The mariner was impatient to continue. "More you may remember, more you will be told. But listen to my warnings, they have the power of revelations. Let us not forfeit this hour. Now to the queen and Dee.

"Her majesty to the liveries of her plumes and the gilt embossments of her carriage, nervous the power of the horses, their trembling flanks. Riders eyeing with jealousies some other's place. Round the ramshackle of Mortlake, roofs of the buildings bowed in staid collapse. The outbuildings' vacant windows without glass, doors unhinged, hung in the teeters of broken angles. 'When my mother dies, this is my estate,' said Dee.

"'But you will be close to court and friends and perhaps the fellowship of a coin or two.' The queen held her hand to be kissed.

"'I am again to France in search of riches in books and manuscript.' Dee kissed the offered hand.

"'And I then to wait—always the patient student—remember your queen, and those at court who would have your friendship to have your knowledge, to have more wealth by commerce. The court is a nunnery sparkling in its gestures to hide a vice.' Ever the confidant to the wise, the queen served her wisdom on gilded lance."

The old mariner struggled a cough into a laugh. "And there is still so much to tell." The river whispering in its eternities. Days later the mariner ripening in his new death. I then the only herald to guide by ink and quill my questions into histories.

Chapter Three

OF ISLANDS FAR AND PRISONS NEAR.

WAS GIVEN FOOD. Already my plans were for escape. Strachey and Argall came to see me. Argall, his purpose undisclosed. Then he spoke. "Your old friend Anas Todkill has returned. He that you sent with Captain Moone before you played the vapor and hauled a disappearance upon the forest. He carries some news. In a day it will be to your smile." Argall's head bowed to some taste of mirth. "It will be fair and pleasing. Be calm."

"Will my beast rise in spoils to another empty heat?" I asked aloud.

Argall smiled, responding, "Forces secret to your defense have conspired. That is all I can say."

Clearing the bile from his throat, Strachey by interruption wove a different mood. "I know of your two books. Much delighted by those who have taken to their pages." Hesitations by an embarrassed silence, Strachey cautioned to his question. "Perhaps you have heard of our Atlantic crossing, the storm, our shipwreck and the Bermuda

Island." Too much to myself, I showed no interest. "My history could grace a chapter," said Strachey.

"That book is yours," I said. "Your eyes have beheld…"

Strachey the prompt bursting. "This drama should have its scene. I believe there are a few moments, and a few new fellows named, that could be worth your ear." Argall nodded.

Strachey told of his voyage across the Atlantic with Gates and Somers and Newport, of the wilds of the rain and howling gales. The storm ripping the sails into threads and tatters. The days dawned dark in a coming night. The fleet lost, its safety scattered. The *Sea Venture* leaking, driven by the changing compass of the wind. Newport captain only to his name, Gates ordering pumps manned. The ship sinking. They had Bermuda in their sight between the mountains of the gray-flung storm. The ship on a reef, the surf cracking the planks of its stricken hull. The ship settling onto the reef, held by the splinters of its broken beams. All were saved, escaping to the island by longboats. Some stores and tools rescued as well.

A happy island, this Bermuda, to an unhappy crew, filled as it was with wondrous fares, wild fruits and woods and tasty hogs. The company sat among their plenties for a month, some wanting never to leave, saying, "This wreck is a better venture than Virginia." In that wait, the company turned to colony. Two babies born, a girl named Bermuda to John Rolfe and his wife, and a boy named Bermudas to Edward Eason and his. The boy survived. The girl had only death. The mother, in her sorrows, coming to her last grief, survived to reach these shores.

Despite all, within some weeks of September, 1609, the longboat was rebuilt into a small pinnace. John Raven and six in crew were to make sail for Jamestown and find some rescue. They reasoned by guess and hope that Bermuda was a hundred and forty leagues from Jamestown, maps being inaccurate and those seas poorly known. The true distance was almost three hundred leagues, or over seven hundred miles. With weather fair and with good winds, Raven pledged to return by the next full moon. "If I shall live, I will return and bring with me the colony's pinnace and with it sweet rescue to this pleasant island." So John Raven said, sailing from the beach. He ran his boat into the swell, fighting the currents and surf-sprayed rocks of the island's reef. Then freedom to the open sea, Strachey and Gates watching from the hill, the sail declining below the horizon's rim.

Three days from the coming of the new moon Gates had beacon fires lit to guide our heroes home. Our fires burned to red ashes in the night, as the Cyclops moon hung its stare across the dark. Its mercies under a darkened lid, its sight the only pledge for our waiting hundreds. For days the fires lit, the moon closing to its sleep. "We waited another month and then another. All hope then lost. Raven truly dead. Mysteries to his name and agonies to his life. Richard Frobisher, a shipwright and relative to the great Sir Martin, began to build a pinnace then. The local forests stored with great trees, he felled what he could. He worked alone, completing one, asking Gates for help to build another. The salvation in our hands. A second pinnace built by the tenth of May, 1610. Most mercy is to those who action for its gifts. The pinnaces were named *Deliverance* and *Patience*. We gathered all and launched our boats upon the breakers, set sails, the shallow rocks of the reefs turmoiling the waters. One pinnace almost sank. We fought to the open sea, holding to the sight of each other by slivers of masts, the sea in waves and we to the crests and troughs of the rolling furrows. In a week the smell of land, the water vined in floating debris, we plumbed a rising sea bottom, sand and stone swept in upward climb to the unseen pedestal of land. In seven days we made the Chesapeake. We sailed in joy of rescue, finding not what we sought, but a colony in its starving. Death here is such a simple trick and we who came for God and glory would fall to eat each other's flesh, but even in our faults I believe we hold the will of destiny to this land." Strachey turned his eye to me. "In this vision all joy ignites our cause. An idea can calm and swallow pain. All flesh that hurts may metal before a thought."

And of the soul? I questioned to myself. *Does that come in iron too, forged unfeeling in the mind?*

"The savages whom we would raise to Englishmen." Strachey rubbed his hands as if searching for his own warmth. "Why will they not be innocent?"

"And why will we not work?" I replied, talking to the candle's flicker.

Strachey pretended not to hear, knowing answer not within his experience, so he continued his tale. "At Jamestown we hovelled with living skeletons and the dead. We brought little food from Bermuda. We sent many of our company into the woods to gather roots and strawberries and such delicacies, the savages bringing upon them wars in arrows and stone cudgels. Two they murdered before the blockhouse, breaking them to bleed in ghastly wounds. One of our boats on the river with twelve in crew they lured close to shore, then threw water on the company to quench the fires of their tapers. The firelocks then useless, the savages slaughtered them all. But this war has a strange account. The next day some savages would come to the fort to trade for corn. Cheat us they would and spy and steal but a small trade we could have. Gates having patience, showing a kindly manner, courtesy for courtesy, hoping peace. But the savages have other minds, brewed by this land to yield only conflicts and deception." Strachey thought himself into silence, then asked, "Would we have shown such restraint to the savage Irish? The answer cries in nay. Here we will not be the Spanish; provocations have little matter, surrounded by war with little food. Gates called a council and so we made our plans to leave, sailing for England on the seventh of June, only to meet Lord De la Warr in the Chesapeake. All else is known." Strachey was quiet for a moment, then spit his words across the candlelight. "Why, Smith, will these savages not be noble?" Strachey's eyes wide.

"All humankind is as a dry twig. That nature more to break than bend," I said. "Dream as you will, but this is no England. The savages here play by a different game. Guide your knowledge to their rules for in its discipline there is salvation. It strikes as deadly as our own, but more innocent is its guile. Here there is little direct attack, except when numbers and opportunity favor; more is done by bluff and cunning. Taking hostages defeats all their treacheries. Take hostages, be firm but kindly—never so kind as to be weak, never so firm as to be brutal. War to the savages is sport, stealing is done for prizes in which their kings share. Murder done to an enemy is like a theft, it is a prize, forgotten until the next surprise. Murder here is an advantage as any other. Take away the advantage, you take away the murder. After death, some trade then some war. All blood here is done for private advantage. Death is not nearly death to them—it is not the single cause for peace or vengeance. All here is done by balance. This is how they live. This wilderness does not rest on our commandment stones but hooks its life in possibilities beyond all our moral meanings. Play upon its temper with sweet brilliance, and time will see us king and our cause as just."

Strachey stood angrily, "I will not be heathen to have a heathen's love."

"It is their respect we want without slaughter," I countered as I rose. "How much of your conscience will it take to make our England Spain?" Argall stood between us, his hands upon both our chests, pushing us apart.

Strachey's face sweated rage, but in that truth that comes to honest men when truth they are shown, his fury changed. He sat again and nodded to himself. "Forgive me," he said. Argall asked more of my dealing with the savages. I gave my advice.

"Kings here rule by custom. Respect them but do not flatter," I said. "Powhatan has an empire but at the edges there is constant war. There are allies there for us if we are wise."

"And of Roanoke? You never said," spoke Strachey.

"We are far from home. Great oceans make all nations but a tender slip. Roanoke is no more." I halved a lie to keep my peace.

THREE DAYS I SAT TO MY RIVER VOICES, THEN NEW SHADOWS CROSSED at my bolted door, a knock on hollow wood, polite in its echoes. William Strachey, greetings to his voice. "Lord De la Warr wishes to meet with you anon. He will send a messenger." Exuberance before Strachey full in the room.

"Anas Todkill," the familiar profile only partially shaded in the darks of the passageway, "I'm glad for your survival and your return."

"I am but a voyager," Todkill joked, "a thief of moments, a bearer of quills and manuscripts and noble secrets." I smiled to uplift a gloom.

Todkill and I embraced. Strachey stood, offered a pat on both our backs, then sat. Todkill talked of his escape with Captain Moone back to England, meeting with the London Company. My letters copied and circulated. "They have given you high office." Strachey nodding. "Protector of the Colony, commander of all Virginia's defenses."

"De la Warr defies the London Council. I am prisoner. Are all our occasions written by a dishonest caulk? All is ridden on a sallow whore of easy prospects."

"You are to be released on some mission of defense." Eager Strachey, his tin cup ever pleading a charmed shilling from a charred consequence. "Perhaps an expedition to bring the savages to some peace."

Todkill uncertain gloomed in thoughtfulness. "There are rumors of a northward river and Dutch spies, secret passages through the polar ice."

"But my expeditions were not by sea," I questioned, "and where is our defense in polar ice?"

"It must be to the savages and a trade of corn," Strachey said.

The questions discussed, the candles spent, the two then left me to my dark. Lord De la Warr chose his council. Lord Percy, his cousin, he made captain of the fort; Sir Ferdinand Weynman, another cousin, was made master of ordinance. With so many Wests and their relatives in the colony now, Virginia seemed a cloister to a lineage of blood. The council full with three knights, numerous captains and for its lord governor and captain general a peer whose grandmother was cousin to Queen Elizabeth herself. All the glitter now upon the lace. Lord De la Warr held to the absolutes of his office. Newport, his vice-admiral; Sir George Somers, his admiral. Upon what cost, I wondered, will the fleet pass to other masters?

All reports now spoke of war. Four of ours killed just beyond the blockhouse. Stragglers cut off each day and murdered. Savages pressed the forest round the fort, hidden in opportunity to bring arrows to the air, or even crawling to Jamestown's walls to bring some slaughter, or coming in excuse to trade, but only to spy and test our strength, seeing to the numbers of our sick and the depth of our want.

Gates, as lieutenant governor, his policy set by London, welcomed all, not understanding the savages and how to commerce in power wisely. His anger rose at each new assault, his patience almost gone. Food ever a problem. I imprisoned. Little trade. For a week, twelve times each day and night, Gates ordered our nets cast into the river. Much lazy effort with nothing gained. The water yielded water but few fish.

Disaster from disaster from the better sorts, I mused. Change is the veneer that sameness gives to simple minds.

Strachey then visited me, complained of the mariners, who at night would row their longboats with well-armed battalions to trade in secret with the savages for furs. All profits to the captains. The company store empty. Strachey angered, sweet in his child justice.

"It is an old corruption, well rehearsed," I said. "Even war holds for that commerce, but for the future, a profit shared by the commons has ever fouled this enterprise. Little for all is none for most. Every house a ruin. We need assurance of wealth by the strength of our work. Private lands for each, and a private fishing fleet." It was never tried. Nor was the digging of new wells. The water, always bad, now claimed the new colonists. Many sick, death floated already in the muddy streets. Bodies to the burial mounds. Still the savages enjoyed their health, their morning baths, the good waters of the icy springs. And we learned by scratch and our accustomed nothing.

Chapter Four

THE OFFERING BAY AND THE BECKONING OF
NORTHWARD WATERS.

HEN A MESSENGER FROM Lord De la Warr. My door unbolted, I to be free. Sweet the chilling breeze, I walked on deck. After those many days in my locked room, I shivered in the treasure of the springtime thrill. Light, colors rapture, as a living paint. My world frantic, I exploded into its landscape. The green of the ship's hull, the white sails, the reds of the painted water lines. Trees, water, skies, vastness of my unencumbered sight. Sensations drink me into my eyes. The sailors climbing, their rags to rainbows in the rigging. The hull's scraped planks re-tarred with black lava. The smell of its heat.

Rowed to the shore. The coming of the ominous fort, its weathered walls filled with fresh logs, wounds of yellow pulp beside the grays of more ancient wood. On the riverbanks an idle of men wandered in the sleep of hunger. A few labored, dragging some newly felled trees, or cannons restored to their carriages. Soldiers rehearsed in their pale armor, played their firelocks, measuring lightning in its powder funneled down the barrels. Practice to an imperfect dream, its ruin all about.

Lord De la Warr sat his office behind a crude table. The small room, an entire hut which would be his castle. Infrequent was the sun through its haze. I was offered an unfriendly smile, then a chair. "I have had some council on your behalf," the lord to his moment and his speech. "Some would have you hung." I smiled. "Few would find the prospects of death so amusing," the lord to the casuals of his power.

"I doubt you would labor through a discourse if I were about to die."

Lord De la Warr nodded. "A waste of rope, and the company has better uses for that neck." The scene in his office now served, the young lord cleared the room. "I countenance a man only by his enemies," he whispered. "Friends are too readily bought, as Elizabeth our queen said many times to me." The "me" having more weight than the observation.

"Every man's politics hangs on the comforts of his purse." My reply to test the lordship's humors.

"Quite so, wit and luck. You have all the mutinies of spirit the common mind despises. See to your luck. You will be adventuring on its circumstance." A pause, the room awash in dust and fallow light.

"The London Council elected you captain of all our colonies' military. Your mission is to protect by all defense this settlement."

"I have served this office in the past as I would now by heart and blood."

"Indeed, I could set you aside and appoint another." His lordship waited, allowing me to weigh his power. "But," he said with a tone of satisfaction, "I will not. I trust less your enemies. They are of a rude flattery. They play above their stations."

I laughed to myself. *It is a fair poison that births its own antidote.*

"You know a Henry Hudson, I believe, even had an exchange of letters?" His lordship impatient in his tale, forfeiting the answer.

I nodded, was ignored, then said, "I rumored on the Northwest Passage, related tales from the savages of a great river, perhaps a passage flowing from the west."

"Last year Hudson sailed, but for the Dutch, his wife being forced to live in Amsterdam, an honored captive while the expedition ships at sea. The Hollanders may plate their map in envies of our English lands. Hudson explored the length of this coast from Canada to the Chesapeake and a little south, making discoveries of two rivers. One he had by a hundred leagues, the other too shallow to gain its bay, or so he said. And so we are stayed, and the question asked."

De la Warr gazed toward me. "And what did Hudson have in discovery?" My words spoken into his stare.

"What, indeed! He sailed in his return not for Holland but to the London docks, and gave our company his reports. Hudson's father being an early investor with Willoughby and Chancellor, so the loyalty not questioned or suspicioned, he being more than kin."

"But yet this tale may be haunted by a whisper of a secret kind." I spoke my thoughts aloud.

"The Dutch paid all Hudson's weight, never a hint of some discord. His wife returned to England. Rumors of the Dutch building of a fort upon that north river. What, indeed, did Hudson map?" His lordship poured two glasses of aqua vitae, offering one to me. "Hudson sails again for us. The prompter as two puppets to play upon a single hand. Voyaging north through the passage Frobisher found before Drake made his circumnavigation of the world. The arctic was Hudson's plot, he sailed again months ago on the Half Moon. No word, no sightings. Does he scheme disloyalties, some treason for his own, or is he lost and periled?

"Find him and what he is about, and that river! Captain Waymouth and his ship are yours. When you have done the chase, return here, and only here, with your report, and be my captain of our guard. But if you fail me, the rope is its own snake, its tongue to play its snap upon the air."

His lordship offered me another glass of aqua vitae, then called for Captain Waymouth. "He is well practiced in long sails and northern waters, having years in the Moscovy trade. He calls himself a child of ice." The sunlight dimmed as Captain Waymouth entered, broad of shadow and thin of lip, a man of beard and little else. His left eye ever frightened, wandered, seeking the easiest path to our captain's most nervous departure. Waymouth played the introduction, his pleasantries cuffed in a plainly hidden annoyance. In his hand a rolled map, which he spread upon the table, after over-pleading permission. He looked only at Lord De la Warr, as he, the surveyor, might, drooling upon a prize patch of land.

"From all Hudson's reports," Waymouth spoke, "I have drawn this chart of the coast. There are some assumptions as to bearing and depths. Hudson noted his fathoms and his leagues, but I am not convinced he determined correctly absolute north. The Pole and the magnetics of the compass have great deflection the further north we sail."

"But Hudson is experienced in polar voyages," I interrupted.

"There truth lips the simple line" responded Waymouth. "Are these logs the logs he kept, the ones given to the Dutch, or a fiction to fist beneath our English nose?"

"Why trust them at all?" His Lordship asked the question I had almost to my lips.

"I trust what I shall see," said Waymouth, holding himself as an imaginary shield.

"Captain, you will be under sail in three days. Ice and cold in polar waters come early. And be apprised, see to Hudson's northern river."

"Three days," Waymouth repeated, bowed slightly, waiting for me to withdraw from his lordship's presence.

I to other minds asked, "The body of the mariner, Jonas Profit, my old friend, buried after the arrival of your fleet. Can you direct me to his grave, or one of the company who might do so?"

"I cannot, but ask who you will." De la Warr remained seated as we left. Already there was the sweat of disease upon his face, the coming pallor beneath his skin, a slight quiver of the hand. Perhaps rank does not take note of its own decay. I thought as I went in search of Todkill, *And where are you now, old Jonas? And so, my friend, death is the only name of our final anonymity.*

TIME ENOUGH IS ALWAYS A TEMPTATION TO THE FATES. ITS HESI-tations weave a demon's scarf. Perhaps one last trading expedition, to seek a supply of corn an excuse, its nobility to shield my secret purpose. My excitements throb. I am reborn a shiver, nervous to the expectations, my love. Can the river's voice lead me to your arms? Can it speak the map, guide the sails? The river to my ears again. I feed upon the currents passing in its mysteries. Its words never sleeping, I dream an awakened slumber. And Pocahontas, where are you from here? What forest trail or hill claims your eyes? The river as ever proclaims its hungers, its watery voice salted in secret orisons.

THE COLONY MULED IN ITS USUAL SLOTH. CROWDS LAZED CONFUSED, diversions in a game of bowls and pins, rags and silks, the drabs of threadbare patches gilded around the fanfares of the gold and scarlet cloth. I found Todkill, ax in hand, pruning logs to repair the fort walls. "I have sea longings," said Todkill after hearing of Hudson and my interview with De la Warr. "A little snow in its sugar might sweeten a dull spring."

"I need your eyes here, your quill to keep reports. Nothing's set. Jamestown is sculptured of an old motion. De la Warr brinks on the edge of some disease. If this plays true, his power will wander to whom and for what purpose? Be sure, it will be against all." Todkill began to protest. "You are to be the ink, the writ to hold this history. I am being sailed into a common death. Those polar waters claimed Willoughby's father. In those fathoms who knows what fates contend. Better you stay and be my voice." Todkill nodded to a stare, the sight in his mind.

"I wish to find our Jonas's grave and to place some fleeting monument, some wooden marker. His name to fester above the worms, his deeds still not forgot." Argall and Strachey stood near the blacksmith's forge watching burning coals bleed their heat. The rough iron clanged and glowed as it was forged into crossbow darts.

"Ah, well freed and a voyage soon to the north," smiled Strachey. Argall hand upon my shoulder in a squeeze of fellowship. The discussion to Hudson and his discoveries, Argall giving advice.

"From Frobisher's strait there comes a great current, an outflow from the west. It portends a deeper passage, perhaps the one Drake sought. But be warned, the year is late for polar expeditions. By September the ice will choke the Arctic Sea and with it any hope of home. For six months in cold and almost perpetual night, your ship is marooned in the blizzards on an ice-bound sea." I in visions saw the mists and swirling frosts, snow in its white ghost, its cold to numb the heat, and of our fur-gloved fingertips.

I asked of Jonas's body and the place of its final rest. "His grave is but common, on the burial mound, like all, unmarked. If you wish some simple stone, be at will. No one can object." Strachey's voice muffled in its drum. Argall spoke of a colonist of some prospect. "We should please a cup and meet. The benefit for all upon your return." So arranged the evening in my cabin. Todkill and I to the burial hill.

"Cinders of the earth, in mounds, all aged to a forgotten death. I weep upon all my kingdoms, crying in the souls of vacant hope. Touch me in passions once you knew. I am your inheritor, and you are my words, and the future of my passing chronicles." And so I prayed to all, to Jonas.

"A stone?" asked Todkill.

"When I return."

Chapter Five

N MY CABIN AGAIN, I hammer my fists upon the prisons of my open door. I curse at nothing, looking into the coffin of its wood. The door creaked, slammed against the hull. "Why plead this noise?" said Strachey in the passageway. Two shadows behind him hung in darkening crepe, like hooded monks of black. Argall one, the other I did not know. There is a loneliness that company makes more foul.

Strachey and Argall familiar in their society, lit two extra candles and chose their chair. "John Rolfe," said Argall finally to cast my way an introduction. Rolfe and I played our politeness reserved but calculated for other's nod.

"I've heard of your sad adventures in Bermuda," I said.

"Yes, yes, the child. My wife now ill." A dead child, a dying wife. Rolfe seemed now departed even from his own grief. A youthful sadness around the eyes, a pleasant inexperience to his face. I thought him a little to the dull, no doubt why the dull gave him some respect. He stared mostly into the bowl of his pipe, an iron needle in his hand to play the ash and rekindle the smoke.

Argall's face, its resemblance so cast we could act as partial twins. His hair not red, he was as my own vapor before my eyes, a theft of my countenance by another flesh. I twinged a moment's hate. Some comedy we are to claim ownership of the game, the dice, and every number carved.

I asked of any charts he had of the northern coast. He said he had none, but thought the people friendly and the land good. The architecture of the New World still a mystery.

Argall spoke of his family, his father landed gentry with several estates, a distant descendent of a king of Scotland. He was the last of eight sons, fifteen children, too far down the line for any hope of inheritance. His father had died in 1588 when Argall was eight.

His mother remarried Laurence Washington of Maidstone, a man it is said may yet spice a great future in his line. And so, through his circumstance, all his friends and connections were well placed. Even Lord De la Warr was married to the niece of his brother-in-law, and Argall's cousin was Sir Thomas Smythe, the wealthy London merchant and principal in England's Muscovy trade. It was to him Gosnold and I had ventured in our supplications on the advice of the Willoughbys and George Sandys to ask support for our Virginia colony. Edward Sandys, George's brother, having close business relations with him. Argall reporting that Smythe was now the treasurer of the Virginia Company, the company's most powerful director, in its most important office.

All my history here seems to come in lines of power and blood. Am I then a descended prodigal, a discard of the flesh? I stood my thought. Argall in the simple raptures of his tale prattled on, his words a javelin through my heart. "The company is still not much for work. Six hours a day—from eight to twelve o'clock, then lunch, then from two to four. Little planting yet done and the precious summer gone to waste."

I spoke to Argall of the need for trade, commerce before war. "Begin to trade where Powhatan's power is weakest—at the borders. Think geographies. Make friends with his enemies. Make his own land his prison. Always exchange hostages. We need the savages at peace, and bartering for our goods, so we may eat."

I thought of Pocahontas. I wanted to seize the stratagems to keep her safe. But all minds breed a cruel delusion. I pranked to my own jest, the mirror clown, the alchemies of the empty flask, as I wondered how much murder there would be before the murder of our love.

AFTER GIVING MY ADVICE TO PROVE AGAIN MY WORTH, I WAS LEFT to the solitaries of my dark. I walked on deck, stars in their shimmering heavens. The sailors lounged with their pipes, the air perfumed in a biting smoke. Fires glow behind Jamestown's palisades, the moonless night on the waters, words of the river flowing in whispers upon the cries of silence. A hush within my warmth. I feel the forever of my life, unquenchable in its springtime ardor. So like me, blind are the braveries of youth. Jonas dead. And Ratcliffe, Gosnold, hundreds more. Whither Jamestown, a calamity upon its name, but no stink for all its syllables.

At noon of the next day sailors rowed my few possessions to Waymouth's ship, the *Black Swan of Devon*, anchored a distance from the fleet. Closer our oars in strained power. Now the water moved as if backward against itself. His ship an undulating blackness, shimmering on the heat. I climbed the wooden ladder onto this ghost of shades. The crew dressed in the usual drabs, uncolored heavy cloth, a few neck scarves charged in purple, red and blue. Scarves about the brow stained with sweat. My chest hauled aboard on ropes. My cabin aft, near the captain's. Small, a closet, damp stale air, the odors merged of smoke, human waste and rot.

Walking on deck again. Commotions, gangs of sailors, barrels on their shoulders. Nets, pulleys, hausers, more kegs caught like fish lowered to waiting hands. By the hull a pinnace, its oars upon the water, ready to return to Jamestown once again. I climbed aboard to find Todkill, Argall and Strachey to make some brief farewells. Waymouth rumored to take the next morning's tide.

Todkill hailed soon enough. We walked upon the beach. "Hear those bells?" asked Todkill. Through the fevered heat, the tones of the Jamestown church. "It is the sound of war."

Now tolls the horrors, I thought.

Todkill shook his head, as if chasing some disbelief. At dawn that day it seems a savage came to the fort to trade baskets of corn for copper. Lord Percy in such a fury that the company had worked so little on its own crop, ordered the man's right hand cut off for impertinence, which Percy called "mischief and other spyings."

"I have given the savages this day some warnings," Percy declared above the marooned hand, bloody, its fingers spread in wide surprise. And so we eat our fears, our guilt porridged with another's blood, corn the forfeit. In excess we starve, the mind's a chapel, its chorus drowns us in the disharmonies of its frantic choirs. Cannot man ever hunger beyond the sanctuaries of his head?

"The colony weakens," reported Todkill. "Many ill. There is scurvy. Even De la Warr has lost a tooth or two. The jesters say he has swallowed his own bite."

"For months I am at sea. What causes here can I avert?" Looking at Todkill I cried at the colony, "What pretense! Bequeath your folly. The grave will bear the inheritance of your bones." No one looked, but one who raised his head from bowls and pins.

Chapter Six

SAILS AND FATHOMS, AND TALES
TOLD UNDER A CRYSTAL MOON.

OME NIGHT, COME TIDES, my river bids me no farewells. Shrill the waves, our wake shimmered upon the waters. The crescent moon paints a lovely meadow through the black.

The ship rocked, the coast passing to our stern. The water rushed. I sat my cabin quite alone, quill and ink, my paper retinue. The crew rumbling their labors on the deck, heavy drums the wood, in thuds and drags and falls. And in the sea, the ever sea, I heard again the cries of whales, echoing through the drowned darkness of the deep.

And you, my love, our silence, our separations in the dark. I wing my thoughts, my grammars change, my passion sings a language exalted into ecstasies, but also I am an agony, a whisper in an exile's ear. My lips turn sand, my tongue echoes to a memory. Not long ago in Mandinga's hand the sword of Coligny, and burned on my breast its wound like a comet round my heart, and I am marked, disfigured to a loneliness.

HOW MANY VOICES FILL THE MINES OF HISTORY? THE PAST RISES again in its blackness, ever seeking a silhouette. Old Jonas stares, his eyes wide, words upon his lips. "John Dee. There are lessons in his life, well to butter upon your philosophies. Be warned," the thin finger of the mariner pointed toward my heart, "even Drake knew some taste of caution, a sugarplum heresy secrets a better lick upon the fingertips than the scowling flames around the inquisitioner's stake.

"The world is a cook of meats, the spice of blood ever near the boil. And how do our immortalities come? By that light, that mystical fire that excites the universe. After our conversations with the queen at Mortlake, Dee set off to Europe, its roads a scratch, a balding line of mud, by cart and horse, and foot. The dangers in the world ignored. Thieves, pirates of the road, disease, filth and stench. 'I have become my quest, to be beyond, to know all that is to know.' So said Dee. A man in search of everything would mostly tie confusion to his map, but not Dee. 'I am a shepherd ordained to be a saint,' he said. Paper bound in leather upon the irons of its ink, words by pages, pages in the libraries of their gathering. Books by cartloads, secret knowledge in transcriptions. Soon the greatest library in all of England at Mortlake.

"'I have the book,' he said to me on his return in 1564, 'and a language deeper than its written text. Through it, the very words which Adam spoke and the names of unknown angels. Whispers, secrets, heavens at our door. The laws of God wielded by us to remake the world, a new Eden. The apple shall consume the snake.'

"At Mortlake books in piles on the floor, carpenters building shelves, texts that survived four thousand years, or held in manuscript almost since the creation of the world. The Eden language lost and now debased. 'I have the book,' repeated Dee. We walked in expeditions through the Mortlake halls. Shadows creep, their frames in sunlight, windows spread their heat tapestries across the floor. Mortlake in its renovations, new buildings, new wings, repairs to floors and roofs, wood fresh in golden white, beams and planks, and how their forest scents the air. 'This I call my open library, my *Externa bibliotheca*,' smiled Dee as he turned, arms held wide as if to encompass by human scale the immensity of the room. Already books on shelves, cream the shades of vellum bindings, the black leather of other texts, clasps to hold the covers closed, no chains to tie them to a post. 'A place for scholars, copyists to have the text by cheap. Knowledge dispensed like silver dust.'

"A single mission makes all philosophies mad, but the shelves of Mortlake held its own reprieve," said old Jonas. "An antidote to its supposed idea. All health believes as it disbelieves. Scientific instruments also up on the shelves, globes presented from his old friend Mercator, decorated with Dee's discoveries and observations, a world in becoming. Navigation equipment, compasses, a 'watch clock' accurate to the second, a cross-staff ten foot long. And more by bottles, jars, distilleries, flasks, and pots, all for experiments, all nature in a revelation, God's text by his mysterious law. 'I fathom divinities by the bubbles glowing in the heated metals. All that is nature must be tested in nature,' said Dee.

I interrupted the old mariner. "Where is my text to open Eden, recast the flames, recount the lisp within the quiet? Do you plaint me fool?"

"First the match." The mariner spoke, his eyes now pits of death. "Leading from the main room of the open library were small rooms Dee called 'appendices,' where oddities and marvels, rarities gathered in his journeys. Liquids brewed in heating flasks, sulfur, mercury, earth of strange chemistries, herbs of medical properties, supposes and theories, and always there was tobacco. Dee led through the narrow halls to a locked door. 'My private library, the *Interna bibliotheca*,' a finger to the quiet of his lips, Dee smiled, 'a privilege only to my very close and the very wise.'

"The room in its darkness, a secret gather for a host of books, and a mirror near a scroll of parchment on his desk, lenses, a crystal ball, several different sizes arranged on a shelf. 'Attend,' said Dee, 'to my private chapel.' This oratory another library—here not public books, but the spiritual texts, transactions of secret alchemies, astronomies, planets, stars and the Hebrew Cabala, the Bible in Latin, Greek and the ancient language of the Jews. 'Here all the known works of Hermes Trismegistus.' Dee caressed the leather binding, the special satisfaction beneath his touch, a smile almost illuminating his skin.

"I sat before his desk. Dee was consumed in silence, as if to speak would embarrass even the portals of his own thoughts. He leaned into the drab colors of his gown, ever decorated in planets and signs of the Zodiac, mystic symbols, more Egyptian, more ancient than the pyramids. 'How our gardens have faded into memory,' said Dee.

"'Gardens?' I asked.

"'Eden!' repeated Dee. 'Hermes had the second Eden almost to his grasp. We failed the gift and played our pleasures puppet to a snake.' John Dee's eyes unlit in humor, their concentrations a weight upon his words. 'We can talk to angels,' he said, 'if we call our invitations, using the language spoken in Eden, and saying their ancient names. I am certain all wisdom and knowledge will be within our grasp.' Dee in the mechanicals of his genius, as brilliant as any Roman engineer. He worshiped numbers, the quadrants of his God. Dee pushed a book across his desk. 'The more ancient the text, the closer to God.' I opened the silver clasps that held the covers of the book closed, the regal lines beneath my fingertips.

"'Hebrew,' I said.

"'The first language of God and Eden. Debased somewhat by the fall, but certainly God's words to Adam and his to God were in a divine and pure form, but this is the key, a rusted key, it's true, but the Cabala secrets angels in its hieroglyphs. Hebrew letters are so much more. They shadow numbers in their sounds. A letter that can be a number is a number that can be a code. I wrote Walsingham of this to better work with spies. All things hidden can be of war and of success. The ancients ever bear to us their many gifts, and also a chance to ordain a peace. The Cabala and Hermes Trismegistus are profiles of our Christian thought, and so we, as they, true by similarities. One religion created new, gathering all, rejecting none, and an end to religious wars.'"

The sea rolls sequestered beneath the black. How sways the deck, the bells call night. Eyes hunt their hungers through the sea, and I in search of one man I scarcely know, thinking on the mariner's face. "Behind the one the many, behind the many the one." The old mariner plaintive to his celestial plea. Every religion gathered into one. Each reformed, its exile healed from the splinters of Eden's fall. How dreamed old Jonas in his many robes and many words, or is all this squeak just a cat playing philosophies with a mouse?

The old mariner spoke his confessions. "I was never the better that is the good, only the sufficient witness to the chase." The tale hangs a moment on Jonas's thought. "Dee pushed the crystal ball across the desk. 'Say a prayer, presume a purity, call an angel's name, then see what mysteries can arise,' he ordered.

"I pleaded my soul, severed from its vanities. But can it serve? Clear, the orb, unblemished by any scratch. I seek in its distortions, divining vapors. I see nothing but the bending of the room, the bowed papers on the desk, a candle, its flame bloomed on the surface of the crystal ball. 'Nothing seen,' I said.

"'Look again. Hold persuasions in a sacrifice,' said Dee. An hour's gaze. My eyes tear, straining in their reports. And so little my revelations only to mix our friendship salted with a tang of animosity.

"'And so have I failed?' I said to Dee.

"'Not an adept, nor I. We must find another.' Kindness in Dee's voice.

"'But I did not call an angel by their ancient Hebrew names. That knowledge may be the herald,' I pleaded.

"Dee shook his head. 'Friend, be at peace, your flesh and spirit are subject to the invisibilities of a different power. As Hermes

Trismegistus wrote, all the objects of the heavens, the metals of earth, its rocks, its liquids, plants, colors, images, wine, sea and salt. As the sun and moon, the stars and planets emit rays, divine emanations, some visible as light, some invisible as the magnet the iron pulls. Each subject and image concentrating certain rays to the specific sympathies of itself. The sun to gold, the moon to silver, and so angels in their aspects to the crystal ball, held there to be seen by those whose soul is crafted to have the eye.'"

As the sun moves so the earth is pitched to its strange occasions, I mused, watching the mariner speak. *Astrology and its dictionary map its hidden rays; vapors housed their energy all about. And so the river's voice and Drake's great sea trembles, living just beyond the common ear.* I saw the old mariner wince to some passing word, or image, not yet staled by age. His face contorted by the thought, he said "Dee was ever in danger. Few knew the sculpture of the knot that held the noose." Old Jonas took my hand, holding it to the warmth of his leathered flesh. "You could have been my son. I have by chance and adventure a little wealth, which is left to you. Captain Moone has arrayed the documents for your hands, assuming you survive. What else I bequeath to you are histories, some most heretical to save our God."

Day sleeps, my evening candles burn. Ash sacrifices itself to become its light. My cabin's squalor, small in its closet, large in filth. The old mariner floats the fevered air, as an imagination speaking in its pieties. "The rumor of Dee's theologies never far from his neighbor's lips. Silence, sometimes not a total friend when ignorance sits its superstitious eggs. When books raised fears in those years ago, a geometric diagram and its mathematical formulas seemed a deviltry. Euclid scorned, but beneath the comedy that burns its clown. Dee believed what Hermes Trismegistus did espouse: man himself could construct an idol, which was a living god. Not the God who could create the world from nothing, but from his laws a complexity of metals, woods and stones, a sculpture that could combine and gather the divine rays of earth and heaven to be itself a divinity. As the ancients could, the Egyptians and the Greeks, so to us our questions and our majesty would no longer be forfeit. Our idols not demons but only of the pure. Still openly agreed by all, Saint Augustine railed against the evil idols, but angels and the good only were what Dee sought. Man again to his rightful place, a seat beside God. A creator of divinities. The puppet has taken the strings into his own hands, burst the dramas to be the play." The old mariner's eyes glowed in the reflections of the kindling fireside. He warmed his hands. "We seek, both Dee and I, as you to be beyond our dominations."

"Am I to be the maker of gods?" my words half-mused. My mariner just smiled.

Chapter Seven

WHAT WORLD IS THIS TO SPOON US
THROUGH AN OCEAN LAKE?

 WALK THE DECK on the *Black Swan* in the crimson of the coming sun. Blue skies paint the water blue. Wisps of clouds in streaks of deeper red, and their western edge still black in the shadows before the rising light. How calm the water's play, the cooling breeze a coming warmth beneath the undertow of chill. I thought on Jonas's words, *What search is there in me? This colony, my love, the river's voice. All my whispers canticle to an uncertain text.* I stand the rail. "Bloom in sun and sea," I cry to myself. "My expeditions now sail to the furthest gate."

CAPTAIN GEORGE WAYMOUTH STOOD THE DECK, A MAN IN THE portraits of his shadow. One eye as ever on his crew, a map on a scroll under his arm, a compass in his hand. "Deep water and fair winds, eh Smith?" I smiled at nothing but the pleasantness festooned in a waste of time. "By midday a landward breeze will swing to and have the coast."

Hands upon the rail. Waymouth a captain steadied by any passing wood. "Ever take sail to the arctic?" he asked. I shook my head upon my appropriate, "Never,...and you?" A question little forward to the plot, as Waymouth gauged the sun by sextant and a sigh.

"Yes, some years back, 1602, seeking the Northwest Passage, my expeditions for the London Company. Then five years later by cloak and secrets along the coast of Maine. Cold and wet we sailed, but beneath our keel treasuries in vast runs of fish.

"Old Jonas held the Pacific sea most far, and the Northwest Passage a schoolboy's taunt on a bogus map."

"Old Jonas, that ancient, featherless duck who played to Drake's quack. Through the Polar Sea, through Frobisher's strait, I in full canvas, my ship against the currents from the east. The savages there worshiped their frozen ghost, mountains, armadas of floating ice, the sea colored turquoise in its blood. The snow, the fog, the chilled discontents, my crew plays mutiny to gain a smile. So a quick return to London and little done."

Excuses lead us as a dog. "Now Hudson gambles upon his open wake." I spoke already heatless in the marrow of my bones.

By mid-day the Virginia coast rose in the swaying grass of its windblown shallows. Green patches and damp sands, breakers tumbling white. Lines in washed battalions, its folds hiss upon the shore. We sailed north, time barring us from the larger bays, but scallop and pinnace sent to map the puddles and spend the clock. Captain Waymouth held the coast always for an easy sail to safety.

Shoals and sandbars, each mile sailed, a lead-weighted line cast into the sea, fathoms counted to the water's depth. A bucket dragged to know the nature of the ocean floor. Black sand, rocks, pebbles, all matters of junk to own the clues to keep us from being beached.

Waymouth to his charts, his deck a wooden sulk, its only recreation worry. I saw the map. "Hudson's own," said our captain, "taken from his person before handed to the Dutch, a copy of a copy, a little to the vague, and somewhat to the false." Waymouth smiled, "But do we know by absolute what papers Hudson gave the Dutch, and are ours true?" The questions he asked are the breeze that sails us north.

IN THREE DAYS WE SAILED INTO A GREAT BAY, HORIZONS ROUNDED in marsh and hills, vast in overflows of water, swift currents from the narrows. "In this bay three rivers pool, or so draws Hudson's map." Waymouth unrolled the chart. Above, sailors called the fathoms, and on the hills the savages marked with smokey pyres to address our sails from the islands to the south and west. "The savages here brought some death to Hudson's crew," was our captain's whisper. "Firelocks readied, caution on the decks." So stammered his braveries, embossed in his nervous heat. The *Black Swan of Devon*, how shrouded the white feathers of your canvas sails, fluttered the light upon the swaying sea.

We sailed northward as if into the shimmering moon of waters, so seated round this curved immensity. *I drink upon the cups of heavens,* or so I thought. Small by Chesapeake, but by fertile land and English harbor, its beauties cleave worlds in wild grandeurs.

Canoes upon the bay, for war or welcome, the question to our mind. We had small rail cannons, these murderers as they were called, not yet with shot and powder. Three canoes, a forth from the start a little shy toward the island. Closer the angry voices did claim our ears. Violent the sounds, the meaning puzzles. Our sails luffed to lie a hull. Trinkets brought, small bells, our hopes in shiny metal tones. We display the gifts, our hands beckoning, peace signs given, sailors in the rigging, and we upon the deck. We court the better silence, but war last year too soon, and Hudson accounts no bargains here.

I spoke the language of Powhatan, it having some commerce with their own. Familiar meanings not quite the sounds. The chatter stopped. "Are you the makers of death, or have you come for fur and trade?" the call, the speaker repeating the French word for "fur."

"For trade and fur." I spoke in French, less the forfeit than our English tongue. The savages council, their canoes by grasp of hand held as one. Waymouth having a long pole brought, a few bells being upon its end, over the side, an offering above the water, a bribe to a moment and its peace. Two canoes approach, caution swallows its bitter fear. The trinkets taken, the savages then to retreat, another council. Then we parley by counter gifts. Furs to us, combs and knives and bells, shiny luxuries rare beside the smoke of the wigwam fire.

Two savages come aboard the *Black Swan.* Their canoes tied along our side. In Waymouth's cabin a feast of meats and biscuits and aqua vitae. A cup of wine more to our new guides' taste. Our mainsail now unfurled, the arms of the horizon beckoning, chains of distant hills flowing to the banks of a great river. I am drunk in wilderness. We anchor in a deep channel, a safe distance from a pleasant beach. "By Hudson's reckoning, this is an island, smaller than the one to our north and east," Waymouth pointed, his chart held spread between his hands. "That is the island of the Mannahatas, the north river bears upon its western edge. If Hudson lied, it is by some hope the northwest passage. If not, by truth, we splash upon the length of a simple river." Waymouth displacing the grasp of certainty with soured possibilities.

So unimagined you are anchored to a fret, I thought.

The savages to their canoes, kindly in parting. "Some hope of peace and trade," said first mate Philip Stacie, who had boarded with Hudson in 1608, the year and voyage before the discovery of the North River and all the islands of this bay.

"More likely we are welcomed by war. Hudson lost John Colman here by treachery. So be at guard," said the captain.

"We should exchange hostages," I said.

"What was played in Virginia is not for here," replied Waymouth, a man who had once kidnapped five savages in Maine for a display to the London worthies. So much we are that contradicts, our actions to themselves. The fog is us, its gathered smoke.

AT NIGHT FIRES ON THE HILLS, THEIR SHADOWS FLAME, CRIMSON on the calm waters. The world in weighted dark trembles to distant chants. Strange these lands, ever in their violent peace. I walk the deck ordering to the crew, "Extinguish all lamps." My footfalls drum, echoing upon their own. Philip Stacie abruptly at my shoulder. "The captain objects to your ordering about the crew."

I nodded. "Reveal ourselves too much and an arrow may find our heart as home. Tell that to your captain."

Receiving my words Waymouth scowled, but anger has its own sulk. He withdrew to his cabin, furious to be reminded of that which he ignored.

At dawn a smoking calm, a tail of dust rising to wag the sky. Savages in hordes to the beaches and canoes, men and women, children, baskets in their hands. Indian wheat, tobacco, fish and fowl, furs by carpets. This to have our trade. Twenty-eight canoes, their oars stroke currents in their advance to the *Black Swan*. Fourteen savages in each canoe, their faces painted in black and red, a bow and quiver filled with arrows, a stone club. Bold and grim in their approach. Captain Waymouth summoned to the deck. "Breathe caution here," I said. A nod, our captain judged the scene.

"We treat them fairly," his words.

"There may be histories of foreign evils come by other ships. Can savages discern a nation by its flag or voice? Be warned, and wary yet again."

Waymouth to the council, silent to himself. "And you, Smith, what do you propose?" speaking as if I were new to the morning's menace.

"A cannon volley of salt above their heads, nothing to kill, a warning friendly said."

"Those furs would bring a royal price in London," smiled our captain, weighing his profits against his fears. Greed salves caution as it slips us toward an open grave. Closer the canoes, oars smoothly dipped, the cut pulled against the water's weight. Among the crew, questions whispered, pointing toward the eloquence upon the bay. Waymouth stood stilled in voiceless wonder. The crew to the rigging, firelocks lit. Some to their cannons, others crouch, crossbows in their hands.

"Falcons prepare to volley. Load blanks with leather," Waymouth called, ever his own man in other's advice, "Command on my warning," our captain's arm raised, "as they bear."

And so the pantomime blasts the morning's heat. The canoes collide, oars drag in many directions on the white surf. "Why do you come in war?" I called out in the language of Powhatan, climbing to the railing, holding to the rigging for support. Waymouth jumped to the spider's web as well, rope ladders to his back, calling in signs of peace. The sparrows playing themselves a sacrifice to the hawk.

In the turmoil round our English galleon, the waters flashed in riots. A passing school of salmon climbed on each other's shimmering backs to pain in frenzy. Golden flesh reflecting sun on the currents here and there. "Smith!" My name is screamed. I turn, a thud, a weave as threads of arrows dart on the air. How dark in their falling strings of black. Waymouth pulls me to the deck.

"Volleys have them far," he said. Too late. Near the wheel a shaft thrust through a sailor's throat. A silence stings in a silent death. Our firelocks burst, flames flee across the smoke. Cannons break thunder in the rainless storm, blasting savages from their canoes, the water stained a floating red. How much war when slaughter accounts the price? Some savages dead, four I guessed. One of ours, a few wounds of not much account.

Our anchor raised, gallant do we advance in our retreat up the bay. The currents in the water swirl. My ankle chills in the memory of my almost death. The canoes have disappeared. Empty rolls the horizon, heavy in its sunlit wait.

SAILING EVER NORTH INTO HUDSON'S RIVER, TOWARD THAT HOPED-for passage built of all our legends. *Oh Jonas, would your geographies were with me now.* Waymouth sent our pinnace some leagues beyond our sight, with lead, weights and line to sound the water's depth. There alone, casting nets, ten great mullets they caught, a foot and a half each; and a ray so in girth and weight it took four men's labor to bring it aboard our ship. We anchored for the night off the island of the Mannahatas. Oozy banks and marsh, but climbing the rigging toward the top sail of our main, inland I could see fair stands of oaks and currents, ponds and clear brooks. And on the height of the river's banks, small waterfalls, their white mists rising against the turmoil of the flood. This surging cataract, such a small cool of breath upon the heat. We rowed ashore, walked a path of packed damp sand, carrying Jack Olver, our slain. A liar and a coward thought by all, but death dominions no contempt, so the burial solemn and forgotten, not even a written scratch to mark the grave.

That night thunder, its storm and winds howl their lost spirits through our spars. Mouthless words, distorted in their screaming frenzies, as if a passing agony now sought its wounds. I sit my cabin, voices in their distant thoughts. All landscapes have a memory, this is mine. Every longing has her face, all passions have her name.

How quickly the candle attends the almost dark. I lie in my cabin to sleep in dreams. Visions now came in fearful portents. We sail the polar sea, the ice in flowing continents, the pink of glowing clouds. The land a haunted crimson, the snow in frigid fire. I walk the deck. Far off Waymouth incoherently babbles, his nervous lunatic beating upon the air. The ice impassible, we anchor to an iceberg. Our ropes stretch, bowed in their own weight, the fragile threads bind us to the blue-white dells.

How swiftly the dream changes in the robes of sleep. Now awakened the day, a warmth, the sea clearing. Our pinnace hauled to venture into latitudes. Unto itself, the pinnace gone, gone from sight, gone to gray and wilderness, a voyage into cold and quiet, and seabird calls. And so the exile's s dreams are woven into the fabric of his solitude.

I AWAKE TO DREAD AND CIRCUMSTANCE, ON DECK THAT MORNING, "No river, this," said Waymouth. "A strait, our passage west. Hudson lied. I knew he lied. I was always the better sailor." The sun in its cloud-clearing dawn, our anchor weighed, our progress north. Cliffs to the east, sharp walls break upward in their palisades from the water's edge. Waymouth ordered a bucket on a line thrown to gather water.

The bucket brought aboard again. "Taste," he ordered, "and discover. The water is salt. The current speaks beyond a river's course."

So certain, so wet, the jealousies kiss, I thought. *How our captain parades himself upon his own adoring deck.*

The river tongues this landscape flat in its broad and silver wash. Salmon in hordes of glitter play beneath the water. Still the waves taste of salt. Four hours we sail ourselves as leaf upon the flows. Now distant mountains roam in round profusions across the sky. The river widens into a bay. Canoes in dart row in welcome, beckoning for our trade. Men and women and children sit within the wooden frames, birch the hulls. So different these crafts from those of the Chesapeake: more articulate in their wood, more craft, more speed. So strange this familiarity, yet so strange. Painted savages, faces in masks and tinted horrors, to scare the children in our heads. Feathers worn as cloaks, or many kinds of skins—some deer or bear—made to civil dress, to modesty and to skill. Women shy and maidens ever bloomed to quiet, as children ever to their play. With caution we allowed a few to board, bringing baskets of oysters, sweet currents, pumpkins, Indian corn, and small furs, beaver and others. The people so loving, so kind in trade. An old man—"the governor of this country," as our captain told—came to us bearing tobacco, calling the name of "Hudson," searching for that frame to fit the profiles of his memory. None discovered, he saddened, asking by sign if we would accompany him to his village as his guest. Waymouth not inclined to any danger, gave to me my own leash and bid me well, saying, "Entertain yourself by this savage and his tricks, and learn of any passage west."

And so I am again by orphan the prodigal. How easily the canoe slips the river on folding waves. Cool water, breathe a pleasant air. The shore sand and rock, an easy step. We walk the grass soft and meadowed, mountains to the east and west. A son again encompassed by the broad fathers of the living land. Nurtures are in this wilderness. I am loved. Our travel was not long, a mile inland, streams and brooks and many planted fields, grapes and berries, sweet rainbows for their food. Pumpkins, corn, ducks and geese, birds in forests. I have seen these luxuries with the hungers of my eyes. In the village furs laid upon the ground for me to sit upon. Great platters of venison prepared, and ducks. Young girls not as forward as on the Chesapeake. Women to themselves. Men a village quiet at peace. But wary always, I know the stealth behind the surface calm. My firelock lit, my pistol set. The language of Powhatan not understood, although a few words had some reach. And so by sign and pictures and some village hieroglyphs, I had the river mapped on a small plain of dirt. The river will divide, that is drawn, but no ocean-sea and no great passage west.

WAYMOUTH, AS EVER, PLAYED HIS CAPTAINCY DULL. HIS CABIN DARK, neat in its poverty: old charts, a table, an old chair weathered by age and damp, rude splinters for the unsuspecting hand. Tin plates for our soured meat, flavored with salt and worms. Hard biscuits for the bleeding gums, armored with the stink of molding cheese. "This is a strait," Waymouth pours himself some aqua vitae, drinks. "Savages and their legends, you call a map."

"The savages told what they believe is true."

Waymouth taps the point of his knife stained with meat into the wood of the table. "Hudson lied, and we will not sail to those dangers north. Not again! I've sailed those polar wastes. Warm your bones, Smith, to a molten red! Flesh does glacier in those wilds." So saying, the captain stood, his forefinger pointing to the deck, as he added, "This river has a tide, its ebb and flow higher and further than any known." I looked my Captain Fool hard upon the eye. *Even the Thames?* I thought. My question never asked.

AT LOW EBB THE BACKS OF SANDBARS ARISE ABOVE THE SURFACE of the river's run. Some far from the banks nearer mid-stream, with shallows all about. The channel undulates, smooth waters, deep ribbons in twisted course. Good winds, the mainsail blooms in its full sheet. Some speed to the western beach. Mountains high in gray assaults crowd the water's edge. Landscape lost, our vistas now forest and a rocky shadow upon the sky.

The pinnace upriver sounded to our safe approach. "Four fathoms," a sailor cried on the *Black Swan*. Depths gauged on lengths of rope. A number offered. The sudden lurch, the swaying mast, the sailors thrown from their feet. A barrel rolls across the deck. The cat screams, racing to catch its fear.

"Beached by sand, we are aground!" Waymouth runs along the railing, head over the side, appraising the damages and his fears.

"No leaks between the planks," Stacie called from below, his relief filling the lyric of his voice.

A cannon fired, noise declared across the shallows, streaked in the crimson boil of a hurled warning. That signal for our pinnace to return. And Drake, you as well beached on the Pacific sea. There canyons rounded in their depthless fathoms, the reef its menace hidden by a slip of water. But here the hurt is but a sandy wedge.

The day slipped by, its hours lost as we waited for the tidal flood. Our captain walked the deck. The sky gray and darkening. A breeze foretelling storm. Some few canoes scatter to the shelter of the sandy beach, its overhanging trees. Anticipations dismiss into quiet, the thunder echoing distance, yellow flashes in its silver lightning. Broad winds furrowing the tide, questing in the avalanche of rain. How cool the fresh perfumes of this world. The river rising to its full. The moment come. Waymouth orders a small anchor brought to the stern railing. The crew soaked to their garments. Every displeasure drips upon each thread. Now by block and tackle all cautious hands upon the lines, respectful of the anchor's weight, lowering this iron grin, its pick down to the pinnace. The currents swell, white crests in violent sweeps across the race. Ropes held wet by their twisted cords, lashed by sweat, greased by the oils of our hands and labors. Perilous the moment comes, the anchor lifted over the stern. The rope breaks, the screams, the falling iron crashes, the rising geyser in its foam of blood. Who is my brother that died this day? The crew to its horror, steps to see its work. The bodies thrash, half-drowned, some submerged, the bubbles exploding around the floating wreck and splintered planks. The pinnace side smashed. The crew flies to rescue, lines tied to weights. Panic and riot graves to a play of grief. The water filled with splashes, calls and thwarted help. Three dead. Two hurt. The pinnace fallen to long repairs. And Captain Waymouth holds the black spot and the crew breathes contempt. "Bear the cheap ropes to save a penny," said one, a little vengeful mutiny in his voice.

How sways the *Black Swan* buoyed upon the river's tide, like a cork in a child's puddle sea. The ship freed by the tide. A waste of corpses in our captain's foolish spite, and so a twin of judgments on our dangled hate. The sacks of our dead carried through the shallows, the weight of dead flesh, our hands strain to grip the legs and shoulders, the bodies of the dead bending, their eyes open staring sightless into their own unknown. Laid on the damp sand, clothes draining, a fresh flood, rough cloths, shrouds to dress a final passage. The graves dug, words follow into the midst of grief and angers.

Spades of earth, the dark loam piles on the pleasant hill above the river. Savages gather into chants to awaken spirits. This land bears no loneliness, excited drums moaning in the sovereigns of their dance.

The shattered pinnace dragged ashore, water gushes between the teeth of its broken planks. Our carpenter and five of the crew felling trees, sawing new boards to repair the hull. On the grassy hill the savages sat, inquisitive in their human sight, a wonder to them this idyll of saws and hammers. Axes flash mighty in our paraphernalia. To the savages our tools were less to labor, more to curiosity.

The carpenter, his repairs, fresh wood planed and nailed, heated tar the black mud to seal the cracks, applied boiling with flat sticks and trowels, this new perfume that bubbles to sting the air. What sweeps within the scent but a memory of old England, its factories, labors in their chemical pots, smoke, flames and a change now births upon this wind. My river, will your voices quench, silent on your flowing lips?

This northern river, so different and yet alike to the river of the Chesapeake, less heat, more and sweeter springs. So cool its meadow, the forest quiet, the dark seas of sky undulate when flocks of songbirds eve on the wing. How calm I am in this mantle of my life. How fearful gloom the thoughts in the undertow. I am grim in this paradise. I am impatient to be alive in the warm protections of her arms. But night dreams flare and bloom in colored vibrance and foreboding, a cold northern wilderness of empty seas and fog, and continents of ice. Visions now; am I prophesied yet again? Perhaps this hint awards from my deepest wounds. In my cabin I slumber into a fearful rest. Nightmares lurk beneath the eyelids' mounds, a painter haunts the mind, his colored shadows awaken fearful in my dreams.

The fog boiled above the calm waters in their quiet wash. Each sound sharp, its brevity cut into my loneliness. Formlessness surrounds in its many grays, a sailor calling the fathoms in their unseen depth. Stacie nods to himself. It is a vision, but I know I sleep. I stood the deck, hands upon the rail. The changing watch, the crew hand-over-hand climbing into the rigging to become as hanging berries on a poison vine. Across the ropes onto the mast, eyes sighted toward the continent of mist, its landscape wandering through the air. But in that watery dust, a shape, more specter, a breath of congealing motion, a ship, a tattered lace, its torn sails fluttering from their spars, all that silent glides spirit-thin upon their ghostly canvas.

"A ship," I cried in my nightmare voice. The watch impatient scrambled to take up my point. All eyes stared into the fog, its clouds in nothingscape, their surface swirls. No ship, only a screen of blank. Then the ship again passing distantly through a cave of thinning smoke. "Heralds to our drums," I ordered. Our trumpets blared. A signal cannon brought forth, primed charged in leather fists, the wild report, the crimson bellows through the smoking blast. No alarm, no stir, the ship sails in quiet evaporation to disappear.

Stacie to the deck, as Waymouth below screamed, tearing at his rope restraints, "It comes the demons of the north. It wants to bear us to our death. I am the captain. I allow the course."

Our crew superstitious but glides the deck. "Our Waymouth is in a captain mood," smiled a knowing Stacie.

"Do we take the wheel and follow to the hunt? That ship most near." I smiled, the answer ready, our rudder set, our tack to plunge full sail into mysteries. How sudden squalled the water's dust. A gale rising to its dramatic now, a freezing dampness to be felt. Our bones cold brace our colder flesh. Grumblings on the deck, fears and unknown terror. Mutiny ever whispers through the armories of the belaying pins.

"We'll beach," a scream, as a white promontory of impending heights, an iceberg off our bow. Clouds of snow and mist in drifts from the wilds of its mountainous peaks. Cracks and growls, the wind in shivers.

All to the sails. The wheel in desperate clock, spins to play the bow upon a different point. Foam exploding spray bursting across our figurehead. The *Black Swan* leans into a deadly turn. Waves flow, rising in thunder, hurl their weight upon the crew. White rivers upon the moving havoc of the deck. Tides and currents wash cold and crash across the listing hull. But slow crawls the digits down the breath, the *Black Swan* to tack and move away from that white death. Our lives pass, exhausted in joy.

We sailed doom to port and the dream breaks. "Was that a ship or mountain that we hailed and sought?" I questioned in my sleep, which answered, saying, "I am uncertain. What law presents."

TWO DAYS AFTER, CAPTAIN WAYMOUTH BREWED HATE EACH TIME he spoke. Our voyage still north. The river no longer fathomed into deep canyons. I sent the pinnace north to gauge the depth of the river.

"There is a tributary, its waters rising in the west. I was told by a *werowance* that might be our best hope of the northwest passage," I said to Stacie, whose nod brought forth a grunt.

Eight leagues we sailed, sounding with weighted ropes. "Beneath the river rise hidden hills, canyons, sandbars and shifting promontories. All that is above secrets what is below," my words like dead leaves swept unheard against our captain's ear. By mid-afternoon smooth rocks glisten across the shallows. Our way almost closed. Only by our pinnace could we venture beyond this rocky bar. "The western branch our only hope." Our crew for its anger had little patience for any danger, but a few for hate of the captain's eyes manned the oars played along the coast searching the western beach. The crew's gift to excuse their sloth. A fool's adventure we had by spite.

I cupped the river's water in my hand. I listen for a noise. No words, only the sun to smile reflections on my fingertips. And yet this puddle has a weight, some binding of a flesh. A living thing with a voice I've yet to hear? As all the seas, are all the waters of this new world one? I touch the river once again. No plaintive speech, no philosophies, no forge to shape theologies, and then the whispers, moistened in the breathless heat.

I am by inundations renewed of birth. Changing ever, never do I sleep, the sleep of memory. The river's words to convalesce my ear. But which river speaks to me, the James or this, its Edens lost? Old Jonas, explain your alchemies. I pine salvations.

We found the convergence of the western branch. Whirlpools circle, waters tumble high backed, more powerful in sight than through its eastern spill. Waves break to foam and surf, we sail on fair winds, our oars plunge. Fair excitements joyed our discoveries. How many deaths to find the strait to the western sea? Not by leagues, but by the splinters of a mile. Soon rapids and rocks, unfavorable currents. We beached, walked the bank, there a great falls of water, mists rising, turning in a field of falling clouds. *This strait is but a river, and we are chained to nothing but retreat*, I thought. *Hudson had his truth. His journals are by some weight the tale, and Waymouth and I just the puppets to the stage, left abandoned but to trace the gestures of its strings.*

THAT NIGHT I FEARED I WOULD TEAR MYSELF AGAIN IN DREAMS, BUT no dreams came, no words. Sleep, my vision, that I might rest! Next day, the sky streaked wide in the crimson and torn ribbons of the night held clouds. Southward the *Black Swan* sped, its bow folding waters. By seven leagues we had canoes in sly circles glide around us, begging trade. Sad at our leaving, they signed with the last of our iron trinkets, hatchets and knives. Trust is a lonely skeleton buried in a drift of sand. Some menace we saw in a well-armed few. These were not let too close. Others who broke their bows and arrows and cast away their clubs, we had aboard with their sweet cargoes of oysters, berries, grapes and tobacco, and a black rock, its sharpness could cut iron, even glass. In water it melted into a fine black for paint.

As ever, Captain Waymouth not such a fool to his own safety, had the crew with muskets to their sides, cannons and falcons readied to be primed. "We have hostages," I said, nodding toward the savages on the deck, "if we have the need."

"These savages craft a better *ambushado*, their menace constant, and hostages of little concern, no halt upon a war," remarked Waymouth. "You are of memories of the east and the Chesapeake, I of Maine and the frozen white and blue rivers of the arctic. Cold in high wilderness, these savages bring war by a slightly different cart."

How sports our success, changing with each cast of the dice, my thoughts upon a world at comfort with its own inconsistent self. As ever, experience hangs its dried philosophies upon a vagrant's pole. I smiled to the thought, as I indulged the brevity of the moment. *The clock is deaf to the movement of its own hands, and the unwinding of its own springs.*

Sailors stroll guard around the deck, muskets played ready in their hands, exhausted in their sleepless tread. Stacie stares toward the river and its raft of circling canoes, toward a point of land where a hundred savages stand dark in their silhouettes.

"For a greeting, or for war?" Stacie questioned, his hand a shield of shadows, some protection before his eyes, the sun a blinding blight in stilled orange blood. Stacie to the stern, peering over the side, the weight of a musket from his shoulder to his hands, aiming. "Thieves upon the captain's window!" Two savages had climbed from their canoe onto our rudder up through the window of Waymouth's cabin to steal clothes, pants and shirts, a blanket, a belt, spoils in their hands, standing on the rudder. Defiance smiled upward at Stacie's aimed musket. The two savages leaped into the flood of the *Black Swan's* wake. The crack, the power blast, the quick thread of fire, its folding smoke. The ball in a bloody fist burst the savage's chest.

Arrows now to lace in blackened darts, the sky filled in lethal falling twigs. The thuds, the snap in slow rolling boom our muskets echoed. The savages on the canoe, bows bent, arrows pulled against the cheek, aimed into coming flights. From the promontories more volleys, our deck a field of feather pins. One of our crew wounded, as our cannons thundered across the water. Our meteors flash incendiary. Canoes caught in wreck as blasted fountains boil the river in a rising white. Two canoes destroyed, some savages dead, others drowned in shock, arms and heads face down floated.

Still from the shore more arrows to lay slaughter across the air. Our cannons salvo smoke in flung sparks. Dirt and rocks explode to dust. How swept these heights as our lightning storms. How many graves to our fallen Eden?

Canoes paddled and disappear. Perhaps four dead on the hill. The savages trading on the deck jumped overboard long ago. We lower our boat, the captain's wares drifting abandoned off the stern. The boat's oars set to their place. Strained upon the pull of the water, muscles bulge in sweat and inner heat. I watched from the deck, my discomfort grim.

The pinnace wallows to our stern. By suddens and surprise, a hand appears upon its side. Violently the waters splash, the crew thrown from their oars. The surviving savage, hidden by our rudder, rages to overthrow the boat. The second mate in the sways of a rugged balance, stumbles forward toward the savage. His sword drawn from its scabbard, cuts upon the breeze. The thud, a gargle in a cry, blood in heavy spit mists the air. A severed hand still grasps the hull. The sword flecked in meat, a scarlet froth. The savage faints to drown in death. Water to salt his hungers.

Chapter Eight

IN THE WEAVE OF MY DESIRES HIDES FATE.

AYMOUTH'S GOODS RETRIEVED, we passed the island of Mannahata. No one seen. No threat. Sailing south toward the lower bay, the sea beyond the final narrows, horizon to a thousand years. Light blue, the sky-painted waters at the horizons, the darkening grays of distant showers. A world content to be itself, the hold of mysteries, and always the hiss that forms the words, the river ever confessing a narrative of itself. "Hudson had told the truth," I said. "There is no treason. Let us make reports and be for Chesapeake and our English Virginia."

"There are more than maps or journals. All who seek the passage know lands of Eastern wealth lie west beyond the frozen wastes. That course follows north, but a closer north in Maine is for our success. Hudson always danced the fool, all his expeditions have come to mutiny. He is done, full sunk in his own wake. But Maine, where I have mapped, there are furs, and on the cheap, all that trade for us. A warmer coin is nearer and safer got." Waymouth glanced the faces of all those who heard his scheme.

Strange this pointed ambition, Waymouth's purpose more trimmed and forceful. And I wonder at the strut behind the play. *The company surely accounts its own agents aboard the* Black Swan, *and Hudson does not sail unpegged. Perhaps our captain's speech secures but his own employment.*

"Frobisher, Davis, Drake and Gilbert. Many have sought the Northwest Passage. Mostly they found but death," continued Waymouth. How unlike my Drake this captain, this scrape. Waymouth licks his words. "Why not for us some riches of a closer wealth in Maine?"

A taste of greed is on his tongue, I thought. The *Black Swan* anchored to refill its dilapidated water kegs. I stood the deck, the words of old Jonas conventioned in my mind. *And where are your magic Edens now, old friend? Embrace the fall, contraries have become our heavens. Loneliness drifts through me. I ache of emptiness. Where is your voice, old Jonas? My wounds bleed some success. I am now of some estate. My possessions have a name. I am ranked in government. And yet I am impelled to dream in visions of the north. A living chill paints nightmares on the phantoms of my inner eye. Gifts no more, what madness gives! A river, cold and prophecy! Am I foretold to die alone, anchored to an icy waste? And John Dee, by what angels did you hear your news? By what crystal ball, by what adept did you see the landscapes of your final choice?*

Old Jonas, I hear your warnings, I am ordained to histories, but are they yours?

"In Elizabeth's court, where ambition fashioned in beauty struts before the gathered eyes," the old mariner speaking secrets few protocols would dare, and fewer knew, "admiration acquires power, and power gains as its illusions grow. But beneath the glitter, the gold is thin, the powder rancid on the fetid cheeks. Their wigs are a vermin's lair, as diseased as the plagues that shadow in the street. Elizabeth and her Court dipped a willing toe in a wizard's brew, some alchemy and a little heresy," so old Jonas said. "John Dee had tutored his dream of our world's resurrection to the most favorites of the Court. All that is important when begun," said old Jonas, smiling through his ghostly words, "begins in insignificance. The cradle rocks unnoticed until the babe, full grown, has burst its sheets. Dee in the service of the Earl of Pembroke and then to the household of the Duke of Northumberland. The Dudley family now had the greatest mind in England to school its line. One of these students, Robert Dudley, was to become the Earl of Leicester. Dee was a college of one, its headmaster and its faculty. He the knife at the pedant's throat, Oxford and Cambridge believing Euclid's mathematics, its geometries just a syllabus of pricks and lines. But on those jots sailed the ships of Drake and the hope of the British Empire. Hammer learning to my mast," cried the old mariner. "Their scrolls are the parchment of my sails.

"Robert Dudley then Dee's student, and later their beloved nephew, the future poet, Sir Philip Sidney. Sidney's alchemies had more than astrologies in their chemistry. Words languaged almost into song, almost into chants, words by images, magics in talismans, and in measured rhythms to change our better speech with sensed invisibilities of a divine light. Sidney then the fulcrum on which our language spins secreted Hermes and his alchemies as its fire. Others of

Angels in Their Silent Gather

Dee, Sir Francis Walsingham, whose daughter married Philip Sidney, and the wizard Earl, Henry Percy…"

"Lord Percy's father, his son that shallow cur?"

The old mariner nodded to himself, saddened. "Greatness dispenses greatness in its single flash. The prodigies are only polished to ferment into rust."

I paced the deck of the *Black Swan*, the forests fleeing into the eternities of a green calm. Hand over hand I climbed the rigging into the swaying cradle of the mast to stand the lookout. How distant the emerald sameness bends. Clouds, swift moving shrouds, blues in golden rays, the sunlight blossoms, descending in perpetual fall. *I am as my old mariner. My garden is a loneliness, I the exile of no one born. And England, its power shared in families, by marriage through the father's or the mother's line. Monopolies consummated in the private chambers of a public vow. By expense and sacrifice, courage earns by luck its genius, and its hour's grandeur. A field of roses is but the moment, its drift is only to decay.*

The tale said then, it speaks now to my memory. Our campfire on the James, the black flickering shadows. The old mariner's eyes glowed in the flames. "John Dee held knowledge as his court. Adrian and Sir Humphrey Gilbert, their half brother, Sir Walter Raleigh, he the blessed of the damned, and John Dyer who assayed the gold Martin Frobisher first brought from that island of the arctic." I held these words by my thoughts, by apparitions, and now I returned upon that history into a strait Frobisher proclaimed the entrance to the Northwest Passage. How many deaths account the casualty that ambition brags? But it was this tale that set Drake to circumnavigate the globe. And now come to me, my Jamestown, my desires not to be swept aside. And Hudson, what decisions do you now mutiny against yourself, on what course are you already set? More the mariner had to confess, the exile giving school to the prodigal.

"Attend to me," he said. "What wisdom old age desires to disperse will not last another's youth. Remembrance is a fragile thing that sits within a dying house." Jonas stared in fascination through the flame. "How to begin with frightful warnings and speak of Dee, desires, and conversations with the angels." Jonas held to silence, digesting hesitation. "The stars and planets, the earth and the sun itself float in a vast emptiness. So it was first writ by Thomas Digges who was a ward and student of Dee. Digges, the finest of mathematical intellect, played himself to scandal defending Copernicus's idea of the earth's solar revolution. But that is where beginnings all begin, and where ideas concede themselves almost to be unthanked. The cosmology of the ancient Greeks and Romans had fouled upon the quill of a new equation: Homage to me that I am the point where the sky revolves. All that Copernicus swept away. Man despaired to be no longer the center of all that is. The sun no longer satellite, and I diminished to be myself. The church sent fire and stake to burn away the truth. Ridicule, a swarm of hate, but truth is a subtle worm. And Copernicus not so forward in his revolution as you may have thought. There is always an illusion that distorts the image behind the water glass. When worlds collide, vision speaks. Copernicus was not to himself the herald of the new, but a high priest of the ancient pyramids, an Egyptian worshiper of a most Egyptian god, the sun. Its light the center of it all."

How chilled was I in that remembered night? The James River flowing through its moonlit mysteries, whispering to itself, as I asked, "By what debate does Copernicus plead angels from Dee's alchemies?"

"They are of one, craving to be the glimpse of true theology, the universal religion encompassing all, excluding none. A family of love in multiple divinities under the supreme and only God. An end to religious strife," the old mariner laying logs upon the flame, his profile in fire and shadow, speaking almost to himself. "Will the dream forgive the dreamer, as he is lost behind its shifting curtain, and there his pantomime is danced? But beware, in double caution, for the servant only serves himself."

In his final revels, Old Jonas hesitant in his revelations. "You must know the geometries of your gift. The dangers beckon, bedded in their angelic innocence." Jonas swallowed, raised his finger as to pontificate a silent point. His hand trembled in the hesitation and nothing said.

I RETURNED FROM REMEMBRANCE, HOLDING TO THE ROPES, AS I sat upon a spar. The wind, the swaying deck, and I webbed in the lines of a delicate balance. How exiled in warm comforts, peace and the sweet salt perfumes, sea birds white in parade, their waddle around the deck, and I lush in suffocations, ponder love and land and resurrections, and always the mariner's voice, claimed always in its histories. "And what profiles in a secret fit, and how the spoils merged to reclaim our Eden. And Copernicus, whose worship was partial to the sun, joined in theologies with Hermes Trismegistus, who spoke of divine rays, effluvia from heavenly orbs, planets and stars, and sun and moon most important. All that is of earth gathered these divine emanations. To Hermes the sun was a visible god, its aspect from the one." The old mariner moved his hand to grasp my cold wrist. "Europe was in turmoils, theologies warring in barbed philosophies. Then the heavens conflagrate, burning a new daylight into the night sky. A star bloomed in white brilliance. For a thousand years heavens taught as set and perfect and unchangeable. And in that evening's moment, a new star, the brightest ever seen. 1572. But a year later that star has disappeared. All that I am is what I know," smiled the old mariner. "What I know, and what I know is wrong. The fever then is in the soul, despair is in the gut. What is my place? I am, but have made myself my own prodigal. Betrayed by God's words that I, the first and only of his love, ever certain as his creation and so my place. Man whimpers to slaughter to reassure himself and his belief. Five years after, in 1577, within days of Drake's sail around the world, there is a glow in a fresh apocalypse, the night burning in glowing heavens, a comet, the largest ever known. Most of the sky consumed. Stars struck to gloom behind this searing light. Words are fragile things, they crack in murder when they defend the castle of our own self-love. Luxurious and grand in the empires of the air, their self-flatteries now kneel before the pities of a single blade of grass. Does all creation thunderbolt to crash our hopes and confuse us into nothingness?

"And how to heal the wounds? How replace ourselves affirmed as the only of his highest love? The stars, the comets, the planets, all that is has heresied against the tablets of our beliefs." The old mariner caught in the desperations of his grief caressed an imagined sculpture on the fire's heat. "Was creation always the devil's garden? The snake the patron to its saints? How far the fall to hang us on our astronomies! And so where lies the resurrection to remake the salvation of it all?

"Hermes' theologies purer, older than Moses, closer to Eden. Hermes who taught his wisdom on the Nile, the Egyptians to his homage and in his debt. So alchemy's rise to build tabernacles on Hermes' name. In rays, some part divine, some part excitements, alchemies gathered by sympathetic aspects of a living earth, whether rock or plant or man, metal, word, or image, or color. Correspondents of our world harvest and intensify those hidden godly vigors. Idols were true gods the ancients made. Those crafted in combinations of this every living nature. All that is, is alive in secret harmonies. Those works of stone, metal, plants and image created from God, the one reconstructed by man into life and lesser gods. Man himself with the one, not as great, for God alone can create the all from nothing. But man by his own perfections had again returned to his central place. But despair ever despairs of change. Copernicus so forward in his cosmologies, but in truth a herald of the past. The sun returned calmly in its ancient divinities to be the pivot where all the heavens orbit in their glide."

The old mariner leaned into the gasps of his weakened breath. "And so Drake by worship of the sea—the sea is of the storm, the storm is of the earth, the earth is of the sky, the sky of sun both dawn and dark. The sun rounded with its planets and its stars. Worship is not only where we bend our knee. To herald one is to herald all. Entities are by hidden sympathies their magics accumulate. And Drake who married the land to the sea, why not script nuptials from the unseen vigors that spirit through creation? Is that so far a thought? Hermes Trismegistus would agree. And you redeemed from silence to hear the river speak. Why not? What words or chants, images and rhythms accumulate in the throbbing speech? All those talismans the savages spoke, there the shadows sound in sly divinities. What is, is a pageant seated in a radiant cloak. Words burst enthralled in the galleries of their power. You, Smith, were trumpeted, exalted in birth, gifts and possibilities. And so the river to your ear."

What was apart now congregates, I whispered to myself. *The simple plot has hatched a field of eggs and on every writ, on every morsel, thought or said, on every living thing or dead, there smiles a portion locked in some attraction to another portion, not fully of itself, different, but in secret divinities in truth the same.*

"And so one God in many, that church had found its theology," I remarked, "that altar universal and for all."

"Time ever unknits the sock." The old mariner ate a shade of irony as he voiced. "Piety is a vice. Self above self beasts in the underworld. Dee was frantic to yield all philosophies in a new Eden. Man by his astrologies could know his character and within the exercise of free will his fate. Man now the author, the drama not wholly writ. Create the words, create the scenes, you are by your own divinities released. And more, the Cabala another mystical portent, that most ancient Jewish wisdom, and in the sounds of its Hebrew hieroglyphics, a speech closer to that illuminated word God spoke when he created all. Language before the Fall, each word beasting in an angelic possibility, a magic to call, to command that which is named. The Cabala surface is the text within the equation of a secret text, its letters more than given in a phrase. Each symbol holds a number. The Hebrew alphabet clothes a divine mathematics. Reform the word to decode an angel's name. The ten powers of God rearranged, all his names, hidden motions toll in silent bells. Discover the mathematics, discover the angel's call. Unseen the light that clearly beckons on the tongue. The angel summoned forth by its true name. John Dee would have his Eden now and speak to angels."

"I am eared only to a river, and Dee to hear the voice of angels," I gloomed, suffocating in a crypt of a lesser self. "Is my river but a bastard angel, nameless in its alone, or a water demon, self-possessed?"

Old Jonas saddened as he said, "Attend to the tale before you whimper to your hell. Be not so proud to pleasure from your own demise. Self-death in a living death. Fool! This is not a sport to theatre in an empty head. Gods drift in consequence, unheralded, while demons dance the playful crowd. It was the stake that could have burned this tale to ash. To Rome and its Vatican, the Inquisition, its pyres lit, in 1486 a young scholar with his Ninety-nine Theses to debate in public spectacle a philosophy toward a new dignity for man. Pico della Mirandola had by cleverness, willful to all authority, enfolded the thoughts of Hermes Trismegistus and the Cabala into a purity of one. The lamb of God, the Jewish text, the ancient idols joined in a new theology. Behind the one the many, behind the many the one. Mandinga recalled in brother to every Holy See. And Della Mirandola not taken to the stake?" Old Jonas paused to have his laugh. "The Pope Alexander VI, who divided the world, condoned the sparks of Inquisition. In his private chambers twelve murals were painted in praise and worship of Hermes Trismegistus. Secrets hold the secrets when we pray. That tug that is a vibrant thought wilds itself beyond any church. Those heresies that seduced the Pope seduced John Dee and our English court. Dee to angels, the Pope to politics and public murder. The heresy in his heart so denied was the fire that heated the cleansing perversions of his executioner's flame."

"Are we all but the divinities that contradicts? Lethal is the light that from the darkness breaks." I spoke aloud, the river whispering in its cataclysms. The old mariner forlorn in his philosophies, his memories distilled to smile a dagger in his melancholies. The silver moonlight, ghost reflection shine toward the horizons on the James. The old mariner to his silence. The river to its thousand, thousand years blanked in waiting, knowing only its sense, its moments as long as the moments of its voice.

I SIT UPON THE *BLACK SWAN'S* MAIN SAIL'S SPAR, HOLDING SWAYING ropes, the rigging beckoning me to stand upon my fear and be aloft. My eyes in persuasions of the sea, rounded in the pallet of its immensity. I am consumed by my own sight; I am eaten by the eye. I continue to climb into the rigging, myself to the gallant height. The world is a breeze in the hollows of the sails. Oh, to feel the wake, to stand and think. Enthralled in power, I purge myself of death. A life again, the old mariner a living vapor who had burst its voice to flesh the sarcasm of his homilies.

"John Dee knew he was not the adept to action angels from the air. First, those secret rays emitted in their invisible divinities would have to be concentrated by sympathetic materials in the proper shape and color, that being a crystal ball. Then the adept must groom in prayer the purest of pieties, a state of selfless grace. 'Discard all pleasures, I am a pauper abandoned to my ministries,' so said Dee. Abstaining from all food and conjugals, a monk of hours before each gaze into the crystal ball." The old mariner sighed. "Pious is the love throttled to announce itself a saint. And so with Dee, universal knowledge the end to the religious wars. Fine thoughts to brace the pagan in a Catholic ideal. But Dee set his plate where ambiguities dance. I was invited to attend one action at the crystal ball. So in heresy we assembled the fears that spy in shadows," the old mariner whispering, leaning into the sounds of his own voice. "What is, rarely tells the full of its own account. Even here on the James where spirits wild, the silence speaks in memories. The air is palpable in its thought. That which glows is not always for the light. I am in the secrets of many things, and in this quiet," Jonas lowered his voice into the hiss of breath, "webs the mysteries of old Bess's throne."

So much I have heard, leashed by the ear, flattered in my heretic to what heathen claim of heaven. Or is it hell? This I thought, my doubts warring with my exaltations. "I have given my blood for a gift I did not want. Why should I now not end the sin and profit nothing for a little sleep?"

"CHILD, YOU ARE HARDLY PAST THE CRACKING OF THE EGG, AND snakes eat chicks to grin a summer's moment. You are not safe. Attend my hopes in gifts of warning." The mariner took breath. "Joys can be the final blindness. Listen and be wise.

"I was for that year, 1580, full in surprise and happiness. The spring, its season budded in bloom. Return now an eventful triumph, the world encompassed, wealth again. I had a claim of friends at Court. Drake the confidant of power, I the wizard explorer, a resurrection and Drake's frequent apostle. So with invitations I attended to Mortlake. I arrived, carriages already upon the gravel of Dee's portcullis. Nervous the bridled horses, flanks a shiver as hooves scratch dust from the barren ground.

"By hardy greeting in Dee's embrace, 'I have hope in empires for our queen and nation,' Dee said upon my arrival. 'We are our beginnings. All that is to know shines, uncaught but for the crystal and another's eyes.' Soon walking in some haste through the house, not even a word to casual a pleasant wait with Dee's pretty wife. Too swift glooms this solemn enterprise. Weighty seriousness, no tub of spirits await in Dee's private study. As I entered, I bowed. John Dudley, the Earl of Leicester, Dee's former student, sat in the wobble of a tattered chair. Also present was another pupil and loyal friend, John Dyer, a man of better inclinations, and Dudley's nephew, Sidney. We all by welcome welcomed all. Clandestines are my brotherhoods." Jonas smiled to forward a little laugh. "Leicester not inclined to be the earl, succumbing to his childhood, Dee's student once again. The parts we play in love, eager do we play again."

Leicester, Sidney, Dyer, names of history. I then wary enough, but still impressed. I smiled, an entertainment to myself.

"'The queen.' At Philip Sidney's words, the company stood. 'Elizabeth twice chosen, both of God and the ever-anointing sun, the moon and stars. She a living idol, a priestess, her powers ordained to every English soul. No closet pope, a catchpenny divine singing platitudes. Our pristine queen, her charities descend imperial to save the world.' Philip Sidney closed his eyes. 'Our queen, our angel sovereign. We are the elect by her hands alone.'

"So much our England coming to its might. It had slipped its church to wander among the alchemies, and so the strength. The Armada not to sail for years, but still the boldness to reap the wisdom from the heresies. Be this, be that, be ever the iron willing to shift its shape mid-thought." Jonas in the Virginia dark, hands upon his knees, straightened into statuary, his eyes watery in age. "And so...," he said, then silence.

I asked, "Of what?"

He shook his head, "Soon enough the warning....We to our seats. The candles burning through the sharp yellow sculpture of their flames. The curtain drawn against the interruptions of the day. We sat, the crystal ball in the center of the table, prayers said. 'Grace me, purify me in your knowledge. Reveal in Edens, remake us from our fall.' So spoke Dee. 'Through churches and theologies, their vestments, their popes, their idols superior in their infallibilities, I seek the angels' voices, provoked in revelations.'

"To myself the wonder spoke, 'Is Dee a Catholic, or a protestant whose words misspend his theologies?' Leicester's eyebrows raised also to some thought. But it was known Dee's belief in one universal church would have a little of all in its mix. The queen, herself, declared protestant ministers should remain unmarried. And so the bloody whirlpool, the old not fully digested by the new. But there is little casual in a war. Ardent for an English Empire first ever to speak that phrase. To cordial rank, Dee handed the Earl of Leicester the crystal ball. Shy to its weighty heresies, Leicester placed it on the table. 'My soul in forfeit for a glance.' The Earl smiled.

"Every soul plays for its eternities. A glance, a peek perhaps to hear the songs of resurrection and see an angel festooned in the brilliance of almighty God. It is worth the chance, is it not? John Dee the loving tutor, his persuasions monumental in their calm. 'Be of ages,' was all he said. Leicester bowed to the glass, his nose and forehead, their curve to touch the curve of clarity of the globe. Eyes closed, the concentrations. 'There is an empty warp, a distortion as in every transparency, whose bulge weighs thick and rounded in the hand. Nothing presents,' said Leicester. 'It appears I am for the court, not paradise.'

"Now each to have his turn. John Dyer, 'It comes to little. I am no skyer.' Anger paints his failure more personally than the others.

"'No angels to me. Not even my fellow ghosts,' I said. 'I am dry of visions.'

"Philip Sidney the last to play his invitations to the angels. 'I see,' he said, 'a great scape in years, dramas that ambition murder, words fearful in their divinities, the inner continent of a smile. This I have seen, but in this crystal just a smudge lingering into an hour's waste. I am an adept, but for a different craft.'

"'I, too, am no adept, but perhaps together we have the society to dance an angel on a twig.' Dee ever to joust a little humor to ingratiate the gods. We stood from our chairs, leaned to be above the globe, looking to its surface, into its lucid glass. After a time, Dee's back straightened. 'Success is not today, but our courage will persist. We will find an adept.'

"'Perhaps Hatton?' asked Leicester. Philip Sidney in some consent, although his expression bolted a question across our many eyes.

"'Tried. Done by happy accident when the crystal first arrived. Hatton here. The man pleasured to hold it before his eyes. So sensed and thrilled, to expand an afternoon's explorations. Glorious in himself, but not our adept.'

"In the study, candles flickered, nervous in the thrills of secret chatter. 'I shall find the one,' said Dee. 'To be upon the way, we must first find our adept.'

"Before we departed, all to the cloister of our private thoughts, Leicester strolled the room, speaking to the question in all our heads. 'How will we be certain our adept once found is not a fraud, here but to catch an easy penny for a pound of air?'

"'I know enough by these libraries,' Dee's hand sweeping across the shelves of his books, 'ignorance happed from silly lies.' So said Dee, confirmed to himself guardianship to the highest gate, and ushered his acolytes to coach and horse.

"'Walsingham has knowledge of what we do, and because his daughter holds the title of Sidney's bride, is disposed to a friendly, but a distant curiosity,' said Dee, entering his private chamber to consider of the moment.

"'Better spies be kept informed,' I replied. 'Hidden knowledge, gained as secrets, suspicions worse.'

"Dee relaxed into the comforts of a tutor's conversation. 'John Dyer has some small poet in him, but had mind enough and opportunity to befriend Philip Sidney and Edmund Spencer when they were all my pupils.' Walking through the many libraries of the house, Dee confessing as if to the shelves, 'Language too hosts alchemies. Distill the sounds, its rhythms lyric music, its images call magic to persuade the soul. I taught them the "how" and the "when" to ink those verbal talismans to account the mysteries. So the page is writ, to express the wisdoms, shadowed in elusive things.'

"In the kitchen, Jane the wondrous of ample eyes, her slightness in womanhood curves harnessed delicious in my urgent thrill. She so much in glow, soft flesh, curlicues of blonde hair, warm reprieves, in canticles of a single touch. And she now puttering at her child's nose. A mother swept into her love. Another child to the innocent cloth. Jane looked from the infant's face. Not a pleasing expression when seeing me. 'Wizards only potion their secrets, and at best a rude expense. I suppose a meal to comfort wisdom?'

"'I can pay my own freight,' I laughed.

"'Oh Jonas, fool and scowl. Here, have an egg.'

"'No, here, have a tickle bag, a little sac of treasure from round the world.' I threw gold coins on the table. 'This gold our Dee's own slice for a loan of navigations.

"Jane to the surprise of great delight, then to clown a miff, a tutored eruption of the female spleen. 'What has the profiles of this coin to you, Master Dee,' taking a gold coin in her hand. 'is to ours but books and alchemies. Not even a horse, a carriage, a new bed, always gold's transubstantiations into paper, our scholar's only magic.' So saying, Jane danced a rough smile in her husband's direction.

"'The message a little curdled, the smile but a ruined pout,' Dee said. And so to the loving discomforts of the house. My own a shattered vacancy. Should I sell its derelict to my jealousies? I envied Dee in that moment."

Old Jonas, the wind and clouds have become the toss of your wild hair. The rippled sea your leathered face. Dissolve your tale. My mind pretends. My eyes see through. Crew to the rigging, canvass to the wind, the *Black Swan* sails. Clouds blur into her imagined arms. I am in the longings of a child's playful dream.

From far away my name echoes from the deck, a call from a world I have sworn to hold in my mastering fist. Waymouth heralds himself captain. Aft he is by the wheel, a chart in his hands, beckoning me. Some conference in his mind to plot the route upon the drawn fragments, waving in his hand.

·   ·   ·   ·   ·

"WE COULD MAKE HARBOR ALONG THIS COAST," WAYMOUTH POINTS
to his chart. "Resupply with fresh water and fresh victuals—nuts,
venison, furs and a little wealth." Our captain sweeps his hand across,
"I made important explorations along this northern coast," pointing to
the map, "some five years past." Our captain smiles a pleasing moment
to himself. "I had their king to England. Well treated. Returned the
next year. Love is our expectation." Waymouth speaking. "These
bays, well hidden and thronged with many islands."

"Waymouth, by trick and a little threat, kidnapped six and that
king," Stacie whispers in my ear. "But, in truth, that royal and his in
a year were sailed for home well pleased."

"It is a fair land," our captain now to the poverty of his pomp. "Fine,
deep harbors, fertile earth in vast forests, furs for trade. The French
sailed this main from New France in Arcadia to the North River, little
exploration purposed, which Hudson in his journals did account. Only
good commerce and profits, we should easy foot and be much forward
of the French. Gold better sits an English pudding than a French cake."
A few cheers, a laugh, then the question to plumb the fathoms.

"Are we for this main," asked Stacey, the first mate, "or, as the
year is late, do we full sail to Frobisher's Strait, and see what is of
Hudson?"

"As the polar summer dies, it dies to an endless night. Barren lands,
no trees, little food. Flies swarm in pin murders on your skin. All this
is but the pipe." Waymouth quieted. The ship's bell tolled the wind, its
echoes through the lower deck. The water's creaking weight against our
boards. "When crews starve, they hunger toward a mutiny. Fables are
not a slice of cheese. Legends will not bake a bread. I've seen the polar
sea. This ship, this crew. Too much to waste upon the few. Hudson is a
clown who captains havoc. Let him inherit rot. Be as you will, but first
be warned. I am for Maine. Better are the easy furs, wealth to hand for
a miser's coin, and no ship crushed in ice to endanger us."

Again to me, I took the voice. "The danger is less if we venture
now. The sun still high. The polar day has little night. The warmth
less cold. We are well provisioned. Fresh water can be gotten from the
ice. Now is now. Later is a flint of never, but the Polar Sea, vast in its
unknown, affords little chance to find Hudson." So I said—around
the table. Continuing, "But I am not for quests, I am for Virginia and
its easy furs."

·   ·   ·   ·

"FRANCE HAS CUT ITSELF A RIVAL SHORT TO LONDON SOUTH ALONG this main. England has a possibility of empire on the Chesapeake. The closest, the easiest estate, the firmer wealth," said Stacie. In every English sailor there blooms a captain, an independent bud begging for the honey bee. The story then spoke. "Did not the queen herself by her own hand present you with a letter to the emperor of China? Where serves that parchment now?"

Ice and mutiny, starvation, fear, haunted Waymouth in his premonitions. So struts the indignities of his failed histories. "Hudson sails the *Discovery*, the same decks we walked in 1602 when we had the arctic and our almost death," Waymouth sneered and balled his fists. "I am for furs and the warmer coasts of Maine."

"And I am for Virginia firesides," I said, fearing the more north the less chance of Virginia, and especially with a hold filled with furs. "I have an office there important to the king and colony."

"The crew of *Discovery* cannot number more than twenty," continued Waymouth, ignoring me. No one for the Polar Sea. Waymouth, the fool, arguing with himself to pipe away the visions of his terror. "When I sailed her north we had but seventeen, in that, three boys of no account." Memory now a conversation but to repaint the past. "She shipped small, shallow draft and easy to the wind, advantage there to lie at hull and pole through the narrow passages of ice." Waymouth quieted to let each strain to hear his argument. "The north hauls to an ever winter season. Sudden storms in snow, rain freezes on the lips, fog floats its dangers hidden."

So are men drawn to their fears that inundate, I thought.

"That northern coast can wait," I said. "We are abroad for greater fortunes. I am a *werowance* to the savages of the Chesapeake. Furs we can have beyond count. I know the tribes. I know the lands. I know the kings." No one stirred the moment to eat the silence. "North are the French and their greed protected by their fleet."

"Foolish is the proven coin. Furs in the Virginia Colony may swing the end of a De la Warr rope." Waymouth tapped his finger upon the table as he spoke. "In Maine there are more and better furs, less threat. And I, too, know some savage kings." Our captain to study the silence on each face. Then the dramatics of a swallowed air. This a captain fearful of his crew. *Mutiny is the haunt*, I thought. I nodded to Weymouth as he continued. "The case is to a vote. Think on it a few lantern hours. At first light I will abide your decision."

And so despondency ever smiles through a coward's mask.

So, let each be in the choice, I thought. *The web threads upon tomorrow, and I shall sculpt Virginia from this plotted clay.*

BY NIGHT, BLACK IN THE ABUNDANT CLOUDS, COLD AND VACANT around the digested stars. Lonely movements of the sea, plunged shadows, then the ripples of the abandoned wake. I stood my watch, an almost captain to my almost crew. Waymouth walked the deck, his hands entwined behind his back. He leaned forward, a man misdirected, but not so wrong.

He turned and hailed me with a nod. Sea birds, feather white, ghost in waddle along the spars, to trowel the wood with their bending heads, wiping the roughage from their beaks. Waymouth now approached, the intent of sermons on his face.

"South is of another earth. It postures only barren hopes, its color only ancient death. Our blood is squeezed, fetid into a blackened crypt. Navigations are by fear. My compass counts degrees in all concerns. Be a dastard wise. I am experienced on the coasts of Maine. Its magnets ever calling easy furs. The French know this."

Waymouth tapped his knuckles softly upon the wheel, a gesture to some unsaid soliloquy. "No moon tonight." The obvious said to halt a troubled thought. "The sea motions in fathoms that never sleep. Attend to the farthest rim." Waymouth pointed. "The horizon, almost a silhouette, its calm to pretend a depth that is at peace." Waymouth almost whispered. "Your persuasion will convince the crew, and hold them an easy hour. But fear and terror own the clock. All our oaths are thin. Our hope distracts, our paths are cursed. To the south, disease, a willful noose and famine. If that is where we go, and if you disappoint, the crew will cannibal their love to pamper hate. This I swear."

"I have fisted men to grip my ambitions more than once. Many times I have been chanced by death, yet I live."

"Empty, sweet and nothing." Little more Waymouth said, but took the wheel and stood the watch.

FOR THE DAYS AFTER OUR VOTE WE LIVED UPON THE TREASURIES swimming along that coast. Waymouth stood an angry watch, a vulture's smile on his face. The crew fished, ate. We sailed before the wind south, then north closer to the coast. Its edges dark and beckoning. The air in its fleeting heat.

French ships in small squadrons, two or three on the horizon. We kept our distance. Their masts, their steady sails a smudge, often lost against the gray turmoils of the driven squalls. Winds fresh, but variable. Waymouth seldom complained or spoke. Only his long stares carried a silent knife.

"What will you pretend when the crew wars for the privilege to cut your throat?" Waymouth said, finally.

I forbore to reply. The *Black Swan* rode on the calm cloisters of the sea. The night, the stars frozen overhead, the blood-diluted moon rising in scimitar. "There is no lie in what I said. The furs there are, and fox and bear and beaver."

Waymouth expressionless, his face sagging, as if surrendering. "You are a fool," he sneered. "Soon this crew will feast on its own flesh. Stacie, take the wheel," he ordered. "I am for my cabin, bed and the pleasures of the wait."

Chapter Nine

I AM THE EXILE, GIVEN OF A MYSTERY.

OR THE NEXT WEEK the sun rose higher in a pensive heat. Days lengthened, folding an early summer upon the waning night. We sailed three leagues from the coast of flowers. The green forest rolled inland toward the commotion of sharp-faced thunder storms. Below the cloudbursts, a violence of grays steam in deluge, and we on the *Black Swan* glide on the cold disturbances of a ruffled sea. Beyond the occasions of sudden storms, broadening tempests in its darkening plates, and at the distant edge streaks of gold, the sun rays fall in broken glows.

The calendar sweeps and we voyage closer to the Chesapeake. Now my spine is to a chill. The tides in currents swirl the outlets of the bays. We drag barrels and wait for better winds. Our sails fluttered stiffly, like soiled shrouds, as they were raised to their spars. Quiet waters played in yearnings about the *Black Swan*. I thought of Pocahontas. Is all this earth her memory? Her face in phantoms drifts the summer squalls, her eyes in moistures, her thighs, horizons curved in hungers of their inviting fire. And to whom my forest love do now your passions court? Or by what insinuations are you still betrothed to the vapors of some ancient kiss?

THE MIND ALONE, THE BODY INTOXICATES, NERVOUS IN ITS ANIMAL, I thought. As ever, agitations linger on the excitements of the blood, and we are carried upon its invisibilities, an acolyte to the theologies of the beast.

All speculations for this country quicken and dilate the distant northern lights at night. The sky, when clear, shimmers a ghostly green, glowing laces, their lights in shading gossamers. How the illumination undulates a swaying curtain upon the wind that rides among the stars. Oh, John Dee, are these the divinities of your rays, emissions from the planets, stars, sun and moon, all the celestial hosts? Have we by some focus of the earth come to see the play of those divine rays, its fire hidden in the blackness of the north? John Dee, are these the flaming cloaks of the angels that you sought? Do giants walk upon the sky, as gods spreading seeds to disperse the days? I thought of the old mariner. Father now of my loneliness, the ship noises upon my ears, waning almost beyond memory.

THE NEXT DAY CLEAR, MOSTLY WARM, A MILD CHILL BENEATH THE heat, as if the sunlight held a winter in its cloak. We bloomed our sails, our ship soon plunging low, the flung bow spray. The rivers rolling words, the living breeze, I exploded again into my youth. *I felt your alchemies, Old Jonas, frantic in their ecstasy. I am alive, its trance consumes, sensed blind in frenzy.*

I strolled the deck, Stacie at my side. "Good morning, Smith, and pleasant day." But to my ear a whisper, "How many days to trade, and we be sailed for home?"

Caution, the better drama to have the better play. "Not long by much, a fortnight, perhaps." So calm in my reply. I joked over the rattle of Waymouth's orders to the crew. "Our captain is in good lung today," I noted. Stacie smiled as Waymouth swore terrors through the fevered odors below deck, shrill words prowling for a common ear.

Stacie nodded to some inner smile and walked away.

The coastal landscapes grew familiar, the Chesapeake wide in the blue sunlight of its waters. Sandbars, hills and forests flats. This my earth, my other self.

The crew to labor on the masts, worn sail tied to spars, only the main to bear a cautious speed in the fresh breeze. A pace in sleep, this tired ship. But to me what affords? My office, a lord of consequence and its histories. And De la Warr—are your promises death? The *Black Swan* by some hours sails upon the James. Walls and ruins hail the eyes, a fleet about, some ships. Life upon the beach, our anchor rides a disappearance on its rope. The depth consumes. The river whispers breathless in its homilies. *I am all that I know, a motion sensed, a current from forgetfulness.*

WAYMOUTH ORDERS HIS CAPTAIN'S BOAT OVER THE SIDE. THE *Black Swan* had anchored near a point of land some distance from the Jamestown beach. Oarsmen now hoist a small sail. Waymouth and I in the center, backs straight. Waymouth's eyes, his face dressed upon an inner stare. Fresh breeze soon in the waters of the James, sweet air to my lungs.

On the beach a crowd gathers in rags and armor, some tobacco pipes. "We are of the *Black Swan* returned with reports of Hudson and the North River," cried Waymouth. Near the shore, vines, leaves dried in rot, death and its discarded vegetation floating beneath the yellow wooden pillars of a half-built dock.

An emaciation of what was Lord De la Warr carried on a litter. to the edges of the water. His sunken eyes in caves, black light on the pallid of his cheeks. Few teeth now, the bite is lost upon a bleeding gum. His words weak, he whispers to an aide, "His lordship commands you to stay from these walls. You and Smith are not welcome."

"We are on the king's service. We seek to bring reports his lordship, himself, has ordered." I spoke, rising to my feet. "Our news portends. We sailed upon the Northern River. We have maps and conclusions bearing on the Northwest Passage."

Waymouth to his voice. "We need victuals, water, a berth for quick repairs."

An attending noble bent to have an ear close to De la Warr's weakened voice. De la Warr, wrapped in the dull threads and blanket tatters tucked to hid his decay, spoke in a hiss. "Give your reports and maps to hand, then go." The noble straightened, ordering muskets raised, their sightless hollows aimed at our chests.

"I am ordained to an office by the London Company." I rebutted. "I have come to claim that power."

"Your office has been disposed to another, upon the lordship's pleasure. If you set foot upon this ground, you will hang."

So much given to be the greater loss, my thoughts in their rude humor. *But this forest sways to more than an English breeze.* Not Argall nor Rolfe did I see. None of mine once loyal, that few, that embattled few. Where stands Todkill now? Over the walls more muskets aimed, the shadows of their throats a sundial murder for their point. "I have not the maps at hand. Send your emissary and they are yours," I said to De la Warr. Waymouth I had by a different thought. I whispered, "Play the night and quiet, I know these waters and the tribes. We could trade and have done with our needs, or seize the colony if we were of the mind."

Waymouth smiled. "A patriot may pretend a pirate with a royal license, but without that seal our necks would stretch as a heated wax upon a rope," Waymouth whispered, then called to De la Warr. "We await your pleasure on the *Black Swan*. There our reports and maps." Waymouth bowed. Our oars in back strokes, the fetid water in white turmoils, we eased into the river's wide flow. No voice pained, no recognition of my return. I have nothing but the hums of some remorse.

EVER THE FAMILIAR IS CROWNED THE KING OF CIRCUMSTANCE. Consequence the toothless whore. A ha'penny for an empty habit. On the deck the grumble of the crew, their death eyes upon me, I played the hate. "Furs and wealth still close enough. I know the land, and De la Warr's nose is where his power ends." The laughter and so the wait. In an hour four boats from shore, armed oarsmen, ten armored worthies and one gentleman dressed in his self-appointed authority.

"We should have them with our cannons," said Stacie.

I, in my knowing humor, answered, "Why waste the expense? In a season it will hap for free."

Lines soon thrown over our decks, the boats rolling slightly on the calm. Ropes tied, ladders over the side. Armed soldiers, boats slipping on the wet lines. The deck a congress of hostile pleasantries. All to Waymouth's cabin. Reports given in their weathered logs and verbal anthems, maps, by what information are my empires ignored?

No suggestions ever from Virginia to the London Company to make claims along that furthest coast. The Dutch and French soon to the north, and we the poorer for being shunned.

Waymouth to his wine, cheese and fish, a lunch of a pondering repast. I to the deck. "Smith, you are the benighted fool," a voice of known spirit. "Todkill," I hailed "Quiet, even the air has spies, and we are under watch." I nodded, my finger to a beckoning, conspiracies to a safer dark, down the forward stairs to the ballast deck. Among the stones and barrels I heard the ill-turned news.

"De la Warr dances to a murderous rope. The savages ill used. The planting little done. Some repairs to the fort. Death comforts many."

"And of Powhatan?" my question cowards on my breath. Words unsaid turn demon in the heart. The mind rebels, dry drunk in denied necessities.

Todkill cautioned before he spoke. "An exile. He offers forest threats and plots. It is a shadow war, but still we starve while he feasts."

"It is as it was," I said, the courtly gesture to the casual that compels. "How then is his daughter, Pocahontas, the one who brought us food? Any news?"

"Nothing seen, nor heard. Nothing by nowhere known."

I nodded, slipping into thoughts and wistful strategies. While our candles burn it flickers in the *Black Swan's* depth. "Are there enough to seize the colony?" I asked.

"No, it is not for us. We have not the allies to bake salvation into this ruined cake. I am determined to be for England, even as a secret upon these ballast stones."

"You must remain sending me reports while I convince the London Company to appoint me once again to be an officer in defense of the colony."

Todkill grim, his anger flushed on the scarlet hardening on his face. "I cannot. This land is doom. Its dreams bear us on its bones."

"You must stay. You are our final hope. Without your news my quill will script only bitter shards."

Todkill was not inclined to be convinced. Resignation comes not as a bravery or a joy, just as an impatience to have the end and some relief. "I cannot." Todkill chilled in his answer.

"If the grave holds our final pleasures," I smiled, "clip fear, play an ancient courage, as a Greek at Marathon. Dare all for all. Become the intrepid eye. You are far from death, and well-seasoned to this earth.

We both shall serve a rescue. This I know." Todkill nodded, knowing death is everywhere close on a London street. He would remain.

"And so forever," he said, "the gold that never rusts," offering me his hand.

"As it was in the east, so it is now." I nodded to the ghost song swirling through the mast. Cries of wind, a river voiced. And when have such companions locked so in their haunted braveries? And when have our duties played so confused as to barter each of us away?

A COOL SEA BREEZE HAS BROUGHT A RISING FOG. TODKILL AND I on the deck again. We walked into the surface of the smoke, voices weighted sharp around us. Sounds of stumbling, footfalls careful in their stride. "Smith!" A name upon a disembodied voice. "Smith, be here towards your name." It was Stacie. By path half-blind in walk, Todkill and I found our first mate and his barking throat. "All is mostly set. The captain made an easy trade, some food and a little water, a beach for quick repairs, but no furs, but me thinks he holds you to your boast of furs and friendship with the savages."

I nodded. "Your Waymouth's knees drag the streets of the quickest coin. Can I go ashore?"

Hard and certain was the *No*. "You be free to have an ease upon the *Black Swan*. You be sovereign to our decks, but," Stacie winked, his voice to a private mirth, "the crew would quest an extra stroke if furs and forest trinkets were the freight."

"I think this night we might have a pound of furs from a small voyage." Thinking how much I am the criminal, in this conspiracy, an illegal trade to hold the crew, perhaps the savages to bear some message to Powhatan. Am I branded in this my last device? My conscience serves a throttled philosophy. I am by what if not for this? I claim a sore to heal a wound, as I did with the sword and Mandinga's son, and with those to have the ear and the river's voice. But this new path slips beneath the foot, too much confused, I fear I am my enemy.

AND HOW MUCH LESS MYSELF AM I, NOW THIS VIOLENCE OCCASIONS on my wayward path. The eye, my sight again, I toil to events. Are my actions spent? I, a foundling abandoned to my empire's weight. On the pinnace our northward sail, the channel a rough of swaying beads of night and moon. "Go fetch your promise, trade for furs." Waymouth's voice hangs in memory. Miles in secret miles above the fort, the *Black Swan's* boats to shore to gather victuals and have the pleasures of the beach. We to wander north. Familiar riverscapes in the dark, the river's words to me—"My currents voice an enticement, moments lost in memory."

The crew from their oars to the mast, canvas lowered into place. Thins of wear upon its bulge, some tears, the ancient mends still firm. Upstream shapes bloom to shadow rocks and trees grotesque, their immensities above the shore in their silent reach. The eye confused, this distant vast. Blue and amber, green ribbons glowing through the blackened sky.

We landed at the Paspaheghs and found the savages not inclined to be of any useful humor. No furs, little corn, no advice but "leave." I sat upon the mats, the campfire warm, its heat changeable in the interludes of the rippling flames. A *werowance* once my friend, the tobacco pipe passing from his hand to mine. "Powhatan is far and in his angers. De la Warr makes a war of little cause. They kill the little ones. The smell of murder is in his voice. Be again their *werowance*. They have to all ears proclaimed your death."

"Send messages to Powhatan telling I still live and that I am the inheritor of his gift. I know the river speaks."

"And where the spirit's breath, and where the spirit's throat?" questioned the *werowance*.

I rose to my feet, my arms wide displaying the river's darkening run. The old *werowance* smiled, rising, "A child's cry. The father yet."

WE STAYED THE NIGHT OFFSHORE BY THE SAFETY OF OUR OARS. At dawn messengers launched their dugout canoes, so different from the birch bark crafts of the northern river. What single eye, its hands, its understanding to bend and form that bark, such a better craft. One vision to itself alone, creating wonders.

The old mariner returned to mind, and the last campfire on the Chesapeake. "What explanations pretend, only masks the snake," said old Jonas. "Poison is not the apocalypse. All is to the worm. The dragon who prowls our gardens also stalks our Edens. This is the history of my final warning. Hear it! My dreamer, my only son! "Many times I visited Mortlake after my return from the Pacific Sea.

Dee ever worked upon secret and hidden revelations. Consumed by pieties and ever arrogant in its humanities, he needed a skyer, one who could see the angels (he could not), call them by their true and Hebrew names into the parlors of Dee's crystal ball. By the Kabala in its divine codes and mathematics, turning numbers into letters, becoming words, an angel's true name. Those ancient sounds herald the power to beckon and bring forth even the archangels to our eyes. All our excitements ventured to bear witness to the One in its grand creation. God is all, and all is God. So it was to Dee to know and hear the laws. Divine knowledge, and Dee to be its chosen, its perfect saint.

"Elizabeth's court ever danced to its deadly favors and protocols. Rumors there can sharpen whispers to the edges of an axe. But rumors too have inner lives, their mysteries may shroud a laconic eye. Those who knew, knew to keep their lips closed upon a deeper silence. Dee's work more a stir of secrets to his neighbors and the shanks at court, but to the councilors closest to the queen, many had sat in Dee's most private study and had placed their nose upon the crystal ball. Nothing seen but the room distorted in the globe. Nothing said, but a quiet search to find the one. Those, the days of much poverty, hunger walked the roads and for an easy plate of food, or a coin or two, many would claim a skyer's gift of prophecy.

"Many times Dee had a wanton at his door, sent by rumor, or by slander, or by a jealous colleague dressing as a friend. None had the rate worth a crust of bread. Dubious is the better mind. Then a note from Dee, 'Attend unto me. Urgent! Haste!' So snapped the words. I to horse the wind. By mount upon the hooves-struck road, dust behind the gallop, I raced into the night."

"'I WANT YOUR WITNESS,' SAID DEE ON MY ARRIVAL. THE DAY TO a warming early spring. My horse in lather led by a stable boy to be groomed and fed. Dee and I walked toward the doors of Mortlake. 'I believe I have by chance found my Godly instrument, my skyer. I am joyed, but still of caution.' Dee stood, a tilt upon a reassuring sense of purpose. A saint is always wise to distrust itself a saint." Jonas stared into my heart. Even in death his words chill. Reluctant in my memories, I am half again in disbelief, but my force of will intrudes to grasp the alchemies.

"Throughout the house children in squeaks of play and interludes of tears, swaddling pandemoniums and runny noses. At the table in the mix of this endearing clamor sat a man dressed as a monk, the hood of his brown cassock covering his head. Next to his chair a staff. He was ominous in his thoughts. He did not look up.

"'A weighty matter?' questioned Dee before the well-mets and introductions. The stranger labored to his feet. 'Edward Talbot' bowed in my direction. I returned the compliment. I discerned his face under the cavernous hood. His forehead and cheeks were scarred with jagged marks. Clutching his staff, he stood, a testament to a leg badly broken, then badly set, some misalignment of the bones. A sudden wince, a surprise of pain. This Edward Talbot had known a stoning in the public stocks. The marks of the pillory across his flesh, a limb smashed by an iron or a heavy rock. All this I surmised," said Jonas. "The question, what other wound in secret did he bear, this unpleasant Talbot of the unpleasant hidden tales?

"'Our old friend Jonas will have witness of our actions today,' Dee announced.

"'As is your pleasure,' Talbot nodded.

"Jane entered the room, still of girlish womanhood, two children born, and as ever a spirit of country milk. With unseen eyes, Talbot's hood moving, following Jane. Fascinations hungering, abiding their urgents in their jungle wait. So much are we aware, our skin can sense another's stare. Jane's nervous eyes, a glance at Talbot, her approach to me so close, a smile to the kiss of welcome. 'So glad, good Jonas, you are returned.'

"'Never quite, but these your hands have claims upon my vagabond.'

"'Sweet indifference, how you play your not-so-subtle self.' Jane stepped away. Such a light within a smile, another glance at Talbot, as her mouth gestured to a clench of teeth. 'I shall leave you to your important work,' she said, begging an excuse to attend the children and have a moment beyond her suspicions. All this my better guess. I stood. My conjectures shrill, my words so within their well, never to be said. We walked to Dee's private chambers. The door unlocked. Its key pounded from the weave of blacksmith's iron, the knob shaped into a human hand.

"The chamber stale with airless dust, Dee crossed to his most private oratory, there to pray. I to myself, a prayless warren. Talbot knelt by a large table on whose top, supported by a wooden base, the dim light dissembles within the Cyclops of a crystal ball.

"Talbot's mouth moved, articulating silence. He bowed his head, his hands held close. He appeared a beggar enjoying the crust of his last bread. A sudden sound, Talbot in a frightened twist, his hood fell from his head, there behind his cheek a gnarl of flesh, a ragged butchery, a missing ear, half torn from its socket. 'This Talbot is a felon,' I thought, 'whose face has paid the sovereign for a crime. A forger? A thief? By what law, to what judgment are you defaced?' I, uneasy, Talbot's head unbowed, rising, indifferent to any revelations. The hood covered his head again, his eyes to the crystal. Returned from his private pieties, Dee said, 'What we shall accomplish here is for God and for the ages. A resurrection, its power to every soul. An Eden is upon us,' Dee shook, 'and I its chosen, its instrument,' he said, his hands offering by gestures their bounties. 'And for you, dear Jonas, a shield of miracles, the swords of heavens, lightning storms to sweep away all death. Your wife again, a child reborn.'

"I was torn by needful worms, congressed to feast upon my despair. My own doubt exhausted, I almost did believe. My life left to leavings, and I the crust of death, a foulness ripe with passions yearning to be blessed.

"'What can be seen in the crystal?' thundered Dee.

"'A golden chair floats in an ocean of fire,' Talbot amazed, his eyes tearing, 'and a voice, speaking from within a silver vapor. No, they recast into certainties. They are wings of light.'

"The curtains wide, the great windows of the oratory blazed as a glass of fire. Shafts of glowing heat, the room swarmed in dust, spinning as burning fireflies. 'Breathe the heavy air,' Jonas spoke almost to himself. 'We are gamed in silhouettes.' Talbot at the crystal. Dee his scribe."

The mariner's eyes filled with memories. What moments shift behind the sights he sees? It is himself passing in a second life.

"'There has come an angel to the crystal,' cried Talbot, 'Regal, in purple robes, silver and gold adornments, a cape festooned in rubies, his eyes sparkling.' Talbot's head shook, his body shivering. 'It is what?'

"'Tell the tale within the stone,' ordered Dee.

"'Another angel even more magnificent has forced within the globe. He has beaten the first, throwing it to the ground, tearing off its clothes, beneath the cloth a monster unmasked with long fangs, curved claws, a face like a wild beast. It is Lundungifa, the demon who in secret stalks this house. The angel has thrown him into a great pit. "So will all the wicked be scourged," he says. "I am Uriel," it says, "the torch of God. I am he who warned Noah of the flood. I am called to be a protector and to hear your words." Uriel stands full in a mighty light, blinding to a perfect brilliance.' Talbot shielded his eyes, looking at Dee.

"'May I ask a question of the angel?'" old Jonas recounted.

"Talbot repeated my words into the globe. 'Uriel says, "Yes, you are most welcome, Master Wizard, as a pilgrim, a seeker and as a scribe. Speak your question."'

"'What can you behold for me?'

"'The whole is a mist in flux, for all are at liberty, even by the stars. But there are some clouds more figured, a woman, an almost queen beheaded by a man in black, and ships in vast companies upon the sea. That is all that can be told.'

"Uriel then disappeared. So helpfully vague, a portent to cheese the simple mouse. But none-the-less all came to pass," said Jonas. "But years later, so compelled to cook my misgivings with a taste of hope.

"For a moment there was a wordless pause. 'Is it done?' asked Dee.

"'I think not. There is a great commotion within the stone. Lightning balls in rainbows, clouds joust in thunder. The sound undulates. It clears, it is singing.' Talbot looked away, blinked and rubbed a cleansing tear from his cheek.

"'Look again,' cried Dee. 'The angels will not harm thee.'

"'But demons,' whispered Talbot, forcing his face to the stone. 'The light softens. The chair of perfection stands on an empty watch. Now, three figures enter: Uriel, and one cloaked in black and another who is in radiance, a halo of falling sun spears, his wings as landscapes gloried in a silver fire. A sword of gold, its hilt of emeralds, carved in Hebrew hieroglyphs. "I am Michael the angel of God." He sits upon the chair, attended by a swirl of golden light. The light congeals to harmonies, its choirs the lesser angels of the air.

"'The figure in black approaches, kneels before the Archangel Michael, his hand upon his hood. It is now pulled back. His face not seen, but has an aspect not unfamiliar…'

"'Why would he secret himself from our watch?' cried Dee. 'Who is this unseen?'

"'The sword is laid on each shoulder of the kneeling one. "Anointed by my touch, as you yield to my words. Arise now the

always blessed." Michael has spoken. The figure stands, and turns…
It is?…You.' Talbot in terror of his joy, looks at Dee. 'You are the one
dressed in black.'

"Dee hammers his fist upon the table. 'I knew! I knew!' tightening
himself into a knot of flesh. Talbot holds his hands aloft to demand
a silence.

"'Archangel Michael speaks these, his words, "You are ever
blessed of God. I am by his commandment your guide. My angels to
you for your doing. The world begins. Quest Eden. Quest the laws
of God. It is done!" '

"The stone now clears. Talbot leaned back into his chair saying, 'I
am exhausted in my soul.' Then he collapsed."

DOES THE MOTH MAKE CONVERSATION WITH THE FLAME, ENTICED TO
words, excited into the poems of immolations? So I pondered. The
old mariner's hands sat stiffly upon his knees, motionless in his
concentrations. Then awakened to the startled silence, he continued.
"'Talbot is the one we seek,' said Dee, smiling like a giddy child,
mindless with his toys. Talbot awakened and staggered from the
room. Dee in other thought showed no concern. 'It is a cruelty never
myself to see within the crystal,' he said, 'so I must paint by ear, with
only echoes to contemplate.'

"'Scholar and friend, we journey within a cloven wilderness,' I said
to Dee. Be cautious! Devils may sow with angels' threads.'

"'This Talbot coaxes some complaint in you?' Dee asked, curious
as to my expression.

"'A clever man,' I said, 'to beg us onward, enticed upon a mystery,
a suckle on our poverties, rounded in a demon's menace. My friend,
will your pride squeeze enough ambition to fill his empty glass.'

"'What think you of this Talbot's gift?' Dee not for my answer,
added, 'An archangel as my guide. Could a coarser or a fraud gall an
imagination to speak as he?'

"'Clever by half and settled,' I said. "Become not a lute tuned to
the harshest scratch.' Dee to his own mind, as I joked. 'Talbot has a
missing ear, mutilated for some crime, I suspect. Let us caution upon
his abilities.'

"'Come, dear Jonas. Sorrow not that I am anointed. Let us together
take the kitchen pleasures and common with a little food,' said Dee.

"Walking through the clutter in the many rooms, Dee spoke more of Talbot and his gifts. 'He is a child of a willful sort. He is provoked, a brat. He has the gift of eye and the sight of prophecy. His talents must confuse. No doubt this lion will eat of many dogs.'"

THE DECK OF THE PINNACE SWAYING, THE SKY GRAY AND FLAT AND low, its turmoil bathed in darkening drifts. My thoughts in divided currents. *I am sighted to the present yet again*, nodding to myself. *I taste of premonitions.*

We sailed from the James up the Chickahominy for many leagues. White mists rose from the perditions of the land. A haunted quiet. Lands of murder. Memory of Robinson, Emry, and Cassen burned alive tied to a tree. My own capture. Histories lie in the geographies of this earth. We had fifty furs in trade at the village of the Chickahominy, another thirty-five and some eighty scrapes from the Mamanahunt. At Amatuck, where Cassen had died, seventy-five fine pelts. Ever the trade, the crew never content. A small skirmish as we rowed south. Arrows fell in hostile shards from the verdant tangles of the riverbanks. A game of conscience to pretend a war and have a friendly moment in Powhatan's ear. Some arrows spent more lethal than the rest. A flash of powder, a noise, our shot gamed a long smile from a hurt.

By dark the James, by moon the *Black Swan's* easy silhouette. We brought one hundred and sixty valuable furs, and some eighty or so scrapes. Good, but not the promise, the crew grumbling. Waymouth smiling into a mutiny and I not much in favor. Greed hates its disappointments, but loves more blindly its furthest hopes. "Our repairs done?" I asked. "Fresh water given, victuals?" my questions to Waymouth and the assembling crew.

"Little of a nothing have we received, some water doubtful in the barrel. No food," the answer.

"Repairs?"

"We are fit to squander a league or two."

"The best course comes at tide. We take the river south to the Chesapeake then north to my friends the Potomacs and other friendly savages of the bay. Some I have cured of war. Others made me, against my intensions, a god. Small now we are in furs, but soon in sweeter prospects, and food and cleaner water. And more messenger to the tribes that I am again upon the land." So I said, but kept to myself the hope that she will hear, and be an emissary to my arms again.

AT FIVE O'CLOCK IN THE MORNING, IN PROMISING HEAT AND daylight, we hauled ropes and anchor, and set our canvas. The time of hope had come to hand. Men in rags hang upon the spars, the many webs of rigging, pulleys, the calls, the freshening breeze, the canvas bows, the *Black Swan* easy upon the light swells. Our wake a white wound through the constant currents. To south and shadows we lay ourselves upon our fate.

Waymouth burst on deck, screaming himself into a sightless hate. "Easy furs and better to the north, sweet water, cold as crystal ice, meat and foods by a hundred weight. And here we pauper, beggars to Smith's calling, and he of no account or home."

I fisted into thoughts of a sunlight murder. "We are here by law, and order of Lord De la Warr and the London Company, if not the king himself. Nail your complaints to the planks of a different door." The crew gathered in quiet juries upon the gathering scene. "Waymouth not forward to any peace, I was not inclined to consequence." Waymouth trips almost into a falling stumble. His arms flung wide, his body turns. He steadies himself, his hands grasped upon the wooden rail about the main. "It was I who saved you from the Polar Sea," he said, now walking somewhat swayed. "I against Smith alone did serve the heat. 'Stay south,' I said, 'but not so south as we would swirl the kettle of a cannibal stew.'" Waymouth staggers.

"Is he drunk?" the whisper on the deck. "Does he steal our aqua vitae?" The crew is in a stomach born of work. Waymouth feeble in his last defiant whimpers. "I kept you safe from the barrens of the polar ice. Tongue the air, it tastes of life." Stacie and Ellis went to Waymouth's side.

"Come, a little rest. Heal yourself in sleep," Stacie said.

The man festers on the fears, I thought, *that worm his living corpse to rot.*

"When he awakes, our captain will remember nothing," said Ellis, "but a comfort a little akin to hate."

THE LAND DRINKING SILENCE, THE SUN TO ITS MOMENT IN MID-DAY heaven. Gulls squawk, circling and hovering, wings lightly canopied, flourish in their feathered miracles. Their prey sighted below, their eyes in determined hungers, their piercing calls, diving in their wave attacking falls.

Ellis to the wheel, his question to me. "By what compass?" the *Black Swan* entering the broad Chesapeake.

"North by west. Hold the coast. In my cabin I have my charts."

"Fair breezes and constant. A good sail," said Ellis. The crew held to its grumbles. None mentioned Waymouth in those early hours, but sudden hangs the rules that we forget. Bastard is the wisdom mothered by surprise.

On the turn of mid-day we set our anchor on the Potomac. I to the pinnace, oars and sail. No shield now upon our hull, no banners. Naked I am returned. Red beard and hair my wizard's sign. A *werowance* true enough, forbidden knowledge, unrequited voices pain my soul. Love and dereliction, a feast of mysteries in their battle.

On the river toward the shore reeds break from the water, casting shadows on the silver sun reflections. The land a clutch of memories. Ducks dance across the ponds of a narrow bay, then take flight.

A cry, "You are alive, my red-bearded friend," from the beach. A savage with a black beard, a child in his arms. Mosco beckoning happily. I stand and wave my hand above my head. The pinnace to the beach. I splash boot-deep into the shallows. Tidal mud holds a slight retard upon my step. Mosco runs, child careful, then a firm embrace. "Again a good sight. We for adventures?" No answer sought. Mosco pushes his son into my arms. "From that Moraughtacund wife, your gift to have end to silly murders."

We spoke of adventures and distant wars. "And where is the old one?" Mosco asked.

"Gone to a lonely grave," my answer. The silence.

"You need corn, venison," Mosco to brighten a question on his face.

"Some," I replied. "Some, but mostly furs."

"Come, let us all be a gather, pipes, tobacco, food," replied Mosco. "Our good trade is later, my old friend."

FIRES TO THE DAY, A HOSTAGE HAPPILY TO THE *BLACK SWAN*. Waymouth a true captain to his table, best at being host. The night to dust the edges of the sky, we finally speak of trade. Furs to blanket decks, corn, fresh meat ready to be cured in salt, sweet water to every barrel. Trade in pins and copper weights, beads and combs, hatchets, knives. I asked the *werowance* of Powhatan. "Far in his new village, he sleeps upon his angry pleasures." We discussed messengers. "Ask that he send his daughter, Pocahontas, and wisest son to show we are still at peace." So saying messengers to the forest. How long the journey? And I not certain when my *Black Swan's* to sail.

Three hundred furs, a greed quiets among the crew, but not the suffice that Waymouth hoped. My return glad in wealth, but not rejoiced. "We are short by many weights," said Waymouth. Pleased I am to wend upon the bay another week. Mosco to guide and translate. Perhaps to him a little wealth, or another wife.

Time always the wayward to any plan. Mosco advises we sail to the Tockwoughs and the Susquehannocks. "Furs, yes. Furs and feathers," his words. More messengers sent to tell of my departure, and where and when my destinations. The moments grind that will not wait.

To the Tockwoughs now, where the fierce Susquehannocks laid the chain of pearls and bear fur robe around my neck and called me "god." I am reluctant in my divinities. A crude idol we seem in our flesh, despite Hermes Trismegistus and the alchemists' claim for us a fragment of a shattered deity fallen from a lesser heaven. And Dee, what path of gilded nightmare do you walk? As we sail into a closing day, return to me, Jonas, tell of warnings, tell of histories and their dread.

Chapter Ten

THE PORTRAIT PAINTS DEEPER THAN ITS INK.

Y THOUGHT IS SWEPT violently by the mariner's words. "Dee's intoxications suspicioned only to the surface of the meat. Talbot was not so slight of mind as to let slip the easy error. Blackened teeth and bloody ear, this man held lightning in his leathered claws." Old Jonas paused. "Demons oft sweet themselves as pretty guests.

"Who anoints himself to be the pilgrim's guide, beware the path, your tread may be of burning coals, and that sweet roast on which you sniff may be yourself the dinner smell.

"The warm impelling sunlight of the private study. That morning early Dee had washed his face, trimmed his nails, shaved his beard, bathed, even abstaining from his wife the night before. Invocations voiced in frantic purities, he now the church and the apostle to his own sermon. Retiring to his most secret oratory, there kneeling, rising, turning to kneel again, four times to each direction. 'I proclaim my prayers in the imagined cross of the compass points.' Dee returning, the action begun. Talbot forever in the snare of his own glooms, protesting, 'There is nothing seen here but devils.' Dee ever reassuring, Talbot's nose pressed to the crystal. Well played his reluctance.

"'Are we with the angels?' asked Dee.

"'Archangel Michael has appeared. He wishes to reveal the governors that work and rule under God. Forty-nine angels whose names and powers are here evident, excellent and generous.'

"'Our wisdom confirmed in numbers,' observed Dee. 'Forty-nine is the square of seven, the number of heavenly bodies: sun, moon, Mercury, Venus, Mars, Jupiter and Saturn.'

"'"This is the first knowledge, mark them... Record them," declares Michael.' Talbot then to expectations. 'I see a gold scroll in winged flight beneath a rainbow of many colored flames. Now a hand, its fingers glowing in ruby and emerald light. The scroll glides to its grasp. The page now unfurled. The calligraphies penned in a black fire. Seven tables of seven rows with seven columns. In each single square a cell, a single letter, or number. These the hieroglyphs that reveal the domains and the angels' powers which govern them. "This," declares Michael, "is the Table of Tables."'

"'But how shall I know the true names to command these angels and their powers?' Dee frantically questioning.

"'"That is soon within your grasp," Michael promises.' The work of much the afternoon to record the puzzle, then Talbot to a long silence, leaning back into his chair. 'The archangel has a wish to speak to me alone.' Talbot's face upon the crystal, he bit in anger on his lips. 'I,...' that word half ground into a regretful noise. Finally, Talbot declared his temper, 'This session now ends.'

"Dee perplexed, if not in fear. 'What were the archangel's words?' he asked.

"'Contrary to my vows and my profession, the archangel has said I should betake myself into the world, and I should marry.' Talbot stood, the fury in his eyes as if an animal caught and chained wild in its hate. So the confession, so Talbot ran from the room.

"'If that boast is not baked in air. Talbot endangers this house, and especially you, my friend,' said I in terror to Dee. 'Is Talbot a Catholic priest and you an advisor to the queen and court? Plots are whispered in the streets of the queen's assassination. All about lies a frailty of trust, and you only a short walk from Walsingham's estate, the shepherd of the intrigue, the queen's guardian and the master of her spies.'

"Dee nodded to my warning. 'I must think on this,' he said, then confiding, 'The queen is considering again the proposal of marriage from the Duke of Anjou, her ugly frog and lesser man. He, the gelding, and to be sure a better country wife.' Dee smiled. 'I have charted his stars and found the match inauspicious, and his death most near.' Dee stood from his chair, speaking to himself, 'Yes, very inauspicious.'"

"TALBOT SAT GAZING UPON A SLICE OF BREAD, SO THE MORNING meal began. His monk's habit a sulk of torn and disheveled rags. 'Last night I was set upon by two demons who berated me and beat me with their fists. I must go. We action only vicious fiends,' spoke Talbot, bruises apparent upon his cheek.

"Dee's calming voice a lullaby, sweet his words, as if to bribe compliance from a wanton brat. 'We are upon the Lord's will, a search for that one religion to cure the world from religious wars and massacres. The all within the one.' Dee's words so much upon Mandinga's own: 'Behind the one, the many. Behind the many, the one.' Dee, more to the forward of his cause, continued, 'We are together chosen to open for all the angelic purse. A child, you may be of a bitter root, but in that crystal ball which only you can see are salvations proclaimed in a living Eden.'

"Jane listened in horror at her husband's words. Talbot, both hands on the table supporting himself as he stood. Leaning across the breakfast plates, his looming face, his eyes a hooded darkness, 'I must go. My quest secrets mysteries and relics of hidden knowledge and even powders that were the philosopher's stone.'

"Standing to his full height, Talbot's cloak unfolded nervously on his arms, like the black wings of an enormous bat. 'Stay,' Dee in anguish pleaded.

"'I am not for a crystal's demons and their angelic games.' Enclothed in his shadow, Talbot rushed from the room.

"Dee labored to stand. Jane's hand pressed her weight upon his shoulders. 'Not by any dare will you follow Talbot. He is a waste, a stench of words.' Pleading to me with her eyes, Jane appealed for my alliance and my opinion.

"'Let Talbot play his dramas for himself,' I asserted. 'His scenes come baked only with a crust.' Jane released her husband.

"'We shall know the truth before the summer passes,' said Dee. 'The stars have chronicles.'

"'And men are blind, but still wield quills,' I whispered."

"'SO MUCH DESIRED, YET SO LITTLE KNOWN, AND STILL WE DRESS our ignorance in a costume of worthless cloth.' Sunlight, the morning coming old as I spoke to Dee as we walked toward my saddled horse. Three days had passed since Talbot disappeared. My sights now for Plymouth and Drake and matters of ship and sail.

"Dee smiled to some commerce voiced within himself. I pledged a penny, a gift to the stable boy's hand. Now hooves upon the high road, the earth trembling upon the echoing hollow. A lone rider, an exhausted gentleman of much ware and disarray, all his rags once of promise. His horse to Mortlake. Soon the stately clap of iron shoes upon the stones.

"The horse held against its speed, raging in a maddening sweat, eyes wide in white pain, the bridle biting obedience in the steed's mouth. All to a trot, then to stand, its head still shaking in violence. Satisfied in his power, the man dismounted. Charles Sledd, a bruise of calamities, a foul twist of many lives and names, a provocative and a rumored spy of Walsingham. 'Hail Master Dee and good Jonas,' Sledd extending the moment of his bow.

"'Examining shoes,' I joked.

"'Your time with Drake has not cut your tongue.' I returned his smile, still unwrapped. 'Quite so.'

"'Master Dee, to the point. There are tales of the comings and goings of John Talbot from your home. I am sent by friends who wish you only good. John Talbot is a coarser and a felon, well educated to many crimes.'

"'Who are these so secret friends?' asked Dee.

"'Friends,' replied Sledd, seeing Dee not inclined to his revelations, adding, 'Friends who marshal documents and who are the shepherds of events.' Sledd to his observation of Dee's face, paused.

"'Your arrival has come of a good noon. Talbot has gone into the forever lost, my guess.' Dee the diplomat, knowing Sledd greeds only coins.

"'My mission tasked a day firmly late, but stand wary of Talbot, he schemes. His name in truth is Edward Kelley.' Sledd sat himself a portrait in a brazen stone. Two fists upon his hips, a triumph. Dee gloomed and shuddered. I to my own shrug, not much surprised. Sledd mostly loyal to whosoever coin he held. I am sure he did the truth, its sovereign's worth.

"'Jane will be pleased.' I played to the ready stage. Sledd coughed himself into a palsied fit, a little blood from his nose dripping on his lips.

"'Come, I will attend.' Dee to his humanities, ever the father and physician to the world.

"In the kitchen my small concerns misspent on this fool of seldom charms. His nose in a cloth, Sledd's head leaning back upon the cure.. 'I must to Plymouth now,' I said after a time. Sledd's hand waved an over-friendly salute. Dee to his pleasantries. I walked from the house, Jane following, asking, 'Is that Talbot for good and gone?'

"'Maybe yes, and maybe no, and maybe Edward Kelley, this Talbot, will crawl himself a pilgrimage and return. Sweet Jane, be of care, even good men, mostly wise, only squeak to the heights of their dearest folly.'"

WHAT THEN DO WE LEARN BY ACOLYTES, BY THE CHRONICLES OF the second hand? The *Black Swan* rolled upon the foam and tatters of a dying thunderstorm. The wash of the bay rose upon our wake. Soon the furthest coast, the Chesapeake closer upon its northeast coast. Never did I reach lands beyond this, our final anchorage. I became now the messenger again, and from the familiar beach canoes as angry logs, in rafts of war. The Tockwoughs circled around us in menace. I stood to the rigging. A flame of my red bead and hair, a werowance, this wizard has come again in a wizard's ship. The Tockwoughs in wild voice call and chant. Their weapons given to me as a sign of peace. The one who knows the language of Powhatan speaks to Mosco.

Hostages exchanged. A few presents—in my good, I have returned with gifts. Celebrations on the beach, fires lit, songs and chants. In the village mats upon the ground. Waymouth and I sat. Across the pleasant fires came words, some unknown, others spoken in the language of Powhatan. My legend recalled. The Tockwoughs wishing to know if I needed corn, squash, or any of their coming harvest. "No," I said after a long, thoughtful silence. "I would trade for furs." The Tockwoughs spoke among themselves, agreeing, asking me to appoint the time to barter. And so I did, the next day at early light. Then I added that messengers should be sent to the Susquehannocks telling of my return, and my desire to trade for furs.

THEY WHO HAD ANOINTED ME THEIR DEITY AND THEIR KING, I AM to beggar now for a cloak of furs. What worships are to free us from our human state? Old Jonas, our campfire flairs once more upon the Chesapeake. Solemn under the flowing harmonies of the dark, and you now unknown in the graves of your last illuminations.

"After my departure from Mortlake, I rode to Plymouth," the mariner said, "and to witness the castings of iron cannons for the coming war. There was no letter from Dee for a month—then by horse, by secret messenger, a note. 'But for the wonders, I am reconciled. Come quickly. The stars proffer to a perfect sky. Edward Kelley is returned.'"

"MORTLAKE, SO PRETTILY MAY A PARADISE HIDE ITS SHAMBLES. Jane had gone to her father's estate, a visit to veil the maritals of a willful rage. Yet Dee in his greeting, hailed me in his high noon spirit. 'Talbot is now Edward Kelley,' said Dee as we stepped into the house. Talbot's foulness lingered somewhere beyond my sight and my thoughts, a haunt of desperation. I craved salvation, my wife and my unborn child. Would I spend my shame, to play and pound the tin to drum a well-forged lie? Every passion loves its squander. Still I by my remorse in fearful pilgrimage, but never would I dispossess myself of doubt.

"In the most secret rooms we found him sitting upon a green divan, his face cloaked, nodding to the quiet. Edward Kelley stood as a brown stink rising from the flesh of a green demon. 'Greetings,' he forced the hiss from between his teeth. I to a slight bow, an empty custom exercised without the form of a true address."

JOHN DEE, DO YOU ONLY ADVENTURE WITHIN THE CIRCLES YOUR shadow marks? I wondered.

Seeing my drift, the old mariner paused, lightly touched my hand. "The New World shall be of thee," he whispered. "Through you its words," he said, the campfire flames, the indolent heat floating in the clear night chill. "Words are drums, they beat of depths deeper than their mysteries." Old Jonas, his gaze transfixed. The smell of burning wood. The vapor glides, the smoke and wisps of embers expire in fireflies. "So bend into the luxuries of the heat and attend the tale." The mariner shallow his breath. To most eyes the surface inundates. But beyond its veils great secrets do contest and play us as nothing in a chessman's sport. The world lies a game board for its snare, as surviving rooks chip their hooves, ignorant of the strategies.

"Dee concluded his orisons, grasped a quill and paper.

"Kelley erupted. 'Undevil me! Demons stalk these halls to have my soul. Hell in panoplies,' screamed Kelley. 'I see a knight. His dark eyes, his face all in fire.'

"Dee's voice calm, his words a purity of warmth. " 'It is an airy fright. Did not the archangel Michael say so himself? Nothing in this house can do us harm.'

"Kelley as rude as the infant child, his porridge almost to its proper heat. The tantrum forgot, wiped away, a sniffle upon this tear of fuss, he to the crystal ball. Too easy this conversion doth convert." Profit scowled. "But I held my conclusions a little to the quiet.

" 'What presents?' Dee almost squeaked his impatience.

" 'A silent man, a king apparent, a lord of clowns, perhaps, lazing upon the chair of knowledge. Curious is this sprite, who winks—and from his fingertips arise speckled birds and floating mice and now a cat to chase them through the air. This simpleton smiles, he seems a fool.' Kelly speaks, his words played a little to the shrill.

" " 'I'm a little of a fool and much a sought for pranks. King Camara's my name, God's keeper of medicines. I joust with bones, trick the plagues. I even flask a little poison cure to joke the grave. I am the quaint, the clown of health, the smirk contestant against the shroud.' "

" 'King Camara stood, stretched the night stiffness from his bones. The stiffness fell in sparkles from his lips. "Good to be up to be bad," he said.'

"'What assurance do we have that you are not a demon?' questioned Dee.

"'How, indeed. How, indeed.' King Camara's forefinger touched his lips, 'No way to grab a certainty, so I guess I'll be off.' King Camara, however, did not leave.

"'Are you here on some command of God to aid us in our search?' Dee not for excess modesty.

"'Don't remember.'

"'You play us tease. You are a demon.'

"'Don't think so,' said King Camara. 'I am of mirth and air. The feather rock that breaks the iron latch. See my cat? Now it's a writing quill, the mouse now its ink, in a shock of smoke all transformed. And the bird, well…still a bird.'

"'Then tell us of the secrets to know the tablet of tablets.' Dee grasped a single purpose.

"'All that glue for a slippery learning. You shall have the knowledge, but you need a better crystal. The rarest stone profounds the clearest sight.'

"'Where can such an instrument be obtained?' Dee wild in his eyes.

"'This gift is mine to give. Perfect this pretty lens, so curved, so desired. It is my gift to you, and with it you shall prevail with all the kings of earth and the creatures of sky and sea. God wills, his living hand upon you. Do not stir, but behold your gift.'

"'I see nothing,' Dee exclaimed."

Old Jonas closed his eyes. Silent, the mariner's judgment, as he shook his head. Then he stirred and continued.

"'There!' cried Kelley, pointing toward the floor under the window. 'It's an angel child, some cherub. Innocent, and in its hand it holds an egg of such clarities, diamonds by compare seem a fog, all our jewels an imperfection.'

"Dee stood, his uncertain steps following the point of Kelley's words. 'I see nothing but a rude carpet, floors and assorted woods.'

"'The angel entreats you to take this stone. Look down,' cried Kelley. There by Dee's shoe an orb of light the size of an egg, a globe, a crystal, almost shameful in its purities.

"'Take the gift. Let no hand but yours and your adept touch this viewing stone. You are in revelations. Soil not what is of God. You are by his will the chosen path,' Kelley exalting in his words. The bubbles on his lips pop in a burst of spit.

"'King Camara bids you be wise in your new gift. All comes as visions to that single eye. Behold your perfect chalice. Soon the map of revelations and its empires.'

"'What portent does Camara...?' Dee's words held mid-throat. The expression on Kelley's face ghastly. The wounded leather of his skin wrinkled, crumpled as a paper shroud.

"'I must leave Mortlake this day, before the pendulum unclocks the hour. I am claimed by the angels to find and dig treasures, mysteries buried in secret crypts, magic cloistered in the earth. I must depart, ordered by the regents of the viewing stone.'

"Kelley stood, a pageant rising, the drama contrived for the thicker skull. Oh Dee, how could you not contest against this silly strut? Are time and wisdom led a squander? And are you in desperation sculptured to be a fool, so self-molded into the likeness of a schoolroom dunce?

"Who awaits the hour hand? Kelley to horse and country road, hooves in their receding gallop. Dee perplexed, grieving as if Kelley was some deathful loss. I keep to myself a needful joke, wondering under what name Kelley would return.

"I lingered some days at Mortlake, so pleasant to its guests. Its library the greatest in England, more tomes than all its colleges. So often Dee reading, quill in hand, notes in the margins of the book. Each day so. He was lost in the learned forgetfulness of a scholar's weave of thought.

"Minutes but prelude an hour, days soon calendar to a week, a month. Every sanctuary recalls my youth, my Oxford student home, then as a don of alchemies, a playwright, poet in dreamy contemplations. My world a dream of perpetual hours, the moon in its growing crescent, everlasting in its only phase.

"So in comfort again, Dee's children, Jane. I was in delight to be adopted by their love, now plundered almost of my regrets. But how familiars war when friends seek to counsel friends. After a month, and Kelley not returned, I wrapped my good cheer in the braveries of an honest cloak and spoke of him to Dee. Jane had pleaded to me of her great concern, and so to secret oratory I came to spend my truth.

"How to approach the forfeit of your worlds. How to conspire against the flatteries? Puzzle the cure, I just threw the dice. Allies by life, by secrets and theologies, and I, like Dee, so eager to believe the revelations within the stone. Kelley had me half-convinced. But the perfect showing stone—I saw its twin, an eastern exotic, in an Oxford hall.

"'We should not tend only to our joyful dreams when deeper suspicion should account,' I spoke, plucking a little drama from a low-hanging hush. 'Kelley is not worthy of our trust. Educated, but his intelligence is used, an easy criminal. It has an anger. There is a danger.'

"Dee's eyes narrowed to biting slits. 'You are turned to jealousy. So early you have tuned your doubt that I am the chosen of the angels, me! Never you! I with God, and you my shadow, my lesser half. Kill me rather Roman with a sword, sling pikes and arrows at my breast! Play me death, my carrion feasted for a dog. I uncount you friend. Vanish to my eyes. I have done with puddle fates. Be gone! Alone, I am with the portents of the heavens. Where I go, I go for all. Even you, lost friend, you should have understood. Be gone, betake your futile path. Become a memory.'"

In the empires of his despair, Jonas watched the Chesapeake's lonely drifts. All shadows float upon the silent currents, those currents glitter, cradling brevities, and wide histories passing through a penny weight of thought. "John Dee had cast a recluse on his mind. That man in the furnace of his distillations sought the secret spices pungent in his medicines. He whose calculations gave maps to English ships had launched fleets to be guided by stars and sextants to claim a world. He to swallow wooden crumbs to have himself be a saint." The old mariner padded the rough earth. "He to a new life of expeditions on a lie," said the mariner. "Eat destiny on the spoils of a maggot's bread. Dee, the grim, had boiled himself a pauper's potato soup.

"John Smith, my almost son," said old Jonas. The mariner fading into the gestures of his schoolhouse yearning. His fingers grasped, holding the tunic upon his chest as a cleric, or a scholar, rags of invocation to a life so lost. Then he threw down his hands, casting as if in its final memory away. "Soon Dee's reputation would be a midnight diamond, the moonlight darkening on a worthless stone." So depleted in sadness, the Mariner bent his head almost to his knees.

Do all our salvations beast? Do all our sins prevail, seated in our theologies? I thought. The bay's perfumes, their odors the breath of salt, the scents of fishes, the water pastured to a slight and fair crescent on the horizon's bow, so small the curve of earth. Beyond that rim to what mysteries are we now enticed? Like Drake, I feel the eons call.

Chapter Eleven

BETWEEN THE WORSHIP AND THE STONE—
THE LORD OF BREEZES.

ARLY LIGHT, THE CAMPFIRE smokes a dying breath upon the cooling sigh of air. A heat hangs hidden in the damp. The tapers of the firelocks lit, held at caution on each sailor's arm. I sit again upon mats. The trade begins. Waymouth kneels, examining the piles of furs. Mosco speaks, knowing most of the Tockwough language: iron, hatches, knives, combs, pins, fishhooks, a bounty of very useful trash. But where there is little known of metal, worlds change upon its necessities.

Five hundred furs, English wealth in measured nods, pleasured excitements smiled. The crew carrying the pelts to the pinnace and to our other boats, then rowed to the *Black Swan*. "More to come," I spoke to Stacie.

"More?" he questioned.

"The Susquehannocks," I cried. "They, the giants of the Chesapeake. Five kings to bid us peace. Dwell upon the thoughts of furs." My arm outstretched, gestured to grasp the distance on the ball of my fist. My determinations action deep to entice Stacie into acquiescence.

Stacie stared into the nothings of his own sadness. "The crew longs for the smell of home. Coins appeal with fallen worth. A presentment is needed soon."

"Five days, maybe four."

"Let us hope we do not hang on our success."

FOR THREE DAYS THE CREW GRUMBLE IN THE QUIET. AND ON THE next, the bay sunlit in its silver hours, light bounties undulate on the water and the life underneath. *What arms to bear your phalanx*, I thought as I walked the beach. Mud and twisted grass broken under foot. I looked into the broad reflections of the sky across the Chesapeake. Thin shadows now dart as iron strings, far off. This way their hardened course. "Susquehannocks," I called. The crew gathered. Upon the hill the Tockwoughs, great dignities in their hosts. The canoes close. I stand the beach. The Susquehannocks cease their strokes, oars at rest. Their songs began, and drums heavy in their voice. *Time swallows pride, but I am again.*

"You are our anointed, beyond all our kings." Words in the language of Powhatan. "Your hair burns in cold flames. You are the lord of fire?"

"I am but a man, a hearer of voices."

"Are you a god?" the words more forced, more angered. "When last you came you were a god!"

"I am a *werowance*. I am of no tribe."

"Are you alone of many births?" the cry. Tears upon the faces of the Susquehannocks.

"I am given the gifts by fathers I never sought. I am no one."

"Then you are rain, the lord of breezes." The call echoed into the hills. The Susquehannocks rowed toward the sandy shallows. On the largest canoe one of their kings stood, draped on his hands a great fur skin and a large necklace of pearls. Upon the beach the Susquehannocks about me, the bearskin gentled to rest its warmth on my shoulder. The pearls lay across my chest. "And yet a god," they repeated as they placed their furs in bounties at my feet.

DAYS OF TRADE, THE NIGHT IN SWARMS OF BURNING FIREFLIES, the embers of the campfires' leaping flames, and night reached into its own dark. The crew content in its constant trembles and complaints. Greed does not come easy to its wealth. Many of the other tribes had joined the trade. No French upon the Chesapeake to steal success, all by more beyond our hopes. "We will sail by two day's tide." Waymouth spoke, his captainsy quite sustained. I little inclined but smiled to some inner thought. "Not all the tribes are seen. There will be those still eager for an iron pin."

Play the moment, play the greed. Waymouth's sour face told that plot had scraped the page. "Two days," Waymouth repeated, "if little presents."

"We may still have messages from Powhatan. Would you cede an empire for a glass of kitchen milk?"

"Our voyage to the north is done. You captain by thy name. Be the better silence. You have brought us wealth. Why displeasure fate? If caught De la Warr could still play the ax. We sail for England now. In months we could return upon a pleasant morrow." So said Waymouth as he stroked the hairs of his bearded gloom.

Stacie sometimes the chatter, sometimes the dagger at any easy back. "De la Warr is ill. A month or two the clock may spring his coffin. So much for so small a wait, and most of it at sea, a sail for home and wealth."

I am more for a mutiny now than vapid coins, I thought. *And will she come? Are lamentations the soul of every mind? I quake in a passion that is only flames. Words in their stricken music fail. You, this land, the only calligraphies of her name.*

THE MORNING COILS IN MISTS TO SWEEP THE NIGHTMARE OF THE dark. I am implored again by the Susquehannocks to remain and ever be their lord. The tribe in tears at our last parting. By wealth and power beyond all histories, shall I emperor against my birth and be a forest exile? Eared to the river, a prisoner to a different fate. But still I am of gifts and the unmarked way. I will not to the Susquehannocks.

Mosco and I in quiet plots. When we sail we will make for the Potomac, return Mosco to his people, and have what news of Powhatan. "Why not to the forest?" Mosco asked.

Why not? I thought. *But with these furs I may bribe a better hearing from the London Company. Wealth gestures best when it struts a dangled excess.*

On the morrow the *Black Swan* to haul its anchor. High tide at dusk. I sit my cabin, accounting flickers on empty walls. "Old Jonas, would Dee approve me as an adept, or some forest sprite with a god-like glow, an idol of pagan cast affirmed in planetary rays?" I smart to my darkening self.

"DEE I NEVER VISITED AGAIN FOR MANY DECADES, I AND DRAKE AT sea, the coming war all that was in the collision of worlds. But much I heard in rumors.

"Whispers now imprinted in the air of new explorations to the west, of double dealings to persuade the queen—she giving monopolies in America to Adrian Gilbert—of Dee's rage and disgust at his former friends, of Kelley's angels, gods and ancient maps and philosophers' dust that bring forth gold. The maps and dust Kelley dug in a decaying crypt at the urging of these angels. Dee offered appointments to the French, German, Russian courts. May what births in shadows one day consume the world?

"The calendar now 1583, that year to beast a savage spring. Two figures new to Mortlake come to honor Dee. The creaking planks of the water stairs, the weight of shoes, above the playful silt and currents. A noble in his red velvet cloth, shoes of some Arabian descent, green with a toe pointed upward in a girlish curl. A polish prince, Lord Albert Laski. So walked together the friend of alchemists and a seeker of an all-inclusive church. 'A family of love,' Laski's kin it's great apostle. And here on the queen's own barge he came wrapped in his treasons and his theologies." The old mariner smiled. "He, who once raised a mercenary army to seize and plunder the vacant Polish throne. So do the shadows stink, in their churchly hypocrisy. God is love, they say, but the world is opportunity." Old Jonas leaned back from the flickering heat. "An odd pairing that day at Mortlake. The other a fallen monk, a heretic and soon burned by the pope at the stake, a scattered ash. Giordano Bruno came to England to debate the Oxford pedants. He of the brilliant mind. He to define the truth: the earth revolves around the sun. The universities as ever the refuge of the persistent ignorance. Those, the dons of the tired learnings, conventioned but to geld their newest mount, and to ape a jungle fit at the passing meteors.

"Bruno was jeered by the Oxford mob. The pedants called him an Italian snipe, a tin pot peddler come to school. But blow not a coward's breath against the hurricane. Bruno disemboweled the petties in their Oxford rags, his scalpel edged in venom, 'You self-gorge by day, feasting upon each other's rot.'

"The world ever costumes to flaunt its power. Two weeks after the Oxford debates, Laski, again dressed in his finest silk, visited Mortlake. Four days the conversations were secreted upon an offer. Finances and protection for Dee and Kelley and their families in the Polish east. 'The court at Prague would be also honored, I am assured, to have you as guests. Rudolf II is of ours. He, too, seeks the knowledge few would dare.'

"Kelley, fearful of an arrest for forgery, played his angels to his cause, worded havoc, telling Dee that Leicester and Walsingham made plots against him. Terror, whispers, suspicions. Only at Mortlake the silence more frightening than the fact. But in truth, Dee's influence at court had fallen from its golden hour. And so eastward toward

Prague, by the mud roads of Poland toward the rising court of Rudolf and its empires of new-found light.

"On September 21, 1583, Dee and Kelley, six hundred books, one hundred manuscripts, children, wives, servants, made to their barges on the Thames. Oars slipped under tattered sails, a cool breeze beckoning to an easterly glow. Laski met at the appointed time and place, set behind the seal of a secret letter. A fly-boat waiting in Queensborough, a night at anchor. Dee and Laski and Kelley, two families, one noble, impatient for the morning tide. Soon to forsake home and England for many years, rolling their eternities on the cast of a loaded dice."

Chapter Twelve

THE WAVES CONTEST A VOYAGE TO
AN UNCERTAIN HOME.

ARS, SEA STORMS, DESPAIRS mould uncounted breaths, unmeasured still the depths that disappoint. Oh, my pondered heart, and you, my Pocahontas, will your father's gift bring me to my destinies? The *Black Swan* tacks toward the Chesapeake's furthest coast. Will she be on that shore? A messenger from her father's craft, or others, perhaps, to speak his law, or am I now so fallen as to be ignored? And what if she be there? I am no one of a nothing cast. Can a princess of the blood flee to England, married to my lesser path. That love would be a cruelty. The *Black Swan* courses south by west. I stand the deck, indulged by the horizons I should seek. So many promises survive only in their desires. Has my world fallen to its true estate? To you, my princess queen, the all of me. The Northwest Passage beyond my hope. By what sacrifice can I now be worthy of your kiss?

AT DAWN THE COAST IS DESERTED BUT FOR THE EARLY MISTS. OUR anchor falling water bound, a heavy echo in the quiet. Nothing breaks, Mosco and I take to the boat, the shore greeting all in its emptiness. Mosco's call, our firelocks lit. We stay the boat a distance in the currents. Nothing meant. Soon the villagers at their fete. No news from Pocahontas, the messenger rumored dead. The wind falls in a scattered chill. Hours pass. "At tide," says Waymouth, "we are for home and England."

A nod to fate, I stood myself a pillory. Should I stay, consume the quiet on the drums of chance? That dice is blanked upon a blind man's bluff. Not the bet a better takes.

Already sea birds gather to jury on the masts, the bay filling its flow with fallen trees. Shall I, by rude, hold this anger to a purpose? In England I shall have the London Company close to bear the reality of the Virginia circumstance. Offer cures where none has yet named the disease. Be physician to the moment. Rewrite the clock. Nurture the New World, its enterprise and its hopes. Cast down its foolish laws and its lazy prodigals. Save our salvation, heal its wounds, chance everything, chance the air. America raises its golden Edens, its shield on my arm, and I, the Odysseus of the wanton birth. My ships, my barges, sail with crews of vulture men, their beaks and their carrion eyes feasting on each other's meat. Blood drips from the brittle of their hardened lips. Eat your festive spice, I have come, the apostle, to captain away your curse.

My baptisms twice, why not? My final wound comes by thrust of water. The river, the bleeding clarity of my burned thigh. Liquid washing liquid. The voices then to cool, to ordain Powhatan's prophecy. The New World awakens to my ears. I am its first apostle, new birthed by exile and by scorn, the knight herald of this new land. I am the first American.

THOUGHTS PAY PLEASURES TO THEMSELVES, OLD JONAS — SPEAK again of Dee and Prague. Coffer now the tales of Prague, cobbled in its winding streets, gargoyled on all its gates.

"Rudolf II was groomed in his uncle's Spanish court. Philip II devised to have Rudolf his adopted heir — Philip's sons all mad by the bigot's blood. Rudolf a horrified witness to the Inquisition at its most brutal, an auto de fe. As ye burn your heretic, so ye burn your every dream," the mariner's fingers into fists.

"Rudolf finally escaping Philip, fled back to Vienna, his father dying soon after. Fearing Ottoman armies at his borders, Rudolf moved his capitol from Vienna to Prague in 1583, a year before Dee and Kelley arrived. There, in the splendor of his isolation, Rudolf's zoo cages of lions, bats, elephants and peacocks, all manner of strange beasts. His library magnificent, his mistresses, art collections, his court painters, enamellists, jewel makers, clockmakers, engineers, artisans, and the hunted philosophers, heretics, alchemists. All in accumulations to the safety of Prague they came, the dispossessed of Europe, drawn to the exile's court.

"Dee and Kelley found refuge in Prague at the home of Thaddeus Hayek, Rudolf's own physician. That house inherited by Hayek from his father, the alchemist Simon Bakalar, who named his residence 'The House at the Green Mound,' decorating its walls with silver and gold hieroglyphs, demonic birds and fish with human heads, fruits with wings held by angels offering their riches to the moon. All in paint and rainbows, silhouettes in glowing hues, madness perfected to fool the eye. 'Shall we pluck a painted apple and deny the garden to the snake?' laughed Kelley. Dee was more for action and the telling stone. Hayek, a rare attendant to hear the angels speak. Diluted were the words with foreign whispers, but Hayek convinced that God had given instructions to Dee, and warnings for Rudolf. Behind the scenes of court the physician pledged his influence. Dee was to write directly to Rudolf for an audience, speaking of his friendship with the emperor's father, Maximilian II, Dee even dedicating his *Monas Hieroglyphica* to the elder.

"Time now in its anxious wait. Three days after Dee's letter, a reply. 'The emperor, well-pleased with Master Dee's service to his father, will grant an audience at two o'clock on the morrow in his privy chamber.'

"What comedies grotesque the contemplative life? The following afternoon, Dee in preparation for his meeting with Emperor Rudolf, when Edward Kelley, in a drunken fit, chased one of Laski's guards into the street, the two throwing stones, drawing swords, coming to blows. The watchman, by threat, making some peace, but warning of future consequences.

"Dee, now an hour late, hurried to the castle, losing his way once inside the massive gates, arrested, held in the guardhouse, finally allowed to send his secretary to find Rudolf's chamberlain, who arrived huffed and nervous, mostly dragging Dee by his tunic through the halls, the dark stone ways within the castle's keep. And through rooms, the apothecaries of the emperor's collections: shadows of exotic shapes; long shelves; glass vats displayed of colored liquids, where floated the drowned, misshapen artifacts of earth, sea and air. And fabulous art: Bosch, Bellini, and naked maidens painted exhalant in their blush of plenties. And enamels, works of silver and gold, with hermetic images to gather the divine and healing rays of sun and star, moonlight secrets all potent in their mysteries.

"Rudolf II, who the pope suspected a willful shepherd, if not a protestant, himself, sat at the council table among his quills and documents, festooned in the liveries of his power. The emperor ordered all to withdraw so Dee might speak in the confidence of a private ear. Again Rudolf told of his belief in the wizard's love for his father and his royal self, the Monas Hieroglyphica being too profound for his own capacities, but he knew of its reputation. All this said, his royal majesty asked Dee of his warning for the eastern Hapsburg throne and the Empire.

"Dee in fleeting sands, his hourglass, its moments almost to the poverties of an empty bowl. How do you stand, a boastful flea, before an emperor's quill? Dee, his only alchemies now were his drunken fascination portraited in the living mud of Kelley's lies. 'With much suffering and great danger, I have come at the request of God, in commandments to me through his angels to speak these words,' Dee began. 'The angel of the Lord rebuketh you for your sins. If you will hear me, and believe me, you shall triumph. If not, the Lord God that made heaven and earth (under whom you breathe and have your spirit) putteth his foot against your breast, and will throw you headlong down from your seat.

"'Moreover, the Lord hath made this covenant with me (by oath). If you will forsake your wickedness, and turn unto him, your seat shall be the greatest that ever was, and the devil shall become your prisoner; which devil I did conjecture to be the Great Turk. This my commission is from God. I feign nothing.'

"'I believe that you do speak to me in love,' strangely gentle, Rudolf's words. Was this majesty humble before Dee's name, a gift against an impertinence of a once great learning; or was there a truth more hidden that soddened the emperor's power? Rudolf's seven illegitimate children by his mistress, the daughter of his librarian, a host of country girls and noble maidens willing to trade a spot of virginity for family influence at court. So declines the aging of a youthful will. The emperor, sighing in his impotence, now only to gaze by painterly art at voluptuous maidens, rather than the vigor of the silken mount. And thus the dying hunger quilts the eye to a passive lust. Dee departed from the emperor's rooms with his head, and promises of financial aid (never given). The condescension of potentates can have its own cruel surprise.

"The next day, Kelley to the crystal ball warning, 'In the eighty-eight, stars will fall in lightning shrouds and the sun shall come a new dawn from the west.' 'Eighty-eight' Dee assumed to be 1588."

But this came to pass, I thought. *Kelley a portrait of a fraud*. In my eyes glanced the river in its moonlight quiet. My words to questions, and old Jonas's reply. "Not so clear, our opinions mount, or do lies and truth again intermix in chanced concessions?

"Kelley pursued his schemes with philosopher's dust (found it is said now in King Arthur's tomb), and soon by slight-of-hand produced a rumor of much gold. Even unto displaying his skill for the papal nuncio in Prague, who, less for gold, but fearful of Dee's heresies and his protestant influence on Rudolf, played schemes with schemes to have them exiled from the city, or at best to have them at the stake.

"Little known of Dee for those years of war," continued Profit. "Cadiz, the Armada sailing itself to storm and doom. Drake spoiling in the victories of his God. All the rumors from the east spoke only of greed, and of Kelley in Prague possessing an alchemist dust that rendered base metals into gold. At Elizabeth's court, Dee's name smothered under the whisper of Kelley's gold. Elizabeth's ambassadors sent to lure him home, Dee to be politely ignored. Greed the triumph, other services quickly forgot. The ambassador sent was your Lord Willoughby. Casuals in incident are the pillars that build histories. Willoughby mentioned your name, John Smith, to Dee in Prague, even before we met in Plymouth on Drake's ship. Do you, my sometimes son, think you were there by accident?"

"But why would Lord Willoughby speak my name? I was of nothing."

The old mariner grinned, but did not answer, posturing in the silence to bring the proper words. "You were known to have visions, angelic child, one of Willoughby's father's polar death. Remember when you went to the great estate?"

"A child's dream, a spriteful innocence," I pleaded.

"You are in mystery, more I cannot tell, other than you were chosen at your birth. Secrets, secrets and revelations, a letter to your hand if you survive. Nothing more! I am sworn now to silence." The mariner into his wizard's gloom. Finally he said, "Lord Willoughby was a witness to an action in Prague. The angels granted Willoughby a question. 'And estates and children?' Willoughby asked.

"'Great with fortunes and earthly honors, but there is one, a son to a borrower of your lands, who will be greater still. Honors and immortalities to your house. By your protections, all are blessed.'

"Lord Willoughby stammering to name his tenants, until your father's name. The angel saying, 'Of his, a new world rises, or that world will fail.'

"But Kelley was a curser, a forger of coins." I then in the storms of wilding disbelief. "They pilloried him," I shouted at the mariner.

"All and more, the truth's to come. A criminal, a fracture of many crimes, but Kelley knew of the Armada, the death of Mary, Queen of Scots. What madness drives the lunatic? What frenzy in a blinding dance, to hop upon the lucky slivers that become the truth."

I wondered at the starless astrologies that guide our lives. A fool's luck, a shill of vagueness, wherein all pretends as a dance of air. And is that our prophecy? Are we but captained by a devil's smile? "Am I but the alchemies of a forger's joke?" My words grieved into the night.

"Forget the wound. Be the child's promise, but cautious in your philosophies. So rare is the man who rises to be his own surprise. Kelley did not return with Lord Willoughby, nor did Dee. It is rumored that Lord Willoughby brought Queen Elizabeth a bedpan turned half to gold by Kelley, and a ring worth four thousand pounds. Our dreams are festers spoiling not much from the chamber pot," said the old mariner.

"In London, more schemes to entice Kelley to the English court. Walsingham sending his spies. But the papacy, fearing for its power not its hordes of gold, sent new ambassadors to the emperor to fix the snares and trap the heretics. Either exile or the stake, Dee and Kelley forced to a meeting with the nuncio. Kelley, drunk, talked of sacred works, actions, angels and crystal balls.

"The dangers now apparent. Burn their angels and their books. Under threat of the papal nuncio, Rudolf disinclined to give Dee protection after their calamitous meeting. Kelley always in drunken brawls. They, their wives, servants, by coach and wagon, fled Prague, wandering through strange lands under every care and hardship, first to Krakow, then the safeties of Southern Bohemia, the Trebon Castle and the fabulously rich Vilém Rozmberk.

"His vast estates, his many villages, his silver mines, his farms all of that earth, its Eden soil rich in shambled love. The snake had cast itself the thorn on a flowered stem. Dee first met Rozmberk on May Day of 1586, in the gardens he had built upon the slopes leading to Rudolf's imperial palace. Rozmberk telling Dee of his three marriages, all without issue. 'My loose life a drab of wenches, fine wines and feasts discarded to the throat. But no son to rule, no daughter, a princess to draw some syllables of my vanished name. All Europe dies, its great kings preside over fruitless cradles. Rudolf, himself, no heir, never married. Elizabeth the queen, the same. The French king a better wife to his wife, no issue. Philip II four times the groom, two mad idiots of small use. Our stars sweep a barren heaven. We are our age's end.' Rozmberk then to alchemy to replenished his line. 'Wizard, be the quest. I am vast in wealth, all my six laboratories are at your command. Be the rain and sunlight to magic a verdant spring.'

"A month later witness his two carriages, Dee, Kelley, children, wives and books upon the road to Rozmbeck's estate. His farms, his laboratories extracting wealth in pure silver from black earth. Alchemies in riches now to birth the alchemies of a legitimate heir. Dee, the wizard, and Kelley to be the one shadow to the only one. But circumstance ever bites the hand of friendly prospects. Kelley more to golden alchemies, more to the sly that tricks the mind, more practical. Dee now pilloried the slight to Kelley's rise.

"In London rumors whispered of Kelley's gold. Lord Cecil ordered his own spies abroad with solemn bribes to entice Kelley's ear. Dee played the useless counterfeit. He who gave England worlds, now the shun of greedy fools.

"All that comes by nothing comes to less. Mortlake plundered of its great library. Most books stolen, finding shelves in nobles' estates. Station and gentility and learning always toward a little vice. All ages wither with grand pretense." Old Jonas swallowed. "In 1589, while I at sea, Dee broken to a haggard wild, a greatness declined, discarded to its poverty, arrived in London to be his country's neglect."

.   .   .   .   .

THE OLD MARINER NOW SILENT. HIS HANDS CLASPED, A CONSCIENCE paused. "I could not visit Mortlake," he said. "Too much war, the court aging into a faltering death: Leicester, Walsingham soon enough, Burghley, Hatton, the queen herself in 1603. A murdering forgetfulness is our greatness's final fall. It is our inheritance. James anointed king. He of small persuasions and teaspoon etiquettes, a drawing room monarch distilling all wisdom from his purse. The unseen in exile. The heavens abandoned, their divine rays dark, their astrologies encompassed in the broken bindings of neglected books. England dies now to its new beginnings. Save us in your memories. As the world falters into its ancient habits, a new world apostles into life. You hear its birth, feel its theologies, your path is given. Take the bible of this living earth, speak sermons in the landscapes of its disquiet. Be the first, its living sacrifice."

Nothing came to me but dread. I am the becoming, the empowered moth to play his pyres into song. This I thought listening to the old mariner in the final act of a failing age.

"Every passion warrens in some nostalgia. In 1605, plague in Manchester, where resided Dee and his family. I learned of Jane's death, three of her children. The wizard himself survived, returning, it is said, to Mortlake after a sojourn and an appointment with Archbishop Whitgift for more than a decade. An exile from court, home to wreck and slander, Dee, still accused of consorting with demons.

"So what is said, is said again. Dee petitioning King James to be tried in court, so he might defend his name. James, disinclined to forward any public foolishness of an old conjuror, simply ignored the fret and planned another masque.

"In worlds of sorrows, my old friendship not quite stale. Why not the curiosity birthed of a thousand better memories? I, being in London then, hired a pinnace to sail up the river Thames. That afternoon, rain flung in fitful torrents. Calm soon, the warmth in breaking sunlight. Mortlake repaired some, its dilapidations spent from the few remaining coins sent years ago from the queen's own purse. Old Bess to the end wayward and loyal in her charities. Up the river walk, stairs half-fallen into the mud and tall grass, my approach to the house a whistle path of forty paces. Excitement, fears, a troubled loneliness. 'Good wizard, are you brewing sunlight from garlic cloves?' I called in jest. No answer. I entered the poverties of the Mortlake dark, walked the remembered familiarities of its rooms.

An emptiness now, a tomb of hollows, shelves without their books, instruments and flasks gone, a broken sextant, Mercator's globe stolen, an age in its carrion, its libraries wrecked.

"'Old Jonas, have you come by hate to drink a smile?' In a corner of the lightless gloom, a shade of gossamer sat and hissed its heat upon the dust.

"'Not for any gloat would I torture an old friend,' I said.

"'There is a chair,' Dee replied. 'Have play of it.'

"I sat into the polished expanse of wood, settling into its loneliness. 'Kelley is taken to his grave, or does he still greed in foreign labyrinths?' Dee's voice an ounce of noise upon the quiet. 'Do all God's Cherubs fly on dragons' wings?' he continued. 'Grotesque this world, a fill of flutter flies, a cabbage for its memory, and I who sought the heavens, a forgotten trash left to idle. I am provoked by this frog, our less kingly James. But still I must bear this fallen earth and the stale divinities of its dust.' Dee raising the viewing stone in his hand, 'My bibles all proffer but a God of nothing.'

"Dee in hesitations. 'Is Kelley truly dead?' he asked, his anger grieving. 'Is Kelley truly rot?'

"'He is a myth,' I answered, 'rumored in a fold of legends. Some say he still lives, working his prompt in Russia. Others, he died by some murderer's plot escaping Rudolf's prison.'

"'He was the greatest of all skyers,' Dee again into his laments. 'What the angels bless, we in our judgment become despaired. Failed, the all of it after the cross-matching.'

"'Cross-matching?' I questioned. That phrase held little sense.

"'The angels,…we are in their fire but to serve.'

"'Cross-matching. Wherefore the action to spin that name?'

"'I was given call of it,' Dee speaking, 'an angel's sacrifice. I was commanded against myself to engorge.' Dee raged, silencing into a spoon of breath, 'By the angelics of a divine decree, I convinced to share all with Kelley, our lives, our poverties, our wives.'

"'Jane, the innocent, so convalesced to be a whore,' my thoughts beyond a voweling stammer, 'Jane?' I questioned.

"'To Kelley in a compliant bed. Joanna to be as mine.' Dee's voice as if a dry smudge. 'One night only to seal the pack. The adulterous dispensations in the promises within the orb.'

A crystal calf, a sin of tongue and throat. I thought, listening to the mariner.

"'What pleases God abjures the stain. The angels command only in their love of us,' Dee said. 'Kelley ever warning, "What is spoken may be of demons."'"

"A conscience vented to be a sly," a gloom on the mariner's words. "When we love ourselves enough, we forfeit every love. Dee clamored to entail the beast." The old mariner's eyes toward me. "Nine months Jane to birth another child. The true father kept as a stilled complaint, lost within the womb.

"So much, so much, the ignorance weaves within the twist." The old mariner's fingers in strange elocutions upon the air, then he laughed. "Kelley now known to be Walsingham's spy, a paid dissembler, a criminal under threat of the noose, a prod of missions, a slither in the ear. Kelley to report on Dee, of much import to the crown. His loyalty not the thought, but who might by craft use Dee to game a treason against our queen. And then so many at his door, as Laski. What counterplots might Walsingham ferment in his sewer's brew?

"Kelley, by threat, thought to follow Laski into the east. Dee stitched to his skyer's side. Perhaps the wizard to drop a little persuasion in Rudolf's ear, to hate a better hate. His cousin the Spanish Philip sent a shiver, perhaps for England treaties and an Eastern alliance of arms. The pope feeling this as well, now his spies pursued the rumors. Rudolf by forced persuasions exiled Dee and Kelley from Prague.

"And you, dear Smith, my wonderment and my almost son, you are the geometries, the stanchion braced to open worlds. Dee is now surely dead, all the old philosophies slumber as a discarded book, our age, an almost toothless mouth, spitting its last blackened ivories at a hardened biscuit on a broken plate.

"The street peddles nothing in its stalls but confections prettied to misinform. A new spring comes, John Smith. It stills the sand, unclocks the hourglass. The crowless cock struts a vigilant quiet upon the earth, but a new harvest seasons in the loam. The old is plowed, turned apostle in its decay. Arise in rot, new figured world, a divine beast wanders drooling of the hunt. Bait the air in homilies around us," Jonas to his feet, arms flung to the horizon's grasp. "These the forest hieroglyphs! Here creatures walk in genealogies more ancient than any royal name. To you, all this is voiced. To you this inheritance. To you the guardian of this last estate."

Old Jonas touched my hand in a caress that sighs of a forgiving hope. Am I not resigned to my mariner's final sleep? I knew his death so close. What consigns the grief to a father's death? The pendulum swings its silhouette by light, by shadow, do all his profiles contradict? And I, in the grammars of the midden heap, unquenchable my thoughts and tongue, moving upon his mysteries.

OUR ANCHOR HAULS, GRIM ITS IRON SMILE. THE WATER DROOLS from off its lips. The golden dusk almost to its crimson turn. Mosco pleads his friendship from the beach. "Break my heart, for I am again myself." I moan in the silence for my other lives, now lost, or forgotten, or sleep a tended waste. How shall I return? Reclaim the destinies of my name. The New World less an Eden now. The savage my contested friends, our wars a child's game of twigs. But this new Eden births a viper in its zoo. No eggshell murders here, the smell is wanton death. A ruined England of a ruined hope, stand with me now, the prodigal.

Tired men on a tired beach, the savages gesture love, its pantomime shining in the shadowing dust. But now the bay and our escape, the sea beyond and England in months. Northward months and east, and hazards of the water.

The wide bay, a basket sea, the sky reflections dome desolations upon the swells. Oh Drake, will the sea take safely upon itself again the almost damned, this triple orphan of the double tale. Jonas, what alchemies will arise in stars? Shall I feast upon the air? Engorge on invisibilities to contend my rank? I am a slight of wisdom, my faith relents. Am I your better fate, or am I berthed a fool as a lesser twin? The river whispers profundities only tuned to the kettles of a chosen's ear. Pretty pins its lexicons. Nothing in its poetries we abide, and yet the river speaks. Is the hearing the only wisdom it imparts? Uncertain, have I claimed the noise, its darkness as my divinities?

THE BLACK SWAN COURSING SOUTH BY EAST, THE VOICE OF THE river diminishing into tremulations. Europe soon, England again. The old world untongued, unheard. Its quiet does not console. Its silence abounds in the rumble of the carriage fancies crushing the litter under wheel on the London streets. It palls the Thames, and how brief its distractions, powdered on the blemishes festered on a courtesan's youthful skin.

I am not of old world cities now. Inclined I am to the forests of haunted spaces. America! You have born me a prodigal, your first apostle!

The *Black Swan* in fair winds. The old mariner left to worm on an exile's beach, and in the empires of my love, she walks conversant with mysteries. Oh, the silken falls of angel's wings bear me once again to those voices that I have lost. And Dee, your alchemies, your secret hieroglyphs, your signs, how they taunt me with their promised miracles.

PART TWO

Ink, Quills, and the Storms of Progress

THE ALCHEMIES OF THE RIVER

The mud drifts of an old wound. The pain sweeps, it is lost. Swift the water flows through the geographies of my forgetfulness. I am a ghost, a vehemence, brief in the intrusions of my passing motions.

Chapter Thirteen

WHAT IS, IS LEFT A SCATTER.

FTER A TWO-MONTH SAIL, I returned to England in the fall of 1610. We made our reports in Plymouth. Waymouth frozen to his prattle, tenuous, shivered in his well-worn boot. Hudson not found, but maps redrawn and expeditions done to his little credit. Stacie bragged himself a self-made fame. Before we parted, we sold our furs, a small portion to us from the London Company. I was now in frenzy to find a ship and return to Jamestown, but that was not a simple plan. Permission seldom writ for a sail to Virginia. Even had I my rank and the excuse, my neck might easy bear a rope. And so I have freighted myself again with barrels of ill content. *Bluff the certainties*, I thought, *I will not be a discard of some whim, I raged. I have power yet to converse the fates and by actions improve my station.* Influence, as always, sheltered in the public alphabets of our family names. Their connections the substance, even when their talent is a little through the door. To gain its power I would have to break into the circle of its blood. I wrote to the Willoughbys, giving some histories of the Virginia project, asking of their welfare, buttering my intent upon a loaf of courtesy, asking of George Sandys and his brother, Sir Edwin, and might I visit to discuss the inclinations of our Virginia prospects.

I had some wealth in London, all that remained from my fortune given to me by Zsigmond for my suffering in the eastern war. In truth, my purse a dust against the memories of its plenties. I took some rooms, made some inquiries, learning Smythe and Edwin Sandys were not in London, but were expected to return in about a month. And so I waited against a dance of shadows, their dramas spent in histories beyond my ears.

A LETTER ARRIVED SOON FROM THE WILLOUGHBYS, HAILING MY return, offering what aid they could. Peregrine chatting always in his happy barbs and his lunacies intoxicating in its cheer. I too grim to be seduced by mirth, but pleasured to be remembered with such kindness. "We knew you were destined for great projects," Peregrine wrote. "Your election as president. How well you have confirmed our pride in you. Our certainty that one day you would move upon a grand estate. We knew of your wounds, some of your troubles; but all that must have passed forgotten, once you learned of the great office the London Company had entrusted to you. By Smythe's and Sandys' own choice (and they, as you must know, not well disposed to each other) to be the chief of colonial defense, third in command under Gates himself. So much we hoped. We knew then there would be a knighthood in your future."

The letter caught me frozen on its ink. I read the passages until the words lost their meanings, all confused in the swim of deeper thoughts. My world, my futures spent upon the profiles of a single coin: Gates and Dale!

Now the plot I never guessed. I was too powerful to be hung. Dale and Gates, both advanced in age, as they succumbed, or were called to other duties, I would have moved in their shadows up the ladder of command, perhaps one day lord governor and captain general. My ambitions not fully set! So close I came, the gift not given, but still it was mine in name.

I continued to read the Willoughbys' letter. I learned my second book was published at the London Company's own expense. "It is a great success," so Peregrine penned his encouragements. I was not so sure, having lived a life much different from its rumors. "George Sandys is just returned from his journeys to the east. Remember, so long ago, we discussed those ventures: he to Turkey, Jerusalem and the Mediterranean, while you to Gosnold and Virginia. Now you both are home. You pilgrims should meet again. I know Sandys would delight at such confidences you could give. He is at work on a book of his travels. Author to author, you might hint advice and quill an inspired page for an old and powerful friend, so versed you are and clever."

WITH SIR THOMAS SMYTHE AND SIR EDWIN SANDYS STILL IN JOURNEYS far from London, I chose a friendly ear and the nearer cause and took my opportunities to visit George Sandys.

Sandys' room assumed the pleasant mirror to a shabby fashion. A scholar's nest, smoke and books in an unclean air, speaking through the smothered light. He hailed me in friendship and kind words. "Ah, my twin, we are both returned, something better for all our journeys. You wear your miles well, and I, in trust, feel fit, obliged to pen a work. And you a hero. My brother and the London Company respect your thoughts, even if your words for their policies are voiced a little forward of contempt." I started to protest, but Sandys' smile held me silent. "I care not what you say of my brother, but for your own success, an opinion too ably said may educate your friends to be an enemy. A word to advise against too much good advice. A tasteful incompetence has never thwarted a good career." Sandys offered me a chair, poured some wine. "And do you like my vistas? A landscape worn of aging fabric. My inheritance from my mother. Two hundred pounds, if I arrived home alive, one year from her death. All that I am, comes with terms, and my brother Edwin's well. So glad you asked."

"I didn't ask," I smiled.

"That is why I count you friend." George Sandys sipped his wine, blood sweet in its salted taste. "Let us talk our books. I've read yours. You have a talent beyond the bastard muses of a formal education. You have vigor, my friend. What most authors lack in genius they try to swindle from a diploma. You write of adventures, storms and exploration, escapes. I shall write an eastern travel graced with long passages from the ancient authors. I am a translator, you an artist. And so again my family and my history steal me common against my better aspirations. I am born to an angry birth. All my life I am but a fret suckled on a borrowed milk. Now, you and I, our paths lie in ink. So much we are like twins of different mothers. Where you go first, there I follow—to the east to write a book, and with my brother's company, why not to the west? I am a shareholder, one share, twelve pounds, some shillings to fill the rate. Why not to Virginia next to seal both our fates; two brothers, twin to one, orphan to the other." Sandys laughed.

"I am more your orphan than your twin. I would return to Virginia if I could by some protection arrange a passage."

Sandys drank upon his own anger, ignored my words. "Hudson is lost on some foolish cruise, and I hear that on your ship came tobacco traded from the savages," he said. "Judged poor, I am told, but not so good as to throw a shade upon our best. Eighteen shillings a pound for the Spanish weed against some pence a pound for Virginia's. But still it is worth in weight the equal of wheat. A small success, a little hope, some profit to the brew. Not worth a ship, but what at first seems a nip may swallow all. My brother Edwin has taken to a tantrum." Then he sipped his wine. "My brother is only for profits of a proper kind. He did not found the enterprise to grow a noxious weed or so my brother treats to the carriage wisdoms protested in the streets. Tobacco less the medicine and more the curse. The king has his own wars with the leaf. Caught by politics, my brother thunders in the Parliament, swearing he did not send Englishmen abroad to grow a vice. But the Company has its losses, and when there are debts, any plan is virtue that schemes a little hope. I have seen such occasions in the east. I would not be so quick to disregard this weed."

I looked at George Sandys. "I know from an old alchemist the leaf yields no remedies. All that's a deadly gossip. But what battle, what battalions march in smoke? I see no heralds in its commerce other than some fools for generals, some pipes for cannonades."

"The east, my friend. There are lessons in the east," said Sandys. "No trifle small enough when man seeks his pleasures. And you, yourself, have made some forward to the plot. From your letters, my dear Smith, well threaded with good advice, the council is thinking to expand the private lands. Three acres to every man, woman and child in Virginia. We, the servants serve, but who the master?

"Let me tell you of the east. Inspired by you, I myself made a voyage to Turkey, then the Holy Land. There, I had some witness. Through the Dardanelles we sailed, landing at Constantinople, that city where once you served as slave, and I now its honored guest. So turns our feeble world upon its feeble consequences, as if all great moments rise from a mockery. I with rank and a brother's wealth came to see the sights, that city having been opened to English trade in 1583. Already Venetian and Genoese merchants had brought their Italian goods, including Spanish tobacco, that herb finding ready pipes in a country used to smoking hemp and opium.

"Soon after our arrival the sultan banned all tobacco, none could be sold or smoked. Tobacco in Constantinople was of a very poor quality, unsalable to English tastes, but judged most excellent by the Turks. Fear was now the cargo on English ships. Hearing that King James despised the weed as unhealthy, the sultan passed such laws as to protect his own. It was widely believed in Turkey that tobacco smoke dried the seeds of men. 'Barren are they who bathe in smoke' was the cry from the palace walls. Torture upon those who took pleasure from the weed. Why all this dread? The sultan proclaimed he feared the chance of fire from the tobacco embers, but that was always a danger and hemp and opium still were smoked. It was said that the leaf was a heathen drug not given sanction in the Koran, but other recreations were so allowed. The truth we speak is always a shadow of itself. The sultan feared the coffeehouse where men did have the weed and talked openly of politics.

"So changeful is man in his thin disguises, the sultan did allow and prohibit the weed three times in one year, merchants and smokers never knowing the whim which was the law. And so the potentate did make his decrees in vacillations, while hundreds died in torture. Tobacco was burned, pipes were broken with picks. Smokers were hung, their pipes thrust through their noses. Merchants, their hands and feet cut off, their stores put to the torch.

"Everywhere in Asia rumors of war against the weed. In Persia, Shah Abbas prohibited the herb, believing any commerce so highly regarded by infidels and so profitable to them must bear an evil aspect. In Hindustan, the mogul emperor Jahanjir brought penalties by mutilations against all smokers, each was to have his lip slit. The Chinese emperor ordered decapitation for those who trafficked with the 'outer barbarians' and sold the weed. Officials at court believed that tobacco ruined the discipline of the Chinese army and was unhealthy, and worse, it was foreign. In Japan it was all the same: tobacco burned, imprisonments, confiscations and death. One hundred and fifty people arrested for selling tobacco in Tokyo, defying the emperor's command. Many were executed, the emperor angered at his own people so besotted by drinking of the smoke. The weed was now the barbarian drug.

"Once you told me of that man, Bashaw Bogall, who bought you as a slave, sending you to his lady Charatza. Of him I have made some inquiries of my friends in Constantinople. He, too, sold tobacco, ignorant of the sultan's new decrees, sat in a tavern smoking. Seized by guards, he was brought before the sultan, who said that he would spare his life if Bogall would judge the quality of a most excellent tobacco the vizier had presented to the court. The pipe so lit, Bogall drank the smoke, approving of its flavor. Rage now on the sultan's face. 'What a drug this you cannot know it from horses' dung!' With that, Bogall was executed, having molten lead poured down his throat.

Ink, Quills, and the Storms of Progress 123

"No news do I have of your lady Charatza Trabigzanda, other than to say that that is not her name, it is a corruption of the words which mean 'a Greek girl.' And so do our memories strangle us upon a broken web. You spoke no Greek, your dictionaries were in a glance."

My Charatza, her name a shift of sounds, their meanings no meanings but to me. The world's a dice, its rolls in chances, with all our passions thrown against tomorrow's wall.

"In Turkey, as in all of Asia," Sandys went on, "tobacco was still smoked, its pleasures in battalions against all persecution. Hidden, its trade brought wealth, a cloaked empire concealed from the emperor's law."

"Tobacco is a fit. Virginia not its farm," I said. "If I can but return, I can, by my actions, keep our cause. I knew a wizard who claimed there were contagions in the leaf, an eater of dreams. Now, its smoke is upon the continents. What alchemies within that men risk death to warm its pleasures on their throats? The Virginia crop, a trade from the savages, still too small even for a commerce with a flea. But if I can be granted passage, I may wrench the riot before we have the curse."

Sandys sat considering, smiling, admiring the rainbows of his influence. "Men always forward the politics they can afford," Sandys talking as he turned the glass of wine in his hand. "The London Company was severed into three factions. The cut, as always, was along the lines of the wealth. The first group was the great merchants, its voice the company treasurer, Sir Thomas Smythe, who, with his many enterprises and concessions, regarded Virginia as one investment that he could sustain in its continuing losses. The second group, led by Lord Robert Rich and his family, his son most importantly, the Earl of Warwick. They were less interested in profits from the colonists, seeing Virginia as a harbor for their expeditions against the Spanish. Already they thought they had such a harbor in the Bermuda Island, which by its charter the company now claims. These wealthy men can hold a loss, while they finance corsairs and sit well in their estates. Despite their airs, they are bankers to a band of brigands. Their hands are washed by others, while their fingers cling to the soil underneath. The last group was the smaller merchants, whose Virginia investment proportioned to a large share of their wealth. They cannot maintain themselves in these losses, so demand some action. My sometimes-beloved brother Edwin speaks for them.

"There is a war of carriages in the Company. Sums clash in jousts of coin, losses contest. And there sits my brother's throne, the lord of Parliament. Purse may battle purse in their shilling wars, but my brother holds legions on his coins. Every faction of the London Council tied to the one resolve. And here the war is civil, but still a war. Defy the king!—the power of Parliament to be the source of all liberty to the nation. Divine right is not of kings but in the House of Commons. These men who sat the council were self-made in vision and luck and craft. To them God elevated more than royalty. So king and common men were made equal to the choice. No station high enough it could not be sought. No power so divinely brought it could not be usurped. It was given all by God to his elect. The king just one, the many behind his throne.

"My brother spoke for all in this regard. In Parliament his voice always to the cause. In the company his following grew. Smythe, with his many enterprises not friendly to my brother, the Company set aside a little, a sneeze less when counted against his gale. Not easily turned to compromise, Smythe scratched a distrust on his growing hate of his peers. My brother, no charm of reason, played counter to the polite and politic. Each faction now a separate drama plotting to have the stage. And so, my friend, you come asking favors from a church that has splits into its divided choirs, warring in its pews, lethal in its homilies, and you, Smith, no glue to this occasion. But if you wish to sit your diplomacies on the couch of this satin war, speed to Smythe. I will help you as I can with Edwin. We, two by two, will make our case. Be wary, your complaints though wise, boast no compliment to the powers of the council."

"Why not my accusations? I was sent to discoveries, denied my office, kept imprisoned with perjured testimonies."

"Please inform me, when were you released? It escapes my notice. Be wise, make your dungeons not your pets. We ever carry them on our backs."

I LEFT GEORGE SANDYS TO DEAL WITH HIS BROTHER ON MY BEHALF. Let blood treat with blood in its exhausted circle. Allies I would gather on the minions of their estate. I hoped my course angeled now certain in the stars, but in truth the hours hung in weighted air. Time had out run the year, my impatience throttling days that gasped to weeks. Where from here does my path lay straight? Always I walk upon a divide. My choices chosen. The map written on a bubbled stew. I smell contagions. It tastes of sugar pendulums, so sweet, its harness on the breeze.

Word now that Smythe had returned to London. By carriage, the horses eager to their bit, I made my visit to the treasurer of the London Company. He greeted me with a secure and ready hand, asking me of Jamestown, and of the colony. I told him the unpleasant tale. The wise are wise because they listen and hold the truth others could not bear. Gather on your marshaled fields, your battalions are in words, your armor is a thought. "Why cannot I find the passage to Virginia to have the office you and the council gave to me?" I asked.

"The lord governor is his own law, a lesser monarch," said Smythe. "His whim is law. He could do as he wished. This was your advice to us, which we granted. We hold you as authority, even with those many complaints and discontents against you. We knew of some imprisonment but we were assured that it was minor and that you were soon to be released. Was it not you who escaped to the savages, went exploring and were wounded, the company under Ratcliffe and Percy suffering starvation, your advice lost to them? Then you returned half-native. This made known to us, we did ignore. We ordered De la Warr again to make you the marshal of Virginia, solely in charge of its defense."

"Ratcliffe was preparing an excuse to have me hung," I said, "and De la Warr withheld the office and sent me to play a Hudson gambit."

"Distance makes willful kings. There all becomes legend. We here in London so far away. De la Warr did not our full purpose," whispered Smythe, "but you we made hero. We published your book, secretly we gave the funds that your chronicle would plead the circumstance of our enterprise. That book was the beginning, the shock to give it life. It was you that sculled the dream to give it mind…and for this, and your import, we gave you a second life. We forged you into resurrection. Be famous, it is our cause."

I never knew until I was returned from Virginia that my second book was printed, not in full as written, but carefully diced and patched to have a lesser truth. Nothing was said there of Pocahontas being the instrument who preserved my life. Much of what I lived was silent, and my criticism of Ratcliffe and Martin and the rest, all the company's policies. When I read the book, I was like a man studying the death mask of his own wooden face. But now, I continued to turn the pages to see the text. Then I placed the lie upon the table.

"That book is not my book! It is a blunt without a point!" I raged.

"Our mistakes are like wounds upon our nation's heart. It bleeds," Smythe's strange words slowly whispered, "but blood is not life itself, only its artifact."

"I have unfinished work in Virginia," I said. "I wish to return as soon as another ship is ready."

Sir Thomas Smythe heard me not. Some conviction in his mind held him upon some other thought. "The London Company has informed De la Warr that the French are planning settlement in the northernmost lands of the Virginia charter, in Acadia, south of the Bay of Fundy along the Atlantic Coast. We are in no humor to have our privileges transgressed, and did so instruct De la Warr. We are told De la Warr has ordered Argall north with ships and troops. That is all that is known. I thought it would be of some interest to you. This is said in confidence. It shows my trust."

I repeated my request to sail for Virginia. "I was to be in charge of the colony's defense. Surely, something can be found for me?" Smythe, awakened to my words, promised to do his best. "I know of the death of Jonas Profit," he said. "He had some wealth, bequeathed to you. Willoughby had trust of the coins. They to me in safe keeping. These said to be the last gold of Drake's great voyage." Smythe stood, walked to his desk, opened a drawer. Two bags he hefted in each hand. "Now to you from all their weighty navigations. Four hundred pounds, and a little extra from Willoughby himself, I believe. But that is a secret, and so the gift."

I held my inheritance, gold by histories, by expeditions, by self and genealogies. Drake to Jonas, to me, and Willoughby a little to the splash, and before the coin is struck, the Spanish, Indian slaves, cruelty and starvation, disease. How much do I touch when I hold a shiny splinter of a muted tale?

"I will see that you have other moneys and means to keep you to a small style. I will do what I can," continued Smythe.

And so our interview ended. The extra stipend I received was never generous, but it allowed a little grace and time to plan. Other friends of Smythe and the Willoughbys assisted. There was other pay, almost nothing from my book. I sat in my room. I thought too much and acted scarce at all. Of Pocahontas I heard nothing. "Argall might bear a message from me," I dreamed, but where was he? Nothing from Smythe, Sandys quiet. I sent reports to the company asking to be sent to Virginia. I was ignored. Everywhere the company called for colonists. Children they sent, and orphans, and men from prison, and women in debt. Privation and poverty sailing toward a wounded dream. Few knew that most died within six months. The company kept its secret close to itself. Everywhere in the fine carriages there were whispers through the tobacco smoke of disasters.

I AM EXHAUSTED IN MY ENTERPRISE. I SANK IN THE BOWELS OF a rotting London, its intestines strangled in twisted mud. "Many a great career has begun in the tower," I told myself, but I sat no tower. Ambition here is the flanks of a beaten mare, its nostrils drowned in its own consuming swill.

Chapter Fourteen

CLOAKED ENIGMAS, REVELATIONS AND THE PEDDLERS OF SECRET HISTORIES.

OTHING SAID, NOTHING HEARD. Rumors bleat the infrequent heat. De la Warr dying, or dead, an aging waste. Hudson lost, no word, his ship not upon any coast, now a bubbled whisper to neglect. Dee to an early winter death. Why had I not taken sail, an easy trip up the Thames to Mortlake, to give some solace and the news of old Jonas's final days?

Home is the nurture we adopt. Why not to Dee? The warning in his tale I know, with nostalgias for what I have never seen. A few coins to a boatman's hand. "Mortlake, if you please," I said.

"Ah, the old wizard, Master Dee," the reply. "Not likely there, but still your coins." Fingers to his cap.

I nodded, a smile on my command. My elegies of Jonas, my thoughts of Dee. *Reflections are the drug*, I mused, *and we made drunk by similarities. Why to Mortlake? What to find? A nothing, its lute tuned to a memory.* My question answered. *We love by fragments, our wishes to make them whole.* Her voice in faraways began their silent cry.

Mortlake its own wreck, in the sty of a rotten clutter. Broken boards, windows askew, walls caked in years of dust. A steep bank upon the Thames, not a hint of stairs or dock . A toss of coins, I had the boatman wait. "It be toward dark," he said.

"Then play the moon," I replied. "Your night will have a richer calling."

Only a bald of some grass underfoot, little green, the wheel ruts indistinct. This Mortlake was a fine house once, ancient but early to its ruin. Walls patched with straw, a thatch of cheap, the roof wormed and sagged with much decay. I walked the thicket of a garden overgrown. I called, "Anyone about?" None the answer, but a witch's laugh and a wisp of smoke. A spy now, I move in stealth.

Behind the house an old woman—thin, skin like bark, fingers the gnarl of twigs—stirs a blackened cauldron, a large wooden oar in her hand, boiling clothes. She raises a tattered dress with the oar, smiling at the rising steam.

"Hail, good mother," I said, as I approached.

"Gone he is, my master. Dead. Most dead," said the woman. "Now go away!"

"Sad to pity. I brought news of an old friend, also passed."

"The name. Some of his are much about. I knew the great. Thirty years I served this place and him, but not in the east. Not the east. Too many foreigners."

By the house many holes were dug. Fresh earth in mounds, a scatter of books bound in white vellum, under blankets of torn cloth, very browned in age and wear.

"The dirt is not a good library shelf," I said, playing silence with a joke.

"Not for your notice. Be off. I have me chores," the old witch, staring hate. "Not for pay, but for him I bend me knee," her head nodding toward Mortlake. "Protecting, that is me, protecting, even dead."

"Here," I said, "a few coins from an ancient friend."

The witch took the coins. "You one of Willoughby's?" she asked. "You have his coins."

Shocked at the name, surprised, the door into secret worlds. I said, "My father rented land on his estate."

"Rent your mother, too, to the bargain, me bet."

"I think not. My mother well born," playing calm to the thoughts of murder.

"The higher the birth, the easier to bed. That's me country motto," she said, holding the coins in her hand. "You ain't gettin' much for them," said the witch.

"Nothing wanted, they are from an old friend, I expect, who bequeathed to me a little wealth." I smiled, "And now a small gift to you."

"Not Willoughby. It's not him," questioning to herself, "oh that Jonas fool, who lost his pretty wife!"

"Yes, a small inheritance for you. He's buried now in Virginia. His death a year ago."

"And my son, he still lives?"

"Your boy? I do not know."

"Anas, I am good wife Todkill."

Where am I in this unknown? "You are mother to Anas Todkill?"

The old witch puffed to brag again the name. "Good wife Todkill, my boy?"

"Loyal, alive, my lasting friend. I am John Smith."

"You are the one he be hired to protect, and me to have the yearly coin." The witch, indifferent to my name, stirred the cloth in its boiling soup. "My son, he lives?"

"A hire, by who?" As I spoke, I kissed betrayal on an anger's ear.

"Parts that have a purse, and he not wanting a single pinch. Be not so split, poison will eat less your gut.

"My foolish son holds you friend." The woman looked me through. I stood the portrait of her gaze. "Small hair, a harlot red. You do not by eye have the plate for all this fuss."

"I may not be by flesh what I am by fate," I replied. The witch gesturing for me to leave.

"I have me work."

"Then wherefore comes the coins, these sovereign moons of gold?" I asked, most quiet.

"Lord Willoughby one, and one called Jonas Profit, and a tickle from Master Dee, when he had the freight. He most easy to dance the monkey pauper before a Kelley's tune. Him you know?"

"I have been told the tale," I said, softly pleading against the witch's stare of hate.

"You look to me a Kelley, squeezed short."

"I account myself not of angels, nor of any viewing stone. I am pledged to a forest, a river and a New World, their gifts a tremor in a water glass. What I possess I would not keep. What I keep is valued against a smudge."

"All sons drunk of their own stink. Their perfume has powdered them a strumpet's bed. Go and mount a drab and pluck me a better child."

Chapter Fifteen

OF LONDON, STONES AND WILDERNESS.

HE THAMES SILENT in its rot and mud. The old world mute, eaten of its own impatient death. And I am of what end? I waited in London all that fall and winter into spring. News that the company was to send another expedition to discover Hudson and make some rescue of his crew. Mad Waymouth again the captain, Stacie his first mate, and some thirty more to play the ropes and grumble, sleeping in their hammocks below deck. And Waymouth, so fearful of the ice and cold and polar sea, now contests his terrors upon a wall painted of whims and ambitions. My musings. Two months after Mortlake the Company published a tract of its plans and prospects, all written in the lofty fonts of a craven hope. It was then I decided again upon another book. My news may not bear upon a fairer breeze. Just returned from Virginia and now in London were Richard Potts, Richard and David Wiffin and Post Ginnat. Anas Todkill still abroad. Ginnat had sailed as a soldier with Argall's northern expedition. At a tavern we met, clasped our friendship with an embrace. Such reports he gave me of that circus war, Argall in his admiral, puffed a clown of strategies, hatching his sorties to battle on still waters. *Bring havoc to breed upon*

his name, my thoughts. The English fleet sailed northward along the Maine coast, fishing as it went. Our admiral told by friendly savages the French were close and planting crops for a late fall harvest. The French also informed by the savages of Argall's fleet fishing near the coast. Commanded by René Le Coq de la Saussaye, the French, took little interest in the news, constructed no fort, made no preparations but to continue their planting and tending of their crops.

All the Frenchmen now on shore. Their fleet unmanned and at anchor. Argall to the coast, falling upon them. He seized their ships, their camp and all their goods, the French running to the forest. He found la Saussaye's chest with its charter from the king of France and its maps. These Argall hid in his own pocket, closing again the chest. Shortly, Argall and la Saussaye met under a flag of truce, Argall accusing the French of being pirates, stealing lands and trafficking in goods given by James I of England to the London Company. The Frenchman retorted with his own claims under charter and protection of his king, Louis XIII. Argall asked to examine his charters and his king's seal. Easy was Argall, calm it is said, knowing the papers were in his own pocket. La Saussaye to his trunk, it quickly opened, the documents lost. La Saussaye confused, never suspecting the truth. Argall making again his accusations, but offering the French an honorable deliverance. "Leave our lands. I shall give you a pinnace to sail yourself to France, or I shall sail you to Newfoundland myself where you may find a French ship, or I will give you a shallop that you may sail where you will with as many of your company as is wished. The rest I will take to Jamestown with me."

La Saussaye, two priests and fifteen of his company chose Jamestown. The other twenty chose the shallop and the sea. And so it was when reaching Jamestown that Dale was in a humor to hang the Frenchmen at once. Argall pleading that he had given his word as a gentleman that his guests would be safe and they would see their country again. Dale, needing Argall for future expeditions, set aside the hangman's rope and welcomed the Frenchmen into the strange lot now walking about the fort.

"But is not De la Warr lord governor still?" I asked Ginnet.

"He is ill, then, dying, as toothless as a shadow. He be back in England a fortnight, I having passage on his fleet."

"And Argall, what of him?" I asked.

"He greeds an ambition."

Our lord governor still a jailer, our visions coming further by faulted inches toward the noose.

"That tale is telling of the dog." Ginnet lit his pipe. The gooseneck clay, the surrounding smoke. "A savage pleasure. I am kin to it," he said, "and this, the Virginia weed," he smiled. "A tobacco of an inferior sort, with no hope of peddling but among the tribes." His eyes gray behind the smoke, which curled upward against his cheek.

"The Indian leaf is bitter, but may be safer to the lungs than Spanish tobacco sold in London," I said, Ginnet staring through the failing smoke, quizzical, his many affections for his pipe. "It is said not one pound of tobacco in five hundred is pure in England now. The leaf costs ten times pepper, it is sold weight for weight for fine silver. With such scarcity and price, merchants sophisticate the leaf coloring it to black. Our gentlemen judge their herb by only two measures: taste and color, black being thought the best, for that is the color the shopkeepers praise as it is the most artificial and the easiest to forge.

"So do cheats now add a juice or syrup of saltwater, and the dregs and filth of sugar called molasses, and sometimes black honey or pepper or the leavings of wine to which they may mix various berries or even paint. These so unhealthy that thousands may be poisoned each year.

"You are safer with the savages' weed," I said. The Spanish, it is supposed, spoil their exported leaf to bring ruin upon us, rubbing the herb in open sores and festered ulcers of their slaves, saying, 'These are for the Protestant pigs.' But why would the Spanish taint their own leaves when our merchants will do it free? It is a rumor to keep us from the Spanish tobacco. There are growers in England and Ireland who want the trade. Two hundred thousand pounds a year are paid for the imported weed. It is said England grows poor, coins now scarce in the London streets. Our gold and silver spent, and we are made destitute upon an ash. The king and Parliament in a rage. Our London Company has some hope tobacco might become a staple in Virginia."

"The best leaf is West Indian," Ginnet spoke, then, "and Rolfe to have some West Indian seeds in Virginia by spring, or so the scheme."

· · · · · ·

SOME TEN WEEKS LATER CAME A LONG LETTER FROM ANAS, TORN into the shuffle of many leaves. Potts and I, to mend the scatter, rebound the pages into a fearful anthem. "John Rolfe being once to see me, he holds an influence here and there, respected in the way the dull respect the dull. He brought news of a pleasant chatter. I listened. 'These seeds…West Indian tobacco seed I promised months ago.' He showed me the lines of soot scattered in the palm of his hand, grounds of feathered dust. 'It is our commerce…teething at my flesh,' his throat a half giggle. He dropped the seeds again into a leather pouch. His hand shook. His body trembled, convulsed in the silence of amazed vegetable lust. Rolfe lit his pipe, drank its bitter heat into his throat and calmed. He wiped his hand across his mouth and inhaled a laugh. 'The savages will not trade much tobacco…and we need food.' Rolfe pointed to his pipe. 'I'll grow my own.' Agreeing to his own nod, he tasted the surface of his desires, ignorant of their own weight. He offered me the pipe. I smoked. The pipe to Rolfe's mouth again. He sipped his own breath in ash. He closed his eyes and spoke. 'This weed thrills its madness to seem a pleasant peace.' He smiled. He touched my hand in friendship. 'In this leaf there is the soul of alchemies to make men sleep.' He gave me the pipe again.

"'There have been many failed to grow the leaf,' I said, 'or perished before they failed.'

"'How many?' Rolfe asked.

"I answered, 'Three or four dead before the crop. Its green not a tangle yet, the worms only at their early feasts.'

"'No tobacco leaf grows natural to be the herb. It seeks to be a weed. In its pit is a witch's stone. To get the leaf it is a constant labor to hold back its weed,' he cried. 'No plant demands from us more time, more tender labor, to prune its flowers, its weak offending leaves to let the leaf grow in leather across itself in perfect sheets, to smell its unburned smoke.' I looked at Rolfe, a man made much less through the narrow of his concerns. 'The London Company thinks five thousand pounds of tobacco could be harvested in Virginia each year if we but had the proper seeds. Less trade to the Spanish, then more wealth for us,' said a joyous shadow at my hand.

"Rolfe to the common of his mind, now told his plan to plant his tobacco in small hills, as was the accepted way. Ten or twelve seeds per hill to let the plants take root and show some green in offering to the sun. The field Rolfe chose where once we planted to ruins our little corn. Now that pasture all disused, the decay soon to grow another tobacco doomed to a fallow spring." Todkill's letter so ended.

Let each man have his prattle, I raged. *An errand in the brain rarely reaches further than the mouth. Rolfe is a man who lives by surfaces, his father's elegy being, he enlarged his world by the proper counting of goods. He sold what England had for what she needed and so he was. The father being the elegy for the son*, a thought. I kept my council to myself, thinking Rolfe dead before summer and its sweat, there being another useless tale unwrit. I gave him nothing but a polite of nothings and held him slim for a man.

In my thoughts, the mariner's words, *Drake was secretly undone by the leaf. Although he fought to destroy the Spanish empire in the New World, the weed he brought from Roanoke in 1586 so excited the habit in England that the Spanish could not supply our wants. Even in war the trade was more than ten thousand pounds of weed a year. Spain so forced to expand their plantations that she invaded by conquest more lands in the New World. On tobacco the Spanish empire sought its heights.*

And so it is the world nurses fools to sour all his pride and snub his easy wisdom in its crib. But what alchemies are in this weed? What venoms there to be the devil's own philosopher's stone?

Chapter Sixteen

LETTERS DARKLING STRUNG,
SING IN DESOLATION'S ALPHABETS.

Y WHAT SCRIBBLES are our lives so writ? Its curlicues proclaim the menace against our case. Richard Potts sat my room, the many letters he delivered from Virginia before me as he spoke this, his choirs into epitaphs. Around me contagions war, my face into the lonely, tender light, its heat barely reflective of the flame. My name never mentioned in Virginia now, I am told. I hear the litany. Potts clerk to the council in Virginia, a herald of education, words power from his simple quill. So comes the little telling, hesitantly, of great consequences.

At Point Comfort a longboat was blown across the James River and run aground. Gates, visiting there, ordered Humphrey Blunt to fetch it back. Blunt took an old canoe. His body working, the paddle straining against the soup of the water, he disappeared to the other side. A group of savages found him there, led him into the forest and cut from him his life, the heads of many axes severing his flesh into bleeding meat.

On hearing the news, Gates was in such a rage that he marshaled murder and led it to Kecoughtan. There, he had in an open field his drummers display some drumming, others to play a dance. The savages gathered to the noise and spectacle. Gates and his company, waiting hidden, fell upon them, butchering six, sending the others to flight, Gates pursuing, burning the savages' village, their mummied kings, their mats, their everything, even to the ruin of all their corn—the corn that by trade or theft we could have had. All lost, and we by war weakening ourselves. The heat of vengeance no friend to our cause. Without you, friend Smith, we are twice bereft, and this but the beginning which holds no end.

Lord De la Warr sick and weak, confined to his ship, captains coming each day to have advice. I heard all this from the mariners or from Strachey. De la Warr sent two messages with a guide to Powhatan to bring a warning, "End all war and violence against us, or we shall have ruin upon you."

Powhatan responded with his own warning, "Send to me a coach and three horses, as it is the custom of great *werowances* and lords to so ride in England, or I shall command my people to war without restraint upon you, to the fill of all their mischief."

Lord De la Warr held to his ship's cabin, the war and its progress all about him. On July tenth, 1610, with grand ceremonies, cheers and banners, Gates and Newport boarded one of our ships. The ship cast off, to sail to England. De la Warr now the only sovereign, no reason or check upon him. His better parts overthrown, he lay in the sway of his disease, his flesh so sweated it seemed to glow in lunacies. His thoughtful moments rare, his orders absolute, he broods his insanities beyond all reason.

.   .   .   .   .

THE *WEROWANCE* OF THE WARRASKOYACKS REFUSED TO TRADE CORN
as was his pledge. The woods now screamed in war each day, its
hours now a count in blood. Lord De la Warr summoned Percy to his
cabin. "Take vengeance on the Paspaheghs and the Chickahominies, a
vengeance without mercy."

"Powhatan is the enemy. The Paspaheghs do his bidding. The
Chickahominies are not of Powhatan's empire. They are independent.
They are at war with him as much as we," spoke a nervous Percy.

De la Warr smiled to the regard of his inner voice. "The throat that
is nearest, that is the throat that is sweetest cut. Ease your knife to my
point or is your blade crossed to my purpose?" De la Warr's brow
raised. Percy agreed to the plan. Percy left, as De la Warr's surgeon
entered to leech his lordship's blood. His physics make his lordship's
skin a powder white.

Percy gathered seventy men and found Kemps, the savage who
at various times had befriended us, betrayed us, fed us—who made
treacheries in such layers no one could know his true loyalty. Percy
had him tied to his lordship's second-in-command, then sailed in a
barge to a beach near the Paspaheghs' village.

The company held their standing pikes as black thorns atop the
swaying curtains of their wooden shafts. On the shore, the company
formed ranks, an officer leading each. Firelocks smoked their incense
across the stately lines. Kemps struggled in his ropes as he was pulled
through the brush.

Percy ordered him to be a guide, a sword to Percy's hand in threat.
Kemps, turning to thought, bore his prison subtle, walking in front in
a rapid pace, dragging his jailer by his own rope. Percy, having some
knowledge of the land, suspected Kemps' treachery. "This is not the
way," Percy said, taking a branch of a tree and beating Kemps across
the head until his face ran in blood and an eye broke from its socket.
The staggering Kemps, a firelock to his back, walked now the proper
path, his blood in ointments to the land as he stumbled.

The Paspahegh village was now in sight. Percy spread his men
to circle it. Hidden and silent, they made their march. The lord
governor's cousin, Captain William West, was given the honor to
signal the assault. His pistol raised into the breeze. The smoke. The
sound, in its widening report. The ranks rushed forward. The savages,
without defense, ran to all the directions that now bore upon them in
armor, wide-eyed the wounds that freshly bled. Sixteen savages fell in

death. The world a feed of blood and smoke. A drummer drummed a short salute. The company obedient to the call, reformed.

"Better justice here," said Percy, "than we bring to all of Ireland." And I held imprisoned on a charge that I did abuse the savages, and never did I countenance such a butchery. The hand that owns the press prints the history, as does its ink pump only venom, its fonts in wanton passion hides its sympathies to the dark?

The ranks in lines, their captain stood for their review. One soldier not yet arrived. Percy thundered at his want of discipline. Others were sent to seek him out. He shortly came with four prisoners: the queen of the Paspaheghs, her two small children and an old man.

Percy looked across the faces of his pride and found himself enraged. "Why have you brought these to me alive?" asked Percy. "The order here was death to all."

The children, holding to their mother's leg, turned their faces to its flesh, as if that warmth could shield them from the blast of rage. The savages, not knowing our language, stood their ground. The queen placed her hands upon her children's heads.

"I brought them as hostages so you may do to them as you wish." The soldier spoke his words as if afraid to speak. Percy nodded and smiled himself into a thought. The old savage he beheaded, the children crying. The ranks of the company murmured to themselves. The company shouting the queen should be next, but Percy refused upon some stroke of conscience.

The company marched to the boat, having burned the village and all its corn. At the river, the company, not yet content, still needed more violence to fill their need. Anger is a wild emptiness never sated.

The day not bloody enough, the company near revolt kicked dirt on the river's edge and screamed complaints again. "Why are the Paspahegh queen and her children allowed to live, when all her subjects we put to death?" Percy, yielding to the murderers' logic, brought not answer, anger and its minions seducing him to powerlessness. He called a council. The verdict given. The children were thrown into the river, volleys of firelocks ripping away their frightened faces to holes of blood, the river in its course drinking white the foam of their drowning breaths.

Their mother's face screaming crimson, she was pushed to the deck and tied by ropes. Percy had all he could do to stop the company from slaughtering her as she wept. The rage soon stiffened to glances of cold contempt. Percy sat. The company took up its oars and pulled against the water's weight. The mother lay, her face pushed against the deck. She shivered, her body boiling in its exhausted silence. Down the river the company rode, stopping once to burn more fields of corn and a few cabins. No one killed. All the savages fled.

Lord De la Warr's ship anchored now upriver waiting their return. Percy, weary of the day and its butchery, sent Captain Davis to tell his lordship of all events and of his hostage. Lord De la Warr, in a fury that the queen was spared, ordered that she be burned at the stake that hour. Captain Davis spoke to Percy, who, sick of murder, had the woman taken to the forest and behind a blind of trees stabbed to death by two soldiers.

Richard Potts leaned into the candlelight, awaiting my response.

WE THE HAVOC'S EGG, I THOUGHT. WE SIT OUR BLOODY NEST AND *beg ourselves not to be what we know ourselves to be. It is my part to have a chronicle. All is absolution in a murderer's game. I was caught by glories. I have failed by truth. Ruin reigns the forest and I am shepherd to the night.*

I nodded that moment into my despair. "I am to write another book, nothing else sufficients," I spoke.

Richard Potts, a solace to his voice, "Have me clerk, my quill to this script. Me but a squint above the candle ledger."

"So in clasp of arms, our calligraphies to field us against the battlements. We must to the continue of the tale," I said, wondering of my forest love, my Pocahontas. I closed my eyes, dreaming of her silhouette. The memory of her voice whispers to me. "Have you but come in spirit, a haunting is only for the dead. Are you come in a rumor of yourself?" I asked.

"I thought you lost...forever dead," said the specter.

"I thought myself in death as well," my thought, as I placed my head against my desk. I spoke into the splinters, my breath upon my breath, my cheek against the wood. Her words sweets in echoes to my ear, her voice buried in faraways. Her breath in phantom lips stroked sounds, her tongue upon moistless air. Words to hold a caress the wash of hands can never touch. What are we but words and glance and touch? Sensation glued by nightmare. Her words spoke as if a throatless voice. Love pleading for its love. I diminished into silence, she to her evaporations. *A conscience makes for poor pleasures*, I thought. My head rose. I leaned against a wall, my back straight, held to its hard comfort.

A QUESTIONING LOOK, RICHARD POTTS LEANED INTO HIS GAZE. "You seem in need of rest." His concern nurtured to the moment.

"I am wearied by many histories." I awakened to my words, sweetened by the secrets of my heresies. But England of still and quiet, and I remain an ear without its melody. Potts coughed and cleared his throat and spoke and cuffed his sorrows, which I harden into my own words.

"AND SO IN EARLY MARCH OF 1611, LORD DE LA WARR RETURNED from Powhatan's old village, now an English settlement. His health had broken into continual fevers, so weak he could not feed himself," Potts continued. "He decided with his council's consent that he should return to England by way of the tropical island of Nevis to regain his strength. Argall to sail as captain for Lord De la Warr. Our canvas loosed, their bundles from our spars—catch wind, cut pains upon the water and depart," Potts recounted, as I, in memory, hear the old mariner once again. He, the ocean mountains' Lorelei, while I on the summit sing songs of sailors gone to sea.

"Percy was given full command again. I sat uneasy, for would Percy let me sail with the Wiffins and Ginnat? He but a sometimes friend to all, his embraces for only power and rank and easy circumstance.

"At the tide, De la Warr's departure near, trumpets sounded, drums snarled, their presentations in angry hails. The savages, seeing the commotion, crept forward from the woods to the edge of the fort. Percy, having given orders to the company at the blockhouse not to stir or march outside, sent reinforcements to watch the savages and stand ready guard. But orders in Jamestown had little weight or meaning past their breath. Not an hour later, Captain Puttocke, the Polander, with twelve, left the blockhouse to display some valor. A few savages, enticing him, fled before his march. He in chase, until six hundred savages hidden in the bush loosed arrows in such swarms, it was said the land stood quilled so thick a man could not walk a pace without stepping on a dozen. Puttocke and his company screamed as they died. The able Captain Jeffrey Abbott with fifty ran from Jamestown to bring a rescue, but too late. All were dead. The savages, dancing as they fled, taunted Abbott with their cries of vengeance: 'Paspaheghs...Paspaheghs.'

"Our ship delayed for the next high tide, then we sailed, passing at sea a ship captained by Robert Adams with a new supply of a hundred men and fresh victuals. He brought word that the marshal-elect of Virginia, Sir Thomas Dale, would soon arrive with a greater supply of men and victuals, and was to have command until a new lord governor was appointed. All this I thought but another change for nothing. A sameness to the root. Men still bowled in the streets, and De la Warr fled east into the assumptions of the dawn."

WHILE RICHARD POTTS AND I SAT AND CONVULSED OUR SOULS IN whispers, the prow of a broken ship, its sails hanging tatters from its spars, cut the waters south-by-east. The motion of its sway was the only gauge of its secret weight. The crew, eight in all, their bone-heavy feet drumming on the hollows of the deck. The hull groaned. The clouds hung canopies in rain.

Luck wars like any war, the edge is to the weapon, not to the wit. Hudson's ship in perilous tack, a beggar of food upon the sea. The *Half-Moon* hailing English ships for scraps. A scuffle haunts, black fire upon the daylight air. The story told. Henry Hudson, his young son, John, and six others abandoned to a polar storm in a scallop. No warm clothes, no weapons, no supplies. A mutiny by the crew. Hudson hoarding, stealing food from their dwindling stores, biscuit, cheese and meat. So the accusations. In truth, ill blood, slander, a winter locked in northern ice and cowards for a wanton crew. But Hudson weak and willful, not a captain much. Each of his voyages, as Waymouth told, ended festered in a mutiny.

Within days the talk of a rescue expedition, and the noose for the mutineers. And more ships sent, nothing found, a slight for trial years later. And no one ever to the rope, or much punishment. Hudson's wife receiving recompense, and so the tale that brought me north. All this begun by me in a letter to Hudson, relating the savages' myth of a river flowing to the Pacific Sea.

HUDSON'S TALE NOT FULLY SAID, THE NEXT YEAR STACIE SAT MY room, a ship's log held in his leathered grasp. "Mad Waymouth made himself a wanton death," he said, his fingers pushing the battered log toward me. I looked at this farce of water stains. Stacie continuing,

"By your book, a chapter to plead a poet's elegy for our unburied lost?" The log in my hands opened. I read the barrens of the script.

"Waymouth chose the way he most feared," I replied, looking up. "Our flame ever dances us the moth, enticed to the curse of our own enchantments."

"Will ye pen the play of it?" Stacie, a full captain now, spoke.

"When ink and opportunity speak a paper moment."

Chapter Seventeen

MISGIVINGS, POVERTIES AND THE RECALL OF WARS.

OW MANY YEARS AGO had old Jonas told me of the first dreams' demise, of greatness strangled and of a man of arms in war against the certainties? It was, I believe, when we sat in Jamestown's ruins among the half-buried dead, some skeleton hands still protruding beyond their graves, grasping toward that desperation they could not hold. The old mariner, his skin pale in a bloodless frost, as I sat to cobble some meanings from his words. His last warning told, all his inheritance to me, on a fading voice.

"It was the summer of 1588. The great Armada half destroyed, its remnants in retreat. The world to its old face, cold in stares. All this we see—all these nations, this earth—is but a struggle between those who have too much faith and those who have not enough. Drake's fame was now beyond his name, he became an idol. Rich, his words spoke law. How many escapes, how many twists of luck did make him who he was? How much could the sea give its apostle before it turned a plaint calling for some deeper test?

"Dom Antonio was the pretender to the throne of Portugal. He believed men would dare for freedom, no matter who brought the chance and with it help. Dom Antonio, half-Jewish, the almost-king to a Catholic state. Portugal then seized by Spain, crushed to Philip's will. Everywhere persecutions and the Inquisition, lives by thousands burned in fire at the stake. 'All men should rise above their beliefs.

We should embrace our humanity with all its faults,' he said, always believing men are better than their politics. But are we better than our religions?" asked the old mariner. "Constant pain made Dom Antonio's hope a resurrecting solace. His supporters in Portugal called for his return. His advisors silent, but to strange advice. Dom Antonio never realized he was betrayed. Philip's spies his confidants, he had fed his enemies and rewarded treason. Gold is stronger than the good. And Dom Antonio was too different to be king, although in the ancients of his blood there were the memories of those who spoke to God.

"That year after her greatest victory, our Elizabeth was almost bankrupt. Her funds and all her reserves but fifty thousand pounds, and she the bank that held the Spanish from the slaughter of the Dutch and the Huguenots and kept the wrecked Armada in its ports. Lord Burghley knowing the fearful truth, many of the Armada's largest ships had survived: seven of the ten Portuguese galleons, six of Recalde's great ships, seven of Oquendo's, two of Bertendona's, half of the Andalusians' and half of the Castilians'. No one certain of their condition or if they could be repaired. Most of their captains and admirals dead. Their crews sick and lost. The ships now docked in poorly defended ports. It was time for England to strike in counterblow and destroy the Armada that still remained. With the Spanish fleet gone, England could seize the Azores and cut the flota's route east and have the New World's wealth for its allies and itself. But Elizabeth had not the funds for such a grand design.

"In August of 1588, Drake was summoned to London. 'Half destroyed and half survived, the whole drowned would be a better half,' smiled Diego, his thoughts, as were the queen's, to have a finish to the war. Elizabeth, with few funds of her own, pledged twenty thousand pounds to have the expedition. She then forming a joint stock company to lure with profits investors to the nation's cause. Wealth and nation and God all spun into the one. Equals make strange equals in their tug. With fifty thousand pounds raised most from London merchants with dreams of the Azores and a Portugal under Dom Antonio's rule, and Drake and his friends and the city of London, all with thoughts of profits from the West.

"The plans progressed. Sir Edward Stafford, the English ambassador in Paris, was a Spanish spy. Nothing said in London did not reach Philip's ear. State secrets were but the gossips on a thousand lips. In England the situation so confused, the reports to Philip so contradictory, that little was learned but something was afoot. Sir Edward loved his queen, but Philip's gold he loved a little more. 'In all things are we in loving treason to our queen,' he said the day they brought him to the block. Now Dom Antonio was receiving word that the Moor Muley Hamed, the king of Fez, his lands in desert wealth across the Straits of Gibraltar, would send soldiers by the thousands and moneys and victuals to battle in Lisbon, if in compensation, Dom Antonio when king would pay double the Moor's costs. This agreed, Dom Cristobal, Dom Antonio's son was sent to Fez as a hostage in good faith.

"Elizabeth always charmed by, but never convinced by Dom Antonio, other than that he was a man of dreams, with some claim to the throne and some support. 'Terceira in the Azores held for him until crushed by Spain,' said the queen, 'but islands are not the nation. They are but dots and Lisbon is a different place.'

"'Are we not that dot that imagination has made great?' asked Drake. Elizabeth, hard to her reasons, spoke again.

"'But he dreams, our Dom Antonio,…and dreams are no shield… and are only wisdoms to the blind.'

"The London merchants and the investors came to Dom Antonio's cause. 'Where else is profit close? The Azores far and the flota not easily found.' Their words were to the Queen's ear, their wealth in silent point. The queen agreed to have a try at Lisbon, but only after the Armada was destroyed in its ports. 'There along the northern coast—at Santander, at San Sebastian, at La Corunna—there we drown Philip in his sewer's nest. Destroy those ships and the Azores are ours and even Lisbon.' The queen's fist hammered upon the map. 'Not any Lisbons before the Armada's gone, do you understand, Drake?' Lord Burghley affirmed with a quiet nod the queen's intent. The queen then promised six great siege cannons to hold the walls of the coastal forts. 'Break the nest and we have the eggs' were Elizabeth's words. On land the queen is law, but the sea is far from any law, and there, there is a different royalty," said the old mariner.

"Sir John Norris, that soldier called 'Black John,' England's greatest general, was to share command with Drake. It was Norris who had broken Parma at Grave, and saved the Dutch. He was all war in the wilds of his thoughts. Too brave for brilliance, but brilliant he was, and cruel and ruthless, and a famine upon all sympathies. The butcher of the Irish and the savior of the Dutch, the two masks upon the single head, and where the smile?

"With the help of Norris, more funds were raised. Eighty thousand pounds now. Dom Antonio, meeting with Black John, had promises from him that Lisbon would not be pillaged or plundered or his subjects abused. 'All that fight with Spain will be given to me to be tried by my law,' said Dom Antonio, who had printed thousands of pardons all signed by his own hand, waiting for the names of his largess. Humanity marshaled in its love against a world of opportunists.

"Drake and Dom Antonio, two men locked in their different faiths to the same purpose. Drake gathered ships, mostly those that months before had fought the Armada in its glory: the *Revenge*, the *Dreadnought*, the *Nonpareil*, the *Foresight*, the *Aid* and others. All were the queen's ships, and soon there would be more. Six pinnaces were being built, John Norris raising thirteen thousand troops, and weapons and stores and clothes and always money."

"IN OCTOBER THE QUEEN SIGNED THE COMMISSION OF JOINT command. The Dutch were asked to provide ships and troops, they then being told some of the English forces in Holland would be withdrawn. The Dutch raged betrayals. It was just, but were the expedition a success, much of the benefit would be for them. Words now across the council's table. Dutch anger listening only to itself. The English were also in a fit. At last a compromise: fewer troops called home, the Dutch to provide ships and men. But as it was, the ships never came and their troops, the Walloons, refused to fight.

"Gathering his regiments, Sir John Norris sailed to find his seasoned thousands, all veterans he hoped well disciplined by experience and war, bloodied to the sword, intelligent to its edge. Few of the English in Holland would volunteer, and in England it was an ill-born crew, weaponless, without proper clothes or uniforms, that formed the ranks. A rabble, an army only in its mind. Debtors, dry leaves drifting on the chance of winds, gentlemen whose families saw for them an honorable death, or wealth by war, their persons saved before the finals of the undertow. A desperate love always reasons in ill logic.

"Many of those who pledged themselves to Norris would have to be released from prison when the time for sailing came. Now the queen was unsure. Vital supplies were not sent on time, vital orders never signed, delays and rumors, investors uneasy. Some withdrew their pledges. More delays and a treasury of neglect, but soldiers must be fed and sailors, and more idleness meant more food, which meant more expenses, and money already not enough.

"The Earl of Northumberland, the wizard earl, perhaps reading the stars, withdrew two thousand pounds from the expedition. The queen never sent the great siege cannons she had promised. Norris, abandoned with only light cannons, now thought and walked his doubts across the council's floors and spoke his fear. He had recruited more soldiers than he had hoped—six thousand more, nineteen thousand in all. Ill trained, ill equipped and soon ill fed, yet still a force, but an extra drain on the pocket. Spanish walls and forts, and he without his cannons. Norris wrote to the queen, begging for the heavy siege guns. Elizabeth was now the pauper queen, and still the nation cried in her ear. History is an action deaf to all excuse. When the cause is the nation, silence is a strange eloquence. Norris was never answered.

"Spies, everywhere spies. Now rumors in the capitals of Europe that Drake was soon to sail. The original plan called for the fleet to be at sea by January of 1589. It was February twenty-third before Elizabeth signed the final orders. Philip, in the long wait of the autumn of 1588, prepared his forts in the Azores and in the west, in Portugal and along his coast. A few cannons to screen the neglect of decades. Spain was the shell that certainty had dried and cracked.

"It was March before Drake and Norris had their final farewells with the queen. Dom Antonio was charming and handsome in new armor of black and gold, a present from Drake. The retinue of his unfaithful few, their wages paid by the queen, their loyalties to Philip, who paid them more, stood by the side of their almost-king, whom they might have truly served if he were more like they. In politics, the worthless make their own prisons and no plot is hatched that is not thoroughly cooked.

"Drake rode through London to his ship in the Thames and then sailed around the coast for Plymouth, stopping at Dover for more ships. One hundred and eighty in all, the largest English fleet ever assembled for an overseas expedition. More ships, more men and even more to come. On their sail to Plymouth, Drake captured seventy flyboats traveling toward France and Spain, Philip's Dutch, those disloyal few who sailed to take up their coin. Drake, needing ships for his victuals and his troops, would make a better use of their treason than Spain.

"The regiments and the fleet assembled at Plymouth by the end of March. The winds then turned in their spite and came south and from the west. The ships nailed to their harbor by the iron breath, as they had been when they faced the Armada the year before. Norris wasting no time, drilled his troops on the fields nearby, hoping discipline would forge an army. The food now low, the winds held and the moneys gone. On April third, only five weeks of food remained, the expedition not begun. Norris wrote to the queen for help, but received instead of food an ink and paper spiked to pin a chorus to delay. Then he threatened to release his angry troops to ravage upon the countryside. Norris wrote to Burghley, who promised help. The final plea for food did not reach the queen for her consent until April tenth. The winds soon coming fair and favorable, the fleet sailed. Its cloud of painted canvas rode silent insignias through the air. The sun broke the sea into its legends. Men cheered and shouted, 'To Spain! To Spain!' It was April sixteenth, 1589, and so we our voyage to cries aloft and below our empty barrels. The queen's extra supplies never reaching us, nor the heavy cannons. Beware the little things, they are small only to their moments, for in their grain the universe is lost or won.

Chapter Eighteen

WE THE PORTENTS OF A DIFFERENT SEA.

IEGO HAD BEEN AT Drake's side for more than twenty years. His hair was now in a frost of surface gray. His eyes quick to the steady of his gaze. 'Our enemy's house is the house of Spain. Lisbon is the jewel but not the blood,' said Diego, who stared into the mirrors of the sea. All horizons filled with our canvas, the sea flat in deadly wait. Drake walked the decks, a pilgrim lost in his own considerations. 'Shall I start our mark upon the masts?' asked Diego.

"Drake, a man drunk in contemplation, never gave his answer, but walked away, the sea blowing its salt wine across our decks. Diego walked to Drake's side again. 'Shall we have our consecrations as we have always had? It is who we are.' In all action there is memory, at its center a spoken prayer. 'It is who we are,' Diego repeated. Drake's eyes in confusions lost. How many eyes had been upon him? How many separate parleys, and for what advice? Desperation makes a man direct," said the old mariner. "Perhaps not wise, but with wealth and station Drake began to court his own success. No longer rash to be a lethal upon the main, he sought the safer way of councils and consents. Men are lost when they sell their best for certainty.

"'There is time enough for sculptures and cuts upon our mast but if it brings you peace, do as you will, old friend. I am on other thoughts,' said Drake, for the first time a man speaking air, without one rock to hold a note."

"THE SKY COMING TO THE FURY OF ITS GLOOM, THE SEA ROSE IN its horizons, the winds screamed in havoc breaking waves in tablets across our bow. What lightning wrote, it wrote in fire. At first the fleet held to its squadrons, but within days ships were borne from sight, dispersed, the coast lost behind the mountains of the swells. Soldiers sickened below decks and in the narrows of the holds the air went bad, and into the water barrels dripped disease from off the planks where lay the stricken many. Smells made the ships rancid huts. At our hulls the storm ran in waves and the winds whipped waters into lines of cliffs, the sea breaking the world into thorns and thunder.

"The ships scattered, making ports all along the channel coast from Dover to La Rochelle. The harbors of Devon and Cornwall and Dorset saw their fill. More than thirty ships were driven from the fleet. Some captains used the storm simply to desert. They and their officers hung when their ships made an English port.

"The fleet was driven far to the west of Santander and San Sebastian, almost across the whole of the Bay of Biscay. The sky rumbled in its threat, and the winds still came. Sails were torn free, their canvas flesh loosed as it flapped. Drake wanted to make for Lisbon and forget the Armada and its wounded plenty. All the world had come to storm. It was a fate that gave weak men excuses. But Drake could not ignore the queen's command, nor could Norris. And no one knew in what Spanish ports their many ships lay to their repairs, or in what conditions. To the investors the Armada held little profit. All their dreams were with Dom Antonio and Lisbon and the Azores.

"Diego poured wine into the sea. The sweet of its red blood blew back into his eyes. 'The sea gives test to those it might reward. All is earned, whether fair or foul. Only chance is blind, indifferent to its judgments,' Diego screamed into my ear, his face bleeding with wine and storm. 'If Drake is lost, I am the last,' he cried into the sea, which hurled wind in its lightning blasts as the clouds glowed hieroglyphics through their low and blackening flow.

"Drake sat below deck, at his table Norris and Fenner and the council. War had chosen its committee. A candle swayed, the shell of darkness sealed itself around them and waves thundered against the hull. Drake plotted on his map. Norris spoke of compromise. Drake's loyalties now ran in earth and land and the stones of his Buckland Abbey. He struggled to hear the sermons in the gales. He rose in his mind to raise himself again. 'La Corunna.' Drake pointed to the map. 'There are reports of Spanish galleons there.' Drake struggled to see himself as once he was. To taste himself anew. Age had made him conscious of what he had lost. Doubt is the worm that eats us to the grave.

"Norris now agreed with the council and made argument for Lisbon. He was co-commander and at equal rank with Drake. 'Surprise is half the victory,' he said. 'In all haste we must sail for Portugal.' Drake sat and spoke of the queen and of their commission. 'The Spanish fleet is at La Corunna, so it is rumored, and it is there I mean to go. It is the queen's law.'

"'And after?' asked Fenner.

"'After is a word which may make decisions for itself,' said Drake. 'I am for one and always the queen's will.' He then rose from the seat. 'The enemy is south and it is Spain.' He walked to the door. Stopping, he began to speak, as if to seal with a phrase the moment in their minds. 'Loyalty, we are our loyalties' was all he said.

"Drake called to Diego, 'The wind braces me in memories.' He, too, poured the wine into the spray, his tongue to his lips to lick the ferment on the blast. The storm having spent its lesson, the clouds began to divide into canyons and great overhanging cliffs, a golden light falling past their crags and shafts in floating beacons.

. . . . .

"ON APRIL TWENTY-FOURTH, 1589, THE ENGLISH FLEET SIGHTED LA Corunna. Drake had brought war to the Spanish coast. La Corunna was a town built on a finger of land that rose to a great promontory. There at its height, crowned with great walls, was a citadel whose cannons cut the fields in overlapping fire. At the lower edges of the town was a smaller wall that held protection all around from beach to beach. And so we closed upon this twice-protected town in its double walls.

"In the middle of the narrow harbor was the island of San Antonio on which clustered cannons and small forts. There were cannons on the opposite shores facing San Antonio and La Corunna. It was a coast built for its own defense. A hundred and fifty cannons and more stood, their muzzles facing across the waters toward the opposite forts.

"Clouds dark with unspent storms passed their shadows across the sea. Toward the land they drifted, patches torn in violence in the gathering heat. Our ships following, swept into the moment. To men about to die, all things have signs and secret meanings. 'It's God's call to battle,' someone cried. From the walls above the promontory, smoke and flashed lightning and the guns of the echoes, a warning and all its anger roared upon the air. The gray walls on the cliffs, the white smoke floating, the infrequent cannon blasts. Trumpets sounded in distant calls. Our ships slow and ready in their approach, our cannons aimed, our gun ports open.

"The cannons from the citadel smoked in their open fusillades. Around us the seas rose in fountains of horned thunder, the fabric of the water broken. We answered with our cannons. The walls smoked in small chips of dust, our shot as spit against a brick.

"The streets of La Corunna now rushed in the turns of panic. Men and women ran in flocks in all directions, changing in midstride to come about to a different path. No road was seemed safe. In confusions some just stood and turned in place, their hands upon their ears to deafen the madness of their screams.

"IN THE HARBOR OUR CANNONS TORE AT THE FORTS AND THE FEW Spanish ships. 'Not the prize we sought,' said Drake, looking at the flat waters of the empty harbor, the smoke of our cannons' fire across our decks. 'But still enough to have a start and please the queen.' There at dock, under the San Antonio walls, was Recalde's great Biscay galleon, the San Juan, and two other large men-of-war, two armed merchantmen, well provisioned, their hulls all full, and two older war galleons, soon relics and skeletons enough to pass into a ready burial. All now brought their cannons to our account, the Spanish guns upon us. Their volleys were a line of infrequent flashes. It was a mockery of war. Most of their cannons stood unmanned. The crews were gone, but down the paths of La Corunna the banners rushed. A caught tide of arms and men raced to man the lower walls. Through the panic a second tide rushed to gain the upper walls. The flags and banners distressed, waving against the counter push.

"Now the sky flooded the earth in rain. Sheets in wet misery fell to quench the tapers of our firelocks. The fire smoked to its cold demise.

"Volleys and cannonballs, the two galleys shattered into wreck. Turning in capsize, they slipped beneath the bay to drown their wounds in death. The *San Juan* held to the punishment of a constant salvo, then, ripped, it staggered on its anchor, its scraps and breaks of hull flung against the protecting walls of the Spanish fort.

"WE AT ANCHOR, OUR SOLDIERS TO THE BEACH. NORRIS ORDERED ten thousand to move forward against the lower wall. Roads in mud, the rain fell through the air in rivers. Our wet banners carried on bending poles, the weight too much for one to hold. We advanced through the alleys and streets past the few deserted houses outside the walls. The Spanish manned the heights and battlements, their banners held to rush and flap unfurled upon the storm. Pikes that quilled and scratched the belly of the wind they held aloft in warning, our shadows facing them across the mud.

"Norris then ordered all to wait. The mud played the streets in sheen and pools, in pocked footfalls, the ooze in our boots. The icy rain ran down our necks, our banners and weapons wet. Men coughed and smelled, and vermin walked their greasy hair. We took shelter in such houses as there were. Our soldiers looted what they could.

"Norris and Drake on board the *Revenge* met in council. The attack on the lower wall would be at dawn. 'Where the lower wall meets the sea,' said Norris, "it does not turn to round the coast but halts, the town mostly open there,' said Norris.

"'A broken fort to save a penny's cost,' said Dom Antonio.

"'You with yours on boats and I advancing from the land…the job is done.' So finished Norris as he leaned into the back of his chair."

Chapter Nineteen

OW FLAT THE SKY seemed in all its dawn, the sun in half light upon the air. The sea smooth, and through its swaying mirrors, the land broke in figures, cliffs and silent promontories, the houses of La Corunna white with streaked repairs of clay and stains of gray. The walls of the fort broken curves of stone upon the table of the land.

"Our soldiers awakened, stretched their arms, while backs arched, slight pain to draw away the sleep. Food cooked in pots, the smell of salt and meat and whiffs of rot. Soldiers took up their weapons, gathering into regiments. The sounds of talk and laughs and iron striking on lengths of iron, war in its spirit was marshaling the monster in its blood.

"On the shore was Norris in his polished armor, patches of reflections on his chest, Drake directing fifteen hundred of his own regiment into boats, his golden armor buckled at his waist. His reputation was now worn in ceremonies upon his heart. Diego in his naked shirt and pants, armorless, his vengeance making thoughts for him of an iron hard enough. War on Spanish soil, and he to the first assault.

"THE CANNONS OF THE BATTERED *SAN JUAN* FLASHED AND SHATTERED the morning into a lethal smoke. She positioned her field of fire upon our gathering ranks. Great wounds of fractured earth broke upward, plumed in dirt and burning powder. Men, and parts that once were men, were split and torn to bleeding scraps. Screams cut to explosions in the throats, the taste of dirt and wet and blood. Panic and bravery and havoc, a thousand footfalls in the mud. Norris's soldiers ran and held their spots or hid. It was a fanfare in deadly fire and so the battle was begun. The guns of the ruined galleon blasted at the earth, as if she would sink the land that created her.

"Among the English ranks flames and storms of rising mist, of rocks, of pastures churned upward into flight and wrecked, livestock slaughtered. Norris ordering cannons brought from the ships to the shore rowed on pinnaces, set on their carriages in a line to salvo in counterblows. Some of Drake's squadron, pulling anchor, rowed by longboats to close upon the *San Juan*. Now the two other Spanish ships sailed from safety to ply their suicide beside the galleon. Plumes and water tore in jagged root, breaking the blanket of the sea in their white contest.

"The cannons on the land joined now with those from the sea. The great Spanish ships staggered in our balled winds of iron. Masts fallen, hulls holed beyond repair, guns coming silent, the ships spread their quiet wakes and ran aground, their crews guiding them to the shore, so not as to have them fall into English hands. Now oil poured on decks, the torches lit. Fire in curtains smoked across their planks. The battle done, Spanish mariners betrayed their hearts by living to their oaths. Admiral Martin de Bertendona of the *San Juan* watched the flames eat upon the ashes of his burning ship. He swore a vengeance, looking across the bay to Drake's ship, the Revenge. His mouth wet, thin bubbles on his lips. He thought in that informed madness, knowing other seas would bring other circumstances."

"OUR TROOPS IN LINE BEFORE THE LOWER WALL. SHADOWS MOTION on the surface of the mud. Pikes rose, tapers of the firelocks smoked. Ladders held by squads to be carried to the battlements. Trumpets announced the dawn of battle. Drums, the lightning in its herald through our guns. Drake's longboats rowed toward the beaches, where steps led behind the walls into the town.

"Our banners flooding the air, each regiment its crest carried in the winds. Badges of woven bravery that called to memories, 'Think on me, your standard.' The harbinger of that gallantry yet to come. No thoughts of the muzzles aimed upon our lines. Walking forward now, they ran. The screams and cries arose as one, as if the earth had momentarily breathed as men, and in that mighty sigh, a relief that finally one would know his fate. The heart pumped to the pounding of the running feet. Guns firing smoke to opposing smoke. Bullets tore the air. Men fell as empty sacks, blood blackening the footprints in the mud. A head torn through into flaps of bleeding bone, a face its recognition lost to the crush of iron. Cries from the battlements, our ladders to the walls. Arrows darkening the air in spikes. Rocks thrown from overhead. Our firelocks aimed aloft, discharged to cut a running shadow closer to its death. Curses, cries and cannonades, the walls splintering into flights of hammered dust.

"We climbed the ladders, lines of lethal men like threads pulling themselves on rungs and pushing their aching legs to gain the heights. Men fell from above like birds cast down.

"Then on the walls swords against pikes, daggers thrown into the pistols' smoke! Hands tore at faces, eyes pushed by fingers into exploding jelly. Desperate banners raised in salute above the rage.

"Drake's soldiers now the streets. On the walls the Spanish turned in fear and fled in panic. Our soldiers on the paths, banners following to taste upon some other's death. Spaniards ran to gain the citadel gates. Having victory, our soldiers now rioted beyond all control. Orders but a waste upon their ears. Officers ignored. Trophies were the Spanish dead, Spaniards caught vengeance in their own cast net. Murdered Huguenots, the Incas and Aztecs, the beheaded thousands and the stake, and in La Corunna, severed Spanish arms were hauled on ropes, and heads danced on poles. Five hundred butchered, but no redress, just a thanks for a battle won. Doors and windows were torn from houses while ransack raged in the narrow streets. Barrels filled with wine discovered. Drinking and burning and drunken soldiers destroyed the corn and stores and all the victuals that would freight our ships. Everywhere there was riot as fires took a portion of the lower town.

"A few Spaniards saved themselves by surrendering to English officers, who by code of honor would protect. Others sought refuge behind the stronger walls of the citadel, which still held. Some escaped into the fields and hills. But in the town, food spilled underfoot, and we desperate in need of what was ruined. Madness then a contagion in the blood. Fire and screams and staggering drunks carrying plunder. Smoke that clayed the choking lungs, bled the streets in confused updrafts. Barrels of wheat were overturned in the mud, cattle and chickens slaughtered that none would eat. The moment was the prize, all thought a treason.

"Drake and some of his captains, hearing of the food, sent men to gather what they could. Norris called for an end to the looting to save the food. Swords and pikes and the muzzles of our own guns—those the threats to clear away our own. Victuals and useful goods were brought to the beach to resupply our fleet. Although much was already lost, there was enough to feed us for two weeks. What waste there was in such a wreck."

"MEMORY IS BUT A FEEBLE SCRAP, TEACHING ONLY TO THOSE WHO already know. Our regiment soon to the countryside. Fires upon the land. The Spanish made war in single volleys, then they fled. Farms we burned, their crops to smoke, their pastures to blackened rings, on their edges the respreading flames. Six thousand oxen we slaughtered, some for pleasure and some for meat. Fifteen thousand rounds of biscuits, three thousand barrels of wine, six thousand barrels of powder and one hundred fifty cannons: all these and other ruins to catalogue against our rage at Philip's wars.

"But the walls of the citadel were still a Spanish keep, and they from the height brought arrows and shot and fire in hosts upon us. Norris, believing great stores of powder and weapons were housed behind those gray stones in that promontory of the town, determined to have it ours. But before this battle there were others yet. War is a wild which holds no human will.

"A Spanish army of fifteen thousand was said to advance upon us. Norris with our thousands and with cannons to the fields to meet the threat. Hills and mountains now the points of a living map. We passed into the valley. Streams thundered in the white boil, their rapids through stone cataclysms of the land. The Spanish used the stone to make bridges across the valleys. There on the river Hero, on the far side of an eighty-foot bridge, near the town of El Burgo, was the Spanish camp, their tents upon the green blanket of the earth, a barricade of rock and brush and overturned wagons on the opposite side of the span. Their camp awake to trumpet calls, as drums broke upon the throbbing air.

"Norris, mad to madness, without his armor stood before his troops. 'There is victory,' he screamed, his sword leveled, his hand thrusting toward the Spanish barricade. 'There is victory before it stands death. I shall have the golden one without the other. Who stands with me now stands with God, eternity and England.' The soldiers cheered, Norris's brother by his side.

"Such words make all death seem a counterfeit and who but the mad would debase it so?" said the old mariner. Around us, a smell stained the air, the smell of corpses fevered in their rot.

"English firelocks in a single volley, arrows in flocks. The air torn vacant. Norris's sword raised above his head. Fabric upon his chest. Iron the bravery and his blind will. 'With me…for England,' he called, already in run toward the narrow bridge. Thousands on his heels. The bridge took the drink of our living men, swords and pikes, arrows flocked in dark shafts against the light. Cannons pushed into the waving banners. Men were dying at Norris's feet, there was a gash in his brother's head, the rose of blood upon his shirt. But the Spanish broke, the bridge was ours. Now slaughter on the fields. Spaniards ran like flightless birds pursued by mobs, cut down by the forests of falling swords. Arms and legs and heads lay orphaned on the earth, rags of flesh, and partial men. The Spanish ran across the fields to wade into the marshes, their heads above the water. They cursed their armor before they drowned.

"A thousand Spanish killed, Norris leaned against his sword to watch the sport. His troops now burned the farms and villages. Fires and flames had become the blanket of that earth. For miles around, the land bled heat and black and columns of rising ash. Cinders fell like rain; smoke became the color of the wind.

"'How magnificent we are that such magnificence should come from our hands,' wrote Lord Ashley of Norris's command to the queen."

"WINDS HAD TURNED AND NOW CAME FROM THE NORTH, STRANDING our fleet at its anchor. No ship could sail against the gale. We became the prisoners of the prison we had seized. Drake in his cabin watched the hours pass. Each day our victuals less, wasted to the wait and change of wind.

"Norris returned from his battle. 'This wind gives an opportunity to have the powder and provisions in the citadel,' he said. 'This time is not a waste.' Norris to his preparation, his troops labored through La Corunna's streets, up hills, on paths of dirt and cobblestones, dragging the ropes tied to their waists, pulling the bronze weight of cannons. The wheels crushed the stones of the road. Men groaned. Dust burst from beneath the wheels. Diego watched the small-bored guns gain the hills, saying, 'More these toys will taunt than bring us victory.' These cannons fired balls no bigger than a fist against the citadel walls which were five feet thick and twelve feet tall. What hope to break that line of rock, and along its face every ordered length a tower rose high above the battlements.

"Flags snapped and winds blew clouds in pregnant grays and white. Their shadows pursuing shadows in the race of surfaces down along the walls among our cannons in their marshaled ranks. Their muzzles locked in lines ready for the fiery assault. Tapers lit, their glow placed against the powder hole. In rows of havoc our cannons flared. From the walls chips of rock burst to dust, but the damage was too slight. The citadel held against our cannons' constant scratch.

"All moments are never done, but secret to return to host a larger life. And so without the six great siege cannons that Elizabeth had promised but never sent, now meant loss of an easy opportunity. Norris and Drake and the council met. Norris planned to bring his cannons against one section of the wall. 'One small breach…and I have victory,' he said. Miners dug a tunnel under a corner tower of the citadel, powder to be placed beneath. And still time slipped and slipped. Almost a week's delay and the winds not changed and nothing of the expedition truly done. And where was the loyalty now for Drake, his queen, his profits or his god? All that sustains us can soon enough become the weapons to our throats.

"Beneath the street, England dug her desperate tunnel. Men labored with picks and shovels. Baskets filled with rock and dirt dragged into the light, thrown into heaps, and powder was carried into the great hole, the fuse ready for the flame. Cannons broke again in one last salvo. The walls almost breached. The great fuse lit, its spark ran its ignitions into the dark. English soldiers were ready for the assault.

"How bloomed the earth in fireballs, the tower lost in smoke and splintered rock. Half-crushed, it did not fall, but held to a fragile stand. One side gone, it leaned. Drake's regiment rushed to the attack, banners forward. Reluctant goes the cloth that beneath it dies the dream.

"The Spaniards to the breach, arrows, darts, our English fell to crumpled rags. Theirs to twist a quietude, ours to stampede upon their corpses. No screams, no groans, just silence and they were still. Men's lives disappeared before my eyes.

"Hands at throats again. Pikes and swords, fusillades and savagery beneath the leaning tower. The cacophony of battle is a broken tune. We almost took that wall and gained the citadel. But almost is a word that within its disappointments carries a greater weight.

"Our banners under that tower of the wall, as along its base men in thrust and parry sport their deaths. Some hundreds of our regiment climbed to slip on dust and blood to hack at Spaniards, who slipped on wet dust and fell into anonymous heaps. And so it was. War flailed its havoc, and then in a sudden quench, it screams in the anthems of the rising dust. The remains of the tower had collapsed. Spaniards and Englishmen now fought against the rubble to gain the air. Hundreds crushed and buried, crawled and clawed, holding to handfuls of dirt on which to pull themselves free. Eating parched clay of the fallen waste, men rose. The battered ground now a stand of sooted men, whose valiant backs peopled all the wreck. Sixty of ours killed. John Seydenham, who held our banner, lost to death. The banner torn, but recovered. The battle done, exhaustion feebled every will, and we in our retreat made for the ships to sleep and sail and be away."

Chapter Twenty

IN THAT LOVE, I AM RECLAIMED AN ORPHAN.

N MAY EIGHTH the wind changed and set us free from that coast. For two weeks the wind had held us to that town. Our supplies now low, our expedition just begun. Sickness was now the issue. Hundreds ill and death the prospect. Thousands of our company would succumb in weeks. Drake and the council met. What loyalty now would be the answer? The queen, who had ordered the fleet to destroy the Armada, which was docked in Santander and San Sebastian, not three hundred miles up the coast, or the investors, who called for profits, which meant the Azores or Lisbon, a longer sail for greater gain for a lesser cause. And there was Dom Antonio, who swore his Portuguese would choose their freedom and revolt and join the English. All this choice, and men still manacled to sly their self-interests. Drake stood upon the deck of the Revenge and faced his sea. The cataclysms of the beckoning waves, the passions of the surging tide, waters white in finger points rolling toward Santander and San Sebastian. Destiny is never the easy choice. He was the creation of his faith. Here his interests cut against themselves. Here profit and duty cleaved. 'What are you if not for this, the final destruction of the Armada?' the water asked in a final sigh. 'You chose to make us one, and now you choose against the choice. Love always brings a bitter peace' said the sea. 'I have no love that is not love of you'

"Drake uncertain in his own mind, his soul never quite for gold, breathed the power of his heresy and looked upon the smile of its depth.

"The council met. All were against an expedition to Santander and San Sebastian. 'The coast is rough and rocky with no good beach to land our troops. The forts are well placed with great cannons and we have no siege guns,' they said. 'The winds are treacherous, the tides uncharted. There is little time and much sickness.' All the excuses to firm a more desperate plan. Lisbon was a greater distance, but there lay profit. Drake was not ready to speak his thoughts.

"'If Lisbon falls, the wound is in Philip's heart,' said Norris. 'Half his empire lost…the East India trade. All that wealth there to us.'

"'And Portugal suffers in its chains, a people without a proper king, soon free. War begs us to their cause,' said Dom Antonio. 'And with my country goes the Azores, a harbor to seize the flota.'

"'Always, Drake, have you not grasped from desperate moments great honors? The sea has been your shepherd, why do you now cast down her staff? The Armada beckons! Its rigging calls. Heed the sea,' said Diego. Near the ships, whales played in the wash of their white rush, their haunting cries in languages beyond all human tongues. The sea rubbed its back against the hull of the *Revenge*. 'Why do all our gifts to men come to this?' called the angels of the surf." The old mariner looked at me as he said these words, pale death spreading on his lips as he spoke in the eloquence of dust.

"Drake thought of his options and the plans and his responsibilities and faced his moment. And what do we lose when men rise to their humanity? The sea loosened its light upon him and gave back to the world a man. And so, the fire divided into its equal flames, the bearer who had been borne by it gently placed again into his own flesh, the alchemies of the sea cast down. 'It is agreed,' said Drake. 'We are for Lisbon.'"

"THE SEA IN ITS RELUCTANT TERRORS FELL UPON OUR FLEET. STORMS in its ghostly waters rose. Waves broke in gargoyles across our decks. White surge raced in hiss. Foam snakes tasted brine on lips, then slipped in coiling wander overboard. The sea's head now raised in viper fangs. The gale tore our sails. For days the weather was upon us. Men grew sick. Many died. Food grew low. We who needed a speedy voyage to Lisbon were now held in the progress, claimed by ourselves a derelict.

"After days, the storm passed to the horizon, the sky coming clear off the Portuguese coast. We found the *Swiftsure*, which had sailed late from Plymouth and lost the fleet. Round her were several Spanish prizes taken while she was ranged off that coast. We all cheered to have her with us once again. On her deck stood Sir Roger Williams, a fierce and ready soldier, all of him for any war. And by his side, in golden armor, his blond hair curled to the glory in the sun, was Robert Devereux, the second Earl of Essex, Elizabeth's favorite for his beauty. He had fled the charms of a queen to make war with Drake and Norris and Williams to regain his fortune. 'I adventured to be rich,' he said. By his fastest horse the earl had ridden by night for Plymouth to catch the fleet, Elizabeth sending messengers to have him back, the *Swiftsure* sailing before the queen's letter was at the dock.

"Drake welcomed Sir Roger Williams and Robert Devereux to his council. The young earl was pampered and foolish, but very brave, and the son of Drake's old friend, the first Earl of Essex. 'Ireland is a long way off, and not my war, but he was the son to a power I once called friend. Memories give strange genealogies to the lives we shared,' said Drake to Diego, 'and he is the queen's most favorite.' Then Drake smiled."

"THE HORIZON TO THE EAST CAST NOW IN A LINE OF CLIFFS. WE anchored near Lisbon at Cape Roca in the flood of the Tagus River, not far from the forts guarding the entrance to the city. There, a council of war was held. The queen, hearing of Drake and Norris at Lisbon, having disobeyed her orders, said, 'What they do, they do more for profit than for service.' Drake had slipped upon the voices of lesser men, forgotten his oath. The choice was wrong, but there was courage in it," said the old mariner, "even though, in truth, he squandered his heresy and cast down his fate."

"Disease had reduced our troops to a fraction. Only six thousand of our nineteen thousand now healthy for the fight. Each day hundreds sickened. Our powder low and our food almost gone. It was a desperate plan to seize luck from circumstance, and land such troops as we had at Peniche, forty miles north of Lisbon, then bring them overland by march to the city gates. 'This march will give all warning for my people to revolt,' said Dom Antonio.

"The remedy is always in the truth, but some truth brings no remedy, and so men make dreams into potions. Lisbon was weakly held. The Cardinal-Archduke Albert of Austria, the nephew of Philip and the Spanish governor of the city, had but few loyal troops. To these were marshaled some thousands of Portuguese whose love of Spain was in doubt. Ten thousand had defended Lisbon in 1580 for Dom Antonio, only to be overwhelmed by Philip. Uncertainty makes brutal men more brutal, which thinking on their method makes them more uncertain. Already Lisbon bloomed gallows, its torture chambers overworked. Its defenses strengthened, yet still weak. But, in fact, weakness balances weakness. Drake and Norris were without siege guns, had little powder and an army succumbing to disease. The walls of Lisbon were beyond the range of Drake's cannons, even if his fleet passed the forts and made the harbor. All had come to this: Dom Antonio's belief that his Portuguese would revolt."

"HOW WHITE THE SURF, HOW BOILED ITS THUNDER, ITS PLUMES in spray, the air about flung with water. The castle stood the cliffs, the town of Peniche further to the hills, a settlement in the flat of a soulless sound. On May 16 our soldiers to our longboats to make the shore. Boats caught and turned and lost in spray, one swamped, the men in heavy armor, anguished on the pull of the insistent weight, their arms loose in flutter to make some swim, the billows of the water upon them. Twenty-five drowned.

"Volleys from the castle on the cliff, the shot stung upon the water. Essex and Sir Roger Williams, not yet on shore, jumped into the surf yards from the beach. Chest deep, they fought against the sickening drag that would have them under. Essex cursed the castle on the heights, his sword held aloft, as if to threaten air. Other men labored to the shore, falling upon the sand like spent beasts. Essex urged them to their feet. Young the fool who thinks valor is his only badge. Shots now skipped upon the rocks. Up the cliffs we climbed, firelocks in our hands, to volley in our defense.

"Almost to the heights, the Spanish fled. The people of Peniche, caught by fear, grabbed panic from the air, running upon the crests of the hills, their rags and valuables upon their backs.

"The castle informed that King Antonio had returned with the English fleet, the Portuguese abandoned their battlements and surrendered. 'What has begun here is but the breeze to lead the storm,' said the man who would be king. A council of war was held to consider and make the final plan. But circumstances had already drawn the lines. Elizabeth had ordered, 'No war or any action will be made in Lisbon until you discover the depth and weight of the love and loyalty of the populace for Dom Antonio.' And so it was we would have no war without a Portuguese revolt. All then was to trick the spark to light the powder. Norris was to march overland, gather what Portuguese he could to Dom Antonio's banner, his progress to threaten Lisbon's walls. Drake would sail to the Tagus and the mouth of the harbor to further the threat and discover what assistance could be had and if the harbor could be seized. All this was agreed by vote.

"The commanders shaking hands, each to his separate way. Drake to the constant of a different sea. 'Am I the prodigal lost to my beliefs?' Drake had forsaken his alchemies and forgotten his sea. He was now a man of doubt and divided loyalties, his direction lost. 'That I am, I am for what?' he asked Diego as he sailed to the castle town of Cascais.

"The answer known. Each knot upon his life, the rope slipped tighter his throat. Each doubt wormed its echo in his brain. The hollow of the skull, that weight, that secred that knows well the proper passage. Our conscience is our compass point. Now point warred with point," said the old mariner as he turned his mind to think upon himself. "My chemistries are soured poisons, all visions are but selfish toys. Heresies are all betrayed. Who shall be my wizard or my guide? Are you, Smith, the living philosopher's stone? Dee, too much Spanish in his sacrifice. Drake, so much less."

"I am but a man," I hissed at the old mariner. "Find your salvations in another skin."

"You are but a child," raged old Jonas. "Fool and child! Gather what is given. The text is yet."

And so the mariner cried aload upon the Jamestown beach, his ancient eyes wild as he spoke. " 'The Armada was the only cause,' said Drake, his hand on the rail, his eyes to the sea. 'I had it in my hand, and I cast it back. Does the bone ever will itself again to be the meat?'"

.   .   .   .   .

"ON MAY TWENTIETH THE FLEET MADE CASCAIS, THE WIND'S BREATH to our backs and for Lisbon. Drake anchored his fleet, showing its threat to the Portuguese, which was the plan. He wanted to leave his sick on shore and his smaller ships in the safety of the harbor before deciding on a try at the narrows and the forts.

"The next day Drake seized the town and its castle. Only a few volleys from the walls to show some feinted battle. Drake then sent these words to Cascais and its council by one of Dom Antonio's Portuguese: 'If you will have Dom Antonio as your king, we are as allies and none shall be abused or hurt.' The council, nodding to our cause, pledged its goodwill. And so a fragile friendship, a peace in which we could delight and purchase fresh food and water. Drake paying all with a ready purse. Our sick on shore, we waited for news of Norris and his army marching overland.

"That army with little food, each man carrying on his back his own powder and victuals, no cannons, in two days five hundred already dead of disease. No army here but haunted pilgrims, yet still they held to their orders and would not plunder or pillage or abuse any village through which they passed. Some hundred came to Dom Antonio, but not enough for any war. The march, the dying and the disappointment, Dom Antonio pleading to himself that desperation to keep his hope alive.

"The army drank stale water sweetened with honey, and so more death was made in its sweet drink. How many dragged themselves from the mountains to stand before the horizon of Lisbon's walls is unknown. Banners on the battlements, heralding trumpets, drums to excite the coast. It was all a bluff of Albert's. There was revolt in Lisbon, but silent executions stilled the will for a more open contest. The great families waited, the city waited, its loyalties open to purchase upon some success. But Norris had no cannons, powder was scarce, an army sick and failing. Dom Antonio thought time was his greatest hope. The English army before the walls would seed revolt, but time had bested his only chance."

"JUST OFF THE SHORE TWELVE SPANISH WAR GALLEYS ROWED WITH battle strokes. Their cannons sparked in harassing fire, our shelter blown to splinters. Mules were torn in two. Men lost arms. We responded with volleys of our firelocks and pistol fire. No threat to the galleys, just an empty cry, not even a slap in all its noise. Norris without his large weapons sat the insults, moving his troops from the beach, the Spanish laughing in shrill taunts at our weakness.

"Essex was in a rage. Dom Antonio begged for time. Norris waited. Messengers now brought Drake reports of the weakened army and the war galleys. Drake, with his voices, listened to his council. He was for forcing the narrows of the harbor, bringing his fleet under the cannons of the Spanish forts of Belem and St. Julian's. 'Dare the guns and seize the waters. All for Norris and his relief,' said Drake. He was now the Drake of old, a flicker that memory had made anew.

"'Remember the words of Pedro Mandinga,' whispered Diego to Drake's ear before the council began. 'The gods are gods because life and death to them is but the same. What is born dies and what is death lives and the anointed are ever so. Chance a memory and be reborn.'

"Doubts have many alliances, and many loyalties lay claims upon the will, but the human voice burns its salvations beyond all the familiar works.

"Drake swept aside his captains' fears: 'The strong forts, their cannons, the armed ships in the harbor, the winds, the tides. We could be becalmed and overwhelmed.'

"'Tomorrow at dawn, our best ships at fair wind. We sail the Tagus and through the cannons to Lisbon.' Drake spoke now as Drake again. 'No man dreams to be a vassal,' he said. 'I find no glory in defeat.' His words now the preparations to each ship. But he was no longer safe in the sea's cloister. The events he had left him but a man. We are each our own shepherd—the sea ever fierce in its judgments." The old mariner looked at his hands. The dream was done.

"Word came that night that Norris had abandoned Lisbon and was in full retreat. Drake had lost his moment. He slept that night as if the day would dawn on a different morrow, but the morrow was the same."

"THE COMET HAD FALLEN TO BROKEN METEORS. ESSEX, IN HIS golden armor, rode to the gates of Lisbon. His sword he thrust into the wooden planks, challenging all to come and war in single combat. The Spanish laughed, their ridicule stung his armor. 'Better it was shot in hail,' said Essex. The ragged army at his back staggered in its disease and retreated toward Cascais. What weapon is a gesture when the drama is done?" said the old mariner. "It is an empty bottle...the potion having succumbed to the disease.

"Our army weak, the Spanish now rode forth from Lisbon. The galleys closer to the shore, the retreat was a hell of *ambushado* and cannon fire. Small groups of ours, the wounded and the sick, slow and separated from the main, ridden down under horses' hooves, slaughtered in a butchery. Their screams faint in the breathless heat. Their severed heads displayed on poles, arms and legs cut to earth to lie in forgotten trophies.

"The galleys volleyed and broke the ground about our feet. A thousand more were dead. At Cascais only four thousand remained. Arguments and accusations, blame enough for all to bear their share of weight. Essex, broken to childhood, raged the curses of a spoiled lord. Norris, his face now of reddened stone, spoke nothing that did not flee his mouth in fire. Dom Antonio blamed the Queen and her instructions. Williams blamed Dom Antonio and his exaggerated hopes. Drake blamed no one but himself. All had lost and all were some at fault. But Drake had spent his better destiny on the foul of an ill-considered voyage, and not enough intent.

"Fifteen bronze cannons we took from the castle at Cascais, and on June 1 Drake seized a fleet of seventy French and German ships, bringing wax and naval stores and powder and corn and copper to Lisbon. Too late, it was the greatest prize of the venture. And so forsaken destiny ever plays its tortures in a fouled circumstance. English supply ships now appeared, commanded by Admiral Robert Crosse, the food Drake had asked of the queen when the fleet was still in Plymouth. On the coast of Lisbon, with all but lost, with what good now. With Crosse was a letter from the queen ordering Essex home and rebuking her commanders for disobeying her orders.

"'How storms that ink,' said Drake, 'and how the weather calms.' Our fleet still on that sea of glass. The Spanish galleys rode from the harbor and made war on our weakened ships. Two of the French prizes sunk. Drake and the *Revenge* pulled by longboats, putting the Spanish to heel.

"But this was a petty war. The queen stood the deck and Essex home to London. So broken and so stiff, he seemed a tail who had lost his dog. We for our own sailed to Peniche, finding the Spanish had recovered the town. Our company mostly dead, hanging in their limp silhouettes from the gallows' ropes.

"We sailed for the Azores, but were held to the Portuguese coast by the wind. We made then south to Vigo, where Drake had success some years before the Armada broke. What agony it is when men must replay old victories. Reliving life is a death of sorts, or at best a sickness in spirit. What we spend cannot be spent again. All things become thin by repetition. Drake held now to the tatters of himself.

"Vigo we seized and burned. Nothing done but ruin. Always there was disease, our dead thrown overboard each day. The army with only two thousand fit. England was the only hope. Storms again, the sea in thoroughfares of rage. The *Revenge* torn and sinking, her pumps throbbed to the beating of an empty heart. Drake just made land again and Plymouth.

"The catalogue of the disaster was told in the names of ships. On the *Dreadnought* only three were healthy of the crew of three hundred, one hundred fourteen dead, only eighteen fit for work. On the *Gregory of London* only four were healthy, on the *Griffin of Lubeck* all were ill, the captain dead, none could haul a sail or hoist a flag. Of the sixty soldiers she carried, thirty-three had died and were thrown overboard, twenty still sick, two dying on reaching an English port. And so it was, ship by ship. In all, more than half the expedition dead, ten thousand gone, mostly to disease. For Spain, their cannons had been less a weapon than our fouled water.

"Norris and Williams strutted London to cock some brag on their success. Drake was silent. The *Revenge* dry docked and repaired, reborn for another death. The queen was in a rage, and then forgave, knowing all were of some blame. Although reconciliation was the word, Old Bess never quite trusted Drake again. The torch had quietly passed from one hand to another."

Chapter Twenty-one

THE CRIMES THAT INTERLUDE THE GREATER CRIME.

O MUCH THE HISTORIES INTERMIX. There the alchemies fester, lingering in an ever engulfing consequence. I sat my darkness. My languors bathed upon remorse. *Some comedy we are*, my thought the single tickle to the blunt. For many months Richard Potts and I gathered letters, reports and interviews of those few returned from Jamestown. Little told of Pocahontas, but much of the colony. What was before repetitions now. "How much murder until we are the murder of ourselves?" I asked Potts.

Keeping his silence as a scarf about him, Potts dipped his quill into the shallows of his ink, and turned from the paper under his hand. "This new book begs a pleading to the nation." Potts in his only eloquence.

"The book is unfinished," I repeated. Potts stood, showing me his tidy script, and the patch and ponder of so many reports. I took the manuscript in my hand. "A work well done," I said, searching for my own quill to mark and have the final jostles on the page.

ON MAY TWELFTH, 1611, SIR THOMAS DALE AND HIS SUPPLY FLEET reached Point Comfort. Dale rowed ashore with Captain Newport to inspect the tiny ruined fort spread along the beach. Log walls circled a few houses, their roofs collapsed, all in more neglect, the litter of a broken enterprise around the barren ground. Men bowled or played at hatchet toss, or lay in a sleep weary even of itself. A few in courage paraded to the beach to beg for food. No crops planted, no nets repaired, no hunting. Ducks and geese flew in squawking flocks. Clams and oysters sometimes gathered. Dale thought murder first before he ever gained another thought. He grabbed Newport by the beard and threatened to hang him on the spot. "Is this the colony's plenty you report in London? The whole council is deceived. If this is prosperity, it is a pauper's dream of such. Even that braggart Smith in his letters told more than you." Dale spent a week at Point Comfort.

He flogged a few for laziness, threatened to hang the rest, ordered the walls of the small fort joined for better protection, divided the company into work parties, each assigned its task at the beating of a drum. Their labors still not heavy, but now an effort.

With a fresh supply of three hundred men, Dale in the suddens of his temper sailed for Jamestown. He landed, saw no work but heard its rumor. In the streets men idled in their endless conversations. Dale raged and thundered threats, looking for an example to prove his word, but one being as guilty as the other, he silenced. He then attended church and had Strachey read his commission. Percy resigned as governor, as was the law, and was immediately appointed captain of the fort. *Still no ax to break the ring, the ring rolled on,* I thought as I read.

ROLFE WORKED IN SMALL PASTURES, HIS TOBACCO IN SMALL GREENS pushing above the earth. He worked for the small gain of a sweeter taste of smoke. On May twenty-second, Dale spoke to the colony. In his hand was a new code of conduct for the company. Law was now to be by the threat of death. All crimes to have a single judgment, whether murder or petty theft or blasphemy. The king giving absolute power to the lord governor. Its liberties unrestricted turned to license. No Englishman in England would have accepted such abuse. But they were not in England and were starved by more than food.

"Pain and fear will remind us who we are. This wilderness, its vastness, comes in seductions to this outpost, overthrows our biles and taints the sense." Dale spoke to the company. "Harsh judgments will bud a violent beauty to the vine. Our eyes ever on the threat, we make ourselves again. Death makes men fear and fear will make us great. All shackles are in the mind. Know my will! This land shall abide my fist!"

Dale held a council meeting, ordering the church repaired. All was to be rebuilt. A new well to be dug, the old one thick with slime and unwholesome smells. Dale redoing what should have been under constant care. He ordered work on new necessities: a stable to be raised, a powder house, a munitions house, a blockhouse to protect the northern island; bricks to be baked to a ceramic red to build a smokehouse for our catch of sturgeon, to season the flesh by wood and so preserve the meat, and casks to be built to hold the fish and protect our food. All this to be done, but he who knew the curing of fish died within a week.

The council made its plans, its designs ever in words. Captain Newport and his mariners to build a dock for the unloading of our ships. Dale to write to London to have mariners sent as colonists because there was none in Jamestown who had the experience to properly sail the pinnaces. Trading for fur and food, even without the wars, was abandoned to the illegal commerce of mariners. Dale ordered with threats that trade to cease, but threats never stayed the lure of profit.

Dale was madness by half. His greatness by slivers now talked of corn. "Working for the common good has brought only a general laziness, no corn planted," he said. "Let us harness ourselves to do ourselves some benefit, and in that single good a general good will rise." He then gave each man and woman, every colonist, a private plot of land to grow what he or she would for personal use or for sale. The company land was reserved for flax and hemp and some corn for the magazine, the work to be done by the colony as a whole and a few savages who labored on our behalf. The relentless circle of the same was not broken yet, but shaken in its rounds.

The next day Dale sailed to see the abandoned village of the Paspaheghs, they having fled to a safer, more distant ground. The land lay fouled with brush and weeds and shrubs where once rich crops and dark soil carpeted the earth. The land too thorned in its decease and brambled. Dale proposed to let it stay to itself, "for another year," he said and walked away.

THREE DAYS LATER CAPTAIN ADAMS SAILED TO ENGLAND WITH letters and reports from Dale and Strachey. Some of which *you* may have seen, John Smith, the words unsigned in such a familiar hand. Todkill's report, better the anonymous shepherd to the murderous sheep. Lord Percy sent a request to his brother, the Earl of Northumberland, asking for additional moneys. "As I am captain of Jamestown fort and must daily set a suitable table for men of fashion, I am in need of further resources," he wrote. "I am aware that you have given to me the generous sum of four hundred thirty-two pounds a year for my many years in Jamestown, which I know is more than half our mother's allowance to you, and is some six fold more again than your yearly stipend to the mathematician Thomas Harriot, who is now in your employ, but I have obligations of station which are incumbent upon us all." Percy sent bills amounting to seventy-four pounds, and orders for clothes including six pounds, eight shillings' worth of gold lace and a Dutch beaver hat for two pounds, sixteen shillings. All this while men died in such numbers they were never reported to London.

AFTER HAVING HIS SPEECH AND HIS COUNCIL, DALE MADE PLANS to bring vengeance on the savages, who in Dale's view still needed lessons. Hearing rumors of Indian sorceries and blasphemous charms, he decided to bring his God against theirs. "Iron is the will of God, as is our sword," he said.

Reverend Alexander Whitaker, who had accompanied Dale from England, asked, "To lift up the heathen there must be peace, but must peace always come in blood?"

Dale gave no answer, but watched his company fit themselves into the rusted and pitted armor and the ancient chain mail he had brought from London. The armor had lain unused in the Tower for years, useless in a war with firelocks and cannons, but against stone arrowheads, stone cudgels and wood swords it might afford a corset of some protection.

A hundred soldiers now turned their magnificence in dents and armor, shine and rust in equal wash across their helmets and their chests. Their limbs cranked against the weighty plates. In some discomfort they made their boats and sailed toward the Nansemond River to have their day.

The Nansemond met them on the water in their canoes. The air a storm of falling arrows, the sky darkening under the hail. Stone against iron, flint sparks and arrows breaking. The helmets streaked with dust and crushed spear points. Arrows struck men and bounced away. Firelocks answered. Arrow points hitting armor could not break the storm of our guns. Some of Dale's company were hurt, their armor only for their chests, their arms and legs exposed, their eyes unprotected. An arrow pinned in protrusion from Captain John Martin's leg. Captain West, an arrow in his unprotected arm, his arm limp, his fingers dripping blood. The battle raged across the miniatures of the boats.

The company in skirmishes fought their way to shore. The Nansemond in the forest screamed their chants to heaven. Priests ran mad with exorcism, their bodies a riot of gestures. In lines Dale marched his company against them. The arrows fell again in thuds, a few of the company hurt. In lines the firelocks came to volleys. Many savages were killed or wounded. Seeing how little their arrows served their cause, the priests sang conjurings and incantations, throwing fire to the sky, asking Okee for a rain to douse our tapers and wet our powder. The sky dark in wanton gesture, lightning came in havocs. The priests frenzied in their delight of power. Then the rain came, falling in cooling serpents. Reverend Whitaker went to his knees, his hands before his face as he prayed. "The sky is heathen. It acquaints with devils," he said, the rain spilling in its clear blisters down his arms and across his armor. The company protected their tapers as they could. The Nansemonds in one last desperate attack, the firelocks volleyed once again. It was a slaughter.

All the villages burned and the corn ruined, as if the food we needed were an enemy. We to destroy what we could not govern.

Many prisoners Dale took from the Nansemond. They were shackled and set to work. Well guarded but in the sly of the Indian ways and the foolishness of the sentries, most escaped, Reverend Whitaker blaming it all on devils and Indian sorceries. But fools in the depths of their hearts, the truth known in soon forgotten flashes.

Dale and the company in expeditions and invasions, their armored host fell upon the countryside and burned the corn. The visions of Drake almost forgot, the orders of the London Company ignored. Reverend Whitaker still talked of conversion, but little of peace. How small is the slip when we fall from Eden. How impossible the return. *Still I would sit my London room, my counsel unsought, given by letters to the London worthies, but ignored, and I had my truth to tear the way, love of her my boundless mercuriess. Make all circumstance a friend, I thought. Move by clever masteries. Usurp the flow.*

Dale now made plans to sail to the falls and build another fort, the other being abandoned. By spies, Powhatan learned of the expedition, sending two messages warning against such an exploration and demanding the release of two prisoners held by Dale. "I will bring such poison in such ways as to make you mad and bring slaughter to your men," was Powhatan's threat.

"Savages will have their forest comedies," said Dale. He sent the messenger back to Powhatan with threats of his own. "I shall sail where I will and I will heed none," were his words.

. . . . . .

A WEEK LATER DALE'S FLEET SAILED FOR THE FALLS. HE WENT WELL armed. After a day, he stopped at a village near the riverbank to have some council with the *werowance* there. Sitting in the lodge with his captains, he was feasted and made to be at ease, a drink served. The liquid to the lips and swallowed. The longhouse burst into rumors and shadows, the world served a lunacy. The company beat upon each other, friends now seemed as enemies, Englishmen turned to savages in the eyes. Sight fouled in its counterfeit. Nothing was as it was as the company did injury upon itself. Then the illusion passed. Reverend Whitaker prayed and called it witchcraft. I knew it was the drink of the *huskanaw*. The village deserted now, darkness hung upon the owl's cry. Only the moon spoke light, as Dale moved his orphans in a lonely search.

After a day, Dale came to the falls. In our old fort, its walls fallen, he built his camp. A protective trench was dug, fires lit, tents and beds spread upon the ground. Flames broke upon the air in crackle. The company had its prayers and ate as the setting sun scattered in crimson through the sky.

Dale surveyed the lands around the falls. Never content with Jamestown's seat, he wished to move the town to a better location. "What madness," he said, "to have us build a town upon a swamp in a river of fetid water? Our wells always stink, disease the common." And so he searched to lord a better dominion.

At night men prayed. The fire leaping in flames and ghostly heat, as darkness spread its moments upon the centuries of the land. Reverend Whitaker held himself grim to his failing certainties, the sculptures of his doubt, his revelations held as war against the wilds of the forest. The men were in fear, seeing grazing devils on the mirrors of the waters. The mind bolts men to panic. In the forest there were cries. Shadows now moved in flashed darkness. Ghosts ran in footfalls on the earth. The night became a spider on the hand. Men screamed to tear away the web. Savages now leaped the trench. The company panicked. The savages screamed and ran among the barrels, displaying their bluff and bravery. The company, gone witless, hid and abandoned their weapons. The savages disappeared. Humiliation and no lives lost. Sir Thomas Dale made his return to Jamestown.

A MONTH LATER, A HASTY LETTER FROM TODKILL, A SMUDGED report, its ink battered and scraped as if by some moonlight demon.

I had not been privy to Sir Thomas Dale nor told his plans. He had been at Jamestown a month before I was ordered to be his visitor. Now Dale sat before me. He seemed a man whose substance was more to his surface than to his soul. "You are in some communication with John Smith, I believe." Dale sat into his threat.

"I am familiar with Captain Smith."

"Friend, sometimes protector. I know the rumors. I wish you to write to Smith of our interview. I have read his letters and his published book," he said. "Are you not pleased?" I felt myself the fly wiggling on the web of his words. He watched me. "Have I not done what Smith would have done if he had the king's authority?" He looked into my face. Power makes all things just, as station turns all actions wise. "You do not brag as your friend," Dale said. "No insolence for your betters?" he laughed as I thought nobility made even fools seem better fools. It is nature's conduit of a reward, it is the ax that cleaves surface from fact. Dale leaned forward. "He deserted to the savages, stayed the winter, the colony starved. He was, as an advisor, a clumsy child. But he has done some service, and I will do it better. Tell him."

Dale then spoke of Drake. "Our enterprise here is to spread our dominion. Our borders are to overflow. Drake brought the world to our plate and our tongue is greased, its avarice upon our nation's lips. Greed dominions continents. Watch upon me, Captain Smith, and see me do your work."

Dale smiled. "God is ever God and we are his plan." Then he stood and said, "Power born from power is double born. I intend to build forts from Point Comfort to the falls to secure the peninsula, which was the idea Smith once voiced to the council. See how well his advice is taken." Then he left.

Chapter Twenty-two

OF FEATHERS, WEEDS AND THE ARMORS
OF SHADOW MEN.

ATE AND ANGER COMPEL a demon's logic, I thought, as I read the letter and its stains.

The day Dale sailed for the falls with a full company to found Henrico, Captain Brewster was to lead his men overland, the companies to meet, our men dressed in armor. The savages understanding its iron meaning. Their gods useless and displeased. Powhatan sent threats. Dale believed it all to be another comedy to amuse his journey. But it is at such times, when gods sicken, that men build their armor from desperation. There came a savage who called himself Nemattanew, whom we called Jack of the Feathers, whose history became linked with ours. As rivers may sometimes run in hidden courses beneath the ground, appearing only to dive again, so it is with some men that when they momentarily appear, the surface of the world is washed in flood and catastrophe and in a bath of blood.

In the clearing near the falls, he first appeared, his body covered in the white feathers of a swan, like the foams of a frozen spray. His shoulders draped in wings, his arms flapped as if he meant to fly. He ran and cried. His company was not seen. He dared Brewster to make his march, screaming, "I am by my gods made iron. Your bullets to me are dust." Then the arrows of the ambush flew in arcs of their graceful darts. From all directions came their attack. The firelocks in their desperate thunder. How webbed the air in the arrows' fall. Englishmen fell wounded. Movements in staccato shouts and violence. Firelocks smoked and flashed havoc. Savages in run, no blood upon their chests. Dart-pierced Englishmen held the shafts that protruded from their limbs.

Jack of the Feathers danced and ran in circles before our guns, as if his body were the spoon to stir the violence to the cauldron's boil. Then he disappeared. The forest silenced, birds flew down from trees to peck upon the earth, as men screamed their agonies through the echoing quiet.

In a day again they marched, Captain Brewster to the front. At each mile now a fresh assault. Jack of the Feathers was convinced he had by his own will and by Okee's voice made soft our bullets and blunted their hurt. The savages murdered and wounded many, but Captain Brewster would have his meeting at the appointed place with Dale. The assaults were constant. On they marched.

Jack of the Feathers, his hates in lunatic, blinded his exalted mind, danced in calligraphies on the battle plain, but he was wise enough to read the pictures in their secret prose. On his choreographies swirled the sweep of coming motions. He would bring by frenzy the salvations of his people.

Dale already at the falls. Around his company the river in curving belts of water swept the horizon on the crest of a flood. Where the river ran on three sides about a tongue of land, the two companies met, Dale and Brewster saluting purpose in each other's duties. Together they began to build a fort.

Arrows now tore the earth about the half-raised walls. Death bore on us in its absolutes. Men suffered in their wounds, surprised into agonies. But what is it in men that even the hard certainties of the world are but a passing toss upon their dreams? Many of our men did ignore the war and would walk the forest paths alone, there to be slain. Many at the fort idled or stole food, refusing to build the walls. Why was it so? Why will it be? Never does our season change. Who has the ax to cleave the clock, change the course, hold the moon, twist the night, let our stars bear us to a different fate? The forest hung in threat. Arrows arced, but still men idled and worked little.

If I am not of that land, then of what? I wept for my passing enterprise. Maybe love could cure my world. My Pocahontas, some simple kiss, the taste of lips, some passion to reperfect my hope. I, who was neglect, so casually we cast ourselves away. Between death and death I chose my coronet. I knew the cause of our delinquent will, our wanton policies. I had by truth the recipe to foreshadow resurrection. I could be again an instrument, if I could but free myself, escape. "Many a great career has begun in the tower," I told myself, but I sat no tower. I sank in the bowels of a rotting town. Ambition here is the flanks of a beaten mare, its nostrils drowned in swill. Have me the latch and I will swing the gate.

DALE NOW PUT FORCE BEHIND HIS EFFORTS TO MAKE MEN WORK. But men still sought safety with the savages, escaping into danger and possible death rather than rub their skins in common toil.

Dale in a fury sent expeditions to find the deserters and bring them back. Many were found. Dale ordered tortures. He fed himself on pain. Limit and the law no longer limits. In fire he quenched his rage. Some he hung and some he shot. Some he tied to wheels, breaking their bones until they died. Some he bound to trees, lighting pyres, bathing them in flame until their screams were ended and they came to ash. A simple laborer who stole some corn Dale had chained to a tree and drove a spike through his tongue so he could never close his mouth. There he was so left until he starved.

All this slaughter Dale presumed because Englishmen would not be better Englishmen, but treasoned to their birth and ran to comforts with the savages. Disrobed, they fled the ornaments of their kind. The converts had converted the apostles. The colony's vision faltering, it became a mere pretense. They weakened and Dale raged murders for the want of law, and they weakened more. They swam in circles to drown ourselves in blood.

THE TOBACCO WAS FRESH IN ITS DARKENING GREEN. PLANTED NOW six weeks, leaves the width of a shilling, its growth spread over the fields, a cohort to the pleasure of a coming profit. Rolfe to his knees. With his knife he hoed the dirt of the small hills, plying its grains, loosening it to damp clumps, looking into the riches of the mud. There he saw a skeletal finger, stained in age and fleshless but for the adhering earth, as if pointing its bony ensign to the whispers of the breeze.

By Rolfe's side was a bucket of water. He lifted the twists of tobacco plants from the hills in delicate care. The fragile roots not pulled or damaged, he placed them to swim on the surface of the water, floating gently, his finger in lover's pull to untangle the twisted plants. The seedlings now ready for transplanting on larger hills, those hills about four and a half feet apart, one plant per hill. Each plant hoed, its surrounding earth made soft to suckle growth. Each mound watered. The weed to bloom and flower through its thickened leaves.

"ROLFE SAT WITH ME, HIS PIPE IN HAND, SPEAKING OF TOBACCO," Todkill wrote in his springtime eloquence. 'To drink upon this unchaliced wine as air, this smoke, this ashen blood that bled its heat through me, its sweet elixir smelling of peaceful madness, all nows for this, all eons held for moments, eternities upon the draws of one sweet breath. It carries through the serpent of the lungs. Its dragon of an almost love.' And so it comes with seducing commerce. Rolfe would have it be angel and the savages would have it be god. And so our divinities mix our love to the same and single coin, just spent upon a different side."

"Are all words the slayers of worlds?" I wondered aloud. A question asked as warning, no answer expected to the ear.

"All histories are heresies that we have come to bless," Rolfe said. "This smoke the final sepulcher, its salvation in transubstantiating fire, its marble glows in ashen hosts, my soul the wafer on its tongue. Eaten to eat. Consuming to be consumed. All the world's a nothing but a sly upon the senses, its philosophies in pleasures, its alchemies in sweating flames and tobacco, the new coin of its prophesy, and would that I could be its apostle, its first, its kiss." Rolfe lingered on his words, then left.

"This land was birthed in heresies," Todkill wrote. "Now each man seeks to be a prophet to his own taste and I still pledged to the one vision that holds us true. And so I think when demons war on demons they use angels as their swords."

"In the tatters our enterprise struggled to survive. The new world was a wild, never could the mind contend to know ever of its peep. Who needs voices? Orphaned from England, we became to ourselves strangers in our derelict. War at the falls meant the savages came again to Jamestown bearing baskets of corn for trade. Nothing was constant, all lushed inconsistent before a zeroing patience. Fearing spies—fear no ally to any sanity—Gates hung those savages as a quick example to keep the peace. "I will, by these deaths, and by fists and chains, keep them from their subtle practice," said Gates. Maybe there was some subtlety of war in these savages, but most of what they practiced just brought us food. Always we were the betrayers of our own success.

"The fort at Point Comfort, by some accident, burned to the ground. Only Captain Davis's house and the store survived. It was hastily rebuilt by Sir Thomas Dale on his return from the falls. It would have been left in ruin but it was the only place we had for plentiful food."

"THE PRIVATE PLOTS BEGAN TO YIELD A LITTLE CORN. MORE LAND for the self meant more food for the public good, but no matter what we grew, the corn was never quite enough. The success so easy, Gates decided to increase the private lands. New settlements were planned, commanders given companies, as forts were to be built along the James and its tributaries.

"Now the tobacco grew in its summer legions. Six to nine feet high it stood like men. The Indian plants grew only to three feet. The savages looked at these trees that offered smoke. The English had brought them messengers in breathing giants. Each day Rolfe labored to the sacrifice of all, holding the plants and pulling the worms that ate upon their leaves as a leafy meat, and fed upon their almost smoke. The worms would kill some plants. The vacant hills had to be replanted, the new plants a garden of endless labor.

"The savages did not pull the flower or top the weed to slow the upward growth so the leaves would spread, vital in their green, but topping gave Rolfe better leaves. Quality came priced in sweat. The market to take the burden. The cost in blood not yet assigned. The savages smoked not for pleasure, but for their souls in message to their gods. They gave no thought to the sweetness of the draft. What sacrifice is worth its pain if it comes too sweet? So Rolfe, for his pleasure, improved on pleasure, his needle to tinker on the hand that held the fiery tablets. Eyes on Rolfe and eyes to the private plots, a chance to grow a little pleasure in the earth and perhaps to feed a taste for an easy sport. Most of the company smoked, as did most of England. Rolfe watched the tobacco grow, others in the company asking for some seed to try their luck next spring. The thought of commerce vague, but becoming clear.

"Rolfe's fields now rich in crops. Twenty to thirty leaves hung from every plant. On his small land grew diamonds, but when to pluck the mine? There was no common wisdom on the cutting of the harvest. Even the savages argued it among themselves. For some, it was when the leaves turned limp and touched the ground, for others when the suckers grew upon the roots, and still others had different clues to guide them in the harvesting of the leaf. Rolfe made no choice, but tried them all. He pulled the leaves from the plants. The wings of the leaf lay upon his hand, leathered and weighted as the dried flight of a bat. He carried them from the plants, stocking them in flat piles on the ground, there to cure and dry under hay. Some he carried to his own cabin, there on a crude table to be cured upon the dark. Rolfe sat by his fire watching the leaf come to its proper flavor. He watched in the uncertainty of what he had done, his crop not yet a harvest but still a hope of one. For weeks he waited, the leaf ripening to its death to bear Rolfe's better smile.

"The company in some excitement. The forest clearing now claimed to pleasure, all deaths almost forgot." So Todkill wrote. "I smoked it first with Rolfe, the sweetness to the caverns of my mouth. The moisture on my tongue coming to a sugared heat. A slight bite in it to deepen pleasure, but a blend that could carry some worth in commerce. 'A success,' said Rolfe. 'Virginia can grow a fair tobacco, not as fine as the West Indian grown, but still quite good. It is a taste to dream upon.' He squeezed his fist as if to hold the pleasure of his joy fast upon his person. 'And the land yields it in such weight that I am sure we can grow it for a profit. In equal kegs it has more worth than corn. Its gold has its glitter in decay.'

"Other crops still tried," Todkill wrote. "Martin raised silk grass, which was something like European flax, but nothing much came of it. A small success for much labor. Silk worms were imported for our mulberry trees to have an industry in Chinese silk. That too failed. Failure all about but the tobacco grew and came to harvest. All eyes now to the weed."

MORE LETTERS, MORE REPORTS. CANNOT THE LONDON COMPANY comprehend what is upon the foot? I wrote to the London Council pleading a commission and a stipend of land. "Have I not invested wealth and blood? I demand some recompense. The New World totters. I have witness and their reports. Your policies are scrubbed in lies. The wilderness placates no fools. Its vengeance will hold the ages."

The Council replied, "You have our ear, your advice well taken. We are not at present inclined by force of debt to lend your passage." My words chipped a warning shot. No one rises who does not have the manor against the Company's fall.

I wrote to Sandys demanding his intersession. "Be patient, friend, I am your ally," so saying in his letter to me. "The Council frets that you have swallowed a wilderness, errant to the London streets." And so the words, and so my loss, but I am of better dictionaries. The Council rings a coward's bell. But what draws men to those fears in which they suicide? And do I not have bite of the same disease? In all that I pursue failure smiles upon its crackling lips. My achievement small against my destiny. I am ambition self-made, sustained dead-eyed in an animal gallop. And the whip upon the flanks, the bloodless scars? The race run to disprove the proof. Are we so ill-starred as we suspect? Have we but fallen to least estate? All fret the plight of knowing, and hide within the haunted quiet. Shall we taste the contagion and the draft and play forgetfulness in the tickle of a peddler's tainted cure? I thought of Waymouth, his madness, his northward course, and now the poetry of his death. Come sing upon the ear a song of corpses. All this to my mind, before me Stacie's report of Waymouth's polar expedition that sailed in the early spring of 1611, before the Hudson mutineers returned.

*W*e to death another moment's feast, a passing crowded interlude. The *Black Swan* in hunt that year in contrary winds, progress turned the endless tack, passed Iceland, Greenland, the sun now high to overwhelm the nighttime clock. Daylight at midnight, the compass less true. The *Black Swan* plunged into the polar sea.

At three in its sunlit morning, the charts upon the captain's table, Waymouth paused in his considerations, then he spoke. "North along this strait between Greenland and the Baffin has been tried by Davis in his three voyages and again by me. Nothing comes of this save ice, trackless in its floating continents, impassible by ship. But to the west I sailed "The Mistaken Strait" that Davis called his "Overflow"; there might be some success for a Northwest Passage in a more open sea, and for a chance encounter with our lost Hudson."

"The crew eagers for furs and wealth," said Ellis, the second mate, his tongue upon his almost open lips.

"Yes, always the easy promise." Waymouth hungers, abiding on the final hunger for his fate.

In what colossals does Waymouth's rage surmount his world? I thought in my London rooms, reading Stacie's simple words. "Waymouth took a madness to us," so he wrote. I to compose to a deeper ledger.

Navigations a wander to the north, the Black Swan then many leagues above "The Mistaken Strait" and its coastal lands of desolation. Ever the morning fog! What phantoms glide within the mist, their profiles obscured, their features lost in the swirling clouds, their colors as a smudge upon a curdled milk. A clearing current, the rising fog, a liquid clarity to see beneath the weight. An iceberg a half-mile wide, the sea foams upon its frozen beach, tumbling into a hissing suds. Blue water calm in pools along its high ice cliffs. Not sand but frost to cup the sea. Danger floats in less than a thousand yards. The *Black Swan* swayed becalmed upon the depthless strait. The vistas spread, the breeze stilled. Waymouth ordered the crew to the boats to pull the *Black Swan* from any threat. "By oars and straining arms and back, creaks the coffin lid. Will it close, clenched upon its lethal work?" Waymouth smiled, his taunt well-savored. "Death gathers to a willful learning. Its spice is schooled in green," Waymouth screamed. "All humour jokes but never past the disease." Waymouth's hands no longer on the wheel. "You are the knave of grace. Take the watch. Be the destructions you avoid." So he said to the nearest manjack of the crew. The truth of his soul nailed to another skin. He walked to the bow shouting instructions to a boat off the port, gauging of a narrow passage. The oars stroked their clockwork scratches on the swells. The crew in chilling sweat, they pulled upon the line. The *Black Swan* slipped a distance from the ice. North by west, wind soon again, a sea breeze near warmth. The long day in its quiet seasons. The seascape opening to a broad sunlight. The world gentles into its mighty sanctuaries.

Our sails bowed, our canvas full, the boats aboard, only the pinnace took the edge, and cuffed some distance forward of our bow. Heavy to the swells, little speed, the pinnace raced as an oxen, a burden on its back.

We anchored in a pleasant bay, traded foods, raw meats, from the fur-clad savages. Metal for victuals, and three kayacks, much to a shallower draft and better for explorations in the narrows, and hunting along the rockiest coasts.

To sea again, Waymouth at the wheel, days in sun long passage. The crew grumbling, in want of food. Cool is a misery eased as it is fed.

A compass in his hand, premonitions walk its clock. Waymouth stands the wheel, fear befriends every lunacy. Blind the vagrant grasps at whims. "The crew plans a murder for an extra loaf of bread."

Stacey looked past the question into the captain's screech, anger and fear thrwart the mind, their icy claws upon the air. "We and the crew with ease could have a better plate. There are fish in plenty we had in trade, and bear and whale, all in every meat. Why take war, when a little biscuit will stew the peace?"

"Why not? Perhaps your mutiny already done! Has the vulture eaten of its rot? This exploration is a fetid waste. Hudson, the fool, only applied himself to command a rope." Waymouth silenced, then the remark, "The crew can eat a little less. Every penny plays my pocket into wealth."

"Shall that be for the crew's ear?" Stacie asked.

"Each of my words is stone. And you, the child squeaks. Has the crew claimed a biscuit for its mutiny? I am no captain to this ship, and you sail a sea which has no name. Disquiet rounds. There is no hope! That rust has played the cinder pot!" Waymouth's reddened face now voiced. His fist knuckled to grasp the belaying pin. Blood and madness bone his flesh, his mouth in screams. Waymouth staggers. "What gulls across my eyes! What floating dust! The world withers and now it sways." Waymouth's hands unsensed, they cannot grasp. "My arm is fouled. My legs disobey." Waymouth's face a jowling plunder, his cheeks falling to a sliding mud. He sprawls upon the deck, his limbs convulsing, foam and bubbles on his lips.

"Bewitched! His demons swell to contagion our deck," screamed Francis Ridley, the carpenter's boy. The crew gathering. "This land damns us with its devils!" The boy caught in his own horrors, accusing all in every shadow, and so fear and superstitions fill its hells.

The crew, not daring to touch Waymouth, slapped the boy and told him "Quiet!" Stacie then knelt a little compassion to blush the raw distain upon his face. "Plague," the murmur from the crew. An easy fear to name, and so the comfort.

"No!" Stacie pounded the certainty in his command. "A fit, like a passing drunk, some babble and some hour's sleep." Stacie nodded secrets, then ordered two of the crew, "Take our captain to a cabin. I will, until the fit is spent, assume the captain's rank."

Stacie, the master pilot, the crew by custom ready to agree. "An extra plate of bread, some meat this night to ease our loss," smiled Stacie, a spike of humor in his voice.

The flows of ice again, and fog and sleet and rain. Cold, the misery deep into the bones. The brief night, strange lights flashed emeralds through the haze. The comforts only worse, a little food the taste of memories far away. Waymouth's babbling echoing through the *Black Swan*.

Stacie at the captain's card, his charts all well-known to the master pilot. "Frobisher's Strait is in truth a bay." Stacie spoke as he pointed. "There Frobisher found his first gold." He, in searching stare, silently asked the question with his eyes, in the quiet. "That take is played to its full folly."

Darkness walked the lower decks, lamps shadow into blackened smoke, as Stacie marshaled all his strategies. "Our captain lies abed. His command is done. The crew fears him lunatic with some devils as his pets." All agreeing. Waymouth screamed words to curse our deaths.

The sea raptured to a soft breeze. Waymouth in his cabin tied to a cot. The cabin as plain as night, stagnant in a breathless damp. Waymouth did not move, but screamed, "You are dead! Howl to your decay. The nuptials of the grave await. Crackle the bones of your bending knees. You may yet lie your mummied rags with a wizened bride."

Small ice in rolling slush and broken sheets, the fog thickening cold. Ten leagues within the Mistaken Strait. Waymouth babbling of a warm beach, the tropics and its jungle heat.

"The captain's hands are badly twisted in the ropes," the cry from below.

"Take care. Loosen the bindings, but be at watch." Stacie at the wheel, considering of the course as he spoke.

A heavy snow fast falling in the suddens of a quicken squall. The gray flutter of the canvas sails, lost in the inundation of the swirling flakes.

"Off to port. A Ship!" The call from the main.

"A ship?" repeated Stacie. "A shadow?" frantically questioning. Nothing seen but whites against the moiling white and grays.

"Heading south, she was," the lookout cried.

"Signal cannon to the ready," Stacie playing full captain in his orders. No one saw the ship. The cannon fired, to hurl a vacant thunder. No response echoed in the empty quiet. Another volley, as we tacked to take up the vapor chase.

Falling was the blind of snow, all swept in repetitions. Then a smudge, a fancy hauled to form. Its lines iced in pallor, its canvas a wander blown as lace flowing in the trailings of its torn sails. "A ship!" The words in whirling hiss. All thoughts upon the passing vapor, a ghost derelict, moving its echoes in the turmoils of a mist.

"A ship!" The watch cried upon the mast. "A ship to port." The snow in obscuring depths. "Swing to port," the call.

The *Black Swan* took up its chase, following upon a guess pinned to a compass point. A sudden sound disfiguring the weighted air. Ellis discharged a firelock, the report echoes into the salvos of a hundred ghosts. Dimmer the blast reverberates, until unvoiced. All is cold and the weather hurts within the bone. Vapors have numbed beneath the skin. All stand as a shiver sensed.

Our cannon's thunder again rolling deeply into the heavy damp. The *Black Swan* calling to its wanderer. How the mist floats upon the sea. The ship obscured. Our compass was our ear. No cannons answering our firelock, no trumpets answering shouts, no drum calls of recognition.

"The ship is death and we follow choked upon its leash!" screamed Waymouth. "Soon enough we will be boned with little flesh." Waymouth laughed.

The snow in white shivers descending through the hush. For a moment, a glimpse, the ship closer off our bow. Like a colorless silk, a weighted nothing, she floated upon the secrets of the unseen sea. "How looms this frozen gossamer? How rolls this shade poised a shape? No sign of life."

Closer now. The shrill in its suddening clamors. "I have torn my freedoms." Waymouth on deck, almost laughing, a madness chiseled in his matted filth. Frayed ropes hanging from his bloodying wrists, and in his hand a menacing pike, its curved edge grinning in its deadly lunatic. "I have chosen of the way," Waymouth said, slowly pushing a kayak with his foot toward the rail and its now open gate. The sea hidden except for the suddens of the mountains of rising swells. Waymouth held a rope tied to the kayak's bow, lowering the leather weight into the wrestling of the undertows, ever holding to the rope, keeping the kayak against the *Black Swan*'s hull.

Nothing said, Waymouth smiled, looked toward the bleached insinuations of a distant ship, his head motioning toward the destructions of its mainsail. Our crew's pleadings ignored. "There! Heaven, safeties and my old friends," Waymouth said, leaning toward the half-hidden coffins of the ship. Then he disappeared, climbing down the *Black Swan*'s ladder to the kayak.

We rushed to the rails. Waymouth, paddle in his hands. Three strokes and he was beyond our grasp. The sea foamed now in an angry rush, blizzards turmoiled as if a suffocation was falling from the air. "The captain, he be rowing toward that ship, he is," said a Johnny of the crew.

"Be damned and all!" Continents of the clouds and snow swirled across the kayak's wake.

"A dream ship, me thinks, a legend made by the cruelties of the snow," said the Johnny in his foolish youth.

"More like a ship pressed in hidden guilts and secret crimes," Stacie's words. "Nameless, without flag, its sails a serpent's robe."

The wind shifted in its course, circles to our face, then from the west. "Changeable this snow typhoon." The remark unheard. The figure obscuring fog, the snow.

"Waymouth gone, lost by the eye!" screamed Stacie.

"He be headed there, in hard paddle to that ship," called the watch. What he said all doubt had any Waymouth to it. The squall too deep upon the blast.

The sea tossed in its battering gale. In fear of capsize, the crew into the masts, sails trimmed to an unknown course. There was no possibility of pursuit. The storm had claimed the ministries and our last rescue.

Resignation is not a bravery or a joy, just an impatience to have the end and some relief. There could be little plot or navigations through the tempest. Such graveside mockeries, Waymouth desperate to forget his terrors. Slowly did he discard the garments of his final worth. Act then your suicides as you panic, I thought, as I set it all to my unfinished book. And shall I have my own immortalities, so like Waymouth through my epitaphs?

Chapter Twenty-three

HOW BLOOMS THE RUIN, EXHALANT IN ITS WEED.

NSULTS THE MARKERS of my path. No pleas in fisted eloquence from me, no letters, no intersession of my friends,
the company held indifference as its pet, while Gates and
Dale sent captains with hogs and cattle and handfuls of
supplies to found settlements at places named for virtues: Hope in
Faith, Charity Fort, Fort Patience, where Reverend Whitaker had
his parsonage, but no lands to me; and places addressed to recall our
histories: Elizabeth Fort, New Bermudas. Some were named for the
grand longings for things familiar and far away: Rochdale, Shirley's
Hundred, Digs, Coxendale, Rockehill. The forest succumbing to an
English will by the force of words. Many companies spread to grow
small crops of private corn. The common kettle almost forgot. Better
the diet, but the crop still not enough. Laziness still the thief of all success. The memories of tobacco a hidden ride upon the companies.

I lost myself in time. My chance of return ever my determined
hope. The winter came. The winter went. A false spring held its
heat upon the frost. Rolfe experimented on those lands to grow best
his crop. Others now tried the same. He sailed the rivers to distant
settlements. In April on some whim and on the tide, Percy sailed for
England, never to return. His passage hard, the ship almost sank. The
food ruined, they almost starved. Saved by a passing English ship, they
were given fish and bread and, for their pleasures, tobacco, in which
they all had some delight. The ship anchored in Dover Road. There,
Percy met with Argall, who was now readying to set sail for Virginia.
The two passed an hour in conversation, then they parted, Percy
to the wars in the low countries, there to be insulted with wounds,
having one of his fingers shot off, Argall to the Chesapeake.

ON SEPTEMBER SEVENTEENTH, 1612, THREE YEARS AFTER I GAVE
up the presidency of the colony, Captain Argall made his third return.
Three by three, the prophecy spoke in its symmetry. The tobacco

grew well that year, the second crop. "Everywhere," Todkill wrote, "lay its dry fruit, everywhere it cured. It lay in small piles under hay or dried in the sun, the leaf laid bare. Even in our cabins it sweated fragrance under blankets. Everywhere its perfume. Everywhere men played to tease a better smoke."

Back two weeks, Argall came to see Todkill with Rolfe and a man never seen before, Ralph Hamor, the new secretary of the colony, and one well jeweled in manner to kneel a service before any noble. Rolfe spoke of tobacco and its yield in weight per acre. All the certainties in numbers and degrees, all the speculation gone to a tally. Rolfe had become a man who sought his God in sums. "Three hundred pounds this year. How much good?" Hamor asked. "One hundred pounds, most lost to our ignorance of curing and a proper harvest time. All learning comes. Next year a better hope. We ship some leaf to England. But our leaf is good, not best, and in that taste is the proportion that holds the gain." Rolfe smoked. They had their pipes and pleasures. Hamor would grow tobacco on his private plot. "Indulgence to this dry leaf, its fruit, shall make this Jamestown a new Jerusalem," he said. "I know few stars that can bring such certainties. We are the egg of a new apostle, our shell in hammered leaf, our birth in the breaking of fragments into flames. What Moses are we to part the seas in fire, our manna on the wings of drying leaves?"

A serpent's chill slithers upon my spine. *Our savior will not be a weed*, my thought. *Be patient. I will sly my cause in secret ways. Be patient.* Words in my own voice. Mine the only resolve. All my visions null.

"Patience is a timid grave. A year spent. Time in lethal hours slips the promise. What is this, but a noose by minutes, a gallows by the hourglass? I will not hold my moment idle for yet another year. I thought by counsel and advise. Be secret but be swift. The forest is a battlement where soldiers are still loyal to my cause," I said.

NOTHING HEARD FOR WEEKS, SCRAPES, AND RUMORS, AND RUMORS of scrapes, but little learned. Then a letter. The corn harvest good, but the stores low. Still the hollow light of winter, the sun in heatless shine upon the hand. There was the fear of famine once again. Dale and Argall had made expeditions to trade for corn with the savages. There was little to be had. Only three hundred bushels gotten, and at the price of war. Powhatan had his way, and Dale almost murdered by another arrow. No one thought of peace.

Hamor always speaking from the easy surface of his mind. "It is not for the colony to provide itself with corn and other victuals, but for the savages to supply it to us. We are a salvation to them, for which some pay is due." Hamor even in his rancid clothes. Most had only what they wore. The gentlemen had three attires of which to make some choice. They were a poor group and no hook would make them seem the richer.

"It is a bad sport to make our own sins someone else's absolutions," Todkill said to Hamor, and then to Argall, "Be as Captain Smith would advise. Go trade with the Potomacs, exchange hostages. Be at peace with them. War serves only a fool's purpose here."

Hamor took offense. The guilty would have us polite to shield themselves from their inner coward's discontent. "All this from a man in London, in his shabby rooms," Hamor said. "Friendless...without true vision." Then he stood and sneered and left.

SEPTEMBER SIXTH 1612—POTTS' FIST HAMMERING AT MY DOOR. He cried the news in bludgeoning words, as the closing of a coffin lid, my enterprise its tomb. "It is learned Pocahontas is married."

"Married. Is it done?" I said.

"A savage captain named Kocoum, that is all that is known."

How simply drained I am of all intent. My anger sorrows in its regret, willful to a willful hate. Does every passion claim its cause? I am abandoned of a soul. I the idle husband to an empty gown. She that falters discards our forest path. All my directions are lonely trod. If I could but relive my life, reforge those moments of long ago, and tongue by sliding tongue the hungers of my bequest.

"Any news of children?" I asked. Potts shrugged and prattled on.

I in loss, grieved to the herald in a secret grief. Other's advice, so distance, an annoyance in the gloom. Convicted of myself by another's act. Have I played my destiny, fretted my life, a forfeit to the one I was to live? Do I love her yet? My passion keeps. And so we move from our birth, guess by guess, to crawl the contagions of our choice.

Where are my visions now? The voices mum a cadence to a silent fit. Not warned she was to wed. No word, no sketch, no colored hint. This giftless joke gives only after the wound is bled. Shall I have my quiet after a candle dies, later in the night by a nightmare post? How does the beseeching pauper pray, naked to his parting angel, perfect in her ruined wilderness?

No news from nothing comes, for months I meet with worthies who have some society with the king and the London Company. Returning to my rooms, I know this is all a diplomatic taunt. Still my quills scratch, paper their feeble meal. Potts and I salute each other in our ink. Digressions play their tired sermons. Jamestown information scarce, but some, as history, pleads its forest retributions.

ON DECEMBER FIRST, WITH PERMISSION FROM GATES, ARGALL sailed toward the Potomac River for trade and to have some exploration. Before he left, he spoke to Todkill of the antimony mine I had found on some voyages of discovery. Argall, using my maps and my old directions, found the mine, and one of lead, as well. All by me through him, he to his own, saw not the wonders of the place. Sailing then on the compass of his greed, his eye but for corn.

He made the Potomac village. The *werowance*, Iapassus, away on some hunt, he waited, piked on his impatience. Iapassus returned in great joy to see an English friend. So he thought Argall's face a brother to mine. An exchange of hostages and the savages' store of corn stood in such feasts Argall ordered a small shallop built to ferry it to his ship. Eleven hundred bushels of corn for the colony's supply and another three hundred bushels Argall kept for his own men to hold their loyalty and keep them in health.

BY FEBRUARY THE CORN WAS AT JAMESTOWN. DALE TALKED OF more violent campaigns against the savages. The colony talked instead of other voyages and other explorations. Rolfe talked of tobacco and on which lands it grew best. "The old Indian fields are richer by far than the new cleared land. The savages by planting many crops on small mounds found that balance where crops feed each other and the soil." Some colonists in their private plots grew, as the savages did, a mix of plants and vegetables on mounds with tobacco. Rolfe always planted his tobacco alone. Not knowing, the soil weakened and the land, in its exhaustions, died.

ROLFE, IN MARCH, MOVED TO HENRICO TO PLANT HIS TOBACCO ON the old Indian lands and to make his trials on different fields. Argall took to building a frigate on the mudflats of the James. By the middle of the month it was near full built. The new tobacco seeds had begun to thrust above the earth. Across the colony fields lay under hay to protect the tiny plants from frost. Early in the months of spring, Argall sailed to make explorations and trade again with Iapassus and the Potomacs.

Argall boarded his ship, the *Treasurer*, on March nineteenth, 1613. With him went Indians friendly to our cause. Argall's ship was no barge or fragile pinnace, but a hull that met the ocean and called it kin. The mast, its sails, cannons on her deck swung into a forest threat. The river speaking histories beneath her planks. *What the ear doth lose*, I thought to amuse myself. I heard no more of him for months. Tobacco grew in the silence of its early spring. It was transplanted to hills, where men hoed the dirt to keep the weed-soft bed. The corn crops on the private plots showed progress. The public lands half planted with silk grass and some already-spoiled corn. No tobacco there. The weed held for richer prospects. Yeardley and Dale and Gates and Hamor had some of the indentured servants of the company work their private plots. The company fields abandoned to neglect, and so by slights comes the consequence.

Chapter Twenty-four

WE LOVE BY FRAGMENTS OUR PASSIONS
TO MAKE WHOLE.

ROUND ME THE GATHERS of my books. The clock clicks its relentless narrative. The quill with its bloody ink assaults each page, and my eye is cast an exile from those Jamestown events. My excluded flesh, my wisdom torn as witness to that distant pantomime. A dumb show, quiet but for the letters, reports, shrill in their untongued script. Pleas marked from terrors in hand, blotched pools of blotted ink. And then Todkill, my faithful oracle, how I feel the doom of this disquiet. His new letter to my desk, I read the apocalypse.

April then in its second week, a morning came in excited talk. Words in fragments. "Pocahontas…made prisoner." In sleep awakened, my mind in disbelief. Senses eaten of no understanding. Laughter all about. "Argall has her hostage on his ship," someone screamed. "We are delivered from murder. Powhatan is overthrown." The company to its excitement. Voices rose on voices. Wild wishes had plundered sense.

More news each day. "She comes as a royal guest, Argall her host and protector." The few women at Jamestown prepared a cabin as her humble palace, Reverend Buck and his wife to be her shepherds. Dale and Gates silent. Argall not yet arrived, having no permission for his purpose, sat some danger. In Jamestown power was to the one whose story first had Gates' ear, and he, the always squanderer of opportunities, sat fast his presumptions.

Banners flew and tangled in the breeze. Ranks of armored soldiers stood line by stately line when Argall brought his ship to the new dock. Gates and Dale in full uniform, all their captains and all the council massed to receive the princess of the royal blood, an emperor's daughter. To Gates and Dale, rank and blood served more than circumstance to guide their attitude. A savage she might be, but a savage of the royal blood, therefore royal, and entitled to all the pomp and dignity of her estate.

They might have her prisoner, they might think her savage, but call her "royal" and the weight of that birth bent their knees. Strange content we are when self wars in contradiction on the self. That struggle vouches mystery. Its tatters the charnel rag house that binds the soul. Blindness does not always leave us in the dark, but sometimes sparks an overflowing light, where happens good.

Pocahontas well treated, not tortured or abused. Hamor and Gates and Dale waited for Argall to make some report.

Hamor had his serpent's smile, and raised his eyebrow, hearing the footfalls of familiar boots. Argall then walked through the door, his body speaking in movements that this was a man who had accomplished some great aim. He sat and grinned, awaiting the approving dust to settle. Impatience now the quiet, the moments fled. Finally Hamor asked Argall to be so kind. He told of his explorations on the Pembroke River, seeing herds of wild beasts like oxen all hung with hair, their large heads short-horned, which the savages called buffalo. "Some of which we killed, the meat being wholesome and of good taste," he said. "Our Indian guide led us to mines wherein the earth has a physic to calm the stomach. We drank healthful water which had a taste of alum. We saw a strange red clay that did float on water. In our explorations I learned Powhatan's daughter was then living with the Potomacs. There was an opportunity vaster than any land. I sailed at once, told Iapassus what I knew and demanded that he betray the girl to me, or I should never be his brother or friend again. Iapassus said that he could not, such a deed would bring Powhatan's armies upon his people. I told him not to fear, for he would have an England as an ally. He went to confer with his great king, his brother, and the council. Their approval given, the snare was laid to catch the bird who would bring the peace and also return our hostages and stolen weapons at no cost of blood. It was a boldness worthy of Captain Smith," Argall said, "the student taught beyond the wisdom of his seer."

Argall had his momentary brag, salted on a little hate. Argall then continued, "Iapassus's wife told Pocahontas that a bearded Englishman wished to speak with her and renew an acquaintance of long ago. Powhatan's daughter did agree to a meeting, coming to the beach where I stood near my ship. She first ran and called me, 'Smith.'"

I crushed the papers in my fist, as I thought, *So much she is, and so much less to be so bought by a costume clowned in a resemblance. But it is not so far the mark for love to unearth a counterfeit. Each glance desires, as passion quakes a solace in a masquerade. We are the presumptions the slights of surface make. The deeper stuff, the kennel for a different hound. Did she succumb to him, thinking him another me? Have I failed my ever love, unworthy even to be my only kin, my life now cast in surrogates, my self strangled on some mirror's whim?*

"Seeing I was not Smith, she said, 'He is then dead.' I made no answer but said she had many friends among the English, and I was one.

"Iapassus's wife then asked to visit upon my ship. I played at anger at hearing her request, saying no woman could go aboard my ship alone. She then fell in full tears and misery as was our plan. I did relent, making this permit. She would go if Pocahontas would accompany her as escort. Pocahontas at first refused, knowing of her father's anger, but seeing Iapassus's wife in tears, she did agree. Aboard the ship we went to a gunner's room, I feasted them, showing all kindness and regard. We left Pocahontas to have some rest. Iapassus and his wife I did reward with a copper kettle and some beads. Returning to Pocahontas we did see her suspicious and much upset. I told her she could not leave as I sought eight of our English held captive by her father and many tools and weapons stolen by the murdering of our men. Pocahontas now stood cold in her dignity, royal in her bearing, no girl or child but a majesty, her blood beating to its truer self. Iapassus cried it was all his fault and begged for forgiveness. Pocahontas pulled to herself in her certain power, in sculptured royalty, eyes upon me high in their silent address, she ignored the pleas of Iapassus. 'Come with me,' I asked, 'not as prisoner, but as princess and as my honored guest. No harm shall touch you, be the instrument of a peace as once you were. Let us be all Smiths to you, our young savior of the nations.' She then calmed and sat and shortly so agreed, I sailing at the tide, sending Indian runners to inform Powhatan of what had happened."

So many cross-purposes in my mind, too many half-spent thoughts. "Does she know I am alive and here, but seas apart?" I asked. Todkill's script not quick enough before the eye.

She now wears English clothes. Some weeks well-guarded in a company of women, given many gifts, treated beyond the call of her royalty. Little thought she would play for some escape. One day I had by chance a conversation. I said that I was your friend, but for fear of death, I could not tell her, except by hint, that you were alive. She spoke of messages to her father that you were sailed upon an English ship, trading along the bay, speaking as a *werowance*. She ran to the rumors, but nothing found, so she stayed closer to the river and the coast.

Are we all the play of shadows? I played at me. Are we all damned by the echoes made of our ambitions? I mused my desperation into philosophies. Her voice far away began to cry into my ear. Another river this. My loves confused. The forest in the passions of her arms, a weave unrequited in their ecstasies.

Then by spite I tried to suggest that you lived. "And your husband?" I now asked. There was only a silence for an answer, then she said, "I am daughter to a king. As any woman, my marriage is ended by my word and the king's consent. I am free, but for that word given but not yet said."

"The time may come for that word be said," I spoke, staring a knowing deeper stare.

That night Hamor laughed to my face. "Such heresies in these easy divorces. Well, if there be no God among savages, why should there be a proper marriage?" Then he raged in disgust, adding, "Oh why should I care how they spend their women?" He looked at me.

"And why should you?" I answered in a cautious nothing.

Then he said, "We should leave it to our church and its iron ministers."

The tobacco planted in separate hills, the roots bit deeply into the darkness of the earth, its growth as searching strangers to the alien soil. Gates sent new warnings to Powhatan. "We want our prisoners and our stolen weapons if you wish your Pocahontas returned." Powhatan sent back seven of our company, well fed and treated fairly, in a better state than most at Jamestown. Although they said that they lived in slavery and in a constant fear among the savages, they seemed not overly pleased to be at home.

With them they brought three broken firelocks, an ax, a long whip saw and one canoe of corn, which brought Dale into a rage. "There are more of our weapons and tools in Powhatan's lodge than we ourselves have in all Virginia." Reverend Buck told Pocahontas that her father refused to trade for her release. "You have another father now," said the good reverend in a stammer, "the lord and king of us all."

"Is my father not my father?" Pocahontas said in a tearful question. "Am I child to what?" Confusions are the prey of easy certainties. "My gods no longer my gods? Okee but a cloth of rags nailed to some wooden log?" Reverend Buck spoke his case, our guns, our iron, the machineries of our altar and the testaments over our covenant. "If Okee is not god, then from whom does my father speak? Do our priests beast upon air and nothing holy upon my life?" A doubt that fractures nations and spills wisdom to its death. A child now uncertain of a father, all authority now a squeal.

The tobacco now stood to heights above men. The weed so quiet in its sentinels, its leaves in wait. Time ticked its digits in its summer's clock. The tobacco harvest soon begun. Leaves in piles, drying in the air. Dreams of pipe making a frantic work for some, while most of the colony rested lazy in the heat. Even the guards mostly slept or walked about, the fort gates rarely locked.

Captain Robert Adams in the *Elizabeth* arrived with more supplies of food and men. Commotion in the streets all night. Pocahontas could easily walk the fort. She stayed to herself. The unloading of the *Elizabeth* cost the colony a week of labor. It was a lazy progress. Meanwhile, the tobacco cured to each grower's taste. Some did not even dry the leaves, but packed them wet in stacks to be shipped to London. Others spent what time and skill they had to thoroughly dry the leaf, then packed them into hogshead barrels, or laid it flat between canvas tied with ropes, the whole bundle called a hand. Sometimes wet tobacco was packed with dry, which ruined all. The cargo was brought to the ship and stacked, death in herald alchemies, the weed piled upon the dock. The magic stilled and readied in its leaf. The ship then loaded. Rolfe stayed at Henrico with his crop. Argall gone to his explorations. He having no opinion of Pocahontas other than she was a strategy, or of the savages other than they were about.

Jamestown now returned to its general laze. The night sharp again in black. The tobacco slept in its contagions in the ship's hold. No sentries were at our door. At midnight she walked upon her lonely shadow. Silence. Some eyes about. She could have escaped.

She stood now dressed, no more savage paintings to her face. A woman like any woman walked inside the heathen shell. She came to the dock. She sighed. (Was that breath for some last hope of Okee's miracles?) Captain Adams and the *Elizabeth* almost under sail. She now gazing longingly into the far-flung dark, dreamily.

I, in London, could almost sense the touch through the thousand other distracting ardors. The sting is soon enough. *I failed*, I thought. *The blight is that nothing holds the mind.*

Footsteps on the wooden planks. Gates and Reverend Buck and soldiers stormed to her side. She screamed as they carried her into the night, Reverend Buck walking after the struggling form, repeating softly, "Please, dear, be at peace. There is nothing meant. You are safe."

Gates running, Pocahontas held by soldiers grasping at her arms. "There will be no treachery with savages here," he said.

As in the hold of the ship lay barrels and flats of tobacco leaf, they soaked the air in smells of a fevered breath, that world of dark reeked of curing smoke. The ship rocked, then cast off. The water rushed, passing across its hull, spars in full canvas sailing toward the moon deep sea, and the cries of whales echoing through the drowned darkness of our fetid sleep.

MUCH OF OUR LIVES ARE THE QUAINT OF SIMPLE TIDINGS, MOSTLY we ignore, the surface but the delay of hidden thunder. Todkill's words a crush upon the ponders of my heart. Are all my desires not for me? What love can cast away its love? I will not fail, my circumstance rages light, rages dreams. Lands and her flesh await. My plans an assembled web, more visits, more letters.

Thoughts of Acadia and northern Virginia now in the London air. Argall to assemble a fleet, sail north into the hurricane and destroy again the French colony in Acadia. South then to spy on the Dutch in New Amsterdam, upon the island Mannahata, where Hudson's northern river flowed, passing toward the sea. And Waymouth, for all your suicide, the English had not the ambition to have it for ourselves. The Dutch too well armed. Argall sailed with his little that was enough, drank Dutch wine, bowed the diplomatic bow and so returned to Jamestown.

Gates pleased, but I will not be thwarted of my wilderness. The letter continued.

Gates to leave to rejoin his troops in the Netherlands, Dale coming to the full of his power. He, never trusting Reverend Buck, sent Pocahontas to Henrico to Reverend Whitaker, more his man, and in truth much the smarter, with kindly eloquence to convert the girl to our Christian faith. She always held to you, Smith. Her thought your faith would bring her closer yet. The forest and its devils to her back, the waters of the river flashed and sparkled upon a sunlit course, she made her voyage north. "The familiar has come as death to my eyes," she said to Reverend Buck, who accompanied her. Strange words, I think, even for a savage, but who's to know their meaning? "A true God will give them life again," said Reverend Whitaker when hearing the report. A subtle man, his charities never held back or overspent, he knew his practice well.

She was rarely guarded in Henrico, treated ever kindly, told by all her father would not trade our stolen weapons for her release, which was true, to the shallows of its truth, but there was more to be said. Our tools were better weapons than anything he could have. "He loves more that rusted metal than your living flesh. Who is it that loves you more?" said Reverend Whitaker. She asked all of their knowledge of you. "Where is he now? Is he well? Is he to return?" Some answered that you had fled to England, others said that you had died, it being said by everyone that you were no longer in Virginia and it was thought you were never to return.

It was said she sorrowed and through her sorrow she begged to some strange hope. Hope ever failing the wear of memory. The world distracts, and we cobble our passions from a tinker's tune. When Reverend Buck arrived with Pocahontas in Henrico, he met again John Rolfe, whom the good reverend knew from the Bermudas. It was Reverend Buck who baptized Rolfe's daughter, Bermuda. The girl not surviving, nor the wife. And so it was on the instigation of a memory that Rolfe and Pocahontas met, Buck seeking out Rolfe and in consequence introducing that fateful two.

Rolfe always to the tending of his fields, as he prepared for the next year's crop, the earth raw and stripped bare. The hills sculptured upward, naked in rounded desolation. Hay lay in stacks at the corners of the fields, waiting to cover the seedlings to protect them from the frost. Pocahontas walked those fields, sunburned the rough straw and dry beneath her feet. Rolfe speaking to her, another Englishman in her life. His beard, his face, one of us like all, but, to her in her memory, confused with you. We live our memories. We see our past in every present.

> The mind is a clockless work. What held her to herself was that
> you still lived. And so they walked those fields together, each in
> a different place, holding to a different time.

Everywhere the talk is thrilled, nowhere lips the truth, that
Jamestown is the word to hide a wreck, its muddy path a wayfare for
the march of corpses. How many deaths to account the ledgers of the
council as a single death? Hundreds now, thousands soon, and then a
message from George Sandys, "Your friend Anas Todkill is expelled,
an exile forever from Jamestown. The excuse, bringing written slander
upon the colony and its governor."

The question now springing upon the clock, when, by what
month his return? Richards Potts and I in fever to see again our
fellow adventurer. What news too dangerous for the quill, but only
for the secret breaths against the ear? And for me, how profounds the
histories that I chronicle? By what lure, chance or fame, did Todkill
pledge his life to mine? A stipend seems too thin a coin, exploration,
and the enterprise a better smile.

And now the wait by month? by week? by sails before the wind,
a voyage to a nation as a silly pup. In weeks, on April 17, 1613,
Todkill's fist came a hammer at my door. Embraced, we the fallen
have embraced the fall. Such an arrival so well met. A company of
three, companions against the thoroughfares, where carriages scrape
their painted wheels, as horses pulled through the riches of the
chamberpots.

Todkill sat, still in his armor. "I am in fear," he said. "I have my
sword not beyond the length of my arm."

I nodded. "The London council is not for murder."

Todkill laughed. "Council? It comes of thieves that walk this
London: pickpockets, way men, mud pirates, whores. The Virginia
swamps have less a fester."

We all in some mirth. "And how goes Virginia?" The question
from Richard Potts.

"I escaped without a knuckle bloodied." Todkill's mood more
tightened. "Virginia is now a pipe, its bowl but for tobacco."

"WHEN CAPTAIN ADAMS RETURNED IN THE *ELIZABETH*," TODKILL
rendered his explanations, "he brought news that the tobacco fetched
three shillings a pound in London. Men then broke their backs

laboring for the weed, those who had never labored to plant a grain of corn. New lands cleared. The earth torn open to be laid bare. With so much death, greed became the only promise.

"It saddens me that with Captain Adams came another rumor of your death, although the captain swore he never said it. The crew saying they heard it without the memory where. A public desire had pleasured its own rumor, I think," said Todkill. "The company itself disbelieving, repeating it just the same. Pocahontas heard the tale all about, Reverend Whitaker repeating it was so. Dale, knowing the rumor to be untrue, repeated it to Pocahontas's very face. 'Pets make better pets when they sleep well in their tether,' said Dale. Rolfe needing Dale and wanting what he wanted, even if he had her by a lie.

"Pocahontas still hoping that you lived. Englishmen spoke sweetly their tales, treating her well. They looked like you, spoke as you. She began to believe."

My thoughts despaired upon the rocks of continents. When does every worth foul its counting house? No chance for Rolfe's lust to fail its bed. He too dull for the boredom sameness stakes. I am bitter to myself, dressed naked in a clown's attire. And so she came to love Rolfe, for he was nearer, closer to the familiars of her past. Passion always seeks a silhouette, the firmer bite left to its demented reason. Pocahontas now walked her courtship, Rolfe by her side. Pilgrims blinded each in their own Jerusalem, their path lost beneath their feet, they wandered toward their histories.

THE TALE TOO BLATANT IN MY EARS, I NEEDED INTERRUPTION. "I visited Mortlake some time ago, spoke to Goodwife, your mother. She then well."

"And so she reigns, a pleasant feeble, if not by rumor a helpful local witch. Much beloved. A skirtful Dee, in a village way, and quite a spiteful tongue."

"I had notice, mostly of the fangs." We both laughed. "She secrets no mind for unsaid thoughts," I smiled through my words.

"Most true, but friend Smith, are we chasing that unsaid question by its rump?"

Richard Potts confused, but ever to his quiet, as I nodded, "yes."

"Lord Willoughby, having associations by wealth, or court, or explorations with Dee and Jonas Profit, and learning of my desire to fight the Eastern Turks, brought a purse by his steward with this request. Sums for arms and armor in a protestant regiment, and I to be of protection and friend to you. Fellows in war and adventure. Jonas, Dee and his lordship having chosen you in some regard. The weapons paid, the purpose done." Todkill's heavy thought upon the breathless silence. "I came home after our separation at Red Tower Pass. I made report of your death to Dee, who said, 'I shall inform Master Profit. Smith was of some noble birth, I believe.'"

What fathers now, scarce remembered, a phrase inflicted wrong. True, my mother of a better station, but some far slip from any scepter or a crown. Perhaps my lineage over said. My father not of any better blood.

Todkill continuing, "When you returned with wealth and desires for the west, you asked of me, learning that I, too, lived, sending me a generous purse. No need for freight, I would have done it for the joy.

"But others, Profit and Willoughby's sons, hearing of the em-paupered Dee, sent some coins each month. Your purse remained for my mother's use." But still Todkill's words are wild dogs barking at my ears. A noble birth, what means this?

TODKILL ALSO CARRIED THE REPORTS AND LETTERS OF THOMAS Studley of the original supply, then dead some years. There were other reports and documents of those still in Virginia. Together we three set our task to write a book of the most complete knowledge and history of Virginia. Enough told to teach the teller. It was a desperate play against all fates. Perhaps I could receive my Virginia passage. Words became me in my revolt. We worked not quite in secret. Samuel Purchas, who was compiling his own collection of English exploration, sought my advice. We became friends, I giving him my firsthand accounts. He having many important associates and influence even to the reaches of the court.

With the great Richard Hakluyt, a friend of Dee, I exchanged letters. Dee, who dreamed of an England overseas, gave the words to knuckle Drake's great fists. It was Hakluyt's books, the work Dee began, which called for English explorations. "We are late to explorations, but our rights to dominion are not any less than Spain's or Portugal's but more, for we are by God and his truth anointed to plunder upon the plunderer and to save the world." He, now aging, wrote to me, "Think of Dee and old Jonas. How many heirs must a great man have to birth an equal?"

"One," said I. My new book was *A Map of Virginia*. The company not wanting it in print, had, through threats and bluffs of suits, every printer in London stand aside. We went to Oxford and there had it done, the book issued with a false date upon its titlepage to protect its publisher.

The company was in a rage, severing all connection with me. Smythe still swore in secret to be my friend. I then at a loss with no means to return to Virginia. Strachey came to see me. He, too, was barred, having written his book, which was passed about London in copies, William Shakespeare having read it, used the descriptions of the great storm which shipwrecked Gates in Bermuda.

A disheartened Sandys wrote me of some events and of my book. "That shipwreck in Bermuda and Virginia now to the conscience of our nation. It slipped to its own meaning. *The Tempest*, our Shakespeare's play, drawn from the consequences of those deeds. His mind raptured in its imagination to its own intent. And I a poet, they say, but a poet by paraphrase, I start my new book, my Ovid in English. I am not as you, my words are to the surface born, my imagination over thought. My feelings denied, then falsely over felt, they jump the gate, come as thin. Passion does not blush upon my work. My rhapsodies break unsensed from consequence. My words crack in hollow shells while yours their meanings bowed, and in that bend there is power. Rarely can I find the language of the inner voice, even the love of their being mine, the grammars not deep enough. And so I come by halves, refrained, never to be the whole."

Chapter Twenty-five

THE HOURGLASS ABOUNDS IN DESTINIES!

 AM NOT THAT MAN who holds himself thin of opportunities. We are to ourselves a circumstance. In 1611 an English ship took as a prisoner a savage along the coast of northern Virginia near Cape Cod. The savage, brought to England, was landed in Plymouth to a great sensation. There was then rising interest in those northern wilds. The English claims in the New World were then divided between two separate companies, each with a king's charter granting them all monopolies on commerce and colonization within their territories. First the London Company, which held Jamestown and Bermuda and all south; second, the northern Virginia monopoly, called the Plymouth Company, which claimed all from Henry Hudson's River north until it held its head under the roof of the French possessions in Nouvelle-France or Acadia. Waymouth's and Argall's expeditions there awakening the prospects of that vast coast. One a fool, the other a thief, but great histories often bed themselves with foul allies.

Samuel Purchas gave me an introduction to the Plymouth Company's most important spokesman and investor, Sir Ferdinando Gorges. "The time does not appeal to me as promising, but soon…our prospects will break upon the west." Gorges sat with the papers of his other interests, a distracted pile, a nothing, a quill's squander across the epic of our English empire. "The time comes once, and it is soon enough, but time never bows a country while to opportunity," I said.

"You are young in your ambition, and that is to the good. But wealth is not gained by worship of an empty purse. Find me investors for your expedition. Sail that first, then we may try a ship." So saying, Gorges would hear no more.

"The age mellows. Be not its regret," I cautioned.

"Find me investors, then we both have a quiet." Gorges fatherly with a gallows' edge. "It is told, Smith, you have a society so mysteriously above your birth, and a willful humor little weighted in diplomacy. A braggart, a rumored liar, who tripped a noose in time to weave its rope into a pretty coat. Self-kept, no firm society, a rogue knight, a dreamer practiced in the world." Gorges leaned back into his seat. "A pocket not so thin of coins, quick against any slight."

"I am what I must. Words may deflect worlds, but to whose lament? The New World's gives fortunes to each to its own elect." I leaned across Gorges's desk. "I abide no genealogies."

"Dangerous, but to me, I account by profits. Coins seldom have the hazards of a philosophy. Go you to London and by hunt fox me some investors."

Humour ever the prod to great ambition, I thought, as I walked again upon the dank garbage in the mud-swamped streets. *No nuptials here in a forest bridal.*

I was desperate to have a ship. And will she wait, as lovers always dream they wait? I drink from the chalices of your imagined breath. How sweet those eyes in fleeting glance, reflected on that imagined wine.

IN LONDON AGAIN I MET FOUR MERCHANTS WILLING TO FINANCE a voyage to Acadia and northern Virginia, there to fish and whale and search for gold. I ready for the plot. Virginia but a name to them, so shortly said, how quickly sailed. North I would sail along the coast voyaged by Gosnold then by Waymouth, then south to Jamestown. I thought myself then a triumph.

The leader of the group was Marmaduke Rawdon, a cloth merchant, rich and well married. Two ships I had from them and another captain named Thomas Hunt. He to the command of the other ship, possessing the manners which prophesized a future gallows.

On March first, 1614, two days before I was to sail, I heard the news (quaint the tones of our devastation) that Pocahontas was to marry Rolfe.

Chapter Twenty-six

AND SHE HAS BECOME THE SAINT
TO THE MURDER OF HER GODS.

O WORDS, NO WORDS, my tongue did shrivel in its root. All my thoughts in weighted brass, all hollow, but for the burden of their press. I walked an empty flesh. A letter then from George Sandys describing the events, his information coming from detailed reports Sir Edwin had received from Hamor.

Captain Adams then in Virginia, having unloaded his supplies of food and what dispatches there were from the London Company. The ship to sail again. Gates on board. Dale to be left a dreg with full power and brutality.

*W*ithin days of Gates's departure on January 12, 1613, Dale called Rolfe and Pocahontas from Henrico with Reverend Whitaker. Argall's ships freighted with one hundred and fifty soldiers, the strategy for Dale to have his final contest with Powhatan. Pocahontas meeting Argall again, she gave him hardly more than a pleasant notice. She had made her choice. Dale was readying a voyage to seek Powhatan and regain his weapons and his men. Months had passed without word. Now it was time to bring the matter to a close. Pocahontas sailed with the expedition as guest and hostage to bait the hook. She went willingly. Her loyalties turned against her father. She and Rolfe were in love. Everything did dance a madman's wander. No joints did fit, but lunacy by its weight did bind them tight.

Dale sailed to have his moment. Upriver, the savages stood well armed on the edges of the forest. Hamor says there were a thousand bows and arrows raised to have a volley. Dale on deck, the whole of the company shouting that they had come in peace to return Powhatan's daughter in ransom for our weapons and our lost men. Dale having suspicions that Pocahontas would never leave us now. The savages laughed their insults, raging in their bravadoes and their taunts, "If you come for war we will well oblige. Remember what we did to Ratcliffe and his men. If you love your safety and your lives, leave us at once."

"It is foolish to remind us of that treachery," shouted Dale in heated reply, "for now we shall come ashore and have our vengeance." The ships no sooner near the shore than arrows fell in lethal pins. The decks porcupined. A man caught by one in the throat, another in the forehead. None dead but wounds enough to bloody the deck.

Dale was in furies beyond control. Firelocks volleyed, cracked in lightning. Hamor gave the tale in his report. "Once we were on the beach the savages ran to the woods, we following, racing through the trees, volleying havoc as we dashed. The savages turning to loose their arrows. Some shot dead as they paused to turn. Six we killed, many others wounded. We came to their villages, we burned their houses, stole their corn, plundering what we could. We carried their corn in baskets to our ships. Pocahontas below deck. If she knew what had occurred, she said naught, but how could she not have known? The baskets on the deck, the murder in the hills. 'It is of a little war and shall pass for the betterment of all. Your people violence upon us, but you are treated well in our love. Who by this example cannot know we are your friends?' said Reverend Whitaker. Pocahontas was silent. Outside, Captain Yeardley boasted of a kill.

"We stayed the night, anchored in the moonlight shallows. The next day we sailed north and west again. The cold dawn brought mists upon the river. We sailed as if through the catacombs. The sun boiled the mist to a hung cloud above the river. We sailed between it and our reflections on the waters. The savages called to us, hidden on the shore. 'Why do you make war? Burn our houses, crops. We are your friends, love you and want peace.'

"'Then why do you shoot your arrows toward our boats, wound our men, remind us of your murders?' called Dale toward the wall of the forest. 'Why?' he repeated. The voice of the savages coming again. 'It was not us, but stragglers of other peoples, ignorant of our desires.' Other excuses they made, but it was all a simple rouge to thinly paint a lie. We pretended to accept the tale. We beg agreements to have a day of peace. We exchanged hostages to seal the truce. We came on shore, bringing Pocahontas as a sign of our good intent.

"She stood and stepped from the boat, dressed as an English woman. A proud head held stiff in regal glance, she walked toward the savages, who gathered in an embracing arc before her. She walked her silent stare upon her people. Not speaking, only to display some displeasure, she passed among them. When they spoke to her, she answered not. The savages murmured and watched her walk the cold of her disregard. Great *werowances* before her, pushing the crowd aside, speaking to her. She looked not on them, but simply said, 'My father loves me not for he would have his swords and rusted guns and broken axes rather than my return. I will dwell among the English who love me. I am now daughter to them as one who my father has so disregarded.'

"The *werowances* having heard the words from Pocahontas's own lips came to Dale, saying that messengers would be sent to Powhatan at once to know his pleasures. Pocahontas now returned to the boat and sat next to Rolfe, surrounded by our English soldiers. Powhatan then far away in his new capital of Matchcot, his answer was a day in coming.

"And so we sat the night upon our boats, the water in wash about us, the silent shadows of the forest ever upon the flowing darkness of the river. The savages told us our captives with Powhatan, hearing of our coming, had run away into the forest, fearing they were to be hanged, but Powhatan had sent savages after them to bring them back. 'If they run to the Ocanahonan, a great tribe far beyond our forest, they will not be killed but taken in and never will you see them again,' said a *werowance* to Dale.

"In a fury, Dale talked only of subterfuges and delays, ordering our ships to sail toward Matchcot and to bring an end to all this savage bravado. We sailed to Matchcot. There on the beach four hundred savages stood, their weapons ready, daring us to come ashore. We in our armor, guns and pikes in hand, we waded into the river, made the beach. The savages, showing no fear, walked among us, demanding to have a council with our captains.

"A truce then arranged until more answer had come from Powhatan. This was agreed, Dale knowing that it was but a plan to escape with more of their provisions. Yet we agreed to have no war until the next day at noon, and only then upon the sounding of our drums and trumpets. Dale more easy than he might be, having Pocahontas as an extra prize to hold against any loss.

"The truce done, two of Powhatan's sons came to have private words with their sister, to which Dale did readily agree. Upon seeing their sister so well and kindly treated, contrary to the rumors then abroad among the savages, their eyes sparkled in the liquids, and the two played their joys open, promising to have their father ransom Pocahontas's freedom and be forever at peace with us and be our friend.

"One brother stayed with his sister, the other went with John Rolfe and Master Sparkes to have council with Powhatan. It was strange that John Rolfe was chosen. Whether it was for him to confess his love to the father, or whether he was but to look upon the emperor and make some easy acquaintance for some future purpose, no one could know. But always, it seems to me, the event hung on duplicitous strings.

"Powhatan in fear, not receiving any Englishmen, had his half-brother Opechancanough entertain Rolfe and Sparkes in his best manner. They had an open council, direct and honest in the proper guiles of a studied honesty. Opechancanough promised to work for a peace and all that Dale had desired. 'Within fifteen days, your weapons shall be returned to Jamestown. Whatever men of yours we have are free. Some, as you know, have fled to the forest and have found refuge with the Ocanahonan. Those are beyond my brother's power. Let it be with the Ocanahonan. Yours are half returned and will have good treatment.'

"When Opechancanough had finished speaking, Rolfe had his moment at playing Dale. 'As for the Ocanahonan, they are but an excuse. All that you promised is not done, and it must, for we shall return after the planting of your corn and burn your villages, and bring such ruin upon your people as none will walk your lands again. This I swear.'

"Opechancanough listened to Rolfe, then said, 'We will do as we can, for we wish peace. Pocahontas shall stay with Dale as his child as she has been treated well and it is her desire, so let it be our seal in flesh upon this peace. But my friend, as to you, beware. It is the emptiest cave that howls loudest in the storm.' With that, the council ended.

"Dale then sailed to Jamestown. Within a month the tools and weapons arrived at the fort gates. Baskets of corn were brought for trade. Every week Opechancanough sent Dale a present and messages of friendship. 'It is my desire,' said Opechancanough to Dale, 'that we call each other friend, and that our friends be friends, as befitting great captains and great warriors, one to the other, each inseparable.' And so it was that the peace began."

*N*ow the tobacco crop was coming green. No longer was the Indian weed grown much, but was almost gone from the English lands. Only Rolfe's West Indian plants grew, they to the heights above a man's head, giving with its own growth visions to those who grew it. Man's imagination half became the leaves, the rustle on the wind, the demanding weed. Now the colony's ears listened to the breeze, our poetry, a dry plant!

Rolfe, twisted in his many considerations, made war upon himself. Conclusions within him few. He intoxicated himself on his own distress. He loved Pocahontas to a short conclusion: he wanted her to his bed. Rolfe, as I understand him, was pure, but had a dull and shallow mind. Such men live upon a violent edge. No imagination to hold upon a peaceful smile. Thus he could love Pocahontas, yet call for the ruin of her people. He was a man divided, and divided men have divided loves, and so he loved more fiercely to hold himself as one.

Rolfe went to Reverend Whitaker—with lust intruding on his thoughts, no thinking brought him ease. "The savages are not of me," he said. "They are insinuations that poison pleasure. I am lost to myself."

Reverend Whitaker set before him a pipe, relaxed, they chatted as they smoked. "Bear not your burden by yourself. Alone we are the easy prey."

"Can I marry with the heathen and myself not be damned?" asked Rolfe. Reverend Whitaker was silent. Rolfe continued, "And will our children be saved? All my wakenings but glorify the beast. I am moved by animal motions. I am crazed as some caught wild bird, flightless on stricken weights. I am mad by madness, an orphan to my God."

"Men tortured to eloquence are not damned," said Reverend Whitaker. "Their souls speak beyond themselves, their reason gathered. The question is, could you be saved by abandoning others to be damned? What mercy is there to speak in that? We are here upon the mission of the one and solitary truth—to found one nation in its many peoples, a diversity by a common cast and so its strength. An English world to be saved by England for itself, a charity by balance, a loving conquest, a Spain without its ruin."

Rolfe, feeling himself come to ease calmly, smoked upon his pipe. His breath drifted in a warming peace. His world now compelled a simpler place. His Virginia exultant, dull in its lust. Reverend Whitaker questioned, "Is it truly marriage that you seek?"

Rolfe nodded. "Yes."

"And is she willing to be your wife?" asked Whitaker.

"She is most willing. She says that she is an exile in her own land now. Her father has banished her from his cruel love." Rolfe looked at Reverend Whitaker and asked, "Do you know what is meant by that?"

"He is an angered father, abandoning his child to the enemy. This new earth makes easy orphans of all its kin. Its spirit cannot be converted too soon. I will help you draft a letter to Governor Dale asking his permission for you to marry with the girl. Have Hamor deliver the letter, tell him of its contents. He is a prudent ally and will be a valuable friend."

And so Reverend Whitaker drafted the letter, showed it to Rolfe, who made what personal additions he saw fit. A labyrinth of religious deliberations, the letter was honest to the level of an acceptable honesty. "I marry not for the ministries of a carnal affection, but to be saved in that salvation of others in which there is a true conversion. Unbelieving though she is, my own belief will make her truly ours. She whose education has been rude, her manners barbarous, her generations cursed, that even am I perplexed by my love, as if another deeper passion has turned to this condescension. It must be God to some greater purpose saying, "Follow through the smoke into the fire and all will be healed.""

As Rolfe wrote the letter in his hand and signed it, the quill snapped upon the table, the feather breaking in two, as if some barrier, a common thought provoked, had rent a new license in the air.

Dale read the letter and smiled. Something had changed. He happily agreed and approved the match. Hamor so informed. One might now marry with the heathen and have them to our beds. Dale sat alone and thought upon the gnaw of a not-so-subtle desire. We never dream what paths we do open by our example. All consequence is a mystery, even to itself.

The permission being more the point than any of its arguments, Rolfe had his way. Hamor carried to him the news. Pocahontas was pleased, it was said, though not so pleased to show overabundance of affection. Strangely displaced, she wandered through the memory of someone else's life. The subject of her other husband was discussed, Pocahontas saying, "With my choice of you, dear Rolfe, the other ends upon my father's consent. It has ever been our way. Marriage is the choice of equals."

Messengers were sent to Pocahontas's brothers and to Powhatan to inform them of the marriage and to invite them all to Jamestown for the wedding. The sky calmed to the powder of a jointless gray. The water of the river flung wide in shades of secret currents. Rolfe worked his fields of tobacco, transplanting the seedlings to their larger hills. Pocahontas studied with Reverend Whitaker for her renunciation and her conversion by baptism. The gods of her youth were now but sightless dolls, the forest mute, its song sung in hush. No Okee to be appeased, never to breathe again his fires upon the world. One god no longer doing good, for it was his way, or the other doing evil, for it was his. But good and bad but a coin for the single god to accept as payment upon some future passage. The gods were no longer willful, they had passed into the one of the terrible judgments.

In ten days Powhatan sent a messenger saying that he did consent to the marriage. Direct and simple were his words. They seemed to speak censure by the little that they said. Powhatan sent Opachisco as messenger, an aged uncle of Pocahontas, and two of her brothers. He was not coming himself, presumably still fearing the English, or perhaps fearing seeing his daughter more wanton and disloyal than he could openly approve.

On April fifth, Pocahontas was baptized, renouncing her old way and its idols, accepting the one power she could suppose on earth and its one truth. Then she stepped forward into the church, Opachisco by her side as her father's standard, and married Rolfe.

By the alchemies of marriage, she had murdered her gods, cast aside her one true love, betrayed her father, her people—all to marry a shadow, a reflection of a man she shaped into a belief, never truly wanting to know who he was. He was to her an expectation that hopeless desires make real. The longing shattered into mysteries and the many ghosts of a thwarted love. How many haunted masks do we kiss before we find the face? She stood in her borrowed English dress. Reverend Buck read words none of the savages could have understood. The old mariner would have made himself a god by recipes, moving by alchemies the same laws as God. "I shall crack thunder from his beard and lightning from his eyes," screamed the mariner in his last hour, those final exaltations before his death. "Where is Mandinga now, and Drake?" All old Jonas's histories upon him. "They, who would purified the world, must gaze into the fire." And so, Pocahontas before the altar would slaughter all her divinities with a simple "yes."

Dale, in a happy mood, gave presents to Powhatan's kin beyond all reasonable need. The day was in the hollows of a nervous heat. Dale danced some tune before the company and drank one cup of wine too much. His excitements bled upon his skin in sweat, as some thoughts made him shiver in the heat. Reverend Buck and Reverend Whitaker well praised the governor for turning this war into a marriage and a peace. "The lord governor has put our swords to a better use," someone cried, then there was laughter.

Rolfe and Pocahontas left to have their private times, Dale to plan some strategy. The word now spreading through the tribes that Powhatan had married his daughter to the English. Now all were brothers to the same lodge. All forest stratagems were at an end.

Chapter Twenty-seven

THE FOREST TO WAFER, ITS SOUL IS EARTH, ITS
RIVER A SUNLIT SILVER BLOOD. PASSION ABIDES, MY
DESIRE HAS SPENT ITS FINAL MASK.

HE STORY TOLD, I sunk into its epitaphs. Nothing now held the hand of naught. Ducks flew, ravens, small birds of many sorts. The air cooled to a crystal sight. Our watch to the main stood in silhouette, an apparition pledged to be the herald of the dawn. This winter ebbs, the days lengthening into a thicker light.

On March third at six o'clock in the morning in promising heat and daylight, we hauled ropes and anchor, and set our canvas. It was 1614. The time for the northern coast has come to hand. Easy our fleet upon the light swells. The freshening breeze, the canvas bows, the wind's ghost through its powerful invisibilities. Our wake white against the constant ripple of the bay. To sea and shadows we lay ourselves upon our fate.

The horizon drinking silence, the sun risen to a pleasant height, gulls squawk violent welcomes, circle and hover, wings lightly canopied, floated, flourished in their feathered miracles. Their predatory sighted below, their eyes in penetrating hunt, their piercing calls, diving in wave-attacking falls.

"A fair breeze and constant," I joyed in my resurrection. But sudden hangs the rule that we forget. Bastard is the wisdom mothered by surprise.

The blue liquid sea on its iron toss swept in rolls and swells. The air bit its premonitions across my cheek. And I by what scrub have come to love an indolent of an imperfect passion. Bedded by the shadow a shadow makes. Does memory take us all a whore, a feeble to an idyll of the mind's caress? And yet a landscape convenes behind the vapor. Forest, mountain, a trackless continent, its rivers whispered. Abandon flesh, the land awakes! The simple perfect of her enthralling nakedness, I cast down the all that is another's. So be it. The river speaks. The New World abides. I am its exile, its lost apostle. Unname me now, I claim my other birth.

I studied maps, and touched with compass longitudes and parallels the profiles of the world. For seven weeks we sailed. Voices now in whispers mixing in the salted winds, and I am an acolyte to a living voice, which squeaked the mind in hides and seeks, its noise the afterglow of an ancient wedding. In April the joint of sea and sky darkened into land. A broad coast swept in cliffs and beaches, bays, horizon to horizon. Harbors drunk cold in deeps, and depths of sparks and shaded beckonings. This land again called me forth to drown me in her earth. Her secret whispers serpent through my mind. I am home again, the lost, to lose myself again.

WE ANCHORED OFF MONHEGAN ISLAND, NOT FAR FROM THE MAIN. The land around rising in bolts of rock, its cliffs white in stone vehemence from the sea. Trees, a harvest on the land, flung their branched webs to the sky, like the heads of some wild rooted beasts. Hunt's ship brooded near to ours, held in its own silhouette, as if it thought only on itself.

"There is the worm that eats upon the bud," said one to me. "Beware, be warned of Hunt," he spoke. "He is a treachery." I listened, looking toward the main. Those waters rushed beneath the cold wallows, the reflections flashed in coils of fleeing life. Great schools of fish darted in silver swirls. I looked through the water's surface into a living wealth.

Samuel Cramton, our whaler, was well acquainted with that great beast. All about our fleet the leviathans rose their backs in giants and their plumed geysers breaking upon the water's reach. So many we saw, their spouts like bursts of water trees, the sea forested in their spray. We lowered a boat to give them chase, Cramton, a harpoon in his hand, a wooden stake with a small iron barb upon its head. *Such a thin pike on which to catch the whale*, I thought. His boat now to the hunt. Men pulled their weight against their oars, their backs spent in agonies. They drank air and crushed themselves to strive. In their thrust the boat tore the breakers into liquid lace. They chased the whale, Cramton standing on the bow, his harpoon raised, his arm ready to hurl the lance. But our lances are not lances to the whale, more like pins to prick irritations upon his skin.

In anger, the whale turned, its spout bursting venom. It rushed upon the boat, its body rising into the air, the sea exploding as it dove. The men and boat swamped like bugs. The sea raged, then settled, then came to calm. The whale, not in a lethal mood, swam off. Cramton, wet but rescued, never for his prey again. "These be the fierce *jubartes* as the French call them, or finbacks, as they are known to us," he said. "Not good for oil. They are not for any commerce that would be worth their trouble."

I still watched the sea, knowing that in its belly there spoons our success. But time had not yet brought the crew to the desperations of an honest toil. Not so paupered in hope that the work became catching agreeable fish. All that flesh could bring us barreled and easy salted profit.

The next day we rounded on the main, traded for furs. The savages being very friendly and at peace traded what they could. Two ships had already played that land, the furs now gone. We made some attempts to search the coast for gold, that always the hot iron of an idle imagination. It was the only hook to snare investors, and so we made our play to save our faith, but nothing did we find. Nor did I expect to find any of the metal.

We now being desperate to find some means to pay the expenses of our voyage and gain for ourselves and for our backers some small profit, I sat upon the thought, knowing the course to the only answer.

· · · · ·

BY SECOND MAY, WE BUILT SIX SMALL BOATS AND BEGAN TO FISH the rich shallows of the coast. Schools in small silvers of their darts fled in knifed turns and panic before our nets. Forty thousand we took, and salted in our barrels. Mostly Poor John, not much flesh but of some value to Spain. Its worth I reckoned at a shilling a pound. Not enough to pay for our voyage and have a profit, but a beginning to strike a spark of some success.

Most of the crew hauled nets. Our catch filled our holds. I thought I would take a small boat and a crew of nine and sail along the coast. How many lost Edens have I found? Free to be, no closures to bind and suffocate the lungs. Drake to the worship of his sea, me to my more accustomed bride, this land, the green and rock of my salvation. My hand upon the soil of its heart. Its flesh to me, its power through my will. This northern coast an orphan as much as I. Neither Waymouth nor Argall ever held it in much regard. Here I would prove myself again. Virginia was closed to me, that company hostile, having sworn all ill against my name. Pocahontas had gone, as Virginia, to be another man's. This land bells to a single echo. Action has the mind forget, and yet I grasp for a peace my ambition never brings. Is vision but the blindness of the wise? And this new coast mostly unexplored, its maps but scribbles. Even Waymouth drew a joke. Nothing was where it should. I decided to have it real and voyage by sail and weight of oars and draw it true, as I searched for some place to have a colony.

I LEFT CAPTAIN HUNT WITH THE FLEET. HE OF A DARK HUMOR, DID his job, but always with his eyes on another man's throat. My boat to the waters, I with my nine sailed first the coast north by east, hearing tales of Frenchmen who had been trading furs. We voyaged into the shadows of Mount Desert Island, where a year before Argall had destroyed the French colony. Then we came west and south. The coast a brawl of mountains, cliffs and large mud flats. At low tide some beds turned to a mirror of a sucking wallow, where weeds choked the water into a thick reluctant flow. All about the land and sea smelled of a hidden life. On some island we saw salt crusting at the edges of a small pool. "A good salt harvest," I thought, "the beginnings of an industry."

Above the sandy beach and in the hills we saw gardens and fields planted in rich corn. Many settlements lay near those tended downs.

Children fished from rocks in the streams or along the coast. Women carried baskets filled with the rough coins of oyster shells. Men burned logs to make canoes, or mended nets. Everywhere there was a peaceful plenty. The world in its sunshine seemed to laugh.

THE AIR WARM, WE STILL SAILED SOUTH. GREAT RIVERS WE SAW filled with the frenzied fins of salmon. Every season had its own fish. Each day tasted of its own delight. Many times we came ashore, traded with the savages, gathering within twenty leagues of our fleet eleven hundred beaver skins, one hundred otter and one hundred martin skins. All that easy, none showing us any will to hurt. South we sailed through the twists of many islands in Penobscot Bay, past the swirling waters of the great river there. Settlements I saw and many good harbors, dark waters always cool, perpetual in its autumn. With the sea in sunlight, the heads of the waves sparkled in crystal tides. Savages fished on the riversides or hunted on the lakes on the reflections of their own wakes, stillness and deer drinking, poised in a living wax.

We went further south. Cliffs rising in their rocky halls, we sailed through chapels' doors. Music sung in their depth on instruments of flung theologies. Fifty miles we sailed against the coast. Trees in pillars broke the earth. The sea surged against the mountains' heels. South we rowed between the islands, the land coming flat and sandy. The soil fertile, the savages planting corn. We passed the river I called the Kennebec. At its mouth, a village called Androscoggin, which I also named the tributary that emptied into the main before it widened into the bay.

Further south the coast now fractured into a still larger bay. These flats of mud flooded into an endless plain. Life fluttered beneath the ripple of its face. Birds walked to peck at the motion of their hidden food. Twenty-five villages I had seen so far, and harbors by the hundreds.

We met a great emperor of the savages called Bashabes of Penobscot, then leader of the Abnakis and the Sagamores and many yet unknown. Another Powhatan he was, but not as fierce. Their language similar to his. South I sailed, drawing maps. So little can the page record. Details are but details, not the whole. Maybe my chronologies are a little deficient, but in the mind all chronologies are but one. Now we came to a thrust of land and at its point a pile of broken rocks. I called it Cape Neddick from the Indian word which means lonely stand. Gosnold had discovered it when he passed this way in 1602 and named it Savage Rock. I changed the name, as many of mine may soon be changed.

South we sailed again along the tidal flats. The land in its great sweeps, its fierce head toward the sea. We sailed its coast, traveling east around to the land's end. That cape I called Cape Ann. I now voyaged into the depths of a great bay, its lands in cyclones around the watery eye. What need I of Chesapeakes when I had this coast?

Birds rose on clouds of beating wings, their profusions a feathered weave in their rising mists. As a quilt of living lights they flew as one in sudden turns to cut the air. So many birds and so many kinds, their calls and cries in cacophonies screaming toward the edges of the wind. The sea flowed in surges above salmon and whales and cod and haddock, sharks and crabs, oysters and lobsters, cold beneath the clarities of those waters. Everywhere in that bay the air hung in a sweet taste.

Eagles hovered above the circling hawks, their eyes dark against their heads and the snow of their feathers. That bay now filled with many islands, all well planted with corn and groves of mulberries, and well peopled with savages and their towns. Gardens and everywhere good harbors, and the savages in great troops, and kind and friendly, fierce in their restrained vigilance, walking to the shore. Three thousand on those islands, I would guess. We met them, trading for what they had. The French, now gone, had stayed five weeks among them, so little there was for us.

Into that bay a goodly river emptied, which I called the Charles. All that land was a garden of gardens, a paradise of that coast, its finest, most fertile earth. I called it by its Indian name, which means "At the Great Hill." I called it Massachusetts.

All about they lived in plenty: deer and turkey, beaver and otter, bears and foxes, wolves and moose. This earth rhapsodies only life. The savages there traveled not as we. They made no great voyages, but traded with other tribes only on the boundaries of their lands. And great forests where cool breezes moved in fertile, humid tastes. And in their stealth, animals called to the world in howls. The trees marvelous in clumps of all varieties and sorts: pine, oak, chestnut, birch, ash and elm, a forest of many to the edges of the sea.

We stayed some days in this country. The savages were for the most part friendly but proud, jealous of any slight that might address against their privilege. And so it was by accident, in trade, there was a quarrel. We had then to sail across the harbor to Cohasset. Three savages followed us in a canoe, coming ashore on a rock near where we must pass. Their bowstrings taut, with arrows to their cheeks, they let fly such darts that we had to answer with a volley. The half-hearted war continued until we had sailed a distance.

We came then to Accomack, which means "Across the Waters," another good harbor and excellent land. There we had a little fight with forty or fifty of that tribe. Some of them were hurt, some slain, but after the war was done we held each other friends. The harbor lay in broad and pleasant sweeps of sand and stone. Of a large rock where I trod first upon this land, I thought, "This stone is tablet, the sea's own step where I rise to feast and drink this earth to its plenty." I called the harbor Plymouth after Drake's home, and that ledge of stone I called its sentinel and named it "Plymouth's Rock."

How many years before another Englishman would step upon that stone, my children orphaned to this found land. They the rejected, rejecting me, and forgetting I named this, they would call home.

Now south again to explore Cape Cod, where Gosnold sailed. I to ship upon his invisible wake. He dead in Jamestown years ago. No grave for him but this name he left and for us the feeling of that emptiness.

From the root of the cape, where we found a village called Chawum, we sailed across the bay to the circled finger of the land. That hook but a rush of sand, and scrub and wild grass. High hills grown with pine, all broke and twisted into hurts; grotesque, their wood screamed into the wilds.

I found another fine harbor, safe from all weathers, then sailed around the head of the cape south some miles, then north toward our fleet, our explorations done. The sea now in gentle swells, we rode the hobbyhorse of the waves. Our boughless cradle swayed, I almost slept. But on that point where sleep and wake ghostly touch. I thought of the old mariner, his voice ever in my mind. His life but known to me and all he served. Is what the world is, this witness now but a ripple in remembrance? And who in future years will dream me from my death? Who will be my chronicle?

·　　·　　·　　·　　·

WITH THE FLEET AGAIN, IN MY CABIN, I SHOWED CAPTAIN HUNT my charts, my new drawn maps. I told of my belief that here on this coast we could found a colony. Hunt, watching the spread of maps upon the table, looked at his ship's master with a curious nod. "I am sure," he said, "this could come to pass and with great rewards to you, but let me study these at some greater length on my own ship a few days." I stayed his hands as he gathered up the scrolls. "No," I said, "let us keep them here and we will speak about it at leisure when next we meet." We then walked from my cabin, I leading Hunt to the deck to have discussions about our voyage back to England. The air about our decks was heavy with the smell of salted fish. Hunt and I talked a moment. His ship's master had disappeared. I thought not much about it. Hardly a notice, until I saw him, his shirt stuffed with bulges of paper as he sneaked upon the deck.

"Where do you go with such bundles so poorly hid?" I asked. The man stammered to some excuse. Finding one he liked, he said, "It was but protection from the sea and spray. Had you not asked Captain Hunt to study them and have them copied?" I took back the maps, Captain Hunt laughing at the misunderstanding. When he left I learned from one of his crew, "Hunt plans some mutiny to have your charts and leave you marooned on a desert island. Be now warned. I sailed with Captain Moone. I am your friend," he whispered. That night against the black mirror of the sea, all was to a perfect stillness as I kept the man with me.

The next day, my crew well armed, I informed Hunt that I was to sail that week. "Our preparations mostly done, you can stay and finish salting the fish and then sail to Spain and sell the goods, Poor Johns having a ready market there." Hunt, his face in a violent red, his teeth bit at his lower lip. He to speak, but I spoke first. "I know of plans to have a mutiny. Any unfriendly word or act, and, I assure you, some will hang." What regrets I had that I did not hang him then. On July eighteenth, 1614, I sailed with strong winds for England. Later I learned that Hunt stayed some days, then sailed south toward Cape Cod, attacking the Indian towns along the coast, burning them and doing as he would. Twenty-seven prisoners he took, bringing them to Spain to sell as slaves. From that day forth, until the Puritans who knew my work stepped forth on that coast, all England would bear that stain. And I always to wonder if Hunt were not a Spanish agent sent to wreck our prospects along that coast.

Chapter Twenty-eight

A SHADOW TO CAST GLORIES IN ITS FINAL DARK.

I ARRIVED AT PLYMOUTH on August fifth, 1614, with my maps and charts and tales of my voyage along the northern Virginia coast. A meeting with Ferdinando Gorges set, I walked to that moment, thinking of Acadia and Nouvelle-France, whose lands overhung that which I wished as mine. Why should there be a New-France and no New England? And so that place was named. "New England," I said to Gorges, "not Northern Virginia. Simple words do make us free. Now we have a colony of our own. With that difference the value of our possession rises." Gorges, on the flames of inspiration, appointed me admiral of New England, and vowed to raise moneys for a colony, I saying, "This New England is no barren desert, as it is often thought, but a garden on which to build a paradise."

AFTER SOME WEEKS OF COUNCIL WITH GORGES, I SAILED TO London. There, I showed the store of furs to Rawdon and his group, and much of our catch of fish. With the salted barrels of dead silvered flesh they were much impressed, there being a ready knowledge of the riches of those waters. But to the furs, that was another matter. The lands of New England were legends then, smacked in rumor and a little fear. Waymouth, never much beyond his coward, only told his terrors. Most believed it was a desert place of stones and barrens and rising cliffs. None thought a forest there, much less a garden. "Those furs were stole from the French," whispered some. "New England is but a foul of sand and wind...and ever death." My ship's master, Michael Cooper, coming to my defense, told as I had of a fertile, watered earth, the sky holding its hands cupped to seed a forest plenty. "And the sea run with endless life...and the land tufted in rush of furred creatures,..." he said. Rawdon's group not fully convinced, suspecting intrigues, and not pleased I had spent such weeks with Gorges. But the voyage showed enough profit to quiet complaints and for them to finance another one. This time four ships, all for fishing and nothing more. I was offered command, but having Gorges' promise of the backing of a colony, I refused. Fool I was, played dunce by better prospects. Rawdon and his group so furious they broke into slanders and accusations upon me. The command offered to Cooper, who made the easy choice.

The fleet sailed for Monhegan Island on January 1615. Gorges and the Plymouth Company, as a sign of friendship with the London merchants, supplied a ship of their own, captained by Sir Richard Hawkins. The fleet brought little profit. The savages, in rage at Hunt and every Englishman, brought war to the beaches instead of trade. So all seemed lost that was scarce begun.

I was in Plymouth the day Cooper sailed. The ships, graceful and fragile in their silence, slipped the sea in breaking wakes heading west. I watched them go. I soon would be their better.

I THOUGHT AGAIN OF THAT TIME WHEN THE OLD MARINER AND myself stood deserted on the Jamestown beach, the clouds rolling in their wilderness, gray to gray they tongued the edges of the sea, and we alone. With death so close, Jonas spoke of death. Words demand a resurrection spice, its alchemy to preserve the flesh beyond decay. Jonas spoke of Drake again and Drake's lost death. Those events closed upon my youth. Jonas Profit now turned to me again and angered of his histories.

"The Drake that returned from Lisbon was a different Drake. Even Diego saw it," he in his confidences said me. "Drake, who had dared so much, so heresied, he threw his gauntlets down before the gods. No gods need judge the saint, he judged himself far worse. He presumed too much defiance and it ate him to the bone. We are ever the disobedient children to the fathers in our heads, as his whispers still whisper in the mansions of his many rooms. The vast silence calls behind the ghostly doors, and we hold in our uncertain steps. Fearful caution is the progress that retreats. And Drake caught on the crucifixion of his own conscience. Caution now the kinder rub, he willed his wilderness into stone. Twice he failed: first at Santander, Drake not sailing there to destroy the last of the Armada, and then at Lisbon, by not bringing his fleet into the harbor to smash those walls with cannon fire, and bring the Portuguese to revolt.

"Deadly is royalty in its distrust. Queen Elizabeth never held Drake a favorite again. The queen understood the essentials of the cause, the final destruction of the Armada. That now failed, the peace far off, this war would swiftly bring its murder. Philip now rebuilt his fleet, his new ships lower and faster before the wind. The Armada's defeat had taught Philip well. These new Spanish ships were Englished in design.

"In 1590 the world still traveled to its continents in war. Martin Frobisher and the Earl of Cumberland on the seas raided the Spanish gold routes near the Azores, but with Philip's new *galleyzabras* trimmer, faster, better armed, this was no longer a simple match. Hawkins always scheming to grasp the wealth, he thought in grand designs where others thought in slights, and so he approached the Queen with his plan to bloom havoc from a pin. 'Blockade the Azores with an English fleet. Those ships on watch only four months then replaced, relieved by another fleet, a constant English net to snare Philip's wealth.' This was Hawkins's advice. The queen agreed, a good profit always to her taste.

"Hawkins and Frobisher fitted out a fleet. The queen was its main investor. But Philip, hearing that English pirates were active along the Caribbean coast, sent word that no treasure ships were to sail for Spain that year. The flota becalmed by dangers. Riches into golden hordes in the treasure houses of Nombre de Dios, San Juan d'Ulua and Havana. Philip in debt, needed that wealth. The queen for her effort with nothing shown for all the costs.

"Each side now blocked wall to wall, holding desperation as a kin. Spies told Elizabeth of Philip's plight. The flota would have to sail the next spring. All this known, another fleet to serve, the blockade to be resumed. The queen cast aside Hawkins and Frobisher. They had not the luck to bring her wealth the year before. Drake's star had set, its course washed so black, he was not a choice. Elizabeth thought of Lord Admiral Howard, who had commanded our navies against the Armada, but this new fleet was too light to bear his great name. And so the queen, ever partial to the Howards, chose the lord admiral's cousin, Lord Thomas Howard, who had commanded the *Golden Lion* against the Spanish fleet in 1588. Sir Walter Raleigh was to be Howard's vice-admiral and second-in-command. But the queen wanted Raleigh at her court just then, he being much in favor. Lord Richard Grenville, Raleigh's cousin, was granted the office, and with it command of the *Revenge*, Drake's ship from the battle with the Armada.

"Is all our life but the fabric of a silver chance and feted accidents?

Who spins our fate? The fabric woven blind, the course of the weave we feel, the pattern only seen in parts. Drake had bought Grenville's country estate at Buckland Abbey. Now Grenville was to have Drake's great and famous ship. And so Drake passed from his death to another death. The sea holds its own legend, forever joked with opportunities. The fleet sailed, Howard in the *Defiance*, Grenville in the *Revenge*, Captain Robert Crosse in the *Bonaventure*, Captain Edward Denny in the *Nonpareil*, all those tinders that had tasted salt from the Armada's blood. Each ship of five hundred tons, forty cannons and a crew of two hundred and fifty. Also sailing with the fleet was the *Crane*, a ship of two hundred and fifty tons, six armed merchants and twelve fast pinnaces.

"In the spring of 1591, Howard not at sea a month, news came of a Spanish fleet of fifty ships, some thirty galleons and six of the new *galleyzabras* of fifteen hundred tons, under the command of the younger brother of one of the Armada's dead admirals. Don Alfonse de Bazan now sought his vengeance against the English. His fleet abroad to destroy Howard's. Raleigh, learning the danger by informants, sent warnings by a fast pinnace. The queen dispatched nine ships to add their weight should a battle come.

"By mid-August the English fleet sat at anchor in a bay off the island of Flores in the Azores. Howard's fleet diseased. The *Revenge* alone had ninety sick. Those who could, sat upon the beaches, sunned themselves or forced pleasures and refreshments from the countryside. The white sands, the blue-eyed sky, a sea of green, linked the palette that closed upon the coming moment. Grenville walked the deck of the *Revenge*, chewing on broken glass as he always did, spitting blood to hold again his legend before his crew. Not years ago, Grenville, in the Caribbean, had come upon a Spanish treasure ship. No small boat aboard to bring his men to the Spaniard, Grenville rowed an old sea chest across the breach. The chest sinking, his men in fear, Grenville and his company jumped and caught the Spanish hull as water licked upon their feet. Power is the cloak to braid the shoulders of those that have the will. With Drake now gone to penitence, the sea now flourished a courtship with a lunatic."

"A SMALL SHIP SAILING INTO OUR FRIENDLY HEAT. LAZY CANVAS fluttered in the almost idle air. Captain Middleton calling from the pinnace with warning of the Spanish fleet. 'Not an hour from here, I have seen their squadrons sailing upon us from all quarters.' No angle of the compass safe. Now in shouts, from our ship a rising scream, we gathered our panicked company from the beach. All warmth now chilled, all the ships in fear, all haste too slow. Some men caught abandoned on the shore swam to make the fleet. Sails snapped in bloom. Some, torn loose, havocked in the wind. Confusion, anchors slipped to make more speed, we sailed to have the weather gauge just beyond the coast.

"In less than an hour our fleet had begun to make the sea. Our flags proclaimed their herald, their ribbons all effaced the air, their banners hailing war. Now ships from behind a point of land, the first squadrons of the Spanish fleet, so slow, progressed in deliberate grace, the horizons all quilted with the white patches and red crosses of their sails. About us now, the circle closed. We caught the wind. Our hearts burst to have the race beneath our keels, water rushing silver in flung spray, our gun ports ready. Our cannons now bore on distant prospects, as they tacked to cut the miles. What once were thumbs of sails growing to threat.

"Grenville, who slipped his cable late, was last to leave the bay. He a small distance from the coast. He could have come about, the wind still to his favor, sailed between the Spanish fleet and the land, and made the open sea. Cannons bloomed eruptions into bloodied flames. Howard was in battle with a Spanish galleon as he fled. Grenville, who raged his war in temperaments, was beyond any fear of pain. He had such riots in his mind, he thought no death could quench his fury. No death such death that he could die. 'Safety is but the wisdom of the fool.' He spoke in rising frenzy, his fascination on himself. 'On this I lay my claim. It is my destiny,' he screamed.

"The *Revenge* now bore straight upon the Spanish fleet. No need, no danger to our ships, we were mostly safely sailed away, a few broadsides to bruise the afternoon, but nothing more. It was Grenville's gesture to marry his twin of madness with the sea. Half believing the Spanish galleons would yield and he would have a path, and half believing he was the only rescue for the English fleet, Grenville bore upon the prisons of the Spanish hulls, his horizons filled with the mountains of their sails. The *Revenge* built low, its keels slipped speed across the Spanish wakes. He held the course. The winds blew gallops in our sails. Our cannons pulled ready. Behind our bulwarks men knelt, heads bent, weapons in their hands, as if in prayer. Grenville stood the deck, cocked pistols in his belt. In the shadows of our rigging, there perched a deadly fruit, men with their muskets aimed upon the closing Spanish ships.

"War now maneuvered in its season of delay. Grenville and the Spanish sought the best position to bear their guns. Weave in counter turns, the wind held close to fill our sails. Galleon behind galleon, the Spanish sails did overlap the horizon in their screens. In rising cliffs the Spanish hulls moved along our side. The *Revenge* so small, still mute before the coming storm. The Spanish close, the distance gone to fist and squeeze itself to war. The *galleyzabras* encircled us, so all about, they blocked the wind. Our sails began to calm and flutter limp. Our speed dispelled, the captain of the *San Felipe*, the nearest Spanish ship, so joyed that he cried and bit his lip. The blood he tasted was his own. The cannons of our lower decks spoke in tongues. Flames and their salvos split the *San Felipe's* hull to ruins. Our bar shot tore her masts and holed the timber at her waterline. But as a raging beast, its power feeding violence from its pain, on she sailed to have the breach. Sailors on her decks, in their hands iron grapples. Smoke now boiled storms. The sea burned in reflections of our blasts. Close enough the air all flung with wreck. The grapples, thrown in winged lines, arched the hooks to catch our decks. Some caught, the Spanish pulled to have us deck to deck, their sailors readied. Their rope lines would not hold. Her hull we cut to murder. Through the gaps the sea drank her full. The *San Felipe* wallowed, filled with weight, and fell away to repair her shattered timbers and her leaks. Tattered sails torn to a beggar's rags. A Spanish citadel has played itself to wreck.

"More galleons to take the *San Felipe's* place." The old mariner, who was with Howard, got it all from such survivors as there were. "My perspective was the air," he said. "All this circumstance so a part of me, I saw it all, I lived it as if it were my life." The old mariner on the Jamestown beach, he saw in landscapes far enough to have its eyeful depth. "I am the last to live the tale." He grabbed my arm, squeezed it into pain. Pain is the only wisdom we truly know. It is the stone whose alchemy has changed the world.

"IT WAS NIGHT, THE DECK OF THE *REVENGE* GLISTENED IN THE blood and mounds of the slaughtered. Cries and whispers crawled their breath through public and secret agony." As the old mariner spoke, he nodded. "The heaps of dead sometimes rose only to collapse, as if someone still lived and moved beneath the weight. The masts of the *Revenge* were all shot away. Rigging in its tangled wreck wove lines of ruin among the slain. Everywhere the deck was coming to a rot. Dark waters, black in shadows, stretched to the small horizon that we could see; grappled to the *Revenge*, the rising silhouettes of the Spanish galleons. Distance cut to shards of distant shapes. Mast beyond mast they tied to each other, then with chains and hooks made fast to our shattered works. The galleons so much higher than ourselves, we struggled in our pit, the Spanish firing down at us. We discharged our cannons into their waterlines, their hulls not yards beyond our muzzles' blasts. Fires, clouds in rising smoke, the action all obscured. Salvos passing iron through the violent winds, air cracked free of air, and through the blackening gap the storm of war walked cyclones in the mists.

"On the decks of the *Revenge*, the company surrounded by the grappled ships. One of the ships was the *San Barnabas*, captained by Martin de Bertendona, who had fought against Drake in 1588 and now sought in a blind vengeance to heal that wound. Grappled to the other side of the *Revenge* was the *Ascension*, holding to her the flagship of the fleet, the *San Andrèa*. All this, and the *Revenge* becalmed in the vortex of the slaughter. Another Spanish ship, no room to cast a line, impetuous to have its touch upon the battle, rammed the *Revenge's* bow, and so brought such damage upon itself it began to sink.

"Fury now, no thought of self. Grenville in urgent race about the decks, rallying in his power. Even our wounded no longer to wait but to rise indifferent to their lot and die a second death. Fallen wreckage, splinters through the air, nets of rigging to our decks. Men fought through the ruins and aimed at waves of Spaniards running riot through the smoke to have our decks. Volleys in crushing weight, men thrown back, torn spurts of bloodied flesh, brains blown free of exploded skulls, eyes open in surprise hung dark in sightless caravans.

"Grenville stood unwounded, the dead about him in their heaps, screaming the orders that seemed to come from smoke. He held his decks and tore free his fate and flung it at his destiny.

"All the upper decks of the *Revenge* now shot away and blasted flat. In our fallen masts the corpses hung in twisted lines. Yielding not an inch to death, they held their place. The main deck a plain of ruins, but in the lattice of the wreck Englishmen still fought, our cannons still discharging lightning through the dark. The *Ascension* began to sink. She cut her lines to drift in her embarrassed wreck to find a private death. Floundering, her decks now low, she passed into the dark. But now our cannons were clear to bear upon the *San Andrea*, which cast a line to grapple and take the *Ascension's* place. In what lance of fire our salvos bore in their final dawn. The night was but a shadow to their smoke. The *San Andrea* smashed to wither in our iron gale. She too began to sink. Four ships Grenville took to death that night and five hundred Spanish lives. And still he stood his deck, covered in the blood of nations, but not his own.

"Midnight in those plaintive hours where reluctant conscience walks its ghosts upon our memories. If ever time had sung its elegy, it was upon that hour. A voice now hailed Grenville from the dark. It was an English voice, the captain of the *George Noble*. 'I have come to bring myself under your command. How can I assist?'

"Grenville turned toward the sea to speak. 'Fool!' he screamed. 'Save yourself. There is nothing here.' As he looked back again to face a different dark, a pain now tore a shrill fire through his side. He fell, a wound bleeding at his waist. They brought him behind a shattered bulwark, laid him back upon the ruins. A surgeon knelt, bloodied instruments at his feet. Threads and needles to tear the flesh again and tie the lips in overlap to stop the blood. The surgeon worked, his knives and saws lying on the deck, his sight fixed on the wound. His eyes caught in a sudden black, his throat exploded into blood and geysered flesh. The surgeon fell, his hands almost to his neck, and died. A volley now cut the deck. Grenville, wounded in the head and arm, was carried to his cabin below.

"Above him the wars now raged in echoes, as the night faded towards the dawn. Our powder almost spent, Grenville ordered the *Revenge* to be blown apart, so it would never fall to the Spanish as a prize. 'Let the prize of all our deaths bring such cataclysms to the Spanish fleet that I will die in peace,' said Grenville. The master of the *Revenge*, himself with ten wounds, weak from pain and loss of blood, spoke. 'The *Revenge* is lost. It will never make a port.' The fighting on the deck has ceased. No cannons, no muskets spoke. The Spaniards too had sickened of all the death and now sought a miracle to end the battle. 'Let those who live, live to bring this war upon Spain another day. There is no dishonor here. Let us make a truce.' So spoke Admiral Langhorne of the *Revenge*. Grenville consented, knowing he had asked enough.

"The truce then made. The English demanding generous terms: all prisoners to be well treated and quickly released, to be returned to England on the first English ship or neutral that passed. This so agreed, the battle ceased. What intoxications were his wars? Is it the human curse that all our sages come reborn from exhausted maniacs, and so their wisdom always seeds a little madness in its swell?

"Grenville sought to kill himself with his own sword. 'And now I claim my death,' he calmly spoke, as he raised the weapon to point upon his own heart. His passing cuffs waved a bloody flower in the air. His hand was stayed by Admiral Langhorne and the ship's master. A struggle, the sword now rose from his chest, the compass of the blade turned safe and pulled from his weakening grasp.

"Grenville was carried to the *San Pablo*. The decks of the *Revenge* a wallow of wreck and slaughtered men. Nothing but pieces of what they were, whether wood or flesh. Blood, the glistening sap, ran as glue upon this decay. Shatters and broken spars lay as boulders in the shadows, rigging and lines webbing the deck.

"A mist now rose, as if the slaughtered spirits congealed a nightmare on the world. Winds boiled in the fog as the Spanish worked to find their own. Their hands now dripping red souped in the butchery. Unsavory the smell, men's innards on the deck crushed under passing feet. The grapples on the Revenge now cut. She taken in tow. Ropes tossed from nowhere, all directions were confused. All the murder and ruins on her deck pushed to slop the sea. Now her wake and all the waters bled with the shatters of a human face."

"FOR TWO DAYS GRENVILLE LAY IN ALFONSE DE BAZAN'S CABIN ON the *San Pablo*, his life living in the flicker of its dying flame. Smoke comes when the fire is quenched. Eyes in sightless gray, his side a moistened wound. Fever palled his flesh. He wished to die and live immortal in his hate. His sickened corpse but a fester to hold claims upon his will. He died, the sighs of cyclones in his breath.

"The Spaniards cheered his death, and with no respectful word or ceremony they threw his body overboard. 'We appalled his flesh and cast the Lutheran sack into the sea,' said Bazan. But the sea has its own ceremonies. Who the sea anoints, the sea will soon revenge. Grenville's body sank, his liquid angers now releasing their fisted choirs on the still waters. The sky grayed to a blackening firmament. The sun spit lightning as it hid. The sea now warred its glories on the world. Cruel winds, and the sea rising, breaking mountains on the Spanish decks. The wind weighted the drowning cliffs of rain, as vengeance cracked its hurricanes. The Spanish fleet dispersed. Ships floundered and were swept to capsize in the surge. 'We are wrecked,' screamed the Spanish. The sea rose red in blood. The giants, their clubs swung in the winds, now walked their demons on the earth. The English far away and safe. The *Revenge* now sunk. Grenville's rotting corpse now rose, exultant in its violent death, his hand sweeping havoc in its ghostly brush. Thousands of Spanish died, the waters pillowed in the slippery white of their bloodless flesh, the beaches of the Azores littered with the decay. The waters ran rancid for months. The surf fouled. Dozens of ships sank. The cost so great Spain was never told the price, only of Grenville's death."

So long ago the mariner spoke, and with the past came remembrance of motions played with other ghosts. "Play not your fate as a weapon. The hurt is double honed. The *Revenge* was the only English fast galleon ever sunk by Spanish cannons. And so Drake lost a destiny of unknown course, Grenville recast the gloom to a bitter irony. And so must all our lives bear a witless elegy."

Chapter Twenty-nine

THE TELLINGS IN THE FARAWAYS.

, THE EXILED CHRONICLER, received reports of Virginia from George Sandys or Richard Hakluyt or even Thomas Smythe, keeping me secretly informed. Mostly they sent copies of letters from Hamor, who was judged the most reliable. Sometimes just quoted from a larger script, enough to entice what never could be said.

Then a long letter from Hamor transcribed by George Sandys, much of which was lost in a circumstance soon understood. I give it now marshaled in paraphrase.

·   ·   ·   ·   ·

After the marriage of Rolph and Pocahontas there came an end to all the forest *ambushado*. Even the Chickahominy, who had always been independent of Powhatan and always at war with him, now asked for peace, fearing some new alliance against them. Two of their number they sent to Jamestown, bearing two large deer as presents for Dale. They offered to become King James's subjects, to change their name to Englishmen, which in their language was "Tossantessas," which meant stranger. The Chickahominy were willing to agree to have King James as their king (they had no king, but were governed by a council of eight elders) if they could still be governed by their own laws when King James did not need them. All this Dale said he would consider, offering the Chickahominy some copper as a present for their venison. This the savages refused, saying what was given was given as a gift. And so they left.

Within days Dale had ordered fifty well-armed men into Argall's ships. On reaching the water near the Chickahominy village, Dale sent Argall to have the bargain. Dale, made coward by all his brutalities, fearing the Ratcliffe fate, hid on board, sweating in his terrors while others signed the peace. The Chickahominy swore in tobacco smoke never to kill our men or our cattle and to return all who fled to them, whether man or beast. They pledged to change their name, be King James's subjects, each of them to bring two bushels of corn each year in trade, for copper and iron tomahawks. And finally they made an alliance to deliver four hundred archers to fight whomever we so desired—Spanish, Dutchmen or the like. The peace concluded, Argall and Dale sailed back to Jamestown, Dale never stepping on deck or revealing himself to the savages.

Argall made his plans to return to England. Hamor, also desiring to return home, asked Dale if he might journey to Matchcot to have an audience with Powhatan so that he could communicate to the council in London some direct knowledge of the monarch's manner and of his court. Hamor's suggestion pleased Dale well, who had his own secret purpose and private message for Powhatan. Arrangements made, Hamor was to have his journey, Thomas Savage, then nineteen, to act as interpreter, and two Indians to be their guides, all to travel overland, the forest now at such peace that Englishmen could walk without fear.

The talk in Jamestown was of the peace and Pocahontas and the marriage. The late spring began to fill the air to the fullness of a summer heat, the cool still then enough to promise a coming change. The tobacco grew to a man's waist. The company toiled. Worms were pulled from plants, flowers and tops snapped from each stem and discarded. The labor each week was more than corn needed for a year. Three shillings a pound pulled idle men to industry. The weed cultivated the earth with devastations of its hungry green.

Ralph Hamor traveled north. At night he slept upon the bare ground, free from any fear of attack by the savages. He gave me the report himself years later.

A cold wander was on the dark. A chill, the fire low, I thought of my strange mission to Powhatan. Dale by law an almost private king, and I to do his cause, a cause no lord in England would privy to a public notice. I made no protest but followed upon his will.

The next day we made the river before Matchcot, calling to the savages to send across a canoe, which was quickly done. On our arrival stood Powhatan himself, four hundred bowmen around him on the beach. "Why come you here?" he said.

"By Sir Thomas Dale's desire," I answered.

"Then where is the chain of pearls that I gave as present to Dale and which he said any messenger from him would bear as a sign of him, as king?"

"I have it not," I said, never hearing of such a chain. "But I was to have it," I lied, "and it was forgot. But see, the two guides are yours and there, that one," I said, "is your own councilor. Surely, I came from Dale."

Powhatan nodded his consent and his agreement, and then looked at Thomas Savage. "You were my child but left me two years without permission. Were you not well treated?" asked Powhatan. "Another disloyal child, but of a different cut of hair."

"I was frightened and I ran away, you seemed displeased with me," said Thomas Savage, almost in apology. Powhatan nodded, smiled, put his hands about my neck as if first to choke me or cut my throat, then gave me salutations, the moment having passed. We followed him to his lodge. We entered, four hundred bowmen standing to their place outside as guards. We sat on mats. Powhatan on his own mat, two handsome women at his side stroking him to his silent pleasure. A pipe was brought. We smoked to a warm sleepiness and had our food. Powhatan then inquired after Sir Thomas Dale's health and his daughter. "Does she and my unknown son," he said, "still have that early bloom of love or is it a tired match already, their liking of each other overlived on too much a common plate?"

"No, she is very much content and very much in love. She would not change her life to return and live again with you."

How then laughed Powhatan, his head thrown back, his stomach heaving. "I am most glad of that," he said. "Now, what brings you here so unexpected?"

"I come on a most secret mission with a most secret message which I must deliver to you in private." Powhatan then ordered all from the lodge but his council and his two wives. I eased the moment closer to my real purpose, presenting some gifts from Dale. Then, leaning closer to Powhatan in the shivers of the firelight, I said, "Throughout your empire it is told of the most excellent beauty of your youngest daughter. Sir Thomas Dale asks that you might send the girl with me, that her sister Pocahontas might visit with her again, and your brother, Sir Thomas Dale, might secure her as the nearest to his heart, companion, wife and bedfellow."

Powhatan, in a rage, began to speak, his face alive. I told him to please hear me to my final point. Several times I quieted him to have my say. "Sir Thomas Dale wishes to bring our people closer yet, into one nation, which this marriage would well unite in bonds of love. Sir Thomas Dale aspires now to live the remainder of his life dwelling in your country. This wedding is but a desire for the general good. Has not love ever been a chalice for a lasting peace?"

I had no need to wait upon Powhatan's answer, which came in swift bites of ill-formed breaths. "I am pleased that Sir Thomas Dale, your king, sends forth to me his salutes in words of peace and love. The peace between us which I and my subjects will abide. His pledges we receive with gratitude and with thanks, but those pledges are not yet so full as to overburden any cup. Though he be great, his greatness does not seek to please in that way that Captain Newport, whom I well loved, always sought. The future now hangs upon future deeds.

"As to my daughter, she has, in these three days past, been promised to a great *werowance*, who lives some distance from my land. He has given me two bushels of oyster-shell beads which we call *roanoke*, and she in the exchange has now gone with him to be his wife."

"You are a great king," I said to Powhatan, "and the one *werowance* to all. Obedience and power stand as fortresses to your might. Certainly you, of all kings, could have your daughter back but for the asking, returning the two bushels of *roanoke* to that king. Dale will give far more by many times, in beads and hatchets and weapons. Far more worth than any beads. No evil to you. Tell that king not the cause, but say in truth the girl is not yet marriageable, as she is twelve years old."

Hamor then wrote an aside to me: "Twelve years old. Sir Thomas Dale well aware her age. This is no second England. Home, in its distance, excites our secret beasts. Our conscience has come a path to darker kingdoms." Hamor's report continued.

Powhatan still refused, saying that of all his children, he loved his youngest daughter the most, and if he could not see her again, then surely he would die. I made some protest, but Powhatan now spoke, "You have one of my daughters with you already, you shall not have another. While Pocahontas lives, she stays with you as is her wish. If she dies, you may have another. I will not pledge more of my flesh. The daughter that you have is gone from me forever. She who once loved me now loves me not. This peace of yours wars in many treacheries. Too much have you had of mine. Too many of my people have died, and too many of yours. I will not have war again, but neither will I give you more. If Dale still makes demands, I shall move again further into the forest, three days from here, with all my people, and so you will be alone. This I promise, as I have promised peace. Now I see that you are tired, and so this business ends." I tried to speak, but Powhatan had risen and walked toward the door. We had no choice but to follow.

Outside, we were led to a small cabin where Powhatan had his men bring us bowls of bread. "We were not expecting your visit. All our food is eaten." We ate the bread, rounded to the size of tennis balls, as Powhatan spoke and drank wine from two great oyster shells. Powhatan gave us three spoonfuls from a mostly empty bottle, the remains of a gift Captain Newport had given him. Then he left us to ourselves and to our meal. When we finished, we lay on the mats given us by the savages. In a half hour such fleas in clouds crawled upon us that we could not sleep. Shaves of torment, they walked through our hair, on our clothes, about us to every inch of skin. It was as if the earth had come to flood in vermin. We stood, shook our mats and stepped outdoors to sleep upon the ground. The earth cleansed, its dirt free of torment. As we lay beneath the branches of a great tree, the stars and the night closed its canopy upon us.

The next morning, Powhatan came to us as soon as we *had* awakened. He asked us of our night, then he brought us to his lodge, where we had bowls of peas and beans boiled into a mushy soup, then bread and boiled fish and roasted oysters, crabs and other shellfish. Powhatan's men still at hunt, we rested from our breakfast with the hope that soon we would have deer and turkey for a feast.

By ten o'clock the men returned with four great deer and two turkeys. While I stood outside watching the turkeys being plucked, the venison skinned, its red and bloody flesh brought upon the fire, a savage walked to me, his face in paint, his hair cut to the taste of heathen beauty, his skin dark in sunburn, a savage distinguished by nothing more than savagery. This I thought, until he said in English, "I am William Parker, an Englishman, taken prisoner three years ago near Fort Henry." I looked at him wide-eyed. This new land had made another orphan. "I am held against my will," he said.

"We thought you dead. The savages said that you had sickened and died," I answered.

"I am watched. I am prisoner. Can you get me free?"

I brought him with me to Powhatan, saying to that monarch, whose face now seemed to be wrapped in stone, "This is William Parker, of whom for years we have made inquiries, only to be told that he was dead. But here he lives and I will have him home. Refuse, and Sir Thomas Dale will know, and in his anger, he will make voyages upon you!"

Powhatan's face, once stone, now came skinned in ice. "You have my daughter with you now, which contents me with little pleasure yet she is with you. But any of yours with me, they must be returned or I am breaker of the peace and our friendship ceases. Peace does not come by threats. If you want this man, take him but I will give you no guides. What befalls you on your way, that blame is yours."

"The way to Jamestown I well know," I said, "but rather than endanger others, I will go alone. If I am not safely returned, Dale will think you did me ill, so expect our vengeance. Accidents do occasion war and even if I arrive safely without guides, all will think ill of you and that you are not to be trusted."

Powhatan then turned from me, saying no more. At suppertime he sent me food. I ate alone with Thomas Savage and William Parker. The day now to its darker half, we sat and talked and finally slept, lying under the lullabies of a gentle breeze.

At midnight, there was a hand upon my shoulder, a savage youth, crying for me to awaken. Before me stood Powhatan, his hands upon his hips, all power in the expression of his face, yet he knelt down the shadows of his form into the flicker of our firelight, and said, "Tomorrow, you will have guides for your return. I hope this will please my brother. I ask that he send me such bounties as I now request."

"Toys," I thought, "to bring an empire to its knees." Powhatan had me repeat the list of things he needed. Then he had me write it in my book and repeat it again, nodding at each word: ten pieces of copper, a shaving knife, a grinding stone of such size that four or five men could carry, two combs of bone, not wood, the wooden ones his men could make, a hundred fishing hooks, a cat and a dog. Cats and dogs there were none, they not being native to the land. For all these Powhatan promised Dale a goodly supply of fur in trade.

In the morning, we ate boiled turkey in Powhatan's lodge. He gave us one for our journey and with it three bowls of bread. We then walked to the riverside. There we were each presented with a buckskin robe, all white, the lay of the hair smooth, combed as satin snow. Two skins Powhatan also sent as presents for Pocahontas and Rolfe. The day hanging in clouds, a coming rain perfumed the air in cleansing scent. Powhatan seemed strangely aged and regal but in a sadness that confused his will. He knelt, grabbed some dust from the riverbank. Holding it in his hand, he let it slip through his fingers as he made some prayers, thinking on the universe of each grain, as if old friends now were lost in its fall. He saddened more. From a pouch he took some tobacco, sighed and crushed it in his fist, then threw it on the water as a sacrifice for our safe journey. Its plant lay still on the current, the color of dried blood oozing through the water, until the current took it wide and swept the crush and the color on itself, washing it in wild race toward the distance and the cloud-colored sea.

Hamor's narrative then falters to some false modesty without seizing on the truth—that this was the last time Powhatan ever received an Englishman as guest.

Chapter Thirty

NOW RISES MY WEAKENED STAR.

HAD NOW RAISED two hundred pounds from friendly investors to finance a colony in New England. Sixteen men, some of whom served me in Virginia, were to be my company and stay with me the winter on the New England coast near Cape Cod. Small, this colony, but my funds were small. Gorges had not raised his share. All about, men would invest for gold and furs and fish, but not for colonies. Few had come to know as I, *This new earth is the savior of our England*. Gorges then visited the wealthy dean of Exeter, Dr. Matthew Sutcliffe, a man who founded colleges and saw exploration as another book whose pages must be opened for all to read. Already he had a seat on the council of the Virginia Company and was a backer of the Plymouth Company. Wealth to him was but a tower from which to trace upon the world a vision.

From Sutcliffe and his friends the final shares were raised. Now two ships I had, one a two-hundred ton, the other of fifty tons, and crews and company. The plan was simple. The ships would fish and whale and trade for furs. I with my sixteen would live near the savages, whose sachem, or *werowance*, Tahanedo, had lived a year in England, he having been taken from New England in 1605 by Waymouth and returned the following year. I had met him in London not long before he sailed. There was a small but ready group of Indians who had been to England over the preceding decade. Even I had carried with me an Indian named Squanto on my first voyage to New England, leaving him on Cape Cod, reuniting him with his tribe. I did not know until later that he was one of the twenty-seven Captain Hunt had taken to Spain to be sold as slaves. But Squanto, escaping his captivity, found his way to England and London. Befriended again, he was returned to New England to be years later of great assistance to the Puritan colony.

Our ships full, our waterlines topped, we set our sails toward mystery and baited our lives once again upon the hook of skill and luck. The seas were high in uneasy roll. Our larger ship creaked, her boards screaming as if in the twists of pain. The masts swayed and bent, the rigging taut then torn loose. The wind then rose in gales and the sea in foam and thundered waves. Thomas Dermer, captain of my second ship, sailed ahead and from my sight. My ship labored in great distress and wallow. The mast then cracked and crashed upon the decks.

Helpless we were, and open to the rushes of the wind. Only our split sail we had. And so we took the wind in spoon and returned to Plymouth on a jury mast, rigged to desperation.

VISION HARDENS MEN TO A FIXED ACCOUNT. GORGES WAS, AS I, not pleased, but not deterred. Another ship we found, smaller and better built. Our crew now was thirty: fourteen and my sixteen colonists. All our victuals and equipment stored below decks. On June twenty-fourth, 1615, we took this bark of sixty tons and made our prayers and broke into the sea-born solitudes.

We sailed now south by west. For some days without sight of any ship, there then appeared one, with a blackened deck and masts and sails as shrouds, a hundred and forty tons, with thirty-six cannons and eighty for a crew. This pirate chased us for two days. Captain Fry, English no less, always his ship hung its tall decks over ours, but the sea so rough no boarding could be made. My ship's master and his mate and the pilot begged me to yield and let them come aboard, but I would not. The chase now swift. Men screamed at each other across the conference of the waves.

Finally, an agreement of which I would have no part. The pirate to search the ship, take nothing but gold or coin. All else—all on which the success of our voyage depended—would be left with us. Captain Fry and some men took to our decks, I stayed to my cabin. Learning now I was captain, several of his having once served with me as sailors, they offered to sail and do as I would bid, but I refused and stayed to myself. Proud fool was I to deny myself this good fortune. They then left, taking nothing, and none was hurt on either side.

WE SAILED AGAIN TOWARD THE AZORES. TWO SHIPS NOW UPON US. More pirates, I thought. We fled before them, we, the only cheese, it seemed, on a sea of mice. They pursued and commanded us in French to yield. My ship's master would have me come about. I refused, fearing they were Turks who would make us slaves, or French who would throw us all overboard. We sailed against the perils of the chase, the pirates about us on either side. Four more Frenchmen now joined the race, and we surrounded. Voices called from deck to deck, my crew pleading with me to yield. "I would blow up the ship rather than lose this chance to found a colony," I said. Why do events hatch such treachery upon me? Should I have made fleet with Captain Fry? More protections with his weight of cannons? Am I my own calamity? And what does doubt restore? A goat that luxuries in his own dirt! Are good and evil but an equal fate? Its ceremonies only pain.

The new world whispered beyond the horizon's rim. On deck I spoke to the French captain in his pursuit. Fans of spray rose above the bows of his ships. We called to each other, the sea plunging on our decks. They were Protestants from the Huguenot stronghold of La Rochelle. With less to fear, their king's commission to seize pirates, Spanish and Portuguese, we dropped our sails. They came aboard. Their captain, François Poyrune, took me to his ship. My crew was taken, dispersed among the other ships. Our provisions seized.

I sat in the darkness of my prison, mariners speaking French, their footfalls on the planks. Somewhere in the sea, a whale cried in its lonely agony, as a haunted thing, a conscience, its voice a drift.

After five days, Captain Poyrune having examined the papers and commission of my ship, I was returned to my bark with all my crew and all our goods, save our weapons, which the Frenchmen kept. I was still for New England, or at worst Newfoundland, where I could trade for what we lost. But the crew and my officers were for home, and ruin. Those that had the hunger of soldiers and those that I had chosen for my colony stood with me. Failure is a habit—yield once, yield ever.

The crew now argued with itself, tearing with words as if they were edged with blades. A French boat rowed near our bark. I hailed it, saying to our crew, "I will have our weapons released and then we will sail to our New England." This seemed the better compromise. The ship's master, Edmund Chambers, too ready to have me gone, said, "The Frenchman is at our rope. Go and see what can be done." The crew growled some consent. I climbed down to the rolling skiff, then to Captain Poyrune. The sky gray and darkening in its blackening threat, winds drove the sea in surges.

On Poyrune's ship he listened and agreed to our request. Edmund Chambers called to me to return with all speed. "The anchor slips, I cannot hold this place. Come back in haste, or, be warned, you will be left."

The sea now boiled in white wilds and convulsing spray. Darkness blew upon the squall as I screamed into the roar, "I cannot command the French to do my bidding. Send a boat. Poyrune will restore our weapons and all we need."

"The boat is split...have the French..." His words cut loose from speech, the winds blew them from my ear. The storm galed as I sat the captain's cabin, the blasts twining the rigging into howls. No danger to ourselves, but only to my soul, my enterprise now a shambles. The dawn was calm, the sea clean and flat. My bark and all my crew had disappeared.

I WAS LEFT TO MY PRISONS WITH THE FRENCH. POYRUNE GAVE ME A cabin. He was kind to the limits of his kind. Soon his fleet was joined by other ships. I stayed to myself, feeling as a worm upon the wood. My colony lost, its moment gone from hope, Edmund Chambers thought me surely dead. My goods, my clothes, my books were divided among those who deserted me. I with nothing swore my vengeance.

I sat alone, my cabin filled by darkness. Shadows hung the walls in tapestries. The candle flickered in its wax flames. I watched its fragile edges lace in dance. "Are we all but whispers of the past?" I asked as I thought of the old mariner. How many years ago had he told me of the dreams' demise, of greatness strangled and of men's vaulted wisdom in war against his philosophies? How desperate I was to speak to him. All his earful inheritance to me spoken on a fading voice.

Chapter Thirty-one

THE DRAGON AND ITS LAIR;
THE CIRCLE CLOSES OF ITS OWN BEGINNINGS.

ILL I BECOME THAT star-raw heaven, abandoned in its firmaments, a gossamer of long forgotten elegies writ in drifting smoke? But no book yet written has encompassed all this English enterprise I've lived. I've seen it full and reported of its future. Now alone, the sea about me in wind-thrown swells. No cliffs, no wide coasts, the ship unclaimed, horizons all about. Oh those last words old Jonas spoke, sustained in his bitter gift. His end so close, in a landscape of his bones. I could see the rot, smell its presence. I rose to leave him to a private death. I thought it was his wish. But he begged me, "Stay. This ends, all my alchemies are not so blunted as my age. I who followed upon three wizards. A second face rises from the ash and the tale is not yet finished," he began.

"It was 1595. Drake had not been to sea in six years. His life filled with all the consequence of his early success. A member of Parliament again in 1593, honors, powers. He used his fame to improve the good and make better what was poor. In Plymouth he reengineered the system of aqueducts to the city. Plymouth's fortifications were rebuilt and strengthened to protect the harbor. All this he had done and more wealth and more powerful friends. Drake's war tolled in distant cannonades, the queen never truly trusting him, the great fleets commanded by other men. Grenville and the *Revenge* all lost, Martin Frobisher dead of wounds storming a Spanish fortress at Brest. This our moment passing, the sands of the hourglass but a river of our own dust. Each age a cannibal, it consumes its own.

"Diego and I were still loyal, and the few who did survive. Little did we speak of what we lived and what we saw. Time has a wanton ear, hungry for its novelties. To each age a new language and a new brew of sloth. We grew stiff in our assurances and dead by our certainties. Many of Drake's new friends were friends only for the convenience of his power. Sir William Courtenay of Powderham was wealthy, well honored; although a Catholic, trusted. As a member of Parliament, he helped Drake win approval for the charter for Raleigh's colony at Roanoke. I never warmed to him. 'In the rag house of the world he is ever the tinder and the match,' I surmised. Courtenay with a secret passion for all private vices, a common eye for women and a stack of coins for whores. 'He is a quick mount. There isn't a saddle in all London he hasn't bounced' was the well-spoken rumor in the carriages. A man who lives upon his own decay is the last to smell the rot. His wife bore him ten children. Drake's wife, dark in the beauty of her eyes, still sweetly moved in the mysteries of her youth, her glance still flamed by the phantoms in her touch. Courtenay, a man of wit, knew how to bank his charm upon some future dice.

"In August of 1595 Drake was again the vice-admiral of a great English fleet. Its compass set its point upon his youth, its course to cut a map to Panama and the Caribbean. Names now spoken as if risen from the depths: Nombre de Dios, Rio de la Hacha, Chagres River. All that was, was to be lived again. But men ever seek their youth where they should not. All things pass. Repetition eats not salvation's meat.

"For two years the expedition had been planned, the queen nervous to have Drake at sea. 'Make all haste. This voyage must be short,' her words. Her eyes saw not the man she once trusted with her nation's fate. But of all her admirals, he knew the coast of Panama, its bays, its mountains. It was the place that birthed his name. It was El Drako's lair. If those waters were to be tried by an English fleet again, it was Drake who would hold command. But the queen, ever fearful of discord, gave Sir John Hawkins an equal commission, and so tethered Drake to Hawkins and Hawkins to Drake. Each his planet spun around the other's sun, the center empty but for their keen distrust. Hawkins was now past sixty. Slow, his caution pinned him fast to safety. All his thoughts well chewed before he would take the swallow. No chance to bite unless an angel sat his side.

"The queen's commission of joint command allowed each to raise his own fleet, supply his own victuals, and his own captains for his separate ships. It was to be a war by council, an expedition by delays. The fleet to have sailed by May first, but victuals not fully received, the queen not sending the twenty-eight thousand pounds she had promised. Drake in the countryside selling one of his own manor houses to raise the moneys to buy needed food. The Spanish fleet were reported raiding along the coast of Cornwall, Penzance and Newlyn burned. Those furies breathed the fearful word 'Armada' again into the queen's ear. Reports of ships in preparation in the Spanish ports. The queen ordered Drake to hold his deck. 'Your expedition must cruise in Irish waters and along the Spanish coast. We would need you home if the Armada sails again.' So wrote the queen.

"Sir Thomas Baskerville, who was to command the soldiers of the expedition and who had invested heavily in the enterprise as well, asked his patron, the Earl of Essex, to intercede with the queen and to convince her to allow the fleet to sail for Panama. 'I am half a ruin by this delay. Few riches are purchased on the penny's worth of fear,' he said to Essex. 'There would be a more perfect consequence if we warred alone, the queen left to her court.' Essex spoke to the queen, arguing his charms against her concerns and his wit against her reason. The queen not persuaded, the fleet held to Plymouth and the dock.

"Diego was old and graying, his war fought by others. Drake not the same Drake whose wounds he had dressed at Nombre de Dios. These old friends almost strangers now. Where was that worship the sea had blessed? To what sea did that finger point on the figurehead Diego once carved on the *Golden Hind*? And that face he had carved into the mainmast—that face that watched Drake, who watched the sea. What commandments now on its brow? And where now was it? The *Golden Hind* lay at dock, dry rot upon her planks turning her to dust.

"NEWS CAME TO PLYMOUTH THAT THE FLAG GALLEON OF THE spanish flota, the *Begona*, damaged by a storm, had made San Juan, Puerto Rico. Her masts gone, her rudder wrecked, she was unable to sail for Spain. But on board her were two and a half million ducats in treasure. The queen, ever in need of funds, took courage from the claw of wealth. Her objections set aside, the fleet sailed in the twilight of the summer's heat, three months late. Those delays, but still provisions not enough.

"Spanish spies, learning of Drake's idle fleet, sent warnings to Philip. Time had swung its pendulum. The destination of the fleet unknown, but speculation had its terrors, and panic reigned across the coasts of Spain. Thousands fled Cadiz. Philip ordered ships prepared to battle legends named again in their ghostly rumors. By

August fifteenth Drake had not food or water enough. Hawkins though ready to sail. Philip now learned the English fleet would sail toward Panama. Five fast ships, a squadron under the command of Don Pedro Tello de Guzman, ordered to Puerto Rico to bring that treasure safely to Spain.

"On August twenty-eighth, 1595, the English fleet of twenty-seven ships let fall its spars and canvas to the wind. Drake on the *Defiance*, Hawkins on the slightly larger *Garland*. Two flagships of two admirals, their two flags in different motion. Drake older, confused, but still vigorous. He a man torn faithless by his contradictions. The sea now rolled indifferent beneath his bow. The sea raged in its plundering silence, its depth too deep, its respectful glance upon him who did betray, as a lover disregards a forsaken love, not quite.

"Drake had not heeded sea when its urgent whispers told him to sail to Santander and destroy the remains of the Armada in 1589. Each man is free until, with freedom, he does lose himself. Drake lived upon his own silence. The fleet at sea not a week, a council called, Drake asking Hawkins to share his store of water. Hawkins refused, screaming accusations. 'You are not mine. Did you not desert me at San Juan d'Ulua? Whatever was your birth, I am not your guardian.'

"Old wounds may scar to disfigured jealousies. Dried in thin crust, they still bleed in words. What hail of speech to havoc our intent. The fleet would be diverted to the Canary Islands to seize its extra stores. 'A waste of clock. Are we not one nation born for this one cause?' asked an exhausted Drake.

"'Slight stitches ever move the grand design. I have not the food. Better to divert and gain supplies,' said Hawkins in his calm, but never again was there any peace in the council.

"Diego stood the deck. He did not cut a face into the mast. The round blank of wood stared its grain into our eyes. 'Why not sculpt the mast as you have always done?' I asked.

"'The face is dead. It will not give itself to becoming whole.' Diego looked back at Drake, who paced the deck. 'Too many eyes to have a face. The hands have swept the clock. It is the time of the return.'

"The air did crack in storms. The rains gray, the seas heavy, rushed in their angry dark. We made Las Palmas on September twenty-seventh, three days before Don Pedro Tello de Guzman. Drake sailed about the island searching for an easy beach to land his troops.

But time unmasked the plot. The Spanish, warned, stood upon the cliffs and watched us wallow beyond the surf. All the island stood by arms a garrison. With no surprise to win the action, Drake by storm would have his futile war. Our boats launched, our troops attacked, the beaches smoked. We heard ours scream as they fell, but the battle would not end its slaughter. Our troops withdrew, many lost and wounded, the high swells awash and choked with the weight of corpses in the battered soup.

"Drake refused to attack again. He would not sail his fleet into the harbor and batter its forts to ruin. He lifted anchor and sailed into the boiling spray, hoping to find a safer beach to fill his water kegs. A war of caution is a war already lost. Drake found his beach, but what is safe when men abstain from danger? The dice are always mysteries, the game is in the toss. Drake's water barrels filled, some supplies gained, but time slipped from his advantage. Don Pedro Tello's fleet, if not ahead, was not so much behind.

"For a month the two fleets raced unknown to gain some advantage. Speed was our deliverance, a haste may rule, but the decision was always the wind's. 'Why am I conspired to be becalmed?' Drake asked. An eyeless sea lay in the mirrors of wildlessness. Drake ordered the boats to tow by ropes the ships. The breezes slight. The sails hung straight. Mercy was a cloud. The wind freshened. The fleet again cut its bows upon the gauntlets of the waves. But the winds had separated our fleet. Two of our pinnaces disappeared. It was October twenty-seventh, 1595, when we made the isle of Guadeloupe. Nothing heard from the pinnaces the *Francis* or the *Delight*, then a sail. The news came a foul. The two pinnaces had come ill hap upon Don Pedro Tello's fleet. The Francis wrecked and boarded. Her surviving crew in chains, certainly to be tortured to learn our plans. The *Delight*, by guess, had found the English fleet. Drake, the echo of the herald's voice, called for English sails to pursue the Spanish fleet and bring battle upon it before it could warn Puerto Rico and the whole Caribbean.

"'The cost of those ships making San Juan, with their extra cannons, men and hope, may have its coin in English blood.' Drake pleaded with Hawkins to sail from Guadeloupe and find those Spanish ships. Hawkins declined in health, his life now a bitter chore, feebled on his leadened will. Hawkins refused to sail. Some men die before their death. Hawkins weakened even as he spoke, his face a tired mask. What life he had but to live, he would live distracted. Drake let Hawkins fade into a peaceful death. The argument was done. The fleet held to Guadeloupe to build some pinnaces and mount more cannons. Three days later it sailed to the Virgin Islands to train our soldiers. Mountains thrust from broken canyons rose violent above the sea. The beaches white. The green of the forest ran in circles close about our camp. Hawkins again safe in the arms of his dying."

"DIEGO SAT ALONE AND CHANTED TO HIMSELF. HE KNELT. HIS words, mysteries in their breaths, did enthrall the chasms of the air. 'The gods speak their dance in masks to shroud their truth and leave men as frightened boys.'

"On November eighth we sailed to Puerto Rico. On November twelfth, no sooner had we made the coast than Hawkins slipped into his last death. The night enclosed him in the nothing of its empty arms. His name forever, his body into dust."

"THE FLEET NOW SAILED IN GLOOM, REACHING SAN JUAN, FINDING Don Pedro Tello already there. For nine days he had strengthened the city's defenses, mounting thirty-five cannons on the stone fortress of El Morro, building new forts of some seventy cannons, arming a thousand men, carrying the treasures from the *Begona* to the safety of the shore, then sinking that ship in the western channel and positioning his fleet behind to protect that entrance of the harbor. San Juan was on a small island, the eastern entrance guarded by four small forts newly built. All this Hawkins had bequeathed by his refusal to pursue Don Pedro Tello when he was still at sea. I would bear the horror to watch the hordes of dead rise up to bear the price of the errors they did espouse.

"How the sea in its glistening dark does swell and roll its claws to eat upon the night. Smooth again, all depth reclined on the cold satin of the surf. The breast rises, then it falls on those sea tides of liquid rolling white. And we again to our sails and the quiet of our oars. Drake's fleet on its muffled strokes passed beneath the cannons of El Morro. Before us Don Pedro Tello's frigates moored in the center of the channel, the points of their lamps casting rude shadows toward our distant silhouettes.

"After our fleet had tried the eastern approach, Drake, not liking what he saw of its small fort, withdrew without a shot. The legend of Cadiz was an old story told, and that man had birthed within his skin another man. That flesh of long ago was indifferent to the surface and the illusion of its circumstance. Drake and his fleet came west, anchoring in El Cabron Bay, but too close to the Spanish cannons. Salvos broke destructions on the resting ships. The *Defiance* hit by fusillade of the iron wind, Drake almost killed, a cannonball wrecking the chair on which he sat. Two at his dinner table dead. Others wounded. 'What Drake is this that so mistaked the gauge?' a sailor asked. The hull of Drake's cabin holed so wide one could watch the moonless stars lay scintillations upon the surf. So close, but yet the voices of the sea held their tongues within the softness of their cheeks. Drake cast out to be the prodigal, his desert now the wilderness of the vast waters. That which made him great washed clean its anointment and left him beloved and human in its wake.

"The voices dead within his ear, Drake decided Don Pedro Tello's ships the only obstacles and the city's main defenses. What we lose with those approving voices is the daring that informs our actions. It is the pull of destiny. The plan to be done at night, the attack by hesitations, the fleet to sail quietly as comes the tide, and burn the Spanish ships. 'Those flames could beacon a dangerous light,' I said. 'Better their anchors cut and we take them whole.'

"'Fire is the safer ruin,' answered Drake.

"Diego sat and sang his songs to a pile of ashes at his feet. His songs in griefs. He rose after dusk, his musket in hand, shirtless, a dagger in his belt, saying, 'I am called to blood. I see my old death.'

"Washed in darkness, our fleet floated toward the Spanish ships. Our incendiaries still cold. Their fires chained within, no torches to burn them free. Closer we drifted as we drifted on. Torches lit on our decks below to shield the light. Passions held to the hearing of a word. 'As they bear' was our captain's call. How eruptions break. The lightning lit with meteors, fled and falling in their trails.

"Bolts of fire arced into the night, launched from the mortars of our iron tubes. We flung bombs with our hands, their fires sparked, their cauldrons ready to explode on the Spanish ships. Shadows ran on flaming decks. The world bloomed in deadly flowers. Masts and riggings, our hulls reflected black against the scarlet of the blaze. Broadsides sparked, their cannons' blasts soon veiled in the smoke. Some of the Spanish ships alight. Spars and wrapped sails burned. Our war glowed a crimson grotto in the night. Our fleet now seen in silhouette. The cannons of El Morro spoke the thunder of a coming murder. Flashes from the distant batteries. Cannons on the beaches now joined to drum the weight of slaughter through our hulls.

"The Spanish gunners had the range. The *Defiance* and the Garland and our twenty-five ships cowered bright in the flares before the burning frigates. Blast and wreckage now began to splinter in the air. Spouts of water rose about our hulls. Men caught disfigured in the iron hail. Faces ripped to jawless bloody hollows and hangs of gaping meat. The soon to die slipped in the blood of those already dead."

Grasping at my shirt, the old mariner pulled himself to me. His eyes white in the wilderness of his tale, he screamed, "Terrible is war in all its beauty!" Then he laughed and cursed and collapsed to lie back upon the earth, to scream again, "The world in its serpent guise ever bears its fangs. Diego on a Spanish ship, the stock of his musket shattered, its splinters red and oozed with blood, the spikes with tears of flesh. He swung the ruin in the air at the head of a Spaniard with a sword. The heat now rose on the wavers of the screening fire. Diego's shadow warred behind the flames. A vision cut. Diego raised his knife.

"How the fire cradle burns the nightingale. Diego was never seen again. Many more of ours dead that night. Drake, broken in the fusillade and with Diego's death, withdrew his ships. Our silent squadrons sailed their elegies down the darkening channel toward the bay. Flashes still bloomed the Spanish cannons in their fading light. The fires of the ships soon rested in the cooling smoke. In the dawn, wisps thin as feathers floated above the Spanish ruins. One Spanish ship destroyed. That towed to the channel and sunk to further block the entrance to the harbor. Other ships scarred and damaged. Everywhere the burn and smell of smoke, but the Spanish still held the town.

"Drake counted his loss in tolls of grief. The eastern entrance to the harbor never really tried. That would have been the man of long ago, who on a Panama beach, to quill the panic of his fearful crew, opened the corpse of his brother, cut back the flesh to enter into the black bile of the lungs and the rotting organs to discover the cause of a disease. Any man so maniac to map his brother's slaughter with his own knife, such is one whose crews will rise in death to heal themselves upon their own beds to face another death. But that man was in his forevers lost. Drake now sat his caution upon the pride of memories 'I know many places where treasure greater than in all Puerto Rico can be had with ease,' he said to his assembled council. Lost in doubt, Drake grieved and played at being Drake, the act of being only half the man. What great men lose in their forgetfulness is that which made them great. How subtly we do walk into our decay. Time bites. We feel unchanged, the illusion is in our memory. Each man is ever to himself the same, even though our hearts beat to an inconstant soul.

"Drake, to save his fleet, set his course to feed his hope upon the memories of his past successes. What should have been done in speed and quick passage to Panama, to strike at the unprepared Spanish, was left to a dawdled war. Drake sailed not to Panama and Nombre de Dios, but to the coast of South America east of Cartagena.

"On December twentieth Drake seized Santa Marta, burned the city, found nothing. We raided along the coast, chased ships, took prizes. Some cargo and some coins we had, pearls, a few gold bars, silver, jewelry in locked chests, a paultry, not enough. We sent it all to England to bring an early pleasure to the queen. But the fleet had not made its costs. Everywhere the murmurs of complaints, the sailors and the soldiers only paid by the plunder.

"How round the earth. Each man his own planet, his life in orbit set. Drake without the sea a man of uncertain voice, unblessed. 'What whispers now to me in love? My star is ghost.' Diego dead, Drake wandered to reclaim the empires in his head. Men should never play themselves in their own looking glass. We are the deception that is ourselves, a faith of accidents, and so Drake, now desperate, sailed for Panama. It was a month after leaving Puerto Rico. The Spanish all well warned."

"'DO YOU THINK HE IS ALIVE?' DRAKE QUESTIONED ME.
"'Diego?' I asked.
"'Pedro Mandinga,' Drake said, looking past the coast and the lit squares of the distant windows of Nombre de Dios. It was December twenty-seventh, 1595. Drake had circled his life upon its turns and come round to where it all had begun. No longer an unknown captain with seventeen men of Devon who had surprised the night and captured an entire town. Now he was an admiral with a great fleet, so much more for less. 'Where are my brothers of a different flesh?' Drake asked. I thought of his two brothers buried not far from there.

Diego dead in Puerto Rico. Le Testu beheaded, sacrificing himself for us to give life to another's fame. Oxenham burned at the stake, and Pedro Mandinga, no word of him for years. Our fleet wallowed in the dark histories of the waters. 'Come to me my lost, my visions to my eyes.' Drake shook his head, speaking to the narratives of the air. A circumnavigation of the world, a life, the maps to bring it flat. Does each man's soul dissolve to be remembered only as a name? The next morning we captured the abandoned town of Nombre de Dios. In a small guardhouse we found hastily burried a bar of gold and twenty bars of silver, and a scatter of some coins. Above this beggar's wealth the round tower rose in its grim of stone. Aloof over our defeat it stared. We ran the deserted streets, following each other like vermin crazed to feed upon our own droppings in the dust. Salvos came from the edges of the jungle near the town. Naked, Drake returned to his hunting ground, now without Diego to guide the way or to steal into the woods to find the Cimarrones. He sought his ghosts as an old lover holds in his imagined arms the warm geographies of a haunted touch.

"The sea wrapped the coast in its discontent. The eyes of the water stared upon the blessed prodigal. 'You have betrayed yourself. Come to us and we will heal your pain' were the whispers echoing in the rolling surf. No Diego there to hear the plea, nor Pedro Mandinga to advise. On December twenty-ninth Sir Thomas Baskerville and eight hundred men marched overland through the jungles to the gorge at Capirilla, thirty miles away, beyond that place where Drake first saw the western sea, then for miles more to Panama City. The jungle a soup of stink, it ate upon its own ruin as it grew. No Mandinga or Mandinga's guides. The air was mute. Fearful the Chagres River well fortified, Drake did not sail his fleet into its mouth to seize Venta Cruces, as once he had done. Ghosts of braveries long forgot rose again in disfigured cautions. Drake crawled his plans for Baskerville to attack Panama City by land. When the city was captured, Drake would bring his fleet into the Chagres as a reinforcement and take Venta Cruces.

"With no one, with nil brought beyond its nothing, Drake having to stay with the fleet, I was the last who knew the jungle. Drake gripped my arm, 'Find the Cimarrones. Find Mandinga.' Through the trees I led the way, the jungle raising in the mists.

"The landscape a swamp of mud, the ooze ate us to our hips. We wallowed and sank, struggling to gain a yard. Such exhaustions, the sweat rotted on our arms. It rolled in a living wax upon our flesh. Everything was wet. Our food began to stink its ruin. Most of our powder damp. The passage through the rock so narrow we could only walk in single file. We crossed rivers, the waters rushing in their plundering white, falling through their tumultuous cataracts. Along their banks we walked, fording where we could. Some men were swept away. They screamed, grasping at the rocks, before slipping into the current's wash, lost forever in the billowing passage of the foam.

"The world no longer a living ornament, but a fiend, monstered to hold us in its deadly grasp. Up the mountain paths we climbed. The road a scratch, a hidden scar upon the earth. The land now rose. We pulled ourselves up, and on the highland flats we swam the ooze and wallowed in the mud. Always the land rising toward Capirilla gorge. There, upon the crest of the hill, a crown of battlement flying all its flags, a Spanish fort across our way.

"We swept now to our attack. Victuals set aside. Firelocks loaded with the little dry powder we had. With forty rounds for each man, we advanced. The Spanish redoubt on the hill a simple tangle of rotten logs. We climbed and slipped upon the petrified cascade of leaves and mud and vines, huddling behind the broken trunks of fallen trees. All the world driven to its decay. And then, in deadly hail, the Spanish brought their salvos. Men cut to rags, they fell as if their flesh were a boneless sack. Some caught, thrown back as if by weighted blows, turning, spinning in the air as they were struck again. Thud and exploded splatter of shredded flesh, life torn to the hydrants of its blood.

"We crawled over our own dead to make the heights, our muddied corpses no different than the soggy wood. We threw them into piles to make our barricades, but still the Spanish held the higher ground. Eighty of ours already dead. The smoke, the screams, the cries, the calls, murdered in their noise. I laid my head upon the stock of my firelock, saw the flash. The smoke dispersing above the charnel of the land. Our wounded thrashed upon the hillside, their fingers convulsing, grasping in the mud. The battle done. Baskerville, exhausted, had enough of war and bravery and of command. We pulled our wounded by the hands or legs or shirts and dragged them from the slopes, the Spanish firing at our retreat. In the chambers of the jungle we staggered through its open tomb. No Cimarrone did I see. The jungle had no human eyes, all glances now were only to our discontents.

"We made Nombre de Dios on January second, 1596. Drake, upon his final history, had come to this defeat. For two days our shards and scatter staggered through the streets. Had Baskerville at Capirilla pressed his moment to its final consequence? No one was ever sure, but still he pledged himself to the last drop of his soldiers' blood, his words but to armor his vacant heart. Drake spoke to his council. His a hollowed will forced to be a will at all. Drake's words, recalled from other speeches said long ago, had an unconvincing tone against the fires of the circumstance. The sea had washed him in its storms, and he in its inspired gales did bring a havoc to forge his profile on the world."

"THE NEXT DAY WE BURNED NOMBRE DE DIOS. IT WAS AN ACT OF spite against a fearful truth. Our sail a canvas of forlorned cloth, the wind slight to breathless against its limp cradles. We made to the bay of Honduras to plunder what towns were there. Drake anchored his fleet at the island of Escudo, sending pinnaces to spy upon the riches of the bay. Reports soon to our ears. Those towns were poor, nothing worth the wind to bring us there.

"Our spies learned that Drake's delay along the coast east of Cartagena and Rio de la Hacha had given the Spanish a month to bring to Panama reinforcements from Peru. Drake now slipped into his dreaded grief. His cheeks were caverns blushed in ash, his face stone white, as if his eyes had sunken into marble continents. We stayed at Escudo for thirteen days, refitted as we could, built some pinnaces, our provisions low. Then we sailed toward Panama. That land, its histories conspiring to have us all again."

Old Jonas looked at me and said, "Through my life I bargained to barter transcendence with my pain. I thought it was the path to the philosopher's stone. What perfect divinities, immortality beneath my touch, its caress to hold some fragment of a lesser god. Touch the stone to lead, it creates gold. Touch pain to thought, it creates all truth. To the alchemist there are two golden resurrections: the gold of metal and the gold of Eden. But my stone has crumbled into dust, and Drake let fall a promise from his hands, an Eden's gift, an apple cleansed. In all this desperation, what hope for me? And how my great teacher Paracelsus, that titan, is now so dressed in foolishness? He the most famous alchemist who ever lived, the first great physician. A century displaced, empires crushed under the thimble of his words. All that is, is born of ruin. He who taught me had changed the world. Imagination was his philosopher's stone. He believed alchemists should set aside their search for gold and search instead for medical cures, saying, 'No metals, only man our chemistry. Diseases are the imperfections of the world.'

"Paracelsus now courted a better truth. He the healing wizard, his hands about the cauldron, his mind fixed on medical fires, burning in portraits only his to know. Ideas have souls, and all our alchemies divine a thought. Paracelsus had created human life. Created life, he claimed, announcing it to the world printed with his receipt: 'Human sperm placed in a glass vial, buried in cow dung for forty days then removed, placed in a magnetic field and fed on human blood for forty more.' The mixture then of human form was called by Paracelsus a homunculus. Educated, it talked, it spoke and breathed, or so he said. Paracelsus the physician watched his homunculus, wondering of his beast. Always he laid his path on deeper thoughts. 'Let the inspired sing their hymns to artifice. It is not art,' said Paracelsus. 'Does my shadow presume itself a portrait of a man?' The homunculus, wild-eyed, shrieked again its name, leaping a monkey dance, his hand holding to a book. 'This masquerade pretends a life.' And so Paracelsus smothered this thing. 'It had the mask of something of a life. It had no soul, only madness its spirit dreamt.'

"And who of us is great enough to strangle his own delusions in their soulless bloom?" the mariner said as he looked at me.

"ON JANUARY TWENTY-THIRD WE MADE PUERTO BELLO AND THE island of Buena Ventura, not far from Nombre de Dios. Drake was now a man searching for his time to die. 'Oh that the world would abandon me to the pleasures of my mind,' he said the last time I saw him on deck. Diseases prowled and sailed their sickness along the timbers of the ship. Contagions by liquid drips, plagues now rattled in the wood. The water fouled. Breezes hot and damp like sweat and fever on the cheek. We would not eat the fruits along the beaches for fear of gaining some disease, and so appalled we stayed our place. Each day our company died in its dozen. The captain of the *Delight* dead, and James Wood, the surgeon of the fleet. Even medicine had cast down its cures. Each day the bodies thrown overboard to salt their death and wash in their slippery gray, bloated, eyeless and stiff upon the coast near Nombre de Dios.

"Drake stayed to his cabin. He would not rise from his bed for days. The ship had sailed the sailor to his sheets. Storms, almost constant dark, clouds growled and flung angry bolts across the bay. Waters rose in mists and scattered upon the rocks. The sea convulsed upon itself, and in the aftermath a haunted fog lay upon the fleet. Drake weakened, his soul no longer in the storms. Gather your scavengers, the immortal meat is now an easy meal. Jonas Bodenham, Drake's nephew, sat the deathwatch, papers and wills in his hand, which, when signed, would make him Drake's heir and executor of his estate. The worth of the man who once saved England had come to be his signature. Bodenham had offered Drake's new servant, Thomas Rattenbury, one hundred pounds to leave him alone with the dying admiral. Rattenbury refused. Drake's brother warned. Thomas Drake hurried to the bedside, standing the deathwatch to protect the admiral for a safer death. Some papers signed. Thomas Drake made executor and heir. Bodenham given a manor house. Drake asked the two to make a pledge of peace. The pledge made, but words have never been the bone to lead the dog.

"Late that night Drake rose, in the last mortuary of his bones, ordering his servant to dress him in his armor. He spread wide his arms as wings draped in the sheets of his bedclothes. As a mighty bird, he waited to be dressed in iron. The servant begged him to take his rest and save his strength. Drake nodded and slipped again into the familiar warmth. It was finished, this futile gesture, but are not all great men futile gestures?

"That night, so late the dawn seemed to expire before it grew upon the air, he died. The news to the fleet. The cannons roared their elegies. Trumpets sang their sorrows in their last salutes. They placed his body in a leaden coffin. So much weight so it would sink. His body not to be swept ashore to rot upon a beach. Into the waters we lowered him, the sea drinking him to its bones. 'I am what fearful consequence,' sang the surf. The sea rolled in its elegies into miles of its last caress. Love had taken the lover to itself."

"THE FLEET SAILED FOR HOME. ITS FAILURE WAS BUT THE SMALLER grief. For months in Plymouth gloom. Thunder there thought to be but drum rolls in the clouds. Elizabeth, Drake's wife, furious at her husband's final will, brought suit in court and had it mostly overturned. She, now one of the richest women in all England, married a year later, 1597, to the lascivious and wanton Sir William Courtenay. How well he played his dice upon her innocent cloth. Elizabeth dying the next year of no cause, it seemed, but whispers. Drake's estate now reverted to his family. Thomas Drake and Jonas Bodenham in court and in foul of each other's blood for years. Thomas, in the final play, gaining all. And so great men leave their estate to inherit greed, the nation all the rest."

As I stood to leave the mariner to his private death on that Jamestown beach, he looked to me and said, "How true Mandinga spoke those years ago. Drake was not for the common way. For him no grave to mark his passage. His ashes to the air, his body ever to roll in the breakers of the sea."

And so the old mariner. His soul had spent its sorrow and he passed into those nostalgias which had swallowed him. I found his body that next morning of so long ago, and now his face fades into forgetfulness. I can but recall his voice. His life, that awakened tear, its globes spill in hurt from that watered eye, the writ and witness of the world.

Chapter Thirty-two

THE STORM'S SALVATION IS BUT TO A PIRATE'S GREED.

EARS FROM THOSE EVENTS sat I in my cabin with the mariner's words. Poyrune's ship at anchor in Fayal Bay in the Azores, those islands Drake's expedition could not have. Is distance traveled but an arc of a battered compass? Is it a sign that I have now Drake's mantle and his flame, the voices of the river, his lost alchemies? Alone, I sat my hours while the French pirates chased the ghosts of Portuguese ships across a sea of taunts ever toward the west. Dark the hungry waters swept me past the last of all my loves, I still desiring to find my way again, my voyage to my lost New England. If there in my mind, why not by pen and book?

I will not sleep in the hibernations of small forms. This book to plan the perfections of another colony, a better Virginia. By ink and vellum, a bound enticement for investors and coin for another voyage.

Experience betters the philosophies of the wise. Ideas are only playthings of the mind. I gained in dirt. The sweaty hand in earth holds fast the ground. From Captain Poyrune I had quill and ink and paper. The sea water from the deck dripping onto my pages, my eyes on the pearls of those many stains. I wrote of the land in its faraways, my marbled calligraphies its continent. Drake left nothing of his words. All of him is of forgotten echoes, but for me in the forever of my books.

All the while I wrote, Captain Poyrune's fleet pursued the distant sails, greeding for ships of the Portuguese East Indies or the Spaniards of the Americas. How far the run of pirates upon the sea? Their sight never past their hands. I wrote of the new continent where men of title cannot rob the industry of the weak. Where poverty is no one's staple. Where work rewards. Where each man is born with the wealth of his own initiative. No riches from Spanish mines, all silver brings but debt. No slavery, no persecutions flamed by greed. No man better, no man worse who is not made so but by lack of work. No titled sloth. Each man, each woman, each child, each the creator of himself. All to rise upon the sea, the New England waters filled with fish to freight the world with food. And there is our living mine, where each can pick the silver from his net, cast equal to any strength. Lands free in abundance, one's labor is kept to labor for oneself. The weakening blood of titles gone. Men to their own destinies born. Each in his own to be ordained.

Food persuades silver from the poor. It is the shield. Have not the Dutch by fishing paid the cost of all their wars with Spain, while the Spanish mines of gold and silver, with all their slavery, left Philip and his heirs in debt? Where famine grows, a coin cannot counterfeit a meal. Food is often overlooked, but its philosophies simple in every gut. And the New England waters have it by the eternal ton. Ships sent to New England with supplies and colonists can refreight by sea, carrying wealth both ways, a double profit; three ways if you add the new colonies to the list. Nothing good is done except by profit, so let its cause be our cause, our ally to our enterprise. All men come to the perfection their wealth allows. But what men of title have attained may soon be lost, their station coming stagnant. Only where all can rise, can a nation never debase itself. Wealth is not by gold alone. I am the apostle of these new treasures. The old laws fail, as I become the will of this new world.

I WROTE BELOW DECKS. I ROSE ON THE WINGS OF THE FALCON'S quill. The weather foul, for days the ships contended with the sea. The water mountained, white spray blew on the gusts. My candle swayed. I wrote. Poyrune's fleet dispersed. The water calmed. Poyrune sighted sail upon the distant point. It was an English pirate named Barra.

Pirates by their hostile greed tack their humors into war. Lightning salvos hailed through their rolling heat. Clouds worked with cinders burned the lungs, while cannons on their many decks broke into cannonades. How cried the fevered screams, the wounded carried from the butchery, the sound above of haste and struggle, silence soon and cheers. Barra to his chains, his ship taken and sent as a prize to a secret port. Poyrune pleased, an extra cup of wine at our meal.

I returned to my writing. The sea is ever a lonely continent. I told of New England. "It is yet a treasure," I said, "set in a band of riches that spreads round the world. From the East Indies through Asia, through India and Persia, to Greece, all one circuit, one circumstance of wealth in fertile ground. The same clouds that watered the species of the Eastern Islands and washed Drake's great bay of Nova Albion let fall their fertile rain on the New England capes." All this I wrote and all the while the schools of fish swam the cold, blue waters of the New England banks. Their waiting harvest bore the force to launch the fleet to sail my colony and bring a common wealth to the uncommon few who would try to mine a purpose from a dream.

And all about Poyrune's ships the sea blushed its mead, dark and polished. Two Portuguese of the East Indies were seized and a small caravel from Brazil, loaded with three hundred and seventy chests of sugar and one hundred hides and thirty thousand reales of eight.

At his table that night Poyrune was in such joy he drooled into his meal. His hunger was ever in his mind. "More," he ordered his ragged servant, his plate held empty to the man. "More is good." He laughed in my direction. "More is very good." When he spoke, he spit his food. I thought of his promise to have me released in the Azores or onto the next ship he sent at liberty to continue home.

"If the caravel is to be sailed to France and La Rochelle, I would wish to be aboard her, and released...as you have long pledged to me," I said.

Poyrune sucked the food stains from his fingernails. "I am having the thoughts of all this." he belched. "I am not against...but not considered to agree. But soon, maybe in the Azores." I argued for my release. I was not in truth a prisoner. Poyrune laughed. He fell then to a contest of our wills.

THE NEXT DAY I WAS SENT TO THE CARAVEL, MY BOOK WRAPPED in canvas to protect it from the spray. "Are you pleased by half, my friend?" said Poyrune. "Your voyage finished is now half begun anew."

The captain of the caravel was Poyrune's thin and nervous lieutenant André Du Pons, who walked his deck like a stalk of brittle wheat, his expression sour on his wrinkled lips, as if his thoughts had the taste of rot. That night he asked me if I would sign a paper which would discharge Poyrune and himself of any guilt occasioned by their stopping of my ship. I set the question aside without a firm answer. Du Pons waved some threat of mischief on his turn of words. "The waters never make good witness," he said to me in French.

FOR THREE MORE WEEKS THE THREE SHIPS SAILED TOGETHER AS a fleet, taking several other prizes, then, in the final days of October, we made for France, anchoring in the Breton straits off L'Aiguillon, between the island the French called Ile de Ré and the main where lies La Rochelle.

There we stayed six days, I held as prisoner. The currents oozed in heavy swills to snake about the hulls. The clouds now clawed upon the earth, the sky darkening. Du Pons came to me again in my cabin, accusing me of being Argall, who had destroyed the French settlements in Maine two years before. But all this he would forget and forgive if I granted his request and signed the papers discharging himself and Poyrune from any consequences of their acts against me. They desired me to further state that I was a member of their crew when on their ship, and so a pirate. It was a plot to keep me from testifying against them in all matters. "It is with the assurance of your silence you buy your freedom. And so by nothing you buy everything," Du Pons said in his French, adding the colored threat to push my ink. "How useless are screams, the water here is deep enough above the throat." Du Pons smiled, his French on the point of his tongue.

I smiled as I said in English while I lifted my pen, "A slight delay, but time will ever be for this agreement." With that, Du Pons left. I gathered the manuscript of my book, wrapped it in cloth, then canvas, tucking it into my shirt.

The winds now whistled through the rigging. The hatches banged, their hinges rattled, the ship swaying and pitching in the rising swells. Rain fell in heavy drifts. The crew below deck sang and drank in safety from the storm. I stole into the shadows of the passageway, quietly, my feet held to careful, weightless steps. On the footfalls of ghosts, I made the ladder to the deck. The closed hatches above my head pounded on their frames and rocked in the fright of terrors beyond the door. I slipped the lock, pushing open the wooden door. Rain in shrapnel stung my face. The sky was in war upon the air. The mood of the tempest fell in squalls, as lightning cut salvos through the dark. Mists ran the earth in shrieking vapors. I found a small boat on deck. It had no oar. I grabbed a half pike, I had no choice. I lowered myself into the turning mill that was the sea.

I rowed toward Ile de Ré, the currents pulling toward the dark of the open sea, the winds and tide pushing toward shore. I laboring by oar, bailing with an old tin pan, to have by luck the beach. My boat almost turned around in fury of the gale. The contest of the current and of the wind and my boat. My life but the fabric of their joke. On I fought, my muscles breaking into pain. The narrows in ghostly swells, the air rushed between the points of land and I sat its race. Shot through the straits, the boat twisted. Waves broke into my face. I drank the salt as a merry wine, the wind's brutal laugh, its frolic to dance upon my death. But still I rowed and bailed, the falling mountains of the waves sweeping in white breakers upon my boat. With my pike as an oar, I rowed the flood, my boat now but a raft, and the waters rising.

HOW THE SUN DAWNS UPON THE EYES HALF-DROWNED. ALL HEAT now wet and frozen to my skin. I found myself asleep in ooze, my shirt torn to rags. The pages of my book were scattered around me on the mud. Ink ran in the water. Words lost or indistinct, their ideas as runs upon the page. I gathered what sheets I could. My boat still one, and I stared on the marsh of the Charente River. Birds flew in hoist, dark blankets across the scarlet east. Hunters found me and gave me heat and rest and dry blankets. I sold my boat for a few coins, enough to make passage for La Rochelle.

In that city, I learned that Captain Poyrune's ship had been split and wrecked on the coast not seven leagues from where I had escaped and he with half his crew were drowned. And so there is no plot to make a dominion safe enough from death, but still I learned that some of the Spanish reales of eight were saved. I, wanting some satisfaction for my months held prisoner, went to the admiralty office to make complaint and some claim on a piece of the Brazilian treasure. There, all good words and French promises I had, little other than lullabies to rest a fool. Always empty breaths and lies are baked well into sweet pastries by the French.

Not long after, leaving the judge of the admiralty, I met by chance some of Du Pons's crew, who thought I was dead, but not being so, I had them arrested to give sworn testimony to confirm my complaints. All these documents I had presented to the English ambassador, who gave me many assurances but little aid. My French lawyers were of better humor, giving me as they could, saying there was a case but "a case is not any assurance of any justice." And so I sat and walked my misery through La Rochelle those many weeks, thinking that law is but a practice to itself, and we who desperately hold it as a chance are but backwashed idlers to the game.

My book was now dry, some sheets torn, with portions lost. I repaired what I could, rewrote what I remembered, redrafted, bringing words to words again from ghastly smudges. This book was a sod but not yet a ruin. Some of it lost forever, but I still impassioned with its truth. Slowly it bloomed again. I called it A Description of New England. By luck I met Samuel Cramton, the master whaler of the New England voyage, a good fisherman, and as always his brotherhood a generous soul. Cramton did more with kindness, loans and influence to get me to English soil again than did the king's ambassador. And so, with a ship arranged, and little prospect of compensation from the French, I left La Rochelle, leaving to my lawyers all the plot that hope could dust, and sailed for home and Plymouth once again.

PART THREE

The All Knowing
of My Name

THE ALCHEMIES OF THE RIVER

*I am of whorls and liquid dust, currents passing in my
genealogies of drift. Beneath azure! It seasons into
clouds and rain, I into a flowing calm. Life worms in
my hollow light. Alive to an emptiness, I fade.*

Chapter Thirty-three

THE THICKET IS A WEED,
ITS JUNGLE GROWS UPON ITS SMOKE.

RRIVING IN PLYMOUTH IN December of 1615, I learned that those who had deserted me in the Azores had looted my clothes and books and arms, and all else that was mine, dividing the spoils among themselves. Many of those who were then about I had arrested and thrown into prison. A few remedied their sad estate by testifying in court before the vice-admiral of Devonshire on my behalf. Much that was stolen was returned. Sir Ferdinando Gorges in a wide-eyed stammer at my return, believing the stories of my crew, thinking I was dead. All that is luck may only be a cheat against the game. How the gambler wagers is not always how he wins.

He who holds ill luck as God's sign is already a forfeit. And so I planned for another voyage. My second ship, which had escaped the pirates, had returned that August well freighted with fish, the company in health. Gorges and the Plymouth Company were never pleased. Little profit had from all the freight. As ever, they filled the air with great promises, but air is air; so I left them to their arid numbers and returned to London.

What creatures are cities to heave their plagues upon their streets? All London's refuse lay quilted in damp and clinging filth, every thoroughfare a wallow, a lake of oozing sewerage. It moves as if it were the city's blood. King James still at war with the weed, but his treasury saved an embarrassment by his tax on imported tobacco. The impost, as the tax was called, had been granted in 1604. Not collected directly by the exchequer, it was farmed to court favorites, they paying the king a yearly sum for the right to gather the duty. From 1604 to 1613 the Earl of Montgomery received, it is guessed, twelve thousand pounds a year from the tax. The king repurchased the rights to his own revenues from Montgomery for three thousand pounds a year for the next twenty-one years. The king then sold, without the approval of parliament, a monopoly to import all tobacco in England and Ireland to two court favorites for seven thousand pounds a year. The trade in Spanish tobacco was then valued at two hundred thousand pounds a year. Such weight of Spanish leaf brought to England, such an export of gold and silver coins to Spain, that metal currency was coming scarce in England. Commerce began to fail. Many thought real wealth in metal bullion was being shipped to an enemy, Spain.

Months before my arrival in Plymouth a pamphlet was published in London, its author only signing his work by the initials C.T., An Advice on How to Grow Tobacco in England. In its pages was outlined the method for growing the Nicotiana rustica variety of the weed in English soil. The tract promised vast wealth and quick rewards for all who farmed the weed. Tobacco farming now spread from the London pale to Gloucester and Worchester. Acreage once used for cereals and food now sported the weed, and famine. Food prices rose.

But that was not the fist upon the king's throat. Domestic leaf was untaxed. An English crop weakened the sovereign's purse. The king always in debt, and in Virginia only tobacco was its small success. Ever in parliament were other politics. "Why should the king choose his own for the monopolies and the gathering of taxes without the approval of the lords and commons?" So quietly the world works its axes through the air.

KINGS ARE KINGS AND DISPOSE OF THEMSELVES AS THEY WILL. But I do have old friends at court, David Hume, who I met in Paris that long ago, giving me letters of introduction to James in Scotland before he ascended the English throne. Others, Sir Samuel Saltonstall, his father Richard, Lord Mayor of London, the Willoughbys. I am braced in influence not inches from the crown, but no courtier, I, no wealth to seal my stamp upon the helm.

Lost by the sliver of a coin, I am defaulted by my name. Old Jonas, your money not enough. Ruin blooms in its petty season. No one mentions Dee, or Jonas, or the alchemies. We, the wastrels, are bludgeoned by a purse. How easily we spend our mysteries, only to be the truant before the only gate.

. . . . . .

ALL THIS NESTED IN SILENCE NOW. SAMUEL PURCHAS WELCOMED me, as well my friends. Purchas lent me news of Virginia. More letters from Hamor came to my hands. I read their lists, a snatch of sense baked into their chronicles. So much the mirror cannot show. The surface presents the tale, its curtain drawn across the inner depth.

Arriving at Jamestown after his visit to Powhatan, Hamor found the colony as peaceful as fear could enlist. Dale was in a constant rage. Free to make his own laws, Dale leased a vengeance as his right, William Parker, lately saved from Powhatan, he wanted to try, then burn at the stake for living with the savages. Hamor and Argall protested. Captain Yeardley, seeing his governor's wisdom, would bow to any murder to gain for himself an advantage. It was said of Yeardley, "He came with nothing, rose on nothing, to become nothing." But, in truth, soon he would become the governor.

Parker was saved from the stake by Hamor's testimony and by Argall. Yet when three deserters were returned by those Hamor called "our savages," they were bound struggling, knowing what awaited them. There rumored another two deserters had found refuge with the Ocanahonan. "Our savages," fearful of the one called "The Alone," failed to press their commission against that tribe. Dale swore vengeance. "I will hold my time until I find their country, then I shall bring the Ocanahonan ruin," he said, with one of our friendly Indians observing, "They are the same, like the strangers, black but of yours. Some speak your tongue. Captain Smith had knowledge of them."

"Captain Smith is gone, blessed with our good riddance," Dale replied, hearing only his own thoughts now. "They are not ours. If they are, they are traitors; if not, they are savages who have broken the peace." Dale took now to his dealing with the deserters, whom he broke upon the wheel, each bone snapping in a crack of agony. For hours he watched them die, the company held as witness. The bleeding plates that once were men shivered, mad with pain, slipping closer to death. Dale brought them heat. He burned them living on their wheels. Their flesh to smoke, their faces to ashes, they screamed their horror, pleading for their own death.

Argall sailed on June eighteenth for London. Dale had fixed in his mind to bring to every slight the reckoning of the whip. Executions were the law in Virginia. English practice forgot. Dale made his whim the canon. Why do men seek to hold others to the surface of their rigid law? A tyrant in the world is a weakling in himself. His actions are the armor to hide the wayward of his soul.

IN THE COLONY, CRUSHED TREACHERIES HUNG UPON THE AIR, and hungry men stood in lazy revolt. In London I heard Argall told the proper lies, that the colony prospered and men now worked. Dale's stain of violence in the corner of his mind, Argall feared returning to Jamestown without the protection that lies could counterfeit. But Argall was accused by the French of an unlawful attack upon their Canadian possessions. The king and the Privy Council met in London to decide the matter, with Argall and his lieutenant, William Turner, and some of the crew called to testify. The Virginia Company held itself aloof, offering little aid to Argall, who protested that all his reason lay in the laws and charters of his king and the company. "Dale was appointed an absolute. Who was I but to obey? Isn't mine but dominion of the yes?" he asked. He was acquitted.

Argall, now free with only a smudge upon his name, raged and embarrassed his own cousin, Thomas Smythe, who had, among his titles, the governorship of the East India Company. Argall sought employment there.

Captain Newport had just returned from India. Humiliated by Dale at Point Comfort, Newport resigned his position as admiral to seek a position as captain in the India trade. The East India Company interviewed Newport concerning Argall's abilities, of which the good captain gave great endorsement. Which was true enough, within the limits of the truth. The moment then was set for Argall to transfer his allegiance.

IN ST. PAUL'S CHURCHYARD FOR YEARS THERE HAD BEEN HELD a small daily lottery. The prizes were of no great sum. In 1567, Queen Elizabeth herself had instituted a public lottery to raise moneys for her treasuries. Her subjects happy then with low taxes. She in desperate need of resources, the new Navy being built. The lottery was no better than an easy hope. It failed, but need rarely abandons the discreet objects of its desires. In 1612, the first lottery was held to raise money for the London Company, the company despairing in its debts. Smaller investors were tasting the salt of ruin upon their bread. The lottery was a disappointment, but still a hope. In 1614 there was talk of another try. A lottery to be held in June of 1616 was first announced in broadside in February of 1615, allowing a year and a half for great sums to be subscribed. Argall, half-seduced by these prospects, held to the avarice that he knew. He by greed, no gambler, stayed to Virginia, his tongue but to taste the prospects before the strike of its poisoned fangs.

In Virginia, men began to rise from idleness: one hundred acres of land for each man, woman and child. In the smoke of tobacco men smelled wealth. Everywhere men wanted to know the secrets to grow and harvest the weed, cure its smoke into its fiber and pack its wealth for England. Human flesh now in measured fields, all labor became a greed for its single coin. The land in fire, everywhere the smell of endless burnings. The forests cracked in agonies as they fell. The landscape regrew at three shillings a pound. Had not the government of the new world licensed men to beasts to their private fancy? "We are not sent to Virginia to grow a pleasure. Tobacco will not be the apple of our Eden," complained Reverend Buck. There are no seductions in which we do not seduce ourselves, and with the easy coin its apostle, always comes the bedded harlot.

The world was an egg in a nervous nest. Men dreamed of crops, waiting for the spring. Dale tortured the colony into quiet. Peace with the Indians uneasy. All this for a shriveled leaf of gold, a vegetable to weed a fortune. Men thought and talked and traded advice, tobacco the ball to roll into its own history. Rumors were repeated into belief, then to legends. Myth became the science.

IN LONDON, THE COMPANY STRUGGLED AGAINST ITS DEBTS. THE king spoke again of silk as the only proper venture for the new world. All past failures ignored, arrogance now choked remembrance, and each ship Jamestown-bound brought worms for the mulberry trees. They died. Shipbuilding failed. The glass factory worked with little prospects. No gold found. Iron was now the grasp among the too few prospects, and still, the company planned. While along the New England coast, salvation swam in massive schools of fish, and gills, and golden flashes.

The company sought its allies in its charities and the gifts of wealth to all, said it would grant one hundred acres of land in Virginia to adventurers who had lived there before 1616. That already done, but who in London knew? To every colonist who arrived thereafter, fifty acres of land when their term of service was done. To anyone who paid the expenses of someone's sail to Virginia, he too was granted a head right of fifty acres per person. But so many had died within a year of their landing, the truth of which was hidden, our cause made blood its exchequer. In his unknowing of all the deaths, Edwin Sandys planned in his humanities to expand the numbers of the colony. The consequence never came to his mind, yet he brought serfdom to Virginia. A servant who sailed at the company's expense, worked company land overseen by a company agent for seven years, giving half his crop to the common store, at the end of his term, he would be allotted fifty acres of land and one month's provisions.

Separate plantations were formed as companies within the company. Any group so doing could buy shares in the enterprise, and was then given a bonus of a hundred acres per share and fifty acres per tenant who sailed to Virginia at the plantation's expense. Those prospects which sought to have such good and such communal wealth brought but thieves and more drunken moods. The law of money reasoned to be the tug to make idle men work. But, beware the law. It is a heavy tablet wherein even itself is crushed.

WHAT CURSE IT IS IF MEN HAVE NOT THE PASSIONS TO INVEST themselves in dreams. I had my book, that penned soliloquy to my other lands, those New Englands. I made more repairs to its drowned pages, my ink stroking confidence across the sheets. Prince Henry, now dead, had been the guardian of the Virginia enterprise. Through Hume, I inquired of his brother, Prince Charles, to be the same for New England, sending him a copy of my map to approve the English names I set there—the "Charles River," "Massachusetts," "Cape Anne"—which he did. Now the project spoke in royal light.

The Dutch engraver Simon van de Passe cut my map to copper, with a portrait of me engraved in a corner of the page. My face now upon the land, my spirit in its hills by the press of ink. The book too was set to type, the pages pulled hard into print.

THE SECOND TOBACCO CROP ARRIVED IN PLYMOUTH. FOUR hundred and twenty pounds more, and better cured. Three shillings each pound of leaf. Sixty pounds sterling for the whole cargo. Fair news to Eden, even a fallen Eden of the Chesapeake. Now all hearts beat in greed. A thousand pounds of tobacco will bring me what? Or two thousand or five thousand? And so Virginia discovered pounds in silver it never knew.

The danger was at hand, but the London Company had little good information, the self-serving reports to England mostly lies. "We will not be vassal to the weed," Edwin Sandys' words no longer the conscience to jury of the cause.

The king announced in a fury, "I will not be the sovereign of smoke."

The company in London, planned to discourage the weed, but would the London Company murder itself by murdering its own child abed? The company, being a wise parent, tried to wean the baby before it ever had the vice.

The council now tantrumed into uncivil wars. Rumors that Thomas Smythe and Edwin Sandys hardly spoke. I heard the news. Lightning broke thunder upon its gossip. Edwin Sandys' brother, George Sandys, to sail to Virginia as treasurer of the colony. Perhaps now I could string the faulted plot and nail my name again to history, return to Virginia with Sandys, protected by his office and his brother. I rushed to George Sandys' rooms. My journey come to me, my map is drawn in victory, I thought. Sandys' welcoming hand upon my shoulder, dead in its unmoving touch. "I have heard the report. Are you to go?" I said.

Sandys, stiff in his thoughts, nodded to the distance. "I am to be the remedy for the disease, the elixir and my family's loyal pawn, sent to Virginia to encourage other wealth and discourage the planting of the profligate weed. Again, my inheritance is but to serve. Others will be the governors. I am left to rise only to the knee. Without much wealth, it is my brother's bribe. Doubly am I stewed in my brother's single sauce. I have already seen it in the east. It will not work, these wars against tobacco." Then Sandys laughed, as if scalding the air with bitter cheer. "But my twin again I shall trespass on your abandonments. I am your shadow. Any letters or messages to those voices in the wilderness, a forest maid, or are you sufficient now in London?"

I looked at George Sandys, wondering what cynics such a misspent heart. Sandys had oversaid his mind. I wondered what lethals in their beginning would haunt Virginia to what consequence. I tried to hold my fears as I respoke my case. "Is there some service I can still do in Virginia? May I not sail with you as your deputy or be appointed some office by you or your brother? I am eager for a chance to be again some parent to Virginia."

Sandys sat in his considerations, his face displeasured by his thoughts. "This decision is for the council. My brother will never risk more controversy on your behalf. Smythe is not persuaded to be your friend. You are too useful to be discarded, but your vision for the New World held dangerous to their nervous prerogatives.

"The company has written a new code of government. The reports of Dale's cruelties are common about London, the whispers discouraging both investors and new colonists. 'Not a second England that would pride an Englishman,' is the talk in the carriages. The new plan has a governor and his council, but with powers reduced, they to be the squeak again of the London Company's prompt. Such a pride my brother's Virginia. My brother to ship his fists over another sea, I the cart to guard the cargo, carrying the new laws to Virginia. I, the discard to a better son, will come again to a strange land."

As Sandys then sat into the shadows of his chair, he became a silhouette. "There is too much profit in tobacco. Avarice hangs upon its leaf. Perhaps I can persuade by wealth a balance for myself against my brother's weight." Sandys smiled. "I would not spend your hope for an office in Virginia, Smith; but I will by the limits of my influence present your cause. New England is the better choice. Seek where others have not plundered." Sandys and I talked an hour more of Virginia. Then I left, he readying himself for his journey west. But by arguments and delays within the company, it would be two years before Sandys sailed. Held by a pin, we both wriggled appalled of hope. Sandys, as ever, raged against his brother's crimes. While waiting upon my future prospects, I walked the London streets thinking, my kingdoms, my loves, ever out of reach.

IN FEBRUARY OF 1615 ARGALL SAILED TO VIRGINIA BY THE northern route. For five months he disappeared, no one quite knowing what he did, or where he kept. Having his part, in his own ship, he was at no one's call. It was supposed he made for Canada to trade furs from the savages. If so, it came to nothing, Argall arriving in Virginia that summer with an empty ship and a bloodied crew.

Tobacco everywhere grew, readying for harvest. Men toiled in the fields, their souls turned to ledgers, now slaves to a vegetable master. More each week became infected with the disease, waiting now for the next season to begin the planting. Rain and sun and land were but the blessings to grow the weed.

Dale was in a frightful mood. The peace with the savages mostly held, but still there was murder. Victuals were scarce. Men planted tobacco instead of corn.

Dale still hung and burned and broke men on the wheel for petty crimes. The company only whispering of wealth. Then Dale called for vengeance against the Ocanahonan. "It will be soon. It will be soon," he said. That rage now deafening all his thoughts. Dale ordered one hundred well-armed men to Argall's ship. Yeardley as deputy commander, with savages as guides, they set forth to destroy the Ocanahonan.

I read the report Argall wrote to Edwin Sandys.

We made the Potomac, the mist swirling into rain. Clouds broke into airy cliffs. We marched inland into the forest, through the undergrowth that weaved their obstructions into thicket walls. The noise of our coming shaking the leaves, still we marched, our savages cautioning us to be silent. We pushed on like pans rattling against a shelf of spoons. Birds fled in horror before the beast of our metal strides.

In days we made the hill above the Ocanahonan town. The place below deserted. "What men are these that build pyramids of mud?" Dale said, looking at three great mounds of earth. A voice ushered in a diminishing cry from the valley. "I am the alone...I am the tribe." The world silent but for the screams of the birds. Dale ordered drums to sound as we moved forward toward the village walls. The voice again echoed from the harmonies of air, "We are but your own. Cast down your murder. We crave but an intoxication. Seek us not for we are spirit. Seek us now and forever lose yourselves." The voice was quiet. We broke the gates. The village was empty. Not a rag. Dale in a final rage swore vengeance even on his own. He reddened in his face, and smashed his fist against the log of the village gate and broke his wrist.

We scouted the countryside for some days, found nothing but another mystery to spice again the land, another tribe to count among the lost.

AT JAMESTOWN AGAIN, DALE, IN A DOUBLE RAGE, BLAMED ALL others for his defeat. Argall, in fear for his life, spent his time with

Yeardley at the town called Bermuda Hundred, where the inhabitants worked the earth to blackened pits, making pitch and tar, which pleased the London Council, pitch not being tobacco.

In that summer of 1615 Pocahontas had her child. The date of his birth unknown, recorded to no testament. A minor act to the marriage that sealed the peace, a child that should have been mine. His name was Thomas, a flesh to eclipse the failing hours of the peace.

THE TOBACCO HARVEST THAT YEAR WAS THOUSANDS OF POUNDS, much of it ruined by growers of little knowledge. The plants were harvested on the fever of many rumors, either too early or too late. Worms ate the leaves to an empty lace. Tapping done at the wrong time, transplanting fouled, proper curing still a mystery. "With a little practice and trial, our curing will bring a leaf as good a pudding as the West Indies," said Rolfe, not yet knowing the Virginia tobacco would never have the excellence of that southern crop, but it would be good enough.

Rolfe was appointed recorder and secretary to the Colony. Dale, encouraged to see men work, encouraged tobacco, allowing it to extend its leaf into the new settlements. "Let work be a habit, and we may soon have a colony," said Dale. Where we English walked, soon tobacco was planted in our steps. Seeking to secure the colony in a better peace, Dale founded more forts along the James. At Jamestown, at West and Shirley Hundred, their companies planted only weed.

Smythe was not hopeful in my struggle to return. George Sandys, soon to sail to Virginia, could do little, or so he said. What rage is mine to any purpose. All my opportunities have come a squander.

BY THE SPRING OF 1616, VIRGINIA LAY UPON THE BUD, THE BLOOM waiting to burst the soft stems. After five years in the new world, Sir Thomas Dale decided to sail home with Argall. In London, the lottery was set for June of that year. Men cast their hopes to paper, while in Virginia men cast their hopes to a weed. Rolfe and Pocahontas and their young son sailed with Argall. He who once brought her as prisoner bows now as her servant. She the princess of an imperial line, the blood of England mixed with hers. Rolfe never suspected that when she looked at Argall she looked through him to see myself. Most of us never knowing we are but the continued refuse to replay another's dream.

GEORGE SANDYS WORKING ON HIS GREAT PARAPHRASE, HIS translation of Ovid, wrote me he was sailing in a month to have his office as the colony's treasurer. "The consternation within the London Company is at a quiet. I am to collect the thousand pounds in unpaid taxes due the London Company. A thousand acres are given for me, fifty servants and a hundred and fifty pounds to pay my way. Those moneys nowhere to be found, I am bribed with an empty purse. So tells my worth. My servants not yet secured, I am to have the loan of those Italian being sent to rebuild the glass factory. And so my life is indentured to my brother's shadow. I am to fix the cream before the cheese is rot—set the colony's finances, send London honest reports and suppress tobacco, the only profit Virginia has ever brought." Then Sandys' words rose into premonitions and confession of a future crime. He did by Ovidian rhapsodies indict himself. "I will sail following into the west. The sea rising, my many ghosts about me, howling to an unknown crime. My old life slipping free, the horizon haunted in darkening clouds. As I sail, cleansed in my growing snake, shedding the cloak of my useless skin, secretly I am purified for the coming sin."

I held Sandys' letter in my hand, thinking it a poetic idle to delight a foul of humor. I put it aside. Sandys in his secret jealousies with his brother, Drake struggling with his father's ghost. I asked myself, So, do all our family wars overflow their estate to consume the world? It was a slight of thought that passed. Its profundities never turned.

By June 18, 1616, my New England book was from the press and bound and ready for the public will. It was then two days later I learned Pocahontas with her husband and her child were landed and in London.

Chapter Thirty-four

A TAVERN, A PITTANCE THAT PRETENDS A PALACE.

OCAHONTAS AND ROLFE and their child were staying at the Belle Sauvage Inn, not far from the stinking lanes around Fleet Street, that thoroughfare where garbage littered dung to ooze so foul a vapor even the rains could never wash the air to sweet. The mist there, heavy with chill, clammed upon the throat and sickened lungs. All about, the crowds, the treeless streets, the sooted stones chalked with reams of dirt. The poisons ever in the humors of the air. The Virginia Company pledged four pounds a week to see Pocahontas housed and fed and well maintained. A pittance to a poverty. The company to use the sight of a born savage princess to raise the plate and call for more moneys for their enterprise. Everywhere Pocahontas was the conversation. In its carriages London could speak of little else. The company knew that whoever guides the fashion holds a filling purse. It was all a plot to play for notice and power, and she alone the prop upon the stage.

There were cold airs that damp spring. Her child, I heard, was not well. Some of the ten savages brought with Pocahontas to England were already dead. Lord De la Warr and Wingfield kept Pocahontas to themselves. In such company I had no chance of seeing her. How soft my thoughts in their painful bounties. Others might have kissed cruelties on her lips, wished her ill, played disdain, but if the pain be mine, let my agonies be sipped in kindness. I picked up my quill and wrote to Queen Anne, and so at our best are we spent by memories. I had no court or acquaintance with the queen, but had my courtly friends guide the letter to her hands. I wrote the history of Pocahontas and myself, explaining for the first time how she saved my life. Why then? Perhaps passion is an embarrassment to the truth. She always to me more than love could itself admit. I wrote how she fed the colony and freed us each week from want. I told what truth I could, and one small lie: that through her, England could inherit a dominion in Virginia. "The daughter of a king, and princess, married to an English gentleman. Where flows the royal blood but to the east, to us. Treat her not so she hates us. I believe an invitation to the court will seize her with admirations beyond all bounds. What we give will be received many times. How many empires have been so built on a kindness?"

But why the dissembling? I wanted her from London and its disease. I wanted her from the Belle Sauvage Inn, a place where men of wit played smug with each other's souls, and where plays danced language to the edges of itself. All words are haunted places, and devils are but memories transfixed, they to terrify from the underneath. The mind's a motion, its language its meaning spiced, grammared on boiling transubstantiations. It was there—during the drama of Doctor Faustus, the actors all on stage chanting verse to verse, Marlowe then fresh dead, and who knows how authors spend their souls. But there, that night, it was said the devil did appear. I think across my histories. I could have been husband to her wife. Everywhere ghosts consort with ghosts and what comes in whisper may one day inundate the thresholds of the world. The new land, its spirit, its voice was once in my very ear. Too much madness is our plate. Better she be safe away. Am I the foil from which the future breaks? Better she be safe away before the inn comes to hatch some spoiled humors for her meat. Better she be gone and I better to forget. But how in my eyes she moves in fire. Better she be safe away.

THE QUEEN INVITED HER TO THE COURT MASQUE LATER THAT year, an entertainment to pamper an evening after a frolic in the afternoon. The playwright Ben Jonson invited himself to meet her at the Belle Sauvage. And so he came and stared for an hour at her without a word, untongued, his mouth open, caught dumb by the power of the sight of a savage maid dressed to the English fashion, polite and regal, speaking English. How our soul loses all presumptions to a special grace. Ever after, Jonson mentioned her in his plays, half-amused by a princess living in a tavern, and that princess once a savage. But never once did Jonson frolic at her expense, he too certain, being English, of where the justice lies.

Samuel Purchas, whose church, St. Martin Ludgate, was but a short walk up Ludgate Hill from the Belle Sauvage, kept me secretly informed of all that occasioned Pocahontas. "Your interest seems more than information can supply," said the reverend, hard to his glance.

"I have curiosities and debts to her. Why should I not inquire after her welfare?" I answered. "I am a man of many facets."

"And such is the perfume ever to the devil's nose," said Purchas.

"There is no devil that is not first born of us."

"My point, but somewhat over said," smiled the smug divine.

ROLFE HAD WRITTEN HIS NARRATIVE OF VIRGINIA AND TOBACCO for the king, a tract I saw from the reverend's hand, a splice of facts in pounds of leaf and acres of the weed, the land shuddered into numbers: the Virginia tobacco crop, twenty thousand pounds imported; the Spanish imported weed more than sixty thousand. By the company's charter and agreement with the crown, the Virginia leaf paid less tax. The king held himself aloof, but soon he would have to listen through his purser's ear. Purchas to condense the work and print it in the third edition of his *Pilgrimes*, that great collection of accounts of English explorations of the world. To Purchas, all things that were of God were worthy of a catalogue. Rolfe and Purchas dined regularly, smoked and discussed Virginia. Sometimes Pocahontas joined the guests, sometimes others of the Indians. Of all besides Pocahontas, Tomocomo caught Purchas's attention. Tall and hard and certain of his gods, England's damp and cold moved him to displeasure at all he saw. The grassless city, the crowds, the dirt, a place where baths were seldom. Indians when at home washed each morning in their rivers. "And where is your God…in his house without a voice?" said Tomocomo. "My Gods speak to me, my Okee, before my hand in human form, his hair long to one side, almost to his feet. What kind of God is yours that will not appear and speak to you when asked?"

Purchas fevered in shivered rage when he told me of their conversation. "I have heard it that all the men of our Roanoke Colony began to wear their hair long to the side, as the savages. What land is this, to bring such initiations? How corruption has fouled the apostles, and we the truth. Their devils conjure superstitions. Pocahontas, quaint in her conversion, has battled a good contest to free herself from demons." Purchas smiled. "She wears well her new English innocence, her regal bearing. She affords a good example to a better purpose. I have discussed her with the bishop of London and he wishes to dine in celebration. She and all the savages are to be invited. But you, Smith, do you wish to be present?" Purchas questioned.

"No, my time is spent, but not for pleasure," I said.

"All London tells her that you are dead. She is well guarded. The Virginia Company hates you, and you are powerless, with few friends. All she hears proclaims your death, but it is rumored that Tomocomo was sent by Powhatan to learn the truth."

"Let circumstance keep me dead for a while more," I said. "This death is not so far from death."

"Beware of lies. There is no telling where we stray in their repeating."

IT WAS BEST I BE AWAY. I TO BE AGAIN! I WAS THEN PREPARING FOR another voyage to New England. There was promise of twenty ships from Gorges and the Plymouth Company. I worked my task to raise the moneys. Pounds I had by pennies. I mined copper by my teeth. From Purchas I heard how small her figure in regal dress, moved by grace, she the object of the bishop's sweet pomp, the festival now a measure to her acclaim, she then the hour. "Never have I seen our bishop so profuse in his hospitality," he said. And so the circumstance allowed the service. The Virginia Company held, all confused. Could it spill the savage viper from its dream? A princess of the blood, she to proclaim what they had long labored to make, a Virginia different from her memories.

It came of night when worlds contest. She walked in a marriage faithless to its heart. Would the ring that held the lie hold our everything? It did, and that shadow to the eye. Purchas now planned to raise moneys to found a college in Virginia for the conversion and education of the Indians. Three hundred and fifty Englishmen then in Virginia, held to the banks of one river, half-starved, growing little other than hope to pay a portion of their way. And now Purchas wanted to have a college. Had ever better moneys lain on a meaner folly?

Pocahontas's health now weakened, Rolfe wanted to take his wife and child to his family home in Heacham in Norfolk. His mother sent messages explaining that such a wife would be welcome only in secret. "She, an apparition from a strange savage kingdom is not fit for a broad, Christian company," the good woman wrote. At the insistence of Lord Percy, Rolfe took a house in Brentwood to the west of London across the Brent River, not far from Syon House, an estate of Lord Percy's brother, the Earl of Northumberland.

That land lay in stone-fenced pastures, wheat waiting for the coming harvest, the Thames nearby, across its waters a few stands of ancient woods. Perfumed silence on the riverbanks, the hollows of the trees, branches holding forth their life, ruins twisted upward before the caverns hollowed in the bark, deep those caves in a rot of blackened wood. In the center of the decay hung the bats. Leaves, twigs and leather wings, dark the sweet corruption. Eternal death is the manure of eternal life. In that place Pocahontas found her health again. Cities are their own disease. Where fair wind cleanses, sweet breezes fill the lungs, and there in the autumn of 1616 I made my visit.

I WAS SOON TO SAIL TO NEW ENGLAND, AFTER TRAVELING TO THE west country and to Plymouth to fix my plans and raise more moneys. My time for London was then quite short. Our only chance to meet soon diminished to a single afternoon. Desperation wings desire. Every expectation forced to the fears gathering in my brain. Already rumors why no visit to reacquaint my past. Captain Martin, then in London, saying, "The savages would not look on him but to cut his throat." I now the offering to she who once offered all. What poverty haunts the beggar who casts aside his wealth.

The house sat low in its clay walls and thatched roof. The sky rolling in its gray. I came to the door. My horse, shaking exhaustion from its flesh, pawed the ground in warning, its head reared, its eyes in wild frights of some imagination. The door opened. Rolfe made cordial greeting, I went inside. I was conducted through the dark and halls into the parlor, and there she stood, a flame cutting a dry fire into the cold, a woman dressed to her womanhood.

In watery black, her eyes, large, seemed to drink all sight. She struggled against the kitchen of her dress, silently she struggled. Her hands balled. She turned away and would not speak. Sobs are more human than any words. She convulsed on broken breath. She would not speak, nor turn about. And I, caught and fevered in my animal, could show but what? Her husband softly thought and spoke his calm. To heal this broken girl would take more than saints, and I was half to blame. What tells the heart? Am I to her now but an open secret, and she married to that fool named Rolfe? My true words I held deep, but still I spoke, "You are a wonderment. My compliments, so sweetly turned in our English cloth." She would not speak.

Rolfe and I left her to the moment to have her composure. For two hours we paced to some different truth. "My wife so ill these last months. I hope you will not take offense at her surprise." How well we tie the tail of our conceit to the fabric of the dog. It is a leash that ever walks the master. We spoke of cold and all ill health and humors. How well the biles bloat the mind. I saw her son. We played to idle time. He looked a son of hers, Rolfe not set into his face.

After two hours I presented myself to her again. She now composed. "And will you call me child, so sweet in firelight as once you did?" she asked.

I blushed to myself to have a sovereign call me such, but I would have been much closer than any blood. She who would have had me to her bed and whom I did protect. Passions mingle where flesh can never touch. I was silent. "Shall I now, a stranger in your land, not call you kin?" she said. "I but in wander, a foreigner unknown of friends."

Draw me forth while I protest, why to myself can I not be true? "I am no kin, no father to your house," I said, "for you are too royal to be birthed on any humble words of mine." I to the horror of the circumstance turned, and my words tolled as if by another voice. "In your arms you gave me life, protected me from your father. We are by those moments far deeper than any kin, but what is, is not. My kinship is to sorrow, my shield is for regret."

"Alone and stranger in Powhatan's land, you called him father, as I now call you. Father you are to me as I am your child? And so you will always be." Pocahontas spoke without a glance at Rolfe. "Always I was told that you were dead, your ship had sunk or you were taken by your wounds. But still Powhatan commanded Tomocomo to search for you and know the truth. Powhatan held you in respect, and your countrymen lie much." Pocahontas came now into the light of the fire's heat. Pocahontas whispered to my ear words filled with lifetimes in their thoughts. "What have I not given to your memory?" Her eyes to mine, to glance accents on each breath.

I could not speak. My words unsaid in crimson. What are meanings but to forget?

Rolfe was caught amused in his own horror. He tried to speak some solemn complaints to bible his wife's willful temperament. How frail is the truth and yet it will not die by hopes. Even to forget is only a demon mused for an uneasy peace. I looked at this, my orphan, the wilderness in her eyes, Pocahontas now of nations to herself. But what of my escape to words? I could not grovel a meaning false enough. She now lost, to ignore the husband and have one secret caress in the silence of our last parting.

MONTHS LATER, I HEARD OF HER AT COURT, IN LORD PERCY'S TRAIN, the pearl to accompany the lord. Rolfe in the party unmentioned, lost to the service to whom he served. He was now the frame and she the prize. She was invited to the royal masque at the Grand Banqueting Hall of Whitehall Palace held on January sixth, 1617. King James had spent two thousand pounds to gild and silver the great room, building grand barriers and separations about the levels of the floor atopped in sparkled balls and reflecting pyramids. Pools of blues painted on the walls to make a sky, and playful nymphs masked to hide their reddened cheeks, and dancing country boys singing songs to other boys, and all the scarlet dance, the room a ruby to complement the king's own rouge.

All this for the masque's many celebrations. The king had been made King of Scotland fifty years before, Prince Charles that November third invested as Prince of Wales. And in its most secret way, the king's most handsome, George Villiers, on January fifth was created Earl of Buckingham, the first commoner to hold that title in four hundred years. In four years how he rose, ordained by a face, too fair his other destinies. And so the masque was called the Vision of Delights. Ben Jonson, its author, held the quill to frolic fantasies to lesser wits. He to make pretty with words, their sly effects and open flatteries, the king to be amused. To court ourselves we do in full; it is our loves we do by half humanities.

THE ACCOUNT I HEARD OF HER THAT EVENING, SITTING NEAR the royal host, bowing when presented, the king having her to his arm, a walk about the room, the music calling its banquets to the air, the dancers swirling rainbows as they danced. Around the room she walked as princess, the lines bowing their moment to the passing king and his honored guest. Food and drink, the wines in rouge bloods decanted to the cups. What fragrance is in the spice, the liquid falls to rise to purge the toasted lips and hide the glance, the king flirts the room, his decoration on his arm.

The chairs now set, the masque to have its play. Rolfe and his sitting near the royal chairs. The stage a blank, its curtains drawn. The room darkened to festival its surprise. What rises now in wanton moonlight, the room to strange vapors glowing in the air. The guests to their delights. The king smiled to his earl. Flat trees now grew in forests where monsters growled and walked on puppet strings. Nymphs flew across the stage on ropes to heights upon the draperies, singing wild their joys, their eyes cast down. The moon changing to wooden clouds, the world darkened to a dance. Maidens, chains of flowers in their hair, sport the monster into death. Heralds sang their pleasures to themselves. The monster dead. Hand in hand they walked the stage, these fantasies of a painted park.

Pocahontas rigid in the stays of her dress, all laced to the collar of her neck. Tomocomo displeased. "How flat is magic that is all device. Our gods do not walk on strings, our air not fabric, our mist not toys." On stage the night now yielded to the day. Shadows lay on squares of light. A great flower rising as the sun, around its bouquet are nymphs breaking into song. Their arms as petals opened, their choirs now blooming into dance. Voices praising the coming of its spring, which was the king. James nodded to himself, about him his applause. Ben Jonson's words sung to suffocations in their silly script. The evening was a great success.

I TO THE WEST AND NORTH HEARD LITTLE NEWS FOR WEEKS. Purchas held the ear for my account. He told me as he knew. Pocahontas was having an engraved portrait cut by Simon van de Passe, the same who engraved my map of New England with my own face in likeness as its seal. His hand practiced some clarity upon his work, but she was more than a frozen silhouette, her life unworn. In the London shops, my portrait and hers faced upon a distance only histories could bind. Our stories told in landscapes, our profiles fixed upon the common mind. How much of this new land is us? So borne we are by implications in our separate flesh.

IN PLYMOUTH I LEARNED THAT GORGES'S FLEET OF TWENTY SHIPS promised in his letters had dwindled to three at dock. So it was three, better than none, and a small supply of fifteen men for me to have my colony. Within weeks supplies began to assemble at the warehouses. I returned to London to say a few farewells. Purchas invited me to dinner, Tomocomo there. Purchas wanted only to speak of Okee and religion. Tomocomo gave me a message from Powhatan. "If he lives, ask John Smith to show you his king and his queen, Prince Henry, of whom he has much told, and his God."

"You have seen the king that night at the great dance we call a masque," I said.

"No...that is not the king. The king gave Powhatan a white dog, which Powhatan fed as himself. I was given no present. That was not the king." Tomocomo spoke of his displeasure. Purchas not amused. "And of your God?" the Indian asked to me. "It is told of your three wounds. Are you not confessed a werowance, the hearer of voices, and whose god now is your kin?" Purchas trembled in a fearful angering.

"I was adopted as a *werowance* by Powhatan. I as his son, he as father and priest, the hearer of the mysteries," I said, paying my diplomacies to smooth a rough Purchas. "I wrote it all in my book and in my letter to the queen," so lightly said, I played the innocent.

"And the voices?" Purchas not to be set aside.

"Is not some divinity in all?" my answer.

"Most dangerous, most dangerous," Purchas' lips tightening. "But this will pass," patting my hand. "You are with us now," his smile toward Tomocomo. "And how do you summon your God?" asked Purchas.

Tomocomo told of the sacred houses where four werowances conjured by chants in language none but they did know. Gesturing, they would make wild movements close to dance, the air filled with tobacco smoke. Okee would appear in the air, a walking human form. Then he, by signs and speech, would have eight more priests brought to the conjuring place. When twelve were standing in a circle around him, he would answer all by conjured signs or words. "So it is our Okee comes to us in human form," he said. "But he has many forms. Ever he is in his fearful hosts."

POCAHONTAS'S PORTRAIT WAS NOW BEING SOLD IN THE PRINTERS' shops. I saw it hung in windows before my return to Plymouth. Standing to my view I heard a gentleman say, "This Virginia woman holds herself some drift of civil blood." Paper is such a poor countenance for a life.

Rolfe readying to sail for Jamestown, Pocahontas was well rumored not wanting to leave. Held to the soft pillories of our memories, I thought. The Virginia Company had met in its quarterly session, Samuel Argall elected deputy governor under Lord De la Warr. Ralph Hamor made vice-admiral. Rolfe himself elected secretary and John Martin rewarded with the title of master of ordinance, and given such vast tracts of land, 'twas an empire within Virginia. He to himself his own tribe, a reward for slander. He the plant to seed our ruin, made our misery into his wealth. And I, who had held by skill and courage the colony to its place, was given what? How it pleases the nothings to reward nothing, for it is all they understand.

IN NOVEMBER I HEARD THAT POCAHONTAS AND ROLFE, WITH Argall as captain, were to sail within a week. Farewells said but beyond the lips. Such a part of me is torn away. What part of me replaced? In Plymouth my ships were at their docks, supplies to their holds. New England now the season, its bloom hinted on the wind. The bright horizon's dusk, the setting sun falling to its beckoning and the thought that somewhere there is another dawn.

Ships are but toys, to the wind a child's play. How idly rocked the hull in its coffined wood. The breezes fresh, the child tantrumed to its rest. The ship I did not notice make the port. Plymouth busy, held to its commerce and its many masts. Sway the forest, the sea rolls by. Pocahontas was dead. "She's dead, the Virginia woman," the cry along the dock. What inheritance to England and my regrets, but the empty portrait of her face. What is remembered is but the shade of what we lived. That ship cargoed through its anonymous wake brought her son. Rolfe no father. Thomas to Rolfe's brother's arms. And so Henry was summoned from London. Better it be done. The child forsaken, his castaway. The father only for lust and piety and the growing of the weed.

"GRIEVE NOT IN SHALLOW WORDS OF GRIEF, AT THIS OUR JOYFUL passage." The minister's arms held wide over the coffin at the parish church of St. George's. Pocahontas had become weaker, more sickly, as Argall's ship had sailed down the Thames. The spires of London paled behind the mist of falling rain, the world had come to grays. In marshes along the riverbanks, fog floated, bearing elegies. The ship rolled in the swells, Pocahontas begging to be taken ashore. Delirium closing upon her, the ship's movement to her a swaying torture. Rolfe, believing it was some passing vapor, held her hand, tending her in their cabin. Pocahontas crying for the shore. The river now wide, marshes filling the eye in rough mounds and flats, the smell of the sea and its mix of death and fish. On the shore was a church overgrown in ivy, half-buried, as if eaten by the earth. Pocahontas in desire for a peaceful death, Rolfe was hysterical in his terrors. Thomas cried his desperate wants at his mother's side. Argall, captain and deputy governor of Virginia, asked the other passengers what should be done. There was a vote. The ship was just before the sea at Gravesend, that rush of water where Drake those years ago had destroyed the Armada. Pocahontas was carried to an inn, soon her life to be lost in death. Tomocomo, singing his own songs to her spirit, smoked the pipe of mourning, burying tobacco to guide his sorrows.

Argall, deciding that the child Thomas could not survive the voyage, sailed for Plymouth to wait the arrival of Rolfe's brother. The plans changed. The child given to the care of the admiral of Devon. Henry Rolfe arriving some days later, after Argall had sailed again, knowing a large tract of land in Virginia was to be given to him and his associates. The Virginia Company had not signed the paper yet, but they would. All this rich account for no good.

How abruptly the wind changes. My ships were ready for their voyage in that April, when the breezes turned foul and came in hurricanes toward the shore. No ship could sail or leave the harbor. For weeks the winds never varied or changed their point. Their wilds were on the land. Plymouth harbor stopped, as Drake before the Armada, the wind holding him to his docks. Lucky he that Philip was a fool. The Spanish sailing, passing into the doom. Argall had taken the last fair winds, and I was embayed with what soured hopes.

For three months the storms held their course. The season lost. The expedition never left the docks. My protests ignored. Fearing growing debt, sailor's wages paid against uncertain rewards, Gorges and my backers sent the ships after other fortunes when the winds changed.

Chapter Thirty-five

VIRGINIA AND ITS SINS NESTED CRUEL AND SIMPLE.

OR MONTHS I WANDERED in my neglect, a shadow exiled to his loneliness. Martin, Argall, Sandys were all to their Virginias, my New England project stalled. My Virginia stricken on a faithless heart. The London Company contesting in its competing needs. Gorges and I now estranged. I sat the quiet of my life and drank its pain. A noble birth. I wondered at those words. A tongue ill-said, or some vapor truth, I thought. A moment to chase an emptiness. No river's voice, no forest to herald alchemies. Ages antique willful to their derelict, and all that magic lost as history's forgotten joke.

What we are, we are by words. Letters from Virginia, Sandys, inspired to his hate, now banged the leaden drum. "Dear Smith," he wrote,

What stars are for me of the diminished seed? Boots are not the best lick upon my tongue. With the great prospects I have taken to the west. Bear witness to my words, for herein is my confession.

Sail we did, the sea in flats seemed a glowing coal, and we ever to the setting sun. The chains of weight lifted from my mind. Upon my face the wind. I breathe the cold and the smell of salt. My old thoughts abandoned. Am I to be reborn a premonition and a vengeance to my blood?

The sea closing to an arc of silver light, we sailed into the Chesapeake. The land in rounded galaxies of its haunted green, the bay, the jagged rush of shore. Gone I am from England, to this my second coast. The James River, the marshes thick with steam and rising birds, the swamp and mud, and there the ruin that reigned upon the reeds. The Jamestown hovels. Low its wreck, its walls collapsed, buildings leaned. Around it in legions, marshaled in its leaves and stems, grew tobacco. Leaves could not hide the sweep of the decay. The streets of the town were filled with plants. Every plot that inched some dirt held the weed. I swear on roofs there grew a few. Men bent on knees, their noses in the dirt like rooted swine, tending their crop to a better growth.

Of all Jamestown that I could see, there were only five houses, the church fallen upon itself in wreck, its roof gone, on its one standing wall a cross nailed, to which was the figure of a man woven in dried tobacco leaves. What idolatry to a weed, images that once were gold now set in leaf.

At the sight of our coming, the company on shore ignored our ship. One man sat on the ground rubbing a leaf against his cheek. Another stood among his crops singing softly to the leafy indifference mute at his feet. Beyond him the bridge across a small brook had decayed into splinters of broken boards. The well destroyed, its stone walls fallen, its water a foul. The dock, sunk into the bay, washed there, its walk in reeds and spoiled marsh. We anchored to a tree and set out ropes.

By my side was a surgeon named John Pott and a gentleman of wild moments of intriguing madness named William Epps, sent from England to escape a debt, or worse. Our ship against the shore, Epps groaned and giggled to himself, his hand playing with the ship's belaying pins, then fussing with his clothes.

From Jamestown walked a group of men, the council, I guessed. Before them, walking in great strides of conscious dignity, a lone man dressed in ringlets of gold hanging from cloth of orange and green, his clothes in rainbows of absurd tints. On his head a hat of sparkles and scarlet. Around it, the air perfumed with sweeps of feathers.. He pranced a dandy on the earth in dainty, thoughtful steps holding lightly to a cane. At his side walked two tall savages, faces painted, carrying firelocks.

The man stopped before our ship and called to the captain, "I am your Governor Yeardley. How many men for Virginia in your company?" The captain stood. A group of men, sunken-eyed, leaned on the railing of the ship, hardly having the skin to warm their bones, living death, so ill fed they moved by the memories of a health once possessed. "Eighty-five," the captain called. The weather warm, the breezes mild enough to sweet the smell of rot. The moneys for the voyage had been paid by the company, but not so handsomely as to provide healthy meals for the five-week sail.

"Fear not. We have work and food," said Yeardley. "The savages whom you see about frequent our fort as they frequent our houses. We live as one and in peace." Yeardley then spoke to the captain. "As for your mariners, as we ask of all, do not trade for corn with the savages. On this I must insist. There are harsh punishments for those who do. What goods you have from the London Company are to be given over to the cape merchant, Abraham Piersey, for our common store, we call the magazine." A man of some grace in his plentitude dragged in a waddle to the governor's side and lifted a not quite elegant hat from his head. He bowed his bald spot to the light, as again the governor spoke to the captain. "Now I must seize all supplies of spirits, whether wine or aqua vitae, for the general good. These shall also be given to the cape merchant, for which you shall be paid at London rates." The governor then smiled, the breeze at play with the feather of his hat. "I understand you have a passenger of consequence, George Sandys, among your company. I wish him to my presence and hospitality."

And so I walked by Yeardley's side through the tobacco fields as we toured the lands about Jamestown. Everywhere the plants in rows, leaves held to have the sun. No corn saw I or any foods. Mad Epps walked with us, babbling wildly of plants and porridges mixed with speeches of noble sentiments. "And where are our fields of corn?" I asked.

"We plant little," said Yeardley. "Tobacco is our work. Our supplies from the savages are most adequate. I, myself, have told the company to enthrall them to our means, plant only tobacco. I will supply the corn. It keeps our peace and progress to the plenty. Tobacco is what we are. Even I plant no corn."

"I am sent by law, by my brother and the London Company, as a second governor, with powers and detailed instructions to secede this colony from the leaf, or at least toward other crops, their industries less noxious to the king and my brother." I spoke to delight the drama of our walk. It is best to play the law before we spend its power. No effrontery to Yeardley yet. Affable, his hand over-graced the air with the sweeps and luxuries of silk. "Ah, yes, the London Company," he said, "and all its considered plans, each thought so far away, each its notions the chamberlain of our ruin. And you as well, George Sandys, sent to us, your servants only half, the one hundred fifty pounds your purse still owed, and your fifteen hundred acres not surveyed or even chosen, and it's so late in the planting season. What love does your brother hold to sail you prodigal into a land of rags?"

I looked at Yeardley, who smiled his question on a cunning. "If I have confessed my mind too harshly against your...the London Company, I beg some slice of pardon, for I am more to solutions and happy coins than paupered dominions and scarecrow colonies. But we are adventurers all, our society not so cruel as to cast out its own. You are welcomed with all your power. I am not such a governor who sits his privilege as if it were his only life. If you desire my office for its remaining term, it is yours. What you wish will be done."

"I am most content to be the colony's treasurer. I seek no title but the one I brought."

"Ah, good, a profitable wisdom. All power needs a mask, some shield against the necessities of tomorrow," Yeardley almost bowed. "Our little band does not war upon itself. We make our allowances and seek a common fortune. And so I have done for you. Two hundred acres I have arranged for your purchase, cleared and fertile. The money as loan against the company's one hundred and fifty-pound debt. The land is cheap. Your servants may begin to work without loss of a day. Plant what you wish upon your own conscience and your own advice—corn, tobacco, silk grass. But if I might suggest, wait for the whole plot before you print a page."

"I was once sold to a marriage for a field, or do you think some wilderness prospect will be a better bribe?"

"There can be many a spice before the bride is to the bed." Yeardley had a look which told of many a knowing vice. "And how much coin will you squander to your genealogies?" he asked.

Some savages in the fields tended the crop. Others with their firelocks braced on iron rests shot ducks as they flew, or geese, all manner of fowl to serve as our food. Englishmen also worked the plants, picking worms from leaves, hoeing, doing whatever they thought the plants loved best. Then Yeardley spoke into my ear. "Corruption is not that we serve ourselves, but we serve nothing else."

"Beware," I thought. "Our race is dull, its sole brilliance is to scheme its pleasures. The wisdom is never slicker than its knave."

*W*e walked then to Jamestown. Such filth in idle sewer puddles, vermin eating at its soup, all about the fallen wrecks, and a few that stood. The houses missing boards, the breaks stuffed with straw. Houses sided of planed wood were scarce. Most were bundled straw tied to poles with thatched roofs. Such tinder built in a day might be burned within a month. Houses here were only homes for the crop. All else there was had passed from filth to wreck to rot.

Yeardley said as I entered his house, 'When there is a general wealth, we will be more to repairs.' Temperance Flowerdieu, Yeardley's wife, a woman of most her teeth and little else, busied herself about the shack with that saintly and haughty air of a woman who knows she has a suspected past. She talked of London and of court and that soon she should travel there in the style of her proper birth. I looked at her face, which had the memories of a forgotten beauty. How men must have dreamed upon it once. The cabin and its palatial offerings were more than the accustomed misery of the place. Here a house so strangely dark, yet on the table silver cups and dishes and silver bowls, not far from a rugged opulence, as if a beggar had dreamed himself a king.

We sat. A servant tended us with a cup of wine. An Indian with a firelock held upon his shoulder brought a fresh-killed duck. "A savage to my employ. He hunts my ducks, the finest shot in Jamestown," said Yeardley. The duck soon feathered for the pot. The savage stayed a moment and talked of corn ready for the harvest. "Opechancanough will live his pledge and only trade with you and those you do appoint."

Yeardley smiled. "With such trust there has been peace," he said to me.

Abraham Piersey joined us for the meal, and Pott and Epps, who now engaged his charms in a not-so-subtle dance of seduction with the self-conscious Temperance Flowerdieu. Piersey watched as Yeardley spoke of tobacco and opportunities and corn. "Pott, you are the envy of us all," said Yeardley, "a doctor in Virginia and free to traffic his cures at any rate, except to me." Piersey laughed. Epps spoke to Temperance Flowerdieu of her eyes and the blush upon her cheek. Temperance sighed in her lost girlhood. Seduction is a game for two. Epps played fondly with a knife "All is tobacco in Virginia, and I supply the corn. If the company has a few coins, they spend them in the colony for corn or at the magazine. The savages here have their firelocks, which supply us some food, and they have corn, which they sell to me...us." Yeardley looked about. "All then by mutual profit we have our peace."

I felt my brother's spirit screaming at my side. "Isn't all that is gained in trade the company's?" I asked.

"They who make the law should live the law. What does London know that they can teach us here? For years we starved with their charters. Their thoughts bear calamities. We are a new thirst that only we can quench. George Sandys, think on this: it is either your brother or yourself. What scrap of land is in his deeded will for you? None? Or some scratch of cinder? Well?" he asked. I stayed to silence. "In Virginia you can have it by the mile. Tobacco and its servants to help you plant and leaf your riches into gold. All this for you. Just play the noose, the means, about the other neck."

My brother's estate by law his own...and what to me? And I too late even to bud a withered prospect. What beggars we are in all our Jerusalems. I sat, the proposition not wholly spoke. "What cares the London drama, the play's for here," said Yeardley, "and here are all of us. Let conscience occupy its geography. Let us not beg more forgiveness than we have the price."

I SIGHED THE SIGH OF LONG AGO AND SAT MY ROOM. DOES NO-thing change but to a better crime? How many Ratcliffes come in dust to sprout again, and we the seed that sows the weed? What alchemies has my mariner reversed? Our gift has turned our gold to a pauper's lead? Cannot my stars persuade some earthly luck that sends me to Virginia to set our futures right?

Soon enough I learned from Purchas that the patents given to John Martin were more feudal than a simple grant—twenty shares as gift, five hundred acres per share, as compensation for all his labors for the colony. But that not half the spike to crucify the colony. The patents so written as to exclude Martin and his lands from all laws, duties and decrees of the company and the lord governor, except in times of war. Smythe and his council, having such good opinions of this man, believed his brag and booted all their sense. By what coronations do we turn our common charlatans into kings?

As I read Sandys' script, its lines cut wounds across the page.

I slept upon the ship that night and dreamt myself to half resolves. Could I but take a few riches without the spoil of myself? My brother's dream had come at my expense. But when does little become too much? Small thefts are not the coin to feed great crimes, I thought, feeling cleansed while I feigned some freedom, dreaming of a judicious sin.

Soon we learned that the Chickahominy would not honor their pledge to Dale and deliver corn to us. Their pledge, being made to Dale, was Dale's. Yeardley they did not know or think powerful. In a rage, Yeardley drooled violence to my face. "Tobacco and furs are wealth, but here corn makes all other wealth the slave. Men must eat. Corn is the mouth that nibbles a helping of all their profits. Men can forget to plant but they cannot forget to eat. It is their appetite that feeds me luxury," Yeardley hissed. "It is the earth. He who is closest to the filth eats its smell, but rolls upon a palace made of coin. The gut is always king, and from its dung all foundations rise. Our footing here is food."

Yeardley looked into my face. "Tobacco brings a general wealth. Let each that can have a bit as long as we have most. What care I if some trade with the savages for furs or baskets or some such trash. Whether it be for guns or beads, it is their cost and we have most the profit. Tobacco makes the sweet pot sweeter. Corn will never have its weight in commerce, but its need makes all their tobacco crop a portion mine." Yeardley smiled. "And yours."

And I, dear Smith, did hang mid-stride before the final step. I had banked my gallows and gladly crossed the line.

John Martin and his patents arrived upon the Chesapeake on the bark, Edwin. He smiled as Yeardley read the company law. The bark owned by Martin's business partner, Captain George Bargrave, they having the right to trade corn and every provision, even with the savages. No decree to bar their trespass. Each word a foul upon Yeardley's mood. And so my brother works against my better prospects. Anger caresses its excuses into war. I now sat the writ to remake the law. I took my bribe, smiled a shrewd love and played myself respected to have the crime.

That week Yeardley ordered a hundred of his best soldiers to the boats to sail to the Chickahominy and to have some council and coerce a little peace. Dale had by his cruelties and harsh discipline forced the company to plant corn in such abundance that at his return to England the colony had a great supply. But Yeardley and tobacco had brought us back to ruin. Corn was seen as a waste. Poor men blinded in dreams of wealth starved to a happier death. There is no worth so small that poverty does not have it a necessity. All for tobacco, the savages' corn a drama that never empties of its plot, and that controlled by Yeardley and Opechancanough. How twines the puppet's string around the master's fingers. Knot to knot, the line does flow. The puppet gestures, movements move, pull against weight, weight against pull, and whose dance is danced? Opechancanough, wanting for himself the trade in guns, intrigued against all the nations so he would be our sole supply of corn. It was he who brought war by trick and lie to the Chickahominy, they always independent of his rule.

Our boats took to the river. There on the shore the Chickahominy taunted Yeardley, saying he was not Dale and had not his power. A coming war mixed to Opechancanough's lies, his bravados and his jeers. The Chickahominy dared Yeardley to bring his men on shore to fight. And so we brought close our boats to the beach, walked the shallows and stood upon the land, the Chickahominy doing little to prevent us. Then we marched inland, the savages staying beyond the range of our shot. Two mobs in their shadowed pace cursed and hurled menace to each other's feet.

At dusk we made camp. The night crawled with screams, the heat heavy upon the sweat of our clothes. At dawn we marched again, the land spread with bundles of newly gathered corn, although most was hidden in the woods or buried all about, so we could have little. The savages stood in troops before us, arguing their cause. Such time we spent, our troops mixing in theirs, and so our companies to their separate pleas, the savages fearing not to be among us, or we among them. All this we might have resolved to our mutual good, had not Robert of Poland, who later called himself Robert Poole, a spy in league with Opechancanough, cried, "An ambushado. It comes, the ambushado." Our men in line, our words cast down, our firelocks spoke in heat into the savage troops. Twelve we killed, their flesh split to ragged, bloody cloth. Two of the Chickahominy elders we captured, Robert Poole seizing one,

Captain Boothe the other. Ten others of no account we had. Marching them, we met Opechancanough, who had agreed to allow this war upon those people. "There can be no peace unless I am made king of the Chickahominy and they send tribute in beads and copper and such to me," said Opechancanough. Henry Spelman, never trusting Opechancanough, displeased, repeated the words, interpreting them in English speech, a foul expression on his face. Yeardley did not agree quick enough. Then Opechancanough spoke in restrained anger of his many works and efforts to bring this peace. Finally it was agreed by all. Yeardley to have his corn for himself. Opechancanough to have the Chickahominy and his supplies and guns. The Chickahominy at peace, their freedom swapped. Robert Poole and Captain Boothe were promised a hundred bushels of corn for themselves to sell as reward for capturing the Chickahominy elders. The reward was never paid, stolen by Yeardley. Poole, now to other intrigues, well served his Opechancanough for other prizes.

And so we sailed again to Jamestown. Henry Spelman warned Yeardley of his fears that Opechancanough had made some league with Robert Poole. "He wishes to keep all the trade for himself, and rule all the tribes," said Spelman. "Robert of Poland is his instrument and his spy, and we caught between, will be his army." Robert Poole, hearing of these words, decided then to have his vengeance upon Spelman.

Our soldiers were anxious to return to Jamestown, they never wanting to abandon their tobacco fields for more than a few hours. Such was the bind that held men to the weed. One boat of eleven rowed ahead, overburdened with luggage and corn, baskets to the gunnel, men forted in their food. Their strokes were on the water, the tide and current eddied on the surface of the reach. Caught in swifts, tobacco phantoms in their minds, they drowned still rowing as the boat overturned. All lost; the corn and the weapons gone.

More than land or crops, it was servants men needed to have their wealth. The weed demanded toil to bring its gift. Land by ruined miles it would bring, but it was that constant need for drudgery that would be the lash upon the mind. Gentlemen no longer starved by idle pleasures. Men schemed on one another to have their labor. The old commons, wherein the wealth was shared, brought but men who would dawdle to their decay. The company ever rested till it starved, or was forced by brutal means to save itself.

Yardley, in his power as Governor, took most of the indentured servants as his own. Abraham Piersey was served his few. The company grumbled in its discontent. The savages came each day to trade us corn. Every nation at our gates to bring us pleasure, fearing now our alliance with Opechancanough. He, that savage chief, moved his plans through the orbits of his strategies, and had his wait. What man he was I never knew, his skin having many layers until the truth. He might have looked the savage, but his ambitions came in the ordered armies of a European king.

All the servants the London Company sent were to plant and harvest the company's land until their seven years service done. This the price for their free passage to Virginia. But Yeardley, with his powers as governor, had the strongest and the best work his own lands, two great plots totaling thirty-two hundred acres on either side of the river. The weakest, or sick, to the company lands, the rest to Piersey, or to favorites, or those who could pay. The company grudged his growing wealth. Piersey and Yeardley, dining on some equal portions, tied their wealth to other hidden crimes.

Yeardley now stole cattle, having Pott cut the brands away and add his own. Discontents ran their rumors now in flocks, the company coming to a rising heat. But the tobacco in the field prophesied a good harvest. Men worked and worked and toiled every minute to content the weed. Their backs in pain, basted in their incessant sweat. With the water bad, the wine and aqua vitae at the magazine were priced at five-times the London rate, as were other goods that brought some comfort to this place. But it was tobacco that swept the stone of hope and had men trust their fates. So close the tobacco to ourselves that its leaf became our second skin. Women wore its flowers in their hair. Men wore its topped leaves as signs around their necks and tied them to their foreheads as frontals to their eyes. They called the crop their child, lit candles to the moon to speed an extra growth and told tales of cures and miracles and of visions walking in the fields.

Piersey was pocketing the moneys from the magazine. In two months, seventy of the eighty-five passengers who had arrived with me in Virginia were dead, or so decayed in health that death seemed a better mercy. "What is divided twice can be divided once again," said Yeardley as an offer to keep my silence concerning the magazine. Yeardley played my avarice at the head, my conscience to the tail. "Here your brother sent you. My brother a tailor, I in wealth. He calls me mean. I call me rich. And what of you? All men are sucked into the mud by too much thought. You choose well your pain. Is it of conscience, or of the pauper's grave? There is nothing else." I smiled at his argument already won. And I, an archbishop's son. I altered but my faith a bit and kept the coins. Virtue preached too much entices the better sin.

In June, Rolfe and Argall made the Chesapeake. Their sails vaulted white, the earth turning in its scented apothecary. The tobacco leaves lingered on the wind, growing into weight to burn as smoke. The sails now, the banners near the shore, ropes cast to the earth, tied to trees. Yeardley and Piersey and I stood on the beach, Yeardley smiling between his two savages holding firelocks. Argall and Rolfe walked down the plank, Argall's foot to touch the dirt. He now the governor. Yeardley smiled. Argall looked at the armed savages. "Who here gives guns to them?" said Argall in a rage. Yeardley stepping, forced backwards, as if by an idea. He began to sweep a reply, his hands gesturing through the hollows of his cuffs. How dangerous was this Yeardley man who dressed himself as a bauble? Argall was not for words that day. "Seize those firelocks," he ordered. The proud savages were disarmed and humiliated, the silence of a vengeance to their eyes. Tomocomo watching, his council always to himself. He was bringing the news of Pocahontas's death to Powhatan, and Argall's arrival, carrying in his anger an invitation from Argall to Opechancanough to join him in Jamestown. He also to bring Opechancanough and Powhatan his impressions of England, of its king, of its God and its people. Always beware how the messenger bears the message.

Argall walked the ruins of the town, ordered the fort rebuilt, the bridge repaired, a new well dug. Savages could no longer enter our gates. No guns to savages, the general trade with them to cease, all that reserved for the governor. The one nation, little that it was, now splintered by the ax of law. Argall took the books of the magazine. Abraham Piersey nervous, sweating, fearing the end of his profit. Yeardley, deciding to sail for England with Temperance Flowerdieu, took his coin and his plate and prepared to leave, wanting the London Company to seal by eternal deed his lands to him.

Rolfe, as secretary of the colony, wrote to my brother. I saw the letter, it said, "All is in peace and good plenty, although, for lack of boats, much is ruined and there is great want." And so Rolfe pleased all power, his contradictions giving pleasure to the moment. His only quality was that he served without contest. When he spoke he was ever a voice without a sound.

Captain Martin, with his thirty servants brought on the *Edwin*, were now building a large plantation called Martin's Brandon on the James. By the privilege in his patents, Martin began trading freely with the savages. The Edwin sailing the river to have the corn and oysters and nuts and other foods, our own magazine Argall's profit a slight and stricken hope. Argall in a rage. "We are two laws by the same book to the same land. There can be but one and it will be mine," he said.

The two men by the same immunities waved their presumptions, and I sat and counted coins and advised such sweet advice that kept the pot a trifle off a salted boil. Peace never profaned an easy profit. What alchemy I am to master my darker self. My rage not so angered now. I guide the knife, seated and slipped to the better cut.

Argall, under the influence of my advice, strangely bent some diplomacies to his cause and called for conversations of the matter with Martin, but all knew that in secret Argall was violent to have his way.

What a sport is dalliance when it leads itself to whores. Argall and Martin to meet and joust their interests on an ever changing law. I to sit and judge the squander of the sport. It was a war of paint, the bounce never off the girdle. I contrived some wisdom and sat the spectacle.

Argall flaming cold against his inner heat. Martin more rage than words. And so they violenced in their masks, Argall speaking first: "I am from Thomas Smythe, himself, and by the great shareholders of the company am made the law. By the king, himself, in grants through them to me. Your patents have no weight but air. I will have no trading on these waters without warrants signed by me. Disobey and you will die."

Martin, hearing death, relaxed into the affects of a smirk. What confidence did the coward know to shield his neck even upon the block? "I am given law and patents and all its license by none other than our noble Warwick." Martin looked at me and then to Argall as if a question had been raised to jolt a silence.

Argall to a calmer tone said, "What was said is said and so the policy. I am sure good Warwick would not raise a dust between us. If you must use the Edwin, sail to the French or pirate upon the Spanish in the Indies, but here I am the law, as Warwick in my policies."

I thought upon Argall's words. Warwick? What rumors on their surface, Smith, that one day may show us their inner bite.

Chapter Thirty-six

ALL THINGS ASCATTER.

O ENDED SANDYS' FIRST LETTER. Ah, my friend, I thought, if only the confession would exonerate the crime. But, in truth, Sandys had only pilfered as the rest. No breach yet to break the back of our enterprise. My energies in fair prospects. I visited Purchas. If I could but heal the secret rift between George Sandys and his brother, I might stay the rage before our Virginia has swung the gallows.

PURCHAS IN A PRETTY MOOD, SAT A SCOWL AND TOOK A LISTEN while he sipped some aqua vitae. "When hate is seated a kiss is but a sting. Edwin has done good offices for his brother—lands, servants, important posts. A hurt that rises from the family, that wound poisons the all." I looked at Purchas as he continued. "The grave is not yet set, but the play is on the coffin lid."

"I hear rumors that Thomas Smythe is much criticized in the

London Company and may abdicate the office of treasurer," I spoke. Purchas smiled and leaned forward.

"What you hear is true. It is said Edwin Sandys will take the vacant seat, thus the company's lord; but there is no conclusion to all this. The king despises Edwin and his love of parliaments. The solution only brings a polity that brews more politics. Edwin and the king both hate the weed, but both need its revenues: Edwin for the company, the king for his own purse. Remember, what seems simple here fouls an easy answer.

"Martin's partner, Captain Bargrave, who owns the bark, Edwin, is now suing the London Company because Argall refuses to honor those patents that gave free trade rights, and so a loss to Martin and himself, while he is also suing Martin for defrauding him of goods sailed on the Edwin. The Virginia Colony is ever a comedy without a joke. My advice to you, Smith, is to seek a better prospect. New England seems the game worth the sport. Try your chances there."

I looked at Purchas. Each life has some contest against itself. The greatness is for the constant battle, never for the final peace. George Sandys, you are bequeathed unto yourself. Am I to leave him to whore upon himself? Inherit what you are, but I shall not desert you yet.

"GORGES IS NO LONGER INTERESTED IN NEW ENGLAND. HE FEARS a loss. It is too early to invest to be assured of any gain, or so he says. He is a man made coward by his profits." I had my say. Purchas, indifferent to the speech, said, "Raise you own monies. Write a plan to calculate the weights of gain and risk. Advertise the New England prospects. Adventure your cause in print and seek a better backer."

"Write a second New England book," I asked, "and be again the chronicler?"

"No, write a considered plan, inventoried with all your beliefs and hopes of profit. Be honest. The gain must see the risks and so the risks must see the gain. Greed is your champion, hope the balance bar."

The conversation done except for some casual asides to the topics we had discussed. I rose to take my leave, when Purchas said, "It is not well known, but Edwin Sandys is in secret a Puritan."

"Here, I don't see even the shadow of a point," I said.

"Just be aware. The Puritans reside self-exiled in Leiden. They rest not happy there. Great occasions are not birthed from stone. Just be aware. That is all I can say."

THE INTERVIEW AT AN END, I RETURNED TO MY ROOMS, LOOKED again upon the curved point of my quill and set the blank pages to begin work. It was to be but a book in brief, a pamphlet to promote my New England enterprise. Five thousand pounds was the price; but from that, furs and fish and other commerce could be had. Wood from the great forests to build the ships of our new navy, the forests of our England now mostly spent. All this I wrote, and of other prospects: wealth not by a common labor, but by initiatives of every adventurer for his own, each to build by work and cleverness his own estate. I wrote the text, had it copied in a better hand and sent it to the Lord Chancellor, Sir Francis Bacon. I asked if I could dedicate the work to him. Such words would quicken the steps to investors with easy purses. I waited. No word from Bacon, he being soon dismissed, corruption the weight on all his brilliance. My fortunes always languish on the threshold of some other circumstance. Now a year had passed since the death of Pocahontas. All our sorrows come by hourglass. It swells the clock and bursts the wait. Our calendar comes lethal at their anniversaries, and we must live again the pain, and so the orbits of our despair run our planets through the stars. The slide is in ourselves, to its moments and its memories.

I HAD BEEN READY TO WRITE TO GEORGE SANDYS TO GUIDE HIM from his folly, when his second letter was placed upon my desk, and I sat my cage, my eyes pacing across the strokes in ink.

Dear Smith, The company is in its discontents. Argall has halted all general trade with the savages, except for Martin who still commands his privileges, even if the Edwin is well anchored to Argall's will. Martin and Argall wear their mutual hates, but duel by lawyers. There is a fearful stay upon this war. I think it is the Earl of Warwick. There, those two are joined by some secret pact, and so the twins are loath to hack each other's meat.

My brother, Edwin, writes to me that great consequences are debated and should be apparent soon. 'You shall see plans to make our earthly paradise in Virginia.' All this the dream, and my brother so ill-informed. He sees not the knife, the air about filled only with his good intents. My brother's dream bettered upon my constructions. If I the pawn, he now the board, on him the play, the game now to me. Rolfe had asked for a continuing stipend for his son, and for himself some grant of land to be his perpetual estate. So asked, my brother to the task. 'It is our prospect to see it done,' he wrote.

I now sit my table behind the straw of my cabin walls, working on my translation of Ovid. Language my estate, blooming as a winter flower, ice its only scent. Brittle, the petals crack. I cannot wizard words as you, friend Smith. My verbs wash cold. I, in fury! Oh but to storm passions in the alchemies of fire. I am resolved to the second rank. Lowful, I am a common tear, a quench of nothing. My world, its destinations are a melt of sameness. And so I am exiled to the surface and its profundities.

The small purse of coins each Englishman could expect from trade with the savages was lost. Food scarce and all having the burden of the expense. Yeardley's plan of a little profit to all in a common greed is now set aside. The savages' trade held for the governor and a touch for Martin. For while Argall could control the Edwin, he could not spend his influence upon Martin's lands; but in its course, all the furs were no longer sent to the magazine. Corn mostly held by the governor and his council and still sold in extortions to have a portion of the tobacco crop. Men cannot eat smoke. Argall's mind now sought a more humane plan. He ordered the planting of corn on a portion of each field. Tobacco he suppressed in part. The company raged, risked death to waste not an inch of land on food. Men who had spoke words in criticism of Yeardley had been tortured and hung. Those punishments put at rest, they pardoned by Argall and released. Still no peace, the colony in a boil at its thwarted dreams of wealth. Argall's crimes were not his corruptions but his reforms.

Slanders all about him now, he did his work in its double edge. The savages in possession of such numbers of our firelocks and expert in their use, Argall seized what weapons he could, the savages screaming war. At Powhatan's council Tomocomo spoke his words in flung spite against the England he had seen. 'What king is he that gives no gifts? Their God is air, their towns cut of stone and wood, diseases cobbled to a stink, washed in rivers through their streets. All this, and they in great numbers.' Argall, hearing of Tomocomo's display, sent reports to Opechancanough to disprove the councilor.

'Tomocomo is disgraced.' So heralded the savage messenger who brought Opechancanough's reply. But in truth, I think not. Fools are they who script their own truth. And all the time my growing wealth, my guilt, my fear. Is it that our corruption corrupts not deep enough? Would I become my own criminal, my conscience to work against my crime?

Powhatan, learning of the death of his Pocahontas, sat in his council before the fires, light no light to him. She was not the daughter he had hoped, but a daughter still. Divorced her own to marry with that Englishman. How spiteful lamentations crawled the memories of she the defiant love. Each child is some child to itself, and we the sculptors who only partly wield the clay.

Powhatan now fled into the forest, across his kingdom to his allies and his vassals on the Potomac. By what abdications do we seek our borderlands? How schemes the grief? Powhatan left the governing of his empire to his brothers, Opitchapam and Opechancanough. Opitchapam, the slower, weaker of the two, unsure, confused by the derelict powers at his feet, soon abdicated his reign to Opechancanough. Now this man was his nation in all its grievance, he not wholly savage, but of a strange combine, as if civil humors waxed his soul. Maybe he was that Spanish captive who freed himself by treachery, for no love had he for us. A titan, he walked in giants upon his lands. He did not flee to far away to find some peace, but spoke his soul in council to himself and planned his war.

Argall now closed the magazine, seizing all its goods, calling the London Company "but an offense" to truck such prices in the colony. Abraham Piersey he dismissed. Piersey writing letters to London telling of Argall's slanders and his theft. Other planters also wrote, speaking of his suppression of their rights to grow tobacco, and of his extortions to have his way. Argall, now even more brazen than before, took most of the colony's cattle as his own, a hundred head. 'It is due me as unpaid debt I suffered on the company's account,' he said. There might have been some truth in that, but no ledgers did I see. Virginia now in confusion and angry fits, Argall sent three boats to trade the Indians for furs and corn. All this to his own account for his own profit, tobacco still having little favor with him. Here was Yeardley without the craft, but why in this now did Argall flaunt his power? He lived the contradictions of a fool, but Argall was no fool. What is the secret plot that binds the play? I wondered as I waited.

Each day some new affront. A few planters who had come free of their service to the company, having served seven years, he held engrossed to new labors on his own lands. 'The men to tears. Argall with threats of torture and abuse against any protests,' said Rolfe, speaking distantly of his ignorance of all matters, always the governor's man. It was rumored Argall had written to London saying that Powhatan was holding all his land for Rolfe's child until he came of age — Argall's crude attempt to gain a stipend for the boy and keep Rolfe's loyalty and his silence.

Argall now raised the rates for goods shipped to England, refusing to allow tobacco or such crops we had, to be placed on the company's boats. 'New ships under a better flag with cheaper goods to supply our needs. All this, we have planned in London, will soon be brought.' So said our governor, but what plans? By whom? To whose account the wealth? When a cautious man comes arrogant and boasts his power, beware. He leans his shadow on the license of the mighty.

Drunk with the belief of protection from his powerful friends, Argall wrote the London Company a letter of such hostile greeting and displays of his willful dealings with the colony, proclaiming that all the company's instruction and commissions were overthrown. 'I have by my own hand and instigation seized all trade with the savages, all furs, all cattle shipped under my sail as mine, as payment for such debt the company owed me. I have rescinded all licenses to the magazine, ended its privilege, opened its commerce to whoever so wishes to sail to these waters to trade and made such policy as to improve those conditions, and heal those neglects, and fix those ruins that first I saw when I arrived. All this I have done by my own hand for all our interests.' For whose eyes, I thought, do these lines bring bright a special meaning? I sat in Argall's cabin. The letter I returned to his hand. Argall looked at me, his voice low in mystery, revelation eager in his smile. To display the power, the tongue does tell the tale. Confession serves corruption best …to enthrall by brag, and dog the stricken conscience.

'The Earl of Warwick, my friend and my protector,' said Argall, 'has been, from the beginning, a major backer of the London Company. He wishes now to gain some profit from his investment. Through legal commissions writ in Savoy he has now privateers in the West Indies seizing Spanish ships and goods. These supplies will be brought to Jamestown as trade to be the magazine. And all the commerce we gather here, all the furs and savage trash and tobacco, that which is in my hands, under Warwick's protection at the council will be sailed to England. For you, some portion for your support and influence. Assistance will bear a better gift than war. For all this, you may do as you wish. No one at court will ever curse Yeardley for being rich and only fools ask a fortune to speak its tale.' Argall finished. He sat, his eyes to mine. 'And what truth do you hear from your brother?'" he asked.

'All I hear could be spoken better by a demented pilgrim,' I replied. 'My brother so far away, his ears so short.'

"Argall nodded, 'To have your own estate is ever the problem of the younger, is it not?' He smiled, calculating my disposition.

'By such accidents of birth have I grown,' I said. 'Necessity baits a better wisdom than any theology.' We both laughed. Reconciled to enticements, I took my pleasures.

And so, I bent my ear and drank the sounds of cynic, much amused. The offer plain enough. I weighed gold against the ambitions of a conscience and so I walked the balance to join the plot. What an infinity of worlds we are. In our skin we demon dictionaries. The pride is in the sin. Shrewd company fears no pains but being caught, conscience being but an affect of the weak.

Yeardley soon sailed with Argall's letter to the London Company. Chests of treasure Yeardley had carried to the ship. So much wealth from so much ruin. The tobacco crop that year was sixty thousand pounds. More ships in their masted squadrons to the Chesapeake to sail it home. More supplies and goods to sell to planters with their eager money. How easy come the coins that slip so fast the fingertips. Men who lived in shacks of straw paraded now on Sunday in silks, their ladies on their arms to strut upon the mud in feathers and hats and dresses hooped in fantastic embroideries. All this in muddied luxury. Even Argall's greed could not control the flow of riches. Ships anchored now with hulls filled with wines and perfumes and dainty feasts to delight our wreck. And I courted hopes, my table lined with a portion of the spoils. And I, my Smith, no voices of the land to fill my ear. Mine, the only voice is cut with magic gold.

The winter came in snow. The earth burrowed in its cold. The soil was frozen into rock, the white patches of the landscape, and blackened lines of trees, the sky a flat of gray. The bay in flow and the shore daggered by broken sheets of ice. Toward the center of the reach the water was free, its black current moving under the reflections of the tide. Still the ships came in such numbers. They anchored in the bay just off the ice, sending boats to the shore, men walking the last yards through frigid water to the land. How many sickened and died? Death so common, it seemed a proper circumstance. We hailed it as another's cost, and not of our concern.

We hearing in London the investors of the Virginia Company now saw a chance to have the colony some success and make a small profit. All hopes upon the weed, but in the carriages and in the stores leaf warred with leaf to gain and hold the market. The best tobacco was the expensive Spanish herb, but the cheap Virginia crop was now demanded in London and the larger cities. The domestic leaf was beginning to find its place, each year a bigger crop. The Virginia Company, fearing the competition of the Spanish and domestic leaf, petitioned the king for protection and monopolies for their own tobacco. My brother would defend the leaf while scheming its destruction. How caught by the noose, we lay laurels on its rope. All the while the king sat his poisoned throne contemplating the revenues of the hated weed as he courted its charities. And so all factions warred in their pamphlets and their confused deceits to find a common interest.

In December of 1617, Captain Stallings, who had sailed to New England with you, my Captain Smith, arrived in Virginia. He having fished those northern waters off Maine for some months. There he had run afoul of a French ship. Cannons spit their fluted tongues in fire and burning smoke. Rage in counter rage, salvoes bellowed through each other's blows. The sea red in rampart war, the battle done, the French ship had been seized, with all its tobacco, furs and wines, and other fine cargoes. That ship brought here, Stallings's own sent back to England. All history turns but upon itself. While Stallings made his riches selling wine and fish and those French luxuries, mad Epps frequented his ship, as did many of our company, men and women drunk upon the deck. Their conversation groaned in the shadows, debauchery but another lethargy in the night. Epps wild in madness, wine excited in his mind. Words were exchanged with Stallings over unpaid bills. The words indifferent to his lust, Epps found a wooden mallet on the deck and, with hammered blows, he crushed the roundness from Stallings's skull. Epps in chains. Argall his friend, he was soon released. With money and large tracts of land and tobacco, Epps bought his freedom. His trial concluded with apologies for its inconvenience.

In this, I was a better man than most. I war not upon my own, I war upon some portion of myself. Anger is a blinded muse. I saw the mallet and believed the charge, but power has conclusions of its own. "It would be unfair to our brothers," said Argall, "not to spare just a little murder for ourselves."

Argall wrote to the London Company to send a proper minister. All ours were drowned. He asked that some of our company play the office. Such was Argall, always to the surface of the facts. To him an act is only to be done, the thought behind of no account.

And soon the early spring, that breath of heat greeds again floods from the melt. Argall sent the company's servants to work his private lands, and those secretly held by the Earl of Warwick. The company's corn to feed them. Argall received letters from London with stiff rebukes. He smiled, setting the pages to the fire. The sun each day now rose to a forlorn chill. A nervous warmth spread to the land, the days perfumed. In the fields, beast climbed to beast upon each other's backs. Flowers broke the soil into bloom, tobacco to its hills. Corn placed to its long furrows. It was April of 1618, and now the news, Powhatan was dead, dying on his own land. How many thrones abandoned? How many capitols cast down? Ruling in his forsaken power, this shattered king resumed his reluctant peace. His favorite daughter dead, thus a haunted man, hunted in his own mind, he had fled to the Potomac River and the friendly king Mayomps, bequeathing his empire to Opechancanough forever and his brother Opitchapam for a weakening moment.

Chapter Thirty-seven

WAR SLIPS ITS STEW TO PLATE AND NEW ENGLAND
PROMPTS SOME PILGRIMS TO A COLONY.

OW THE MIGHTY WITHER under a mightier hand. Powhatan the beginning, now has come his end. His daughter dead, now so he. How many lineages kept his blood? How many weights of tobacco blessed his soul? All was changed in such subtle poise, the rock hardly seemed to slip before the avalanche. Opechancanough was the emperor. The peace, now old, came brittle before it snapped.

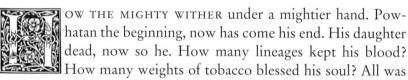

Argall long since had stopped the trade of guns to the savages. Peace here secrets a lethal intent. Richard Killingbeck of the first supply and four other adventurers were lured from their boat into the forest, enticed by the Chickahominy with stories of great stores of corn. Songs of food and thoughts of women, Killingbeck danced the string, led by the throat. The Chickahominy, in vengeance for those Yeardley had slain, shot Killingbeck dead and cut him and his party into bloody heaps, their formless skin to dress the earth. The savages then raided upon the countryside, attacking their own, stealing even the treasures of their own dead kings. Violence spiked into a maddening hate, they rampaged near our settlements, slaughtering five children at William Fairfax's house not far from Jamestown. How small their skinless frames nailed to the wooden walls. At the sight, the mother so distraught, she bit into her hand and drank her own blood.

Argall sent messengers to Opechancanough, demanding justice and the lives of the savages responsible. Opechancanough assuring Argall that he would never break the peace, promised to deliver the heads of those murderers into Argall's hands and to please all his satisfactions. 'These, our own, have robbed from us as well and done murder here.' And so Opechancanough told his tale by messenger, but never did we see those heads, or hear that justice was performed. Tale to tale, the lies now entwined, and we to wander in its landscape, all conscience set aside.

I *have now received your letter,* my friend Smith, your sermon, your clever pleadings. I would never slight the sin to ignore the crime. If I am reasoned to be not quite the knave, I am certainly not quite the saint. Have I not made initiatives of my life, as you would have wished? Am I not the hero of our book? I no lazy gentleman to eat upon the work of others, nothing built for nothing gained, my complaints confound all sloth. Let the commons murder themselves by sleep, groan salvation from another's meal. I am risen, the pillow tossed to air. I am the other alchemy of the other path, I am your book written to another plot, sit the course and watch the play. If you are love, so be it, my compassion's gone, I am distilled, a brew not weakened, I stratagem in my hates. We are still friends, twins if you prefer, our enterprise struck on the same coin but wagered to a different toss. Never to me the river bleeds its voice, silence is the land I wear."

Argall made maps and divisions on the earth. His grants of land now called Argall's Gift or Argall's Town. It was known to you, Smith, as the land of the Paspaheghs, those savages long since having been driven into the wilderness. By four incorporations and parishes he set their bounds: James City, Bermuda City, Henrico, Kecoughtan. The earth now cut, gripped in our lines, its names now ours. Is not our great translation but a lend of words? My angers blot the ink. I sat in my cabin distilling Ovid into English verse. All my works are of a lesser quill. I am but the folly to rouge some better's lips. Its voice not a voice of mine. Is the world too silent for me to speak its mysteries? Will the knot ever slip my tongue? Will I ever be a music of my own? The probable is a common 'no,' but my sins golden in their compensation. And all those little strings that suspend me from a forsaken heaven, swing me very rich.

More Company's servants now worked Argall's land, the common land left to ruins while other towns were founded, named, their boundaries drawn: Martin's Hundred, Flowerdieu Hundred, Martin's Brandon, Weyanoke. Argall appointed officers, men of quality and some gifts. His days at sea still held him to some reason. Laws were made more lenient, his advice not wholly sour to our cause. Wells dug, houses built, some ruins repaired.

Our corn supplies low, but no one hungered who had its price. The servants were fed from the company's supply, they to labor and grow tobacco on private lands. Our theft is never wanton when it remakes old laws to the benefit of ourselves. Those who had paid the passage had their labor for seven years of service. Most died within six months. Those that lived made their masters' wealth. John Rolfe keeping numbers to ledger the growth of riches. One man could tend on poor land two thousand plants, which harvested five hundred pounds of tobacco leaves. On good land, three boys could tend plants which would yield three thousand pounds. Crops and weight of the harvest differed. In the fields, a man's experience, the soil, the rain, the labor of his servants, all changed the numbers; but certainly one man could earn two hundred pounds a year from each of his servants, more money than could be made in England in a life. And servants were the means, and servants were the prize. The land might be ruined by the weed, but the earth provided plenty more. Our houses never sturdily built, a man's wealth was constant only in the trinkets he possessed, silver and a copper spoon, and others that he employed. It was riches told in servants, and those that had the power and the means stole them from the company, and soon we stole them from each other.

Even servants begged for servants, that they might grow a portion of the wealth. The company sending twenty to serve the indentured servants. Land now cheap, all hope now weighted in labor.

How much of England we did cast aside. There, a laborer sold his work for only one year, guarded by the courts, his service valued at standard rates. A master feared to displease, or none would work for him again. All this well practiced and codified in law. In Virginia, the key was blood. There servants sold themselves for the cost of passage for four to seven years. Their terms of long labors set, their passage seen as debt which must be paid, no penny forgiven, no pound forgot. Iron chains contract against all circumstance, even a master's cruelty. Most servants were almost lost to starving before even reaching the Chesapeake, so little was allotted on the voyage for their food.

Even with provisions and the voyage, the cost of a year's work for a servant in Virginia was less than in England. John Rolfe, his Bible in his ledgers now, prayed his numbers and kept accounts.

'The cost of passage to Virginia is six pounds sterling,' said Rolfe, 'With clothes, some food, another four pounds, or at most six. For the tally, let us say twelve pounds the price of each servant. A four-year service is three pounds a year, a seven-year service is one pound eighteen shillings a year, but in England a year's labor costs is one and a half to two and a half pounds. We have not squandered any advantage by being here. Each servant may yield his master seventy-five to two hundred weight of tobacco. At the least, good profits, at the best, riches.'"

So many servants died, but so many lived enough to oil the hope of wealth and keep all others laboring to have their freedom and their own chance at servants and at fortunes. Some servants were sent by private funds to work the private lands, those grants we called the hundreds. The passages of the rest were paid by the Company. It was those we stole. 'And we to save the freight,' Argall said, that idea already well explored.

All is balanced on the leaf, and greed, corn and profit. How much land to sacrifice for food? Corn could be bought from Argall, who had the savages' trade. How much profit planted today would you use to eat tomorrow? But food was freedom. And so each to his own plan, his land so divided. In Virginia hunger now not common, but a separate foul of every man's judgment. Most chose tobacco, and so starved, their bellies crawling across the weed in their blind idolatries. A few would have plenty of food and be poor, finally selling food and becoming rich. Some would starve in wealth, giving most of their riches to buy food and be poor. All by sums, the balance never moved.

'As asked by London, we have brought some hold upon the weed,' Argall spoke in a smile, 'We have done our commission well.'

We are not Spanish yet, my thoughts in London, reading Sandys'
letter. But words make better hide than any mask. Fools are we who
so cleverly persuade ourselves.

Letters now received from London that Lord De la Warr
was again to sail to take up his commission as lord governor.
Argall to be replaced. Two hundred and fifty new colonists to
be consumed. Argall sent letters and salutations to the London
Company on the returning ship. 'If you bring such a new supply
of men, they must have provisions, victuals and clothes, or all
will die. We have not the stores ourselves to keep them well.' It
was all untrue. We could have borne the cost, we had the corn.
Argall smiled to me. 'Let the company provide the gain, and we
will keep the profits.'

Rolfe was seized with love again, he courted now his Jane, the
daughter of two ancient planters, William and Joan Peirce. How
rare women, so few in the colony, and Jane, how dry that face in
its blank, her expressionless eyes, dull her stare, the world but a
watery wonder through their glass.

I see the courted nuptials as a dumb show prank. My thoughts
of Rolfe—how sits a man his passions all asleep? Pocahontas, his
life's one great cry. Never did he seek the savages again. Rolfe,
neither cruel nor kind, indifferent to their state. Conversion
to him but to bring her to his bed, and she in love with other
thoughts and other memories, and so are our contracts drawn.

Rolfe walked with Jane, his nervous hand at his side. And
how to decide the touch at first. The tobacco leaves he caressed
as he spoke to coo the treasuries from the wet fields' furrows.
Their figures drifting between the plants, lost to the horizons of
the weed. Rolfe well-played his familiar part and married Jane.
Tobacco his ecstasy, a woman's flesh an occasional taste.

Never did he see his son that Pocahontas bore, left to
Plymouth, raised by his brother, well provided for, that Thomas,
from Rolfe's wealth and Opechancanough's gifts. But never did
the father seek him to his side and Rolfe now with a new wife.
The tobacco leaf veined upon his hand his love. He to harvest its
life and cure it to the proper burning within his pipe.

Chapter Thirty-eight

THE NOISE, THE CLAMOR, THE ACTION—ALL THE SHREWD ORBITS OF THE BLIND.

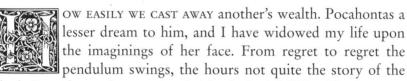OW EASILY WE CAST AWAY another's wealth. Pocahontas a lesser dream to him, and I have widowed my life upon the imaginings of her face. From regret to regret the pendulum swings, the hours not quite the story of the clock. I sat the strokes surrounded in the invisibilities. There are no new lands that do not whisper her. I sealed another letter to Sandys, waxed the lock on its paper cage. Is Virginia to its fate? Does that earth still hold to her, to me, to something of us both? Can passions divide and not dispel? Can I protect and love, love and be betrayed? Time has countered every hate. The river speaks but of itself. And I crave still a consequence. So much, so much, my desires founder on desire. Two I have, Americas both of a different wilderness. She of dark eyes cupped in mysteries, measureless even upon the eons of the land. That land, that other self, forests to my alchemies. Twins of many, and who is the one? That first love is the deepest spent. Behind the one the many, behind the many the one. Love contagions a love confused, and who the only or the most: she, my Pocahontas, or the New World? I smile in my disease. I, the true apostle, swept aside. Chains loosen, soon no anchor to my life. Still, I am enthralled to be possessed. New England is my only country now. To it, in chronicles, I scheme to bring it full.

I HAD NOT SEEN PURCHAS FOR SOME MONTHS WHEN I RECEIVED an urgent note to visit him. What Purchas greeted me with no sweet wine to ease the moment, his patience hanging salted on his meat. "All this I tell you in confidence," Purchas said, then paused to gather his excitement behind an ominous dam, the calm then split. I had the verse. "Edwin Sandys is in secret negotiation to bring the Puritans to northern Virginia. The story this: the Puritans under a double threat in Leiden, first from a renewed war with Spain and second from the humanity of their Dutch hosts. The Dutch having too much toleration is an annoyance for their guests. And so we persecute that tolerance as we beg its favors. So it is, and so it was. The Puritans in fear of becoming more Dutch than Puritan, sought a place to have all to themselves by isolation. We die by purities, my Smith," Purchas smirked, continuing, "And so your part," I smiled, ready to speak. Purchas with a nod held me silent. "The story is not done. The Reverend Whitaker you knew in Virginia is a Puritan. He by note keeping his fellows informed of the Virginia enterprise, especially of silk and worms and mulberry trees. One of the most important elders in Leiden being a silk weaver, he seeing the threads of commerce in that tale, even if the crop failed in Virginia. Among the Puritans it was still a hope." Purchas looked at me. "Hope is the devil's shepherd," I said. We laughed. "Men greed their dreams with more avarice than their coins," Purchas continued, not to be thought less.

"The Puritans soon decided for Virginia. By agents and secret interventions their brethren Edwin Sandys was informed. He to speak to George Abbott, the Archbishop of Canterbury, the archbishop having friendly inclinations toward the Puritans. 'Our Puritans to pilgrims it seems,' so quipped the Pilate as he consented to use his influence with the king.

"Now the story is a chase. The Puritans having drafted seven articles elaborating their attitude toward King and government and the Anglican Church. As you know, these well received by all. The pen well served the diplomacies and what is not known is Edwin Sandys has appointed an agent believed to be Sir John Walstenholm, the merchant, to negotiate the matter with the king." Purchas relaxed into his chair. "Northern Virginia, friend Smith, northern Virginia. Seek out the Puritans. Persuade them for your part. There is a New England colony to be had, and you the experience and they the thought."

I looked at Purchas, my strategies plated on the battlefields of the air. "I have my second New England manuscript never published, only sent to Francis Bacon. That could be a printed book to adventure myself and claim the Puritans as a prize." As I spoke I watched Purchas.

"Be not too superior with the Puritans. They too are certain. Beware and be gone. I am tedious with too many good works."

I rose and thanked Purchas, who waved me out, saying, "Think not for the nation, Smith. There is little here but problems for your stomach." A sweet man, Purchas, more presumed than cynic. I had my task. I returned to my rooms. I began to recast my manuscript for a greater good, detailing the economies of my plan, fishing to replace tobacco. Food the sovereign against the vice. I called my book *New England Trials*. Purchas kept me informed of the Puritans and the progress of their negotiations, all the complexities and of a policy contested in the swirls of competing needs. And where the hook to hold it right? Edwin Sandys the secret prompt, the plot is urged upon the proprietor's fingertips. And then came a letter from Purchas. "Thomas Smythe has asked the king to replace him as treasurer of the London Company. That office now in doubt, Edwin Sandys is the presumed choice, but the king not warm to him and all his parliaments. Stay your hand and finish your book. I would not approach the Puritans as yet. Too much public may be the ruin of the prize."

Events ate upon events, their progress if at all in a fool-bound stew. In April of 1618 Sir Edwin Sandys confirmed as treasurer of the London Company, the king's reluctant choice. Good sense had enticed some peace, and so with all the wobble, the two sat their separate thrones, my plan coming to their point. I wrote to gain some interview with Sandys or the agents for the Puritans, and then suddenly the rumors of arrest, the king, learning of Sandys secret dealings with the Leiden group, crowned the thorn of treasons on his head. While politics played their private sport, I dawdled my hours into weeks. The Willoughbys again to the rescue, and to pay the expenses to print my book, but the money stayed until the king and Sandys resolved their paper wars. More delays and politics all the waste.

IN SEPTEMBER A FAST PINNACE REPORTED LORD DE LA WARR'S fleet had made the Chesapeake that July. His lordship dead some weeks after he arrived, his grieving widow with her servants, her maid attending at her hand. Argall saved to be governor once again. There was no one else.

The report not full. No words to insinuate the truth. There were no ready houses, nothing built, the new supply of men was scattered to the woods to live under hedges. All wild in the open, the heat and rain washed across their bones. The strongest and the best were taken to work the private lands. All the reports were a fare-thee-well and prank. Lady De la Warr being given a house, her many able servants about her. Then the mumbles, the rumors and the silence. Nothing heard for months until Captain Edward Brewster came home to England to speak his accusation. The story this: Argall, seeing Lady De la Warr's strong and healthy servants wasted on her small needs, ordered those servants to tend his tobacco crop, the Lady De la Warr angered to see her own abducted without her consent. The lady protested. Captain Edward Brewster, an old acquaintance of her husband, in a gallant gesture to the memory of his friend, told the servants to disobey Argall. "Stay by your lady. Our lord governor, though dead, his commission still protects."

Brewster spoke his heresies with justice but he, no angel to the governor, was arrested. Silence is their law, where concealment is the fragile peace. Argall called the council to sit its court, the jesters soon to sit in judgment. Sandys voted with the rest. How much the secret rage is the murder of all our hopes? Brewster sentenced to be hung. The colony fixed to riot, everywhere protests. The new ministers begged mercy. Lady De la Warr threatened Argall. The governor spared Brewster, sending him into exile, home to England, with a pledge never to speak ill of Virginia or its governor.

Pledges made by threat are rarely kept. Once in England, Brewster spoke against Argall to the commons and the London Company, calling for him to be replaced. Everywhere he spoke. All London a single echo of Brewster's accusations. The public armed its mob to have its justice. Argall sent more letters to rage defiance at the Company, he not knowing how other powers wobbled the arrogant crown upon his head. Warwick's influence too light to hold the balance. Brewster brought legal charges against Argall into court. How soon we sip before we drown. With Lord De la Warr dead, the office of the lord governor was vacant. Empty as a whistle in the wind. The London Company, with no choice left to choose, made Captain George Yeardley their new lord governor and captain general. He who strutted the London streets to boast his wealth, twelve liveries at his call, dressed in fantasies the low thought regal, taste lost to the cheaper plate. Now he strutted ordained to real privilege, the power of the London Company called to nest beneath his painted feathers. Boast yourself and brag your riches. You are led by others' vanities. Tell your tales upon the street, how those of little gifts have farmed them to great careers. And what cabbage will not brag himself a king? Men have ever put aside their judgment where greed and hope are mixed.

. . . . .

GEORGE YEARDLEY WAS KNIGHTED BY KING JAMES AT NEWMARKET in Suffolk. Six days earlier, November eighteenth, 1618, Yeardley was finally given the authority to found a council of estate and a general assembly for Virginia. This parliament was instituted as a congress for the colony where representatives from the parishes would have a voice to fulfill the common good, and could pass laws with the approval of the king and the London Company, all to the prosperity of the whole.

The world is an irony and we the puppet dance on depleted strings, all our reasons are but a congregation of competing barnyard recreations. The king hated Yeardley and all parliaments, but even more he hated Sir Edwin Sandys who said, "The king is a man ordained by our histories to be a man. No more God in him than in the histories of the rest. Equal in equality divinely blessed. God no less a choir in our anointed voice than his. The pretensions of the king all swept aside. His divine right gone. We are by our fortunes free for our common good. Law and wealth and privilege to the parliaments."

Yeardley was disfavored by the king for being Edwin Sandys' favorite, Sandys always admiring Yeardley's abilities. How often wise men boil their wisdom to overcook the meal. Yeardley's grasp his only cleverness. Crude men ever confound the wise: whose visions ever to the sky, wisdom rarely sees what wiggles at its feet. And so the king spooned Yeardley's limits to his mouth and sucked the bitter taste. The king created a hated parliament in Virginia to salve the great investors, hoping he could control their laws and better tax tobacco. The lord governor was to call a representative assembly every year to make laws which would be finally adopted after the approval of the London Company. This assembly to have two burgesses from every settlement and plantation chosen by the inhabitants themselves. Two by two they stepped into the ark to breed their laws. It is by dots and scratch we join the lines, the script soon to be the page and what the text? The choice we choose always bears a hidden consequence. Beware the surprises the surface hides. Too much the policies contradict. Confusion now the lord of circumstance. I was never considered for any post. My opinions a foul of provocatives.

The throne sat its violence through its policies and warred its conclusions upon itself. And so the document was called the great charter. It lowered the tax on Virginia tobacco, the weed now half the rate of the Spanish leaf, encouraging the expansion of the fields while only slightly hurtful to the king's own revenues. All this was done for the general good, but in truth were these blessings just another inspired curse? Seeking to make an imperfect world more perfect, Edwin Sandys made it worse. Now the council moved to free the colony from all taxes, and so devised a plan of benefits which would improve the common wealth. All officers would receive no pay but would receive allotments of land and servants, those being the company's own seven-year indentured. The lord governor would receive three thousand acres and one hundred servants from the company's supply to tend his land; the admiral, fifteen hundred acres and fifty servants; the marshal, fifteen hundred acres and fifty servants; the vice-admiral, three hundred acres and twelve servants; the ministers, one hundred acres and six servants. George Sandys as treasurer was to be reaffirmed his fifteen hundred acres and fifty servants. All this and no taxes to the whole. But no one saw but I, now all were party to the coming sin. How largess comes by generosities only to corrupt. What was done for charity made legitimate half the crime. Now the officers stole servants because it was their right. The law is always the better prompt to improve the crime.

GEORGE SANDYS NOW SOUGHT HIS COLONISTS IN GREATER NUM-bers, from the prisons, from the poor, from the starving in the streets. Each English parish to give its exiles, and they in Virginia to feed and fill the bellies of the appointed greed. That rabble was sent to be the servants and harvest the weed. Strange benefits there are in charities.

DAYS BEFORE YEARDLEY DEPARTED, A FAST PINNACE SAILED FROM Plymouth, one of Warwick's ships to warn Argall and have him to safety in Bermuda. The London Company had ordered his arrest. Across the Indies, Warwick's fleets of privateers plundered the Spanish trade, spoils from the despoiler, seizing all goods and property. Bermuda was their haven and their port. This was Drake of a lesser kind. Simple humanity gone from vision. Profits now the only weight upon the tale.

It was war against the fallen. Spain dying, suffocating in its Inquisition. All who could have made her great expelled or murdered.

Rising debts, her coins debased, her military power on the ebb. Portugal rebelled to free herself. France's star rising on the bigot's continent. King James made a peace. England had mostly won her war, but wars do not die in ink. The Earl of Warwick and others of his mind would still have their sorties to have their gold, victory not plain enough. Spain truly still a threat. Vengeance to some makes a fairer justice, but Warwick's vengeance was kindled on a greed. Beware in wars how soon the bloods do mix, and we become our enemies.

Chapter Thirty-nine

ALL THIS AND WEALTH, FORGET THE OFFENSE, IT SWEETS THE DANCE.

YEARDLEY'S FLEET SAILED FROM Plymouth on January nineteenth, 1619, with a fresh supply of three hundred colonists and adventurers for the Virginia Plantation. The lord governor at sea, unknown to him, in that secret race with Warwick's pinnace. The sea ever baring its fates upon the land. In Virginia the weeks did pass, the weather drifting into spring. I could see it all described in Sandys' letter. The tobacco crop set to its hills, the seeds to womb in earth, the soil dark with loam. Even the streets and doorways were pocked with the rising nibbles of the weed. Masters beat servants to have them obey and do more work. Backs made raw with lashes, the tongues of the whips, the bleeding scars in grotesque smiles. How maps the pain in flesh when tobacco owns the will. Men all drank and staggered to their fields. Women sold their laughter for the pleasures of its taste. Indian girls were now fearful of the settlements. Diseases of the loin did drip in the mercuries of their pasts and stalked the streets. Some men married with the savages, but only with daughters of the kings. All the world is but a feed upon some new example, and so another to our Rolfe.

Argall still held his office, not yet warned. It was March 1619. The day clear but for the river and the green reflections on its silver waters. The world waiting to be inspired to its foul. In London I walked the threads of my neglect, nothing to hold me to a smile. While in Virginia, Sandys, the scribe of action, composed the history. Sandys' letters in my hand, his to quill a confound of telling upon the page, and homage the thrill of his dereliction.

*O*ne *of Warwick's ships, the Treasurer, its sails* bowed in power. The pale push of its bloodless flesh, its hull as a black seed, cleaved its monotony through the bay and had our dock. It had come to trade. We bought the trifles she had. Reprovisioning her, Argall gave the captain, a Dutchman named Daniel Elfrith, a commission to sail to Bermuda and return with salt and goats. Elfrith was in truth a privateer, and sought more than goats.

Some days after the *Treasurer* sailed, the fast pinnace arrived. Argall in all haste and panic appointed Captain Nathaniel Powell acting governor, and fled with all his wealth toward Bermuda. Some twelve days later, on April twelfth, 1619, Yeardley's fleet entered the Chesapeake. How pleased the company was to see Yeardley again, he always more prudent in his greed, more humane in his tyranny. Nothing truly changed but the tack. Yeardley knew government governs best when all the criminals feel they are masters of the crime.

*T*he *tobacco crop* from the year before cargoed many hulls. The corn we grew was of no account, for all Argall's rages. We still relied on the savages to supply us food. Although the land was rich and moist and easy to our plows, and one oxen could sow forty acres, we had not have enough irons for the plows or harnesses for the cattle, and what should have been a plenty to our barns was but another waste. We starved. Even the corn we grew we harvested last. Tobacco always had our labor first. Our corn rotted in the fields, shaken from its stalks or eaten by the rats or cattle, untended in their ramble.

Still no shelters for a new supply of men. They ate what we gave: Indian corn from the company store or roots or last winter's nuts or salads made of leaves, even leaves of the huskanaw plant. Madness to they that ate, rude humors to their brains. Soon to drool and scream and run in defecating frenzy, their urine flung in warm rivers down their knees. Men would laugh, "It is the Jamestown salad in their gut."

Yeardley and the council surveyed the acres the London Company had allotted. A hundred servants on three thousand acres were added to Yeardley's thousands of acres already owned. Grants of land to all others of the council and all the tending servants. I too acquired more lands, more wealth, more power. My father's hold in York now but a pin to prick a smile. Such estates came now to verge on empires, but with death so common, where to find the servants in their allotted numbers?

And so began the thefts. How different England was. Masters there ran from servants, the courts and common practice of the law putting burdens on their backs. They to hire in numbers they did not need. Masters faced with ruin fled. The employment lost, the servants to the fields to starve or rob. These brigands and the unemployed were seen now as the company's supply, my brother's dream of a commons risen from a common fall. The jails empty, the gallows still, criminals no longer pushed to crime.

The world does not come easy to our dreams, although we always seem to dream. In London the company floundered toward bankruptcy, begging the king to grant Virginia a monopoly in the tobacco trade, the English tobacco farmers more a threat to us than Spain. The king's own rent of the tobacco tax, a yearly sum of sixteen thousand pounds was in jeopardy from the domestic leaf. Policies are born when interests merge. In Virginia we all waited on the king's pleasure, while a few made fortunes and many had hopes. Several of the ancient planters, William Spencer, Thomas Barret and some others, having served their seven years, were set free, to choose such lands as would content them and there to plant and build as was their desire.

The tobacco all about hung its leaves like sleeping bats, the ears of its flowers turning to cries of those who tended upon its needs. What master this weed, that gentlemen grovel at its roots and ships sail oceans to have it home.

On all sides now, my brother is betrayed. John Ferrar, his London deputy, secretly sent a ship financed by a company of his own to the Chesapeake to trade with the colony. Wine and silks, pleasures sold to procure the tobacco leaf. The captain of the ship, William Tucker, grim, his spiteful cheeks sunken in their cruelty. His ship a sly of dice and gambling, cards well-marked in villainy to steal our crop. The wine watered to a colored swill, and beer foamed in poison, brewed badly in London. Hundreds sickened at its taste and many died, but still men sat the tables, squares of cards as coffins in their hands, betting tobacco leaves in pounds, in next year's crop. Debt pushed men to madness. When the tobacco was gone, masters waged their servants or sold them to cover their bets; men and women, their eyes cast down in the candlelight, their flesh a currency, their terms of service a ripening gold. All wealth had become the weed. Fearing poverty at home, the king decreed no English coin could be shipped to the colony. So much silver and gold had been sent to Spain to pay for the weed, all coins were for home, none for export. We forced to barter smoke, our currency the weights of leaf, and the servants who could make it grow.

Captain Tucker sold his freight. The tobacco gained, he traded against other goods, kept the profits, never sending an account to London, and pleasured himself buying lands and servants, Virginia now his home. Nothing foul enough, it did not seem fair when balanced against the leaf. With his ship and a license from Yeardley, he traded corn with the savages and made even more. The tickle of avarice his tended itch, scratched into fortunes and a little murder.

Within a week of the new supply, most were dead, the cords of their unburied flesh lay in the fields for days, torn by beasts, who eat us as a feast. So few survived, so few seasoned to the heat and swamp and bad water. If three of ten had made the finish of a year, it was a blessed lot. Men lived in shacks, beat their servants. Death now but death and hardly worth the notice. Virginia is not a place to stay but to escape.

As treasurer of the colony, I chose for my servants those men and women who seemed to have most health, keeping my accounts against their cost in food and clothes. A shilling a day, I wrote my brother, was their price to me, but in truth I spent but a sliver of that coin. Their deaths no debt, their cost to me so small. There was always a new supply, my brother emptying the prisons and collecting the paupers from the streets. Newgate Prison opened its doors to loose its locust feast. John Throckmorton, hat thief, sent; John Carter, horse thief; James Knott, convicted felon; Daniel Francke, malefactor;

fifty lewd women; and thirty who walked the streets after ten at night, all shipped to Virginia. All badly clothed and fed, the London Company without the means to tend them well. Their deaths a secret, not told in England. The enterprise must survive. How many harvests make a dream? Eleven ships in the first six months of 1619, enough adventurers to harvest the crop. Always we were moral to our greed. There was no slavery in Virginia, for who would own a man who soon would die, never paying back his costs? Death was our commandment, greed our lord.

I sat in my cabin in the candlelight, translating words of Ovid's, all ripening into their English sweet. What an easy garden is the mind, its grotesques grow a futile pose. Each hope imagines us to be better than we are. I not even a shank of Ovid's genius and yet I thought myself as good. All this to dissuade me from the conscience of my crimes.

In Virginia there were servants of three kinds: tenants who labored for the company or associations which bought large tracts of land, called hundreds, the tenants to have half of what they grew; bond servants, who were provided with food and clothes and nothing more, their masters keeping all their harvest; and "duty boys," so named by me, many having arrived upon the ship *Duty*, they to work seven years for any adventurer paying ten pounds for them, then seven years more as tenants, with half shares of what they earned. All this seemed fair, but what the practice. A "duty boy" who committed some crime in his first seven years will be forced to serve another seven years as punishment. And so the practice weaves a willful license. Even a master's death could not free a laborer, for he is quickly claimed. Even those who sailed to Virginia at their own expense, free to plant tobacco on their own, bought land. They, too, have hazards of this place—bad crops or debt. Soon, by hunger and in need of clothes, they are forced as tenants to another's land. Freedom here is the quest and luck the grail, and our knaves all made the better knights.

Yeardley within days of his arrival sent messages of peace to Opechancanough, inviting him to Jamestown to have wise council and renew their friendship. Opechancanough refused. Rolfe and some adventurers wondered if the peace by halts and tiny gestures was coming to an end.

The fabric of the land now squared in our tobacco fields, and we so spread along the James. But our parishes so far apart, and settlements ten miles or more, little help were we to each other in a war. So thin we were, like a mist about the dragon's jaw.

Jack of the Feathers was now seen dancing near our forts, his arms and shoulders all laced in down and feathers. He screamed before his evening fires. The moon full, rose to deflect the night, its halo a grotto around the wooden blaze. "Your leadened shot calls to me no death," he cried.

In Jamestown on Sundays after church, women strut their rough fur hats, silks and other corsets of their wealth, pearl bands to belt their hair, husbands on their arms, arrayed in their blush and exorbitant clothes, colors all to promenade success. "God did not decree so we could flaunt his day," said the minister in a rage. Where men sold men like cattle into years of servitude, small morals make some feel safe.

To ease the stick I played my pittance to a qualm and did the surface of my estate. I did my brother's policies, raised such works, egged ideas to become an infant industry; built iron works, glass works, salt works; planted vines and mulberry trees, figs and cotton wool, potatoes and pomegranates; explored for the copper mines; sought good supplies of sand for the glass works; and even wrote such letters home to encourage such investors into adventurers. All this as I gathered land and collected taxes to bankrupt the small and take their servants.

But I was not the only one, the governor now traded guns again with the Indians, we always in desperate need of corn. Opechancanough always in greeds of longing, engrossing all our weapons to himself. Robert of Poland was Yeardley's agent and Opechancanough's squeak and pander. Where his loyalty lay, no one knew, but for me it was the freshest coin just placed in his hand. So wanton this Pole that if he had been a woman of the night, he would have pushed away a mount in mid gallop to seek a bigger coin and a better tickle. And so, in the grill of the summer heat, the Potomacs sent word that they had corn in mountains and wished to trade. Opechancanough, fearing some guns and shot and powder would not be his, sent Robert his Pole to bring slanders against the Potomacs. "It is an ambushado. They call for two of our ships, not to freight with corn but to seize the guns and have us dead. Ruin in their words for those that trust."

Henry Spelman spoke in defense of the Potomac. He who had lived among them, they who had given him shelter, traded him back to Argall and, for the love of the strangers in their land, plotted against Powhatan, giving us Pocahontas. All this Spelman did remind the council. "Why would they now betray us when for so long they were our only friends? What has changed? Nothing but Robert of Poland who is a traitor!" So Spelman spoke, and so do fools waddle in the truth, all that inconvenience with so little gain.

Yeardley deaf but to where his interests lay. Too much makes cheap, and corn was as wealth to him as tobacco. He controlled the trade. Another source, a squander, his commerce weakened.

A nod and a wink from Yeardley, Robert the Pole now spoke his slanders. "I have seen Spelman in the forest with the Potomacs. There he planned his betrayals," said Robert Poole, accusing the innocent of his own crimes. "For promises of wealth and forest pleasures, he has spoken against the council, calling them thieves and cowards, inciting the savages in their hopes. His lies here will come in murder. It was this Spelman, when but a child, led Ratcliffe to his death." It mattered not what was said, the sentence already set. Robert Poole smiled in his anxious sweat, he shivered his excitements on his face, he blushed. So small this criminal, he is but his crime.

How weak the truth when framed upon such offense. Spelman spoke in his passions to save himself, but all was drawn before it was ever begun. Yeardley rose and had his say. Spelman to serve another seven years as a servant. "And so the punishment for any who would plot against our enterprise and the king's law." Spelman screamed then went to silence, broken to live his truth in toils. Robert Poole glowed in the shadow of Yeardley's power. He who conspires, then rests beneath the sword, had better watch the blade above his head.

Opechancanough's supply of guns now safe, Robert the Pole received promises but little else. So Opechancanough worked his vengeance against all at no cost to himself. How wild is that mind. He knew our ways, he warred by spies, he intrigued his stealth by subtle stratagems. A Spaniard would have done no less. Maybe he was that boy the Spanish took and educated as themselves, only to be repaid in massacre. Oh, Smith, more than thought does foul the air, and we are strangers in this land. We may sit its plate, but hidden histories are our swill.

Chapter Forty

CONTAGIONS IDLE IN OUR GEOGRAPHIES. THE
PLAGUE SEEPS, ITS SEEMS AS A CURE.

READ SANDYS' LETTERS, thought them a surface tide. Are we by our own creations so betrayed? Our laws by government but an instrument to do vengeance upon ourselves? Self-interest ever sets too close, the general good dispersed, even freedom easy turned a license to do another crime. And where the halt to this decay? I encumbered in a pod and so ignored, truth the lost, no constituents to speak its tale. I sat at my desk, a single candle as my grail.

Soon another letter from Sandys. My reply not penned. Sandys now boasted a little poetry, played the words to coo a compliment. But I had the freight before Sandys' thoughts unboxed, the story from Purchas. I combine their tales.

The winds fresh and plenty to cut their ciphers acrossthe bay. Two ships, their masts blighted with patched sails, their hulls with rot upon their timbers, decay torn in gnashes on their heavy planks. All this and their shadows trailed upon their wakes. The waters fled from their bows, waves swallowing waves in backward rush, as if they would not be touched by such a thing. Fleshed skeletons they were that would not sink. What hell that sails in shrouds does come our way? Death not dead enough to them. They made our dock. The Treasurer had now returned in the company of a Dutch man-of-war, captained by a man named Kerby. He no more than pirate, but he held by some means a commission from the prince of Orange. Two ships, their crews half-starved. Captain Elfrith of the Treasurer and Captain Kerby now on shore, Captain Elfrith demanding to trade for food. "I am in the employ of the Earl of Warwick, his lordship, as you well know, on the council of your London Company, this ship part owned by him and your lord governor Argall. I seek what his lordship would expect—prompt compliance with our desires." Argall owned a piece of the *Treasurer*. All heads nodded silently on the news. It was no wonder that the *Treasurer* was so quick revictualed and so cheap.

"Argall is displaced and gone," someone called. Yeardley now walked forward to have his introduction and to boast his authority. Captain Elfrith used again the names of Warwick and Argall and made again his proposal in the subtle of his threat. Yeardley, always meek when hints of power were displayed, invited the captains to meet with the council and have their say. All walked toward Jamestown's walls.

The full story Purchas had by whispers and his friends at court.

*T*he *nation squanders* when news must come as gossip. What I tell you, Smith, is a most secret report.

The *Treasurer* when first she sailed from Jamestown sailed not to Bermuda, but to the West Indies, there to plunder the Spanish main. This was a war on Spain and against the king's wishes. Diplomacies were but a fret. Warwick wanted this new land as a port to thieve upon the Spanish. "War is better when it battles upon a treasury," he said. In the Indies, the *Treasurer* had met the Dutch ship, Captain Kerby having already seized fifty blacks and other booty from a vessel under the command of another Dutchman named Youpe. That ship known by no flag, with no commission to trade in those waters. Youpe's cargo forfeited to the luck of the cannonade, the booty lost to Kerby. So thieves did pray on thieves and ate each other. Youpe to sail his silent way for home with no complaints. He had his life, the law no redress, and rarely does the criminal praise the better crime.

The Caribbean wide, its soup salted not to Kerby's taste. Low on food, he had come upon the sails of the Treasurer. All the world is an accident occasioned to any simmer. After friendly conversation, a partnership formed, Elfrith exchanging food for a portion of the booty. Both ships in need of victuals, they sailed to Virginia for Argall's protection and for trade. And so the council sat, darkness flickering on the edges of the light, the devil's candle glowing. What angels there, all sat appalled. Elfrith offered to sell his Negroes as slaves for a hundred pounds apiece. John Pory of the council spoke. "We are not sent here to forward any Spanish custom. There will be no slavery in Virginia. We are still Drake enough to call ourselves our Cimarrones. Our hope not lost, our will not so corrupt. I will not have Spanish thoughts. Are we to free the world only to have it slave?"

And so the sparse and light of Purchas's report. Sandys more lyric now enticed the scene.

Elfrith calm, his eyes pearled in a desperate anger. "His lordship, the Earl of Warwick is law enough for any English court. He will expect some account and action on his property. Do you wish to trade? I and his lordship wish to know."

What good men live is the memory of what they wish themselves to be. What fails us supports us some. The council might crawl the dirt to lick the filth to have their wealth. It would buy and sell men and boys as cattle, but only for their terms of service. Seven years by contract is a servant, however roughly used, not a slave. Words cut many a distinction to save the conscience but to betray the soul. "When England comes to be a Spain, then I will consent to this," said John Pory, the council nodding. Yeardley thinking, weighing each option on the weight of leaf. "A hundred pounds is too much," Yeardley said to the Dutchman, "when we have our servants for ten pounds, the cost of their passage. Why pay more when death takes most? It is a drag on profit when men here live only months. To own the flesh is but a loss." The leaf to have its weight on the balance for the just, beware the leaf might shift its wings ever changeable to a fairer breeze. Yeardley then offered Elfrith ten pounds apiece for his blacks, they to be as any English servant, seven years of toil then their freedom to build and harvest as they wished.

Elfrith found his hands almost touching the profit, but not enough to please his avarice. He cast down the name of Warwick again as a challenge. It was a cause well lost. Elfrith sold us twenty blacks for food and provisions. The blacks to be servants, no different than the rest. They came ashore: six women, fourteen men and one infant, all sweating in the heat. Mysteries rescued from places foreign and away.

I, John Smith, sat in London, while in Virginia they sat now surrounded, realized in the dream of Drake, his great alliance— Indians, blacks and English—all formed in might against ruined Spain. The world ready to be freed. Slavery there was in the Spanish colonies, Indians dead by the millions, blacks ripped from their own lands to work as beasts. We the forgotten now to have the pendulum slipped to us. But moments flee to moments and memories pass away. The clock's great metal gears click even in their muck, hidden they crush by turns the hour and alter all by their subtle rounds.

And so we bought their freedom with the company's supplies. They to work not the common lands, but the private fields. Five men and three women to Yeardley; four to Abraham Piersey; a husband and wife and their child to William Tucker; one man to John Rolfe; the others to the officers and the council. The servants so divided, no different than the rest, laboring for the weed, Englishmen by their side. Equals in equal toil, with shares of the same abuse. More labor for the weed, the world as ever idling in its recreation. Nothing different, nothing strained. They were like us, they ate with us, they worked with us. Indian, black and English, the three plates of the great balance. Drake's vision now across the body of the land. The world breathless in its uneasy peace.

By fall of 16-19 food was very scarce. Captain Ward sent to the Potomacs to trade for corn. But those who had always been our friends slandered by Robert the Pole were no longer eager for our good regard. So changeable our adventurers were. Not to be sent away, Ward brought his will by force of arms, and stole eight hundred bushels of corn, took some captives to work our fields. "I shot one myself," said Ward, "called Mosco, who claimed a knowledge of Captain John Smith, and spoke of villages built on hills and of their fallen prophet, an apostle risen called the alone."

The All Knowing of My Name 325

And so, my Mosco died. What lives do we forfeit to serve our easy brag? Captain Ward perhaps, by chance, I shall encounter with a little death, a slight, a knife upon the throat. So happy blood, his shirt a stainful festival.

THE OLD FIELDS OF THE SAVAGES PLANTED ONLY WITH THE WEED. No longer many hills of beans or peas or vines of herbs and roots, but all to the one leaf. New land cleared. So turmoiled the new soil beneath the hoe, such a wound upon the soil that fresh dust was infectioned from the new turned earth, vapors tombed for eons swam the air and danced in sunlight premonitions on the breeze. What a wizard is the land. What alchemies does it fester from its stones? In festers the land now rose, and you, my mariner, where in all your craven jars are such lethal chemistries? The sickness came to man and beast. Deer in herds died in the woods. Hundreds of the colony sickened. The land defending itself with plague. What words from the soil would I have heard? What song does contagion sing? The savages also died in numbers beyond our own. Okee the devil made lunatic with their tribes. Their priests chanting powerless words, no dance brought gestures to physic any cure. The land in revolt, tobacco still planted on its shrouded seeds. Sandys told the harm and had the story.

The savages, once sickened, always died. We had many who would return to health. Our true blood its own defense. God has made his truth manifest in us. The land depleted of its game, the savages starved. We still weak. Three hundred of the colony dead. Some plantations abandoned to their ruin. The earth came in death. For what crime this a punishment? For what fault this sacrament of blood? The savages lost, and we, more accustomed to disease, lived on.

Reverend Stockton called in his fevers, "To what God do I pray? I, the deposed. Would the savages pilgrim to us from their powerless Okee?" His eyes wide, his veins flowing, burned as the veins of the tobacco leaf. "A slit throat is a better conversion than any Christ," he screamed. The other clergy, seeing only devils in his talk, prayed for his salvation. But in truth, he spoke for many in the colony. And so the love warred with hate, as Drake's dream with the tobacco smoke.

Men shamed in their beliefs make wars by mysteries. Jack of

> the Feathers still danced by his fire, declaring himself immortal in his feathered armor. No English shot could pierce his flesh. He now Okee's messenger on earth. Where we wore iron armor, he wore feathers, the sign of Okee's herald. How puffed the apostle sits, a strumpet of no God.

I smiled at the letter in my hand. In London, Edwin Sandys raised two thousand pounds to build a college to educate the Indians. Said George Sandys: "My loving brother, always our father's son, and I shepherd to a different sheep." "As treasurer, it was I who oversaw the glass factory and its Italian glassmakers. It was they who made the glass beads we used in trade for corn. Our coin was glass. I and the council used the beads to have the corn to sell and keep the profits. What joy it is to betray a brother, and flaunt your father's God."

But Edwin Sandys would have his college. He and his deputies, John and Nicholas Ferrar, promoted their sacred cause. "Most honorable is this our Christian work to exhort by example and raise up the savages," said Sir Edwin. "So civil the process of our God through the light of his truth. The heathen arrow breaks, his sword withers but to bloom as a Bible in his hand. This college our University of Henrico, God's instrument on earth. For what blessing it is to spend our wealth on such." And so every English parish gave, and the mighty and the weak, we above all would be the salvation of the world. Mary Robinson gave fifty pounds for the construction of a church at the college; there were donations of silver plate, vestments and finely bound Bibles; five hundred and fifty pounds by an anonymous member of the London Company to convert any Indian age seven to twelve from their faith to our own; then more moneys to pay for their apprenticeship to a trade until they reached twenty-one; three hundred pounds to educate ten Indians; an additional twenty-four pounds a year to the colonist who would guide their instructions.

"The whole nation rose to the cause of my brother's charity," wrote Sandys. "How demons glee to witness foolish men being good."

Reverend Patrick Copland raised seventy pounds from passengers on a ship, the Royal James, on its sail to Virginia. The next year, sixty-six pounds were raised on another ship. All England had come sick on this self-awarding purpose.

*H*ow the stomach rots in its own bag to hear the tales of these fair men bearing folly. And good they were, and kind, and sometimes in their foolishness even wise. Money offered to educate Indian children in London was refused, our climate now known as lethal to them. An Indian maiden living in Cheapside in London, since the visit of Pocahontas was granted twenty shillings a week for her care. She quite ill. Requests denied from certain Virginia plantations to have some Indian children live in their homes there to be instructed in our faith, because the children might be fearful, having no acquaintance with those colonists. Plantations selected were carefully chosen and known to be places of calm and nurture. All ministers sent to Virginia were well practiced in the church, known to be of superior mind and saintly disposition. Their wages generous. Their faith to be strong. Most ministers were dead within two years of their arrival.

And all of this plan was air to soap the wilderness to a London street. Did my brother really believe that Opechancanough would bring his children to our homes so we could make them strangers to their own? No father was ever such a heathen. No lunacy ever came in maniac quite that much. 'Wings to the savage soul, his conversion is at hand. All England thrills.' Words—are they always sermons to self-approval? Everywhere words, intoxicating words, my brother nailed to his own congratulations.

John Rolfe, his new wife now great with child, lamented on the moments past. 'How little we tend God's works, our mission not forgotten, only much less sought.' Pious Rolfe, who made his name from lust and his fortune from tobacco. Yeardley did what he could and so too the council. Some wished to lie down in justice and sing to angels; others saw it all a waste, grew tobacco and cursed the savages. The colony was of two heads, each walking in its opposite direction, the single body in a split.

And so in London my brother sermoned, and we in Virginia squabbled with ourselves. Men always better deceive themselves while they pursue their greed. The building of the Indian college delayed, begun, then postponed. The thousands of acres for the site well plotted on maps of Charles City. The hundred servants to work the land. Day laborers, their rates too steep for our treasuries. The whole project left, but thoughts have currents, the tide ever through our gates. Sermoned such, the will of the nation must be done. We had no choice. Tenants we allotted to do the work. To cleanse the servants in their sacred task, Reverend Buck refused to allow them to grow tobacco even for their own needs. Bitter then the protest, no work for weeks. 'How can we ensure that we have food or clothes? Without the weed next year we starve,' they cried. The golden calf in its weed, its meat even to the altar of the church. Reverend Buck set the law, the law not stronger than the leaf. The workmen had their crop.

The savages dispersed into the forest to have other villages and plant other grounds, but the best and closest to the river is mostly ours. The savages not inclined to war, the peace still holds. Yeardley has found ways to have two crops of grain a year: one of European wheat, the other of maize. The crops small, but the promise great. The contagions and the sickness gone, the land bloomed in power. Yeardley asked the London Council to relieve him of his office, screams of food and the weed ever to his mind. Wealth makes power seem but another cost against a gain, and the weed always had its purchase beyond its price.

I read Sandys' letter and heard the subterranean whispers between the lines. The king never warm to Yeardley who was considered housed in Sir Edwin's pouch, the court played its hates and snapped its presumptions at Yeardley's heels. The political game not worth the freight. The lord governor had his title and his wealth. Why not keep them both and abdicate the joust? Contentions with the crown too uncivil for his coins. His vision by sums, its laws by averages, his ambitions proclaimed in numbers. He set himself aside.

The office now an empty derelict, and who to fill Yeardley's place? The murmurs hint, the mumbles trace suggestions on the slips of plots. Could I at last be considered for the hobbled throne? I not aligned with the Sandys faction or that of Sir Thomas Smythe. A compromise to the middle way, neither friend to the weed, nor seen as enemy to the king. My experience without question, I wrote Purchas and the Willoughbys to learn what influence could be used on my behalf. The letters no sooner writ, the war on the council came in trilogies. John Bargrave, in his rage at Martin's patents, hated the company, called for the king to govern the colony directly. The king, wanting Sandys replaced when Sir Edwin's term expired, had him arrested briefly and then released. In the council, factions constantly warred upon themselves. But with all the twists, I still hoped the company would turn to me. All I plundered was but stone. I called charities to my name, wrote to the ancient adventurers still alive: Todkill and the rest, all those I had saved from famine.

Upon my life I hunger. I am a memory. Too soon our forgetfulness, too late our recall, we are but the simples of the disconnect, and so we choose the redemption of the familiars in our rest. Lay me on the thorns of my birth and burn my flesh. Sir Edwin Sandys chose his own, a cousin by marriage, a bedded guest, Sir Francis Wyatt, a nothing to Virginia but perhaps not a mistake, just not the better choice. Wyatt had married Margaret, the daughter of Samuel, one of the elder Sandys' brothers. Sir Francis, himself, was heir to a fair fortune and a grand estate, a member of parliament and a poet of enthusiasms but small abilities. His great-grandfather was a notable sonneteer during the reign of Henry VII, his grandfather having led a rebellion against Queen Mary. In all, Wyatt was a man of histories, his portion more than slight, well trained to his inheritance. I sat my rooms, my disappointment close about me. Feed action, my anger burns. I wrote to George Sandys telling him the news of Sir Francis. I smiled to incite a little pain. I sculptured rot, wondering was this more the shovel to feed Sandys' rage? "Bettered by a cousin, an interloper of the sheets," screamed Sandys. I was told my small accomplishment.

I live between the spaces that contraries bring. I suffered by neglect but more by my thwarted blinding energies. I became the wish that kept me whole and danced my tune to some slight success. The Willoughbys financed my New England book, it now in the press. "Ever it was our father's wish to bring some service to your life. You have fulfilled his hopes," so the Willoughbys wrote. "We are as much as common sons." Pleasant, warm and gracious sounds these words, but I made my own secret messages to the Puritans. Purchas the phantom herald to whisper in their ears. Alchemies are in the mind. There imagination is a philosopher's stone.

THAT SEPTEMBER OF 1620 WITH THE TAVERN SHIP, HER PLEASURES no secret on her soiled decks, and in her hold the first shipment of a new gun. Not like our firelocks, no burning taper, but a spark to ignite the powder, a hammer to hold the flint to fly its scratch against rough iron, the flecks of fire to fall into a pan containing the powder.

We called the weapon a snaphaunce, a machine with a mechanism precisioned like a clock. As the hammer snapped forward carrying the flint, the iron which covered the powder moved back, the strike to set the charge alight. How the click of the iron, this new earth falling to its hammer, the spark now in the powder. Before the English armies in Europe, those in the new world had this weapon. John Martin changed all his firelocks to the new flints. Within three years, of the thousands of muskets in Virginia, all but fifty-seven would be snaphaunces.

Sandys ever Sandys, his crimes to him never fully gained unless they were confessed.

So it said Sir Francis Wyatt will be our new lord governor. As always my brother fumbles at his wisdom. Whatever moos in London, here it will be an easy strangle of the cow.

An old friend we saw October last. Jack of the Feathers came to Yeardley and the council with a message from Opechancanough, his shoulders and arms downed in feathers overlapping as an armor. He seemed a bird of some exotic wing. His face cold in its painted rhetoric, red and black and white squares in sharp lines on his face. His skin moved as leather when he spoke. His hatred burst from his eyes. "We the Pamunkey wish ten of your English to be as allies with us, well armed with muskets and clothed in their metal skin to join in war against those who are above the falls." Jack of the Feathers contemplated the depth of himself, then added, "This is Opechancanough's wish, that from this treaty…a peace more lasting."

Yeardley looked about the council. "And what of the Chickahominy who murdered Killingbeck and the children? Why have we not had satisfaction for those deaths?" he asked.

"It is for that revenge Opechancanough makes his request. The Chickahominy are innocent. It was not they who were the murderers. Was it not that their own burial places were looted, their offerings to the bodies of their Kings stolen? It was not the Chickahominy, it was the Pamunkey. It was our own who did it all who then fled above the falls," said Jack of the Feathers. "Opechancanough offers you one hand in peace for a common vengeance." Jack of the Feathers hesitated. "Ever have you wished some of our children to live among you. Opechancanough sends these words. Some of ours will be yours to raise in your ways."

The council talking among itself. "Opechancanough so long aloof from us, we all had doubt of his regard but this, an opportunity to seal a treaty and in God's gift, a path to an easy conversion," said Reverend Buck. The council disposed to grant the expedition.

"If Opechancanough is a great king, his people ever fearful of his anger, why did these, your Pamunkey, violate his law and break the peace and do murder upon us?" I asked, our translator turning toward Jack of the Feathers.

Thick in its mystery, the answer came. "There were those who fled with Opitchapam, loyal only to him, not Opechancanough." The story so strange, we hearing it in rumors. The dying Powhatan had been no longer strong enough to have his old tyrannies, beaten by age and the desire for the pleasures of his wealth. All things to such men become their toys. Opechancanough, wanting power, conspired against his brother. Powhatan fled to safety, visiting the friendly tribes at the borders of his empire. Such safety was not kin enough, old age bearing in its wings his death. He died. His brother Opitchapam was in name the emperor, he to share the throne with Opechancanough. But Opitchapam was weak, Opechancanough seizing all the power. Jealousy draws no boundaries by blood. Insurrections warring Opitchapam's mind. Brothers turning against their own. Opitchapam had murdered Killingbeck to bring our vengeance upon his brother. Our minds all consumed upon the weed, we too confused to make our war. Opechancanough offering us justice and, to help slip the ax, a little benefit to him as well. So royal these sovereign wars, we thought them European. We sent the men. In high hopes they sailed away. We never seeing them again. Ambushado in the land of the Nansemonds was the tale—all dead, their weapons stolen. The council blamed Jack of the Feathers. Opechancanough claiming innocence again. The story of the ambushado he said was true. But who held the knife, whose arm let fly the blade? The tip of the sword baited with children's meat. Was this but an incident or a prelude to what? We smoked the question and stayed the clock, watching the season turn.

The winter crossed the air with flights of snow, white against the gray, how hushed the fall. Now the land rested again, hard in its frozen sleep…

It was a haunted peace in Virginia. The remains of Sandys' letter were all water stained, smudged ink and polite regards. While in England, it was a war by a penny wage. Those who rented the right to gather the king's tobacco tax grew alarmed at the size of the domestic crop, no tax from that weed. The Company, wanting protection for the Virginia harvest, called for monopolies. Sir Edwin argued for that policy in parliament. All who hated the weed were in its debt. If Englishmen will smoke, the king will have his tax and revenue and plunder of the weed. King James then wrote to the College of Physicians asking, "How healthy is our English grown tobacco? Is it not that the more southern crops from Virginia and the Indies with better soil and more sun have natural vigor in a sweeter leaf and less poison to those who drink its smoke?" The physicians, knowing the politics as well as the herb, replied that indeed the English leaf was an inferior leaf, and of little benefit and much hurt to the nation. Lands better used for cereals. "Food not sport should be our crop," they wrote. And so the clergy, at the king's request, did sermon against the domestic growth, pamphleteers to spread with vitriol the common wisdoms through the streets. Smokers were not in high regard, although their numbers grew as if they were the weed themselves.

Sir Edwin and the London Company beseeched the king for protection from the domestic tobacco and the Spanish weed. The king played his time and his revenues in a smile. In a proclamation, To Restrain the Planting of Tobacco in England and Ireland, the king barred the weed from being planted in London and Westminster, because the English tobacco was most unhealthy, more so than the Virginia leaf. Physicians having attested the claim. "And so much agriculture in the smallest villages is now given over to the weed." Further, the document declared the Virginia and Bermuda colonies might lose the trade in their most important crop. The king's revenues were mentioned as a passing thought, not half a plea, a digression in a footnote to sweet a sympathy in the street. An offer was then made to the Virginia Company, the king willing to prohibit the tobacco crop in all England and Ireland if the company would agree to the tax of a shilling a pound. James then decreed another monopoly: all tobacco to be imported into England by a company formed by his favorite, Sir Thomas Roe. And so Sir Edwin Sandys had the choice of holding the weed his enemy as his kin, or betraying his parliament. The king also groveled to love his hates. The friendless weed lusts more power than any charter. The company to debate the king's offer, and so in talk they slipped the winter by.

I SENT COPIES OF MY NEW BOOK, *NEW ENGLAND TRIALS*, TO THE great city companies, to the great merchants, to those who had interest in Virginia, begging finances and the assistance to settle New England. I spoke before the Fishmongers' Company in their guildhall. "This enterprise is of the sea, its success measured in the great catches off my New England coast. Who would benefit, but you?" Most men think themselves to sleep. Nothing done but timidly. For weeks I sat in my chambers, pulling answers from the air. Hope was my only company. "If others act on your plan, so shall we," was the message from the guild. Other companies promising a less of little, bound in an excuse.

Disappointments awaken and then are forgot. I heard from Purchas important news. The Puritans' plan for New England was complete by the fall of 1620. Through the Archbishop of Canterbury and other wealthy and powerful men at court, a grant of land near Hudson's River was given not directly to the Puritans, but to the Earl of Lincoln, then assigned to John Wincob, a gentleman known to the earl. Then by all winks and legal frets permissions were allowed to the Puritans. This arrangement not satisfactory, a new patent of lands sealed by pledge, the paper handed to one John Pierce, the London agent for the Puritans. It was through him and their other representatives that I offered my pilgrim services. As a favor to Purchas, I was granted an interview.

In how many rooms have I sat abandoned, these to be my legacies? All the world is a whore who virgins by pretense. Who are these men without the sense but have this power? The world made derelict as fools sit thrones, their heads wreathed in rusted crowns. I spoke to the agents of the new lands, of the waters, of the labor that bound in such enterprises. I spoke of Virginia, of the company's mistakes. Before me their determined eyes, they asked me if I was a Puritan. "No," I said, "but ever have I been a pilgrim." They scowled to each other, as if to disrespect a smell, then swallowed and looked away.

How darkly moved the lines across their brows in the profiles of their prejudices. "I am the chance which has been sent to you. I know these lands, the Indians. These many times I have saved Virginia against all circumstance. Yet I survived, as did the colony. Bills and stores, barrels and the necessities of provisions, of weapons and diplomacies and of trade. Building settlements I understand. I had the power then, I did protect. Who else is so prepared? I pledge my honor to you. But this enterprise must be a divide. All matters of faith are yours forever. All matters of our colony in the world, its harvest and its toils, are mine. On this I can tolerate no interference. In Virginia, councils were but opportunities for delay." So I spoke and was politely thanked.

The pilgrims bought my books and maps, a thrift less costly than my hire. Dead thoughts upon a page, which I could have given light. A book is an interference that can be closed and put away, ignored, and I, who would not have rested until all New England was secured for them, was set aside. The pilgrims aspired to have leaders more easily led. They already a flock of shepherds, and all the sheep were in the captain that they chose. Four years younger than myself, with no experience in the New World, a proper captain, titled to be captained by his colony. He the twist that should have turned the other key. His name was Miles Standish. Not will enough to use the knowledge that he had. The pilgrims landed in a place in Massachusetts I had named Plymouth Rock.

I AM NOT SO EASY TO BE PASSED AWAY. I AM THE CIRCLE THAT life makes flesh. *Where my beginnings end, there I shall begin again,* I thought. I wrote to the Virginia Company and in formal petition asked for some reward, either in stipend or in land, for my service to Virginia. For years I had not much contact with the London Council, but if Martin and others were so rewarded, why not myself? Perhaps I could return my prodigal robes and clothe my resurrection with a laurel wreath.

Chapter Forty-one

BLESSED FOOLS AND SAINTLY MANIACS.

 LETTER NOW FROM George Sandys, without a squint of moral purpose in all his vision. He was a man licking sweets upon his doubts, as he drowned infested in his sugars.

Ah Smith, I am too well accommodated to be a different kind of saint. A monk who builds a cloister of his crimes still lives a cloister. My conscience unhorsed for someone else's gallop. I am to myself, my own. Pain is to me a delicacy to fever pleasure.

My Smith, friends should not decay their love by arguments, transgress the psalm and eat upon the dainty. There is now in Virginia a man of such nobility that I am sure within the month the forest will have their own vomit as a meal. He came as if the dusk, in confidence of a returning light. George Thorpe, Esquire, the eternal hope and fool. No sooner had his ship tied to our dying tree, our dock, than he made his proclamations that he was God's anointed benefactor and shepherd to the savages. Why do good men speak sermons from their hopes and less from their judgments? What fear is there in wisdom that men do shun it so? Each man who comes to this new land to seed another virtue services only to harvest another vice. Better to harvest first the vice, and let the virtue barren on its own. Virtue, me thinks, is the last calling of a lunatic.

And Thorpe, a man of wealth and connections, a member of the Parliament and the king's Privy Chamber, an investor in the eight-thousand-acre James River Plantation of Berkeley Hundred. Abandoned his wife and children to convert the savages and better his own plantation, he set to be an example to us all. His Berkeley Hundred had fallen onto the path of ruin. Upon his arrival Thorpe worked to bring it right. His eye ever on the savages to bring them by kindness to our God. Thorpe was a man of commerce, making experiments by distilling Indian maize to a pleasant whiskey. Among the common drunks of our company, it is a popular drink, so local, so easily had. We called it bourbon. So his first discovery was a better, more fulfilling sin. This whiskey quenched more the soul than our English beer and aqua vitae.

Men made drunk staggered in the woods and chased the forgotten touch of women through the trees, but Thorpe had dreams. With little progress made on the Indian college, Yeardley appointed Thorpe to see it done. "By will, make a finish to our plans, make wood and stone the architecture of your pen," said the governor. "Make right the college's laborers, the proclamation." Excitement to Thorpe, his moment come. Ten thousand grapevines he had planted to barrel wine as a revenue for the college. He oversaw the creation of the ironworks there, paying a mason from his own wealth to see the project done. The London Company spent five thousand pounds to have this industry, the college to be self-sufficient. How good this Thorpe, our Drake in small, no sea winds to wilderness his mind.

And you, Smith, have often said the savages only respect the strong. How many charities does it take to forge the knife that cuts our throats? I walked the college lands with Thorpe, saintly the angle of his smiling face. His chin tapering to a point, his eyes black upon their black, his thin hand in joy reached toward the horizon. "Our work is progressed," he said. Around me in the fields great lines of corn and beans, and hanging vines of grapes lay to the distant trees. English tenants hoed in the heat or stooped to weed rows of corn or tend the tobacco hills. Thorpe's eyes averted from the weed. "A small sin to smooth the path to salvation," he said. "Even God has his works done by revenues."

In the fields the Englishmen worked, their white shirts stained with sweat, and so, too, the women in their skirts, dressed heavily in the heat. These lands were different than the rest. Indians also toiled here, many dressed in English clothes, men in pants and shirts. "Allure the heathen heart with English goods," said Thorpe. "From English fashion it is but a stop to the English God." How little of the savage remains in civil clothes. The women no longer naked, but sported their figures in the bridle of our cloth. I for myself missed the dance of the bodice of their flesh. "Gifts of pots and housewares and kindness. The world moves on the apparel of our true God," said Thorpe. Never did many Indians wear our clothes, but there were enough. Mostly they just used our guns and did our hunting, frequenting our lands to trade, sometimes even sleeping in our bedchambers as our guests when their village was far. "Give me means and time and money, these Indians will be more English than our own," said Thorpe. "Soon in Virginia there will be but one tribe, and that will be an England."

Kind he is, my Smith. Does Thorpe's virtue reflesh your Drake, or is his virtue just misspent? I sit my desk and face the page, your voice I do not hear. Has my better conscience vexed you to a ghost? But Thorpe is saint. When an adventurer in a drunken rage beat an Indian, some of ours laughing at the sport, Thorpe had the man tied to a stake, one of his ears cut off, those that laughed publicly whipped. The Indian wronged and his whole tribe to watch the punishment. Some colonists cursed Thorpe's name, but he had a mission beyond any censure or rebuke. When our guard dogs, all large mastiffs, in wide-eyed growl lunged their open jaws at the savages, so frightening them they ran away, Thorpe had the animals killed. "All this," he said, "so our people will converse and labor each among the other. They to grow in liking and so to the loving of our way and be brought familiar with our true knowledge and our God. Only truth that has within it pleasures and English goods will ever break the strangle of their priests and heathen customs."

"And so you think the savages will sit upon the ground, well Bibled, and calmly cut their own throats with a cross?" I asked him once. "Their priests and elders are savages, not fools. This is more than God to them. This is themselves." Thorpe not wanting their corn, nor their lands, he wanted only their souls, their bodies husked to our God.

*G*overnor Yeardley now proposed that some money be used to buy Indian children from their parents and raised by the colony. The college, being built, had yet to find a student. The council in its doubt agreed. "Do you think savages are so base they love their children less than we?" I asked.

Reverend Buck then answering, "By their false gods, it is my belief that natural light within us all is deflected in the savages to some dusk, the light not pure, and so their feelings much profaned."

I nodded to show the council I held some thought upon his words. What I thought was this: Our God so infinite that sometimes the sinner has better vision than the saint. But what I said was, "Beware of any belief that makes you more by making others less." And so my small conscience had its squeak.

We received letters from London. The fool added its fleeting wisdom to the ashes of our shattered book. The company bankrupt. Little could be raised, only for the college. Donations from the parishes, and gifts of books, even libraries to our cause, funds to educate the Indians and convert the savages to our world. My brother demanded that we build rest houses to aid the colony's sick. "A hospital to ease the pain of adventurers when first they land in Virginia, that a necessity and yet nothing done." It was all a posh of perverted pretties. The London Company, continuing to wage its war against the weed as it fought to have our tobacco a monopoly, bargained with the king to prohibit the farming of all the domestic leaf. The company ruled by dread, seeking to destroy what it wanted to protect, passed laws to limit the size of our crop. This to please the king, but laws writ in faraways are not so easy to enforce.

The crop this year is sixty thousands pounds. The company agreed to pay one shilling a pound as tax, which was half the rate on the Spanish leaf, if the king would, as pledged, extend the prohibition on growing tobacco to all of England and Ireland. All this was made law. The king through his monopolies decreed only fifty-five thousand pounds of Virginia weed could be imported. Such limits on our own weed, my brother now called betrayed and sought to have the Privy Council redress the wrong. While in Virginia we tapped our fingers and looked a better circumstance, shipped our entire crop on Dutch ships to the Netherlands, finding another market on the continent for our leaf. Then we wrote the king saying we were ever loyal to his law, and asked that all fifty-five thousand pounds of that year be imported from Bermuda, "that island so dear and so in want." I wrote the phrase myself. And we planned to smuggle the leaf the next year both to England and our new friends the Dutch. The king, learning what we had done, raged laws at us, ordering all

English goods to be shipped to England first on English ships. Most of this we will do when convenience pleases. What you hear in London I do not know, but for me I have changed my life by an infested church. To me salvation is ever urgent in the crime. Our wealth known at court, the king will relent, saying he has no desire to harm the colony. Despite the king, men still drank and flaunted their wealth, and spent in hours on clothes and gluttony sums not earned in years in England.

And you, Smith, since your time no explorations have been done. Our adventurers stay upon their fields, bound to the sweet scent of the weed. The company demands discoveries. But too much greed holds men only to the known, and dirt is dirt, and that in hand was dirt enough. Unlike Drake, I did not hear the world beckon me to its unknown. I claim a darkness of another sort. Do not have me ill. Only apostles breathe in ink. My brother ever lives in the gladness of his paupered faith and I with four plantations and more servants to make me rich. To me, wealth always sermons better than a poem.

And always there was that Thorpe. Saints make better fools than pleasant virgins fresh from school. Magnanimous Thorpe and his angelic expeditions, goodness ever in his pouch. He had now gone lunatic. After giving every assortment of English apparel to the savages, he made by one gesture the cast of all his dice. Thorpe, as a gift, gave to Opechancanough as a present an English house, built for him of wood, with all the metal works upon its windows and its fireplace, a lock with a key to bolt its entrance, hinges to open up the portal and let in the English light. Extravagance by self-pursuit. Opechancanough is said to have locked and unlocked the door a hundred times a day, ever admiring the strange machineries of lock and key. Thorpe so excited in this telling, he said to me, "He dotes on the house I had built. Such good entrance I have made into his affections by this gift."

And Opechancanough at the door, opening the lock, the key in turning clicks of the metal clock of years, no pendulum to swing, the hour tolled in memories. In what fascination men witness themselves. Are we but repetition's ghost, and Opechancanough, at the door, clothed in an English house? Would he be a prisoner of Thorpe's largess? Cast down his history to hold the key, the lock now tried? And what if it be true and Opechancanough were the savage who escaped from Spain, the Don Luis of legend, the child taken from the Chesapeake to Madrid, raised as noble to be a monk? I can see Opechancanough's eyes, his sight upon the past. The door before him opened and closed and opened yet again. And what his thoughts? How do you close the moments in a life, and now the English? Don Luis converted only to the depth of cloth. His mind and soul kept to the whispering in the earth. His priest danced Okee's spirit into flesh. His Gods spoke to him in voice, gesturing to him on those silhouettes moving in the air. An idol without history is but paint. What is God to Opechancanough without a joyful song and stories speaking in stories of his land? No God to him is god who does not know the bee, the feather and the fish. What is the rain to him but sermon, the corn his catechisms. The whole world was his church. Opechancanough a *werowance*, the hearer of these secrets, the messenger of the forbidden world. Through his initiation his people held to him, the giver of the law. The Jesuits had him to educate for years in Spain. The anointed do not change. The Jesuits, fooled, brought him back, they to be betrayed and murdered. They who would tear the fabric of the world died. Their blood was Opechancanough's proclamation forever to his god.

I am the prophet of the mud. Thorpe too kind to see the warnings. Opechancanough in dangerous seductions was half seduced. Would he bend to England what he could not bend to Spain? We or Spain, a conversion of equal deaths. To lead his people to be a people no more. No king could so advise such sovereignty. A people without their own beliefs are covers of a book closed upon an emptiness. Opechancanough, in wait, waited to the last to war his certainties. He called to Thorpe by messenger to come to visit and have some conversation on the practice of their lives.

Thorpe delayed, offering Opechancanough instead a fine English garment of red cloth and black, emblazoned in designs of sewn gold, and helmets and iron armor for his chest, "as would befit an English gentleman," said Thorpe in his message to Opechancanough. "Our God rewards us in goodly things. He wishes to be to you as he is to us, a blessing in his miracles.

Let families of yours live on our plantations, on our lands, that kindness can bend with kindness, and our two people live as one, as Pocahontas, with all her nakedness forever dressed, and the false god set aside."

When good men act as deaf, their words pushing daggers through another's eyes, what do they expect? To Opechancanough, Thorpe's kindness was a dance of cruelty. The London Company approved the plan to have Indian families living among us, but warned of neglecting our defense and allowing the savages a dangerous familiarity with our homes. In Virginia we believed the Indians were defeated and at peace. Thorpe declaring their conversion would be soon at hand. The trade in guns had contented all. Our cannons no longer mounted in our forts. Our soldiers never exercised or much practiced in their weapons. The savages doing all our hunting, many of them better marksmen than our own.

Again Opechancanough asked Thorpe to come and sit with him in council, Opechancanough to plumb the depth of Thorpe's danger. The savages now everywhere and underfoot. We cursed them as a defeated waste, and ate their corn, bought their fish and deer. The colony still sported wealth and died. Half my servants dead within six months. The waters bad with fouls of ooze, the disease, the heat, the swamp where vapors flew in swarms of gnats. Vermin all about, but all the wealth. And still we spent this year's tobacco leaf before we had it dry. Planters in debt, always drunk. Their lazy servants beaten to make them work. Women on the ship bought for promises of next year's crop, and in the woods men did at times chase the Indian women to lay by strength their weight on nightingales.

Thorpe called upon the council to issue warnings to protect the savages from all abuses. This proclamation was made in words. How nobly our empty justice sings. Opechancanough sent messengers for a third time to have meetings with Thorpe. How slip the seconds on themselves, moments gathered to their fall, as ghosts ready to be born, violent in their philosophies. My brother now raged distantly that no explorations had been done on the Chesapeake, a project abandoned. "We know little more of the land, its geographies and its situation, than we did when Smith drew his famous map fourteen years ago," he said. Yeardley, to satisfy the threat of my brother's authority, sent

Pory and ten adventurers to voyage up the rivers of the bay. Pory not returned these weeks.

And so, my Smith, you are still remembered by the profiles of the land you mapped. Keep that coin for some further prospects, my brother might yet give you some reward. Crime is not my cause, only my misspent alchemies.

Chapter Forty-two

THE GODS SMILE, LETHAL ABOVE MAN'S DEBATE.

READ SANDYS' LETTER, writing to him, "Be to your brother, speak to him of my employment." For myself, I made my own plans. On May the second of 1621 I attended the "Great and General Quarter Court" of the Virginia Company, held in London, to bear witness, and perhaps aid by diplomacy, my employment, or my pending petition for a grant of land. There in silence I sat and watched slip the monasteries of their closed debate. No purpose in their words but to move the air. But revelations are not always spiked on lightnings, or on the trumpet's blast. Sometimes they come plain in common speech, ignored always as walls cave inward.

Captain Martin walked into the hall, lately returned from Virginia to defend his patents and all their extraordinary grants. As he passed me, he turned. "I hope, Smith, you have enjoyed your neglects as much as I. Have you come a pauper to beg a coin? I have land, Smith, and exclusions of law. By dominions I am lord. By power I exempt myself from need. Here, a few shillings." He tossed me coins. "Be bought and be gone."

I took them, felt the weight. "You have always purchased your friends too cheep before you cut their throats. I prefer to live safely as ever your enemy." Then I threw the rounded insults back in his face. "If you wish a duel, I propose it now."

"I want nothing of you," he said as he walked away, much blushed, tottering in his shame.

Thwarted in his own brag and slander, the London Company dismissive of any pretence, Martin had raced the circle and confused the finish with the start. The company wanted Martin's patents returned, replaced with new ones well-bribed with lands and incomes to sweet a fair reward for any common knave. But Martin, seated with uncommon greed, refused the play. "I will not surrender my patents for some easy peace, and to the foul of my better prospects."

Sir Edwin held the calm, a thrust of power silkened on a lethal point. "Your patents, Captain Martin, are illegal, never having been approved in any quarter court, the only congress so empowered to issue such grants. Take the compromise, or leave with nothing."

Martin knew the law. He flirted to himself and thundered some, but took what could be had, begging some special charities, an extra five thousand acres for his important services to Virginia. All was denied. Martin bowed and groveled to his exit, the door open. Outside he screamed slanders at all the company and raged a lunatic so fierce some thought his brains would burst blood and break convulsions from his ear. *This is not the last of this,* I thought.

A CAPTAIN JOHN SMYTH OF NIBLEY ROSE TO SPEAK, HE THE servant of twenty years to Lord Berkeley. All knew in those words were the broodings of Berkeley's power and his thoughts. The company listened. The good captain proposed the company write a history of itself, "to nourish by good reports, and advance the healthy opinion of the colony among the commons, remembering the worthies now deceased and their parts, displaying for all a tale rescued from neglect."

I sat and listened. *Who is more anointed? It is the only by which I am known. I am witness, the story mine. Play words, play chronicles, ink bursts in philosopher's stones.* That night, my papers round me as a fort, I swept with plans the designs to hold the work. All my books published as one volume, all revised and brought to date. The histories of New England and Virginia, continued to the latest voyages, supplied with descriptive letters, an annex of those eyes upon the story. I visited Purchas, who agreed to assist me with the book, lending me copies of maps and letters and narratives, some never published, some published only in parts, some passed through many hands to Purchas, used by him in his encyclopedia of English explorations, *Purchas, His Pilgrimes.*

And I sat the float of hours in his study, all this of Virginia and New England given to me. The chronicles beneath my fingertips. So much, so much, but all this not enough. The work had outrun the plan. How do you frame a world that is not confined to a single all?

I held copies of Ratcliffe's letters to the London Company, and Wingfield's defense in his apology for himself, sight of script drawing whispers to my ears of that once adopted world. This earth tells its tales in ruins, and we are the passage writ upon its bricks and mud. So soon forgot, and I the memory. "I thought of you," I wrote to Sandys, "and of your book, *The Relation of a Journey,* that account of Turkey and the Holy Land, of Italy and of tobacco. All those lands described with quotations from learned sources and verses of Latin poets. So much and so much more. 'These lines are flat in politics, the poetry translated dead,' you said. But still to me it was a fountain from a cup of dust, a golden skeleton on a painted sky. It was the sketch that defined my plan. You were my source. Are we not all singers of borrowed songs? Only the great may have some escape, but I not great enough. Pilgrims touch as pilgrims pass, parting to our separate destinies."

I am by right the living tome, by consequence of how I lived and how I saved Virginia, and sailed the then unnamed New England coast, up Hudson's river toward the endless north. I the exploration, my trials through air and rain, I have fought the deluge with my will. I brought no slaughter on the savages. We lived together in ill ease, yes; but we lived in some progress of being one. Allies maybe not, but always that deadly knowledge—that balance is respect. All this without the weed, that useless plant. I would not build a nation on a vice. I know it brings a profit now, but too uncertain is its cost. That one is not the only healthy path, and in Virginia, when it was mine, men sold not men. All this the dealings of my book. I told the history, I spoke the remedy. Elixirs are not always an easy swallow. The plan now seated in my mind. I showed Purchas the first completed chapters of what I called *The General History of Virginia and New England and the Summer Islands.* "It is a fair ghost of a foul haunting," Purchas said, but did approve. I added the story of Bermuda, the Summer Islands, their tale so twisted tight in the other two.

ENGLAND THEN IN BAD TIMES, MONEYS SCARCE, THAT BLAMED on the import of the Spanish tobacco. Sir Edwin spoke in Parliament to that very point, proposing to end all the importation of Spanish leaf. Almost now he was the puppet dancing across Virginia's tobacco smoke. "I feel his fate, I taste my riches on his humiliation," wrote his brother to me.

The company sent us in letters its rage. "You hold your tobacco too dear for a quality so poor. Of the harvest last year twenty thousand pounds was of such trash it could not be sold for eight pence a pound. If we are by agreement to pay three shillings a pound, all ill-conditioned leaf must be burned. Even our factors in Holland report they cannot dispose of such dregs again." So the company spoke while trying to wean us from the leaf. We will appoint inspectors (hate is our spiteful governance), but, in truth, we will still sell the weed. The quality, I suspect, never improving much. Lax in our lives, lax in our vices, and yet we will make our profits.

October last the new governor, Sir Francis Wyatt, my beloved cousin, arrived with a fleet of nine ships. He quickly taking possession of his office, Yeardley's term expired. A new cape merchant also sent, as corrupt as the last, and so the bulls of our enterprise have bred themselves a proper calf. Rolfe's child by his English wife now one year old, she a daughter called Elizabeth, a name so sweet for one so weak. I fear she will be a memory before another year.

On November eighteenth Wyatt was sworn in, in solemn oaths, to be our lord governor and captain general. He to his formal chair to read more letters and declarations from the London Company, his council about him, Thorpe, now on the council, taking his place with the rest, his reward for his progress with the savages. My brother, always dissatisfied in his milk, has ordered by law a limit on each colonist's tobacco crop yet again. (Don't good fools ever abjure their own foolishness?) Only a thousand plants per man and only nine leaves per plant, one hundred and twelve pounds the total weight of leaf. How powerful men of decrepit judgments make monuments in their minds, their authority whimpered on a dream. Do they believe, by will, they can guess the dice? And so do men over-play their power, scheme it to a noise? Corn by law to be priced at ten shillings a barrel instead of five shillings for the same. The more the profit, the theory said, perhaps men would not neglect it so. And we with the best lands now would supply corn to the savages. That was the thought, but not to us. Nothing gave us as the leaf, and with the leaf scarce in the fields, the price in the barrel rose; even if we obeyed the law, which we did not. Always London was at war with tobacco while it paid us fortunes to drink its smoke. We in Virginia at war with ourselves, as the savages stood aside in wait. All their secret purposes increased in a lethal smile.

John Pory now returned from the Chesapeake with a China box traded from an Indian who said he had it from the north from another king. The company now believing China was as close as a neighboring tree. "I am certain that we sit not far from Drake's western sea. I can almost hear the Pacific in the breeze, its fragrance almost calling on the wind," said Pory. Too many are fools. Nearly fifteen years of Virginia and they not knowing where they were. Pory with his stories of escapes. The savages were still not all our friends, and word came of lonely speeches whispered in the forest and through the trees, stories of black Indians who spoke to English heathens. "What conversions are we ourselves converted to?" said Pory. "I swear I heard an English speech and sorrows for one who died they called The Alone. There is more wilderness in us than is ever spoken in our elegies. And who would be so much like us and yet so different? And where do they go and how do they come?" The question asked, we thought Pory mad, but with his connections and his power, we let him be.

Wyatt then sent Thorpe to Opechancanough to bring words of greeting and of peace. I was asked to accompany the saint and bear the witness of an apostle. We traveled by boat down the James, that river already peopled with our many histories. The fabric of the waves silken in the undulations of the light. What ghosts before my eyes. In what haunting the mind speaks to itself. I watched, feeling myself called forth. I held in my animal, transfixed. I escaped into the ear of water. I jumped into the river. Cold, the dark surges drank me to their throats. No words heard I, no words to me, I who lived in words. Hands to my shirt, arms lifting me to the deck. Crimed by rescue, I lay wet, coughing, as I whispered, "I slipped. I almost drowned." I lied. What could be more soiled than my death by my own self-murder? What currents are in the mind, and we caught unsuspecting in the undertow? How easy are we lured into its blindness as we race toward the illusions of a door.

We walked inland to the Pamunkey village, the land cleared and flat, harvested to its scraps. We walked on a path between the circles of the overlapping walls that served as a gate. Once inside, there among the thatched cabins, was an English wooden house, Thorpe's gift to Opechancanough. A growth alone with sorrows left to sing. How strange this familiarity seemed to us, a flower from another plant. Some of the Indians dressed in English goods, with English iron pots upon their fires. Most of the men with guns. A people no longer the people you would have known, my Smith.

We sat in the great lodge. Opechancanough offered us the clay tobacco pipe, six feet long in heavy gray, feathers and bands of copper decorating its bowl. We toasted to our own truths in the blessed weed. I smiled to see a heathen sacrament laid on the altar of the smoke. How commerce they with God with the victuals of a common trade. Thorpe took the pipe but hesitated, as if a little too much heathen might tarnish his beliefs. Opechancanough watched. Thorpe's mouth not upon the stem to drink the ashen wine. "Opechancanough will suspect you are here but to lie," I said. Openchancanough eye to eye with Thorpe, who smiled as he bit upon his breath to have his full of smoke. He coughed; strong whiskey from Indian corn was his better vice. Opechancanough leaned back into the arms of his women. A lion of a devil's wood, he sat his silence, waiting for Thorpe to speak.

"So much has changed in all these years since our two people have come to know each other," said Thorpe, "and respect the peace, which we both now do love, for it is God's will." Opechancanough listened, showing nothing of himself but paint. "Now the time has come in our meeting for conversations of great importance. In me I carry the words of God, in his voice to my tongue to you," said Thorpe.

Opechancanough leaned forward from the arms of his ladies and said, "I too carry his voice and have seen his spirit in the air and had his signs before my eyes in the dark where no sight should be. A *werowance* is more than king. His are the lips that speak the words. I am the servant, the messenger and the message."

How sweetly Thorpe sang as he plucked the poisoned apple from the serpent's mouth. "A servant is judged by whom he serves, and I serve the one, the only, true God, the only path which is the right." Thorpe did not cast away the fruit, but bit into its cheek and tasted of the apple's blood. Opechancanough stood, Thorpe watching him rise saying, "Okee is not a god but a confusion sent by the devil as spirit to lead you wrong. Does not Okee do only harm, your other god who is but good ignored? I am sent to lead you only to the good, who is our God, whose voice is silent here. We are not so different, you and I, two men on a journey, the way sometimes dimly seen, our God the road. I am the sign, my hand to you." Thorpe reached out his hand. Opechancanough sat and smiled, his arms folded against his chest.

"And where in your God is there a God that is not a man?" asked Opechancanough. "And how many perfections are there in his one to make him all? One voice however loudly sung is not a choir; one dancer is not the dance. A spark, but a lesser fire." Opechancanough looked at Thorpe as if he searched his inner life.

"And how do you know of choirs?" asked Thorpe, confused.

Opechancanough did not answer but said, "All that life is, is born of life. All that is the world is born of some part that is itself, as the tree is tree. As a river is born of water and the ocean is the rain. All that is gives up part of itself in birth. And so the many gods that are the world live in the world as the multitude of one, in many names. The tree cannot be the bird. A bird who would be the tree is doomed. The path is never one, the path is always clear and many."

I watched two men now speaking in their theologies, and I who had surrendered my beliefs to the vestments of my coins sat in sentimental passion, wishing all that sermoned here had not my father's face.

Thorpe, ever in his kindness, brought himself to a silent stare, sitting back to think of arguments never thought. No is not a conviction strong enough to convert the faith of this new land. Here the Bible is the earth, its roots cloistered deep in the loam. How apostles Zion in trees, its persuasion in the hills. All that is is Sabbath, and Thorpe, who never understood the good are not necessarily the wise, trod in his kindness upon ancient deities, and so to Opechancanough made war by piety against the earth. And tobacco, which to the Indians was a sacrament, was now defiled by us as a weed to plunder from the land. Thorpe in his simplicities made the world so simple. "And the house I gave you, is it not a fine gift?" he asked.

Opechancanough acknowledged of the gift and of his pleasures. Thorpe then smiled, as if sensing a truth. 'Are not our things better than yours? Our God, who is the one truth, who created all, does he not love us more than you? See our clothes, our combs, our needles. Look upon the house I gave to you.'

"All that you say is true but we in our gods did not starve on this land. We could feed ourselves. We kept you alive that now you make us small." Opechancanough spoke his voice in a baited hook, his peaceful smile such lore.

"Your charity was a grace and proof you are not fallen wholly to the devil. You are of those sweet perfections I would see bloom," said Thorpe. "Take my hand. I offer it yet again. Be not the pauper as your fathers."

Opechancanough sat in lion's stone, moved not. Thorpe continued. "Worship not your human dead, your father's withered skin, those mummies in that hut, priests to tend their empty sacks."

"Those dead are our books. Our memories and the memories of our people are written in their flesh." Opechancanough spoke so calmly, no anger in his voice. "Would you have us forget?"

"In all of us is a memory of the one true God, a flicker of the returning God. If forgetting is but a step to remembrance, then isn't it best to forget. Our God's promises are kept, his love is real, his gifts we wear and carry about our bodies. Aren't our guns better than your bows? In him our power rises to its source."

"Is your God a gun?" asked Opechancanough. "Is his love but another agony? What gift is this that makes a better murder? And those who do not believe as you, are they not burned living at the stake...as in Spain?"

"We come to save you from that Spain," said Thorpe. "Our kindness is your protection, our one true God is our shield. Change will come. Love converts all to itself."

"And so in Spain love comes in murder and so by losing what you call a little, I lose all." said Opechancanough.

"Gain all…a soul and heaven," said Thorpe.

Opechancanough nodded. "The souls of our dead kings live forever in the west, following upon the sun."

"And so now all will live forever in our God," said Thorpe. "The devil gives us gifts that he might possess us. Forget the devil's trinkets."

"How am I to know your gifts from the devil's trinkets?" asked Opechancanough.

"Ours is the better way. Lay down your fathers in the ground. Let their evil sleep."

"And there is no other way but this to have some peace," said Opechancanough.

"This is the way," said Thorpe.

The silence between the two men, each speaking to their separate thoughts. What divide there is in a word—from ear to ear its sound is a false bridge. Thorpe offering again Opechancanough his hand. Opechancanough looked upon it and said with cynical thunder in his sigh, "Your voice has shown me. I know what must be the path." Opechancanough spoke as a man caged by the necessity of his reason. Behind the mask of paint, his face spoke without expression. His words drifted on the course of some future compass. 'God is love, for he has given me the desperate truth through you.'

Thorpe's eyes wide in joy. All that in him believed, believed in its own miracles. "And now you know that God loves us best."

"Powhatan's way was wrong," said Opechancanough. "Our families must live among you, close among you, to be familiar with you, as ever was your wish."

"Truth is our shield, our will superior because we hold the right. God triumphs through me, his exalted servant, that I am made my own apostle," said Thorpe.

"Ever I believed there could exist no other truth. This our proclaimed inevitable, and now it done. Your fathers will be now forgotten stones, but a true lord and father you shall have. Joy with me in this your living resurrection." Thorpe gulped upon his words as he drank them in one belch to himself.

"How this savage surrenders so easily to our works," I thought. "No war less fought. Perhaps a profit here to him, who closer with us lies." Opechancanough now spoke of concluding treaties with us on trade and exploration and land. "All fields along the rivers not planted by our people can from this day forth be seated by the English. In exchange I wish many English families to live among the Pamunkey, to instruct us in your God." So easily the doubtful bubble bursts, so cleansed our minds in certainties. "One more test," I whispered in Thorpe's ears. He nodded and spoke my words. "And will you now renounce the ceremony of your old god, Okee, your fathers' bones and the service of the huskanaw?"

"All this I do renounce. Our fathers' bones are the bones of any dead, our stories vacant, the bear a bear, no god in him, the river its voice forever stilled. The huskanaw, that life in Okee's dream forgot. We are the tree where blooms the fruit, we cast down the serpent," said Opechancanough, "beneath the points of the shepherd's hoofs."

"You see in him a religion coming right," said Thorpe. "He knows more Bible than ever we did think."

"How much known and where the teacher?" I did have the passing thought, but in all Thorpe's joy it was soon lost, knowing later this passing doubt was the only wisdom.

In Jamestown we rejoiced and had such sermons in thanksgivings. "The Indian has come in peace to his conversion, new tribes in God to hold his light." So spoke the reverend in his church. Wyatt, his hand in benedictions upon Thorpe's hand. New lands for the weed. The peace so securely won. That year twenty-one ships had anchored in the bay, four hundred sailors, thirteen hundred men and women new to our plantation, many children, eighty cattle. Yet death still kept the freight, our population along the rivers only fifteen hundred. When the common grave was heaped, our increase tilted towards the none.

Words now whispered in the forest that Opechancanough had changed his name. "What ceremony is this?" I thought. "What rebirth, what resurrection sounds in him, a spite to all his history? Consumed by some intent, he calls himself Mangopeesomon. How cleansed we are to marry to another name, but what the purpose that holds the mystery?" Thorpe thought it a good sign, a new name to person before his new God. "Change the bread, hoping for a better meat," said Yeardley.

More rumors speaking of Powhatan's brother, Opitchapam also having a new name, Sasawpen. "This is some sacrifice,"

I thought, "some mutilation before the world, a gift of great value to what end, this self-tongued murder?" The council sat well content. "Indians are savages still. Why should they not practice in their hellish ways? Soon their devils will be spent." No one thought of it much. True causes are not the wonder of the self-content.

Plans were made for Pory to make another exploration south along the coast past Roanoke toward the Chowan River. From the eastern shore of the Chesapeake a werowance sent warning that the Pamunkeys were purchasing the service of mercenaries among those tribes with a promise of guns. Messengers also spoke of Opechancanough in his new name seeking to trade for a poison which only grew in the east. As you, Smith, were so poisoned years ago, did Opechancanough now seek to poison us? All this was told. Wyatt presumed upon the peace. "No war," he said. "Concerns there always are when all goes well." So it was with regards so casual we set the walls of our defense.

Pory sailed into his second voyage, south into that uncharted coast. He was not gone three days when one final warning came from the eastern shore: "Opechancanough gathers all the tribes, having had Powhatan's mummied bones brought to him and the bodies of all the great kings, their ghosts to war their spirits through the air and come in a mighty choir against your God. Be warned." So the messenger said. It was war by histories in arrows of belief. Still the council not much concerned, the Indians at peace. Some small marshaling of soldiers to march light practice in the fields, but not much. A warning sent to distant plantations, but weeks passed and the peace held at its usual calm. The stories soon forgot. The weed planted for the beginning of its new crop. Pory returned with reports of silk grass, great forests and voices in the wind. "Has the land all risen in its mighty spirit to cast us out, or was it our lost of Roanoke seeking to be lost no more?" He asked the question, the answers too unpleasant to be thought. Pory was silenced with a glance, his name spoken ill in weekly sermons.

On March sixth of our year 1622, John Rolfe reclined toward his death, sick in his bed, his young daughter crawling at the feet of those that tended him. How little intrudes the light in his final cabin. Yeardley and his wife to bear witness to his will and testament. Rolfe's hand too weak to sign the page. His servants in the field, working at his crop. The master more mortal than the weed. Rolfe called to Pocahontas. In delusion now he spoke to ghosts. Weakness enfolded him in its easy wash. To Rolfe the gift of weakness was to see the truth. "And why did you love…that I was not your love?" Something in the world was passing on and no one wise enough to stop and grieve its elegy.

Miles from Rolfe's plantation, not far from Jamestown, there slept the moment before the drum. A small house of an adventurer named Morgan, fields in tobacco, several servants to work the plot. That day Jack of the Feathers appeared, down about his shoulders, the dark nervous bird of his eye, asking Morgan if he would care to trade for such goods as the Pamunkey had. Morgan, always ready to ingratiate himself with luck, agreed. In his red cap, Morgan followed the savage into the woods, toward the Pamunkey village. The feathered back of his guide moved, rolling on the pace, as if white the snow of the mountain beast rumbled on the earth. The two disappeared into the forest. After three days Morgan had not returned. His servants unconcerned. Jack of the Feathers then seen near the plantation wearing Morgan's cap. The servants gave chase, surrounded him, asking where was their master. Jack of the Feathers proudly saying he was dead. Men in rage think rage their shield. Immortal their deafening screams, to them they are immortal. Jack of the Feathers believed no English bullet could kill him, his tribe the audience in his mind. Morgan's servants grabbing the savage to have him before Thorpe. A great struggle in the dust, a snaphaunce drawn to quell the battle. He who in his soul had pledged his own death to defend his people. We create our fate by subtle wiles.

The gun discharged. Jack of the Feathers struck, the blood leapt from his chest through his grasping fingers, like any man's mortal blood. Surprise on the savage's face, so pathetic this wound to bring him hurt. His life now chained to its mortality. He was dragged to a boat to be rowed to Governor Wyatt.

He lay on the wooden deck bleeding, his blood now a path to death. He spoke to the servants. Dark around him in its nothing. His own life an evaporation before his eyes. "Bury me in an English grave," he said. "Tell no one how I died. No one must know I am killed by a bullet. Not by an English bullet." His last words were to beg his fantasy into another life. He died, no death so final as his own.

So much mystery there was in him. His people holding such belief that he was the old way soon reborn. Opechancanough swore such threats and vengeance on hearing of Jack of the Feathers' death that Wyatt's messengers returned to the lord governor bird white in trembling voice. Wyatt sent other messengers asking if the peace was lost and forever was it war. Opechancanough, still now to a thoughtful calm, said, "Our peace is the root of mountains, it holds aloft the sky. Forever I swear my love. Nemattanew is dead. I care not if the English cut his throat. One death will not break my vows." The plantations nervous for some days, but the tobacco fields in need of tending. All forgotten and put aside but the necessities of the weed.

SANDYS' LETTER SLIPPED FROM MY HANDS. THE FOREBODING ink a river beneath his words. The shuffle of the paper at my feet, the silken flames of the candle glowed satin in its heat. I thought of Opechancanough and of the contest of our wills. No war did we ever make upon each other's beliefs, and so war stayed a child's sport with all its lethal toys. But Thorpe in foolishness had tripped upon the canticles and cursed the ruins of the Pamunkeys's church. This would be a war by alchemies. I know if I were there I could stay the ax and hold the arrows in their flight. But I was not, and no possibility of my return. I wrote again more never-answered letters. Perhaps luck will hold the bloodied rose before its fall and let the dangers pass. For what magic do we seek in all our murders? Are but the salvations and the proof, that the whispers of our doubts are wrong!

In London I sat my exile, Virginia's salvation squandered at my desk. The news of the company but the same. Martin still plotted to have his five thousand acres and his old patents, now petitioned the king, who gave the problem to his privy council to make the final judgment. The king in disgust at the company, as its council drowned in its own soup. I, in truth, schemed to search the heraldries to discover what birth is mine. Uncertainty in the mind seeks solid holds to grasp, to have a wall against the agonies. Mine lines on parchment, inked in painted shields and heraldries, but nothing could be found.

All that is, circles in its ever. And I so sick of thought. Memories come of memories but to forget, our escapes come to nothing but the wordless turmoils of the air. My quest fills with a sudden haunting. The mariner's ghost, his garments a weave of mist, his finger pointing frantically at what? The calligraphies of my name. "You are of fathers but of no house." His voice empty of heat and breath. He disappeared.

Chapter Forty-three

PROFUSIONS BURN. OUR EMPIRE IS A RAG.

NO WORD FROM George Sandys for months. Sir Edwin writing, denying me a grant of land. The excuse was the debts of the enterprise. "No gift until our finances show a better coin." So said, so done. At last, the third of July, 1622, a letter from Sandys. Such thick paper I had never seen from him. I opened the bloodied ruby of its wax and read its open grave.

The plot has flung its carrion to my feet. Bear to me and listen of the doom.

The calm heavy, the weighted days, the savages demonstrating their love as guides and as our hunters. On March twentieth the Warraskoyacks returned one of our youths, well fed and happy, who had been sent to learn their language. The Pamunkeys guided a group of our own through the forest, all in peace. Savages borrowed our boats to row across the James to hold council with their own on the morning of March twenty-first. By this, in our normal day, the world held back its breath. We thought it peace, but in truth it was a swaddle to clothe a history.

Evening. The sky rushes to the red glow of its diluting day. The Chesapeake calms to sweet the dusk. Four ships dock upon the images of themselves. It was the approaching night of March twenty-first. Jamestown lit in the squares of windows. Night came full in blackness and in weight of its forgetfulness. I had supper with Governor Wyatt. He only a cousin by borrowed blood, by marriage with my niece. Yet the distance of the genealogy not far enough. He was a family too close, and as such a strain upon my policies and a danger to my wealth. So young he was, no experience in war. To his own standards honest, by ours naive. Hints of bravery about him, and a relentless energy. I wondered if corruption would make him wise. Supper done, we chatted to ease the while. I then left, Wyatt not confirmed as a friend of the weed. Night had slipped its hollow voice across the land. I went to my house and slept.

Fists thundered at my door. "Sandys, Sandys, awake." Commotion and cries in the street. The light breaking in the east to seduce the dark. A face before my open door. "We are betrayed." The words in mists, the morning cold. "Those hellish savages have planned a slaughter." I dressed. My snaphaunce to my hand, I went to Wyatt's chambers. There stood an Indian boy named Chanco, dressed by conversion and by baptism to us in civil clothes. He was with a planter, Richard Pace, whose hand rested upon his shoulder to calm his fears. Wyatt ordering Englishmen to warn the neighboring plantations. Barricades quickly set to renew Jamestown's walls. Men in groups struggled to place cannons again in rotten carriages. Panic screamed its fears, curses against the savages. Wyatt now stood before the crowd. "How young his green face, how tight his whitening lips against his teeth. His words coldly spoken in their logic. Men might yet follow him," I thought as he addressed the disquiet and our vengeful terrors.

We are by our own love betrayed, but it is that love that shall bear us through. Time is short and dangers all about. The young Chanco was told yesterday by his brother—that this morning at eight o'clock the nations of Opechancanough would rise in murder to slaughter our entire colony—every child, man and woman. All this to be done by cowardly ambush and surprise. Chanco ordered to murder Richard Pace while other savages were to murder Chanco's master, William Perry, in his own plantation nearby.

Chanco small, his shadow large. He seemed to huddle against himself in the cold. Men nodding to themselves to understand the words. War was crawling toward us in the rising light. Pace had always been kind to Chanco. Well known he was for the gentleness and kindness of his manner. Chanco told Pace the story. Pace then saw to the defenses of his two-hundred-acre plantation, sending warning to William Perry and such planters as he could. Then he rowed across the James at night to alert Governor Wyatt.

From Jamestown runners now dispatched. The dawn well gone, the day broadened into the spring light. Boats from the ships and pinnaces of our own assembled to bring warning and rescue to plantations further up the rivers. We spoke of friends and manned the Jamestown walls. Some cursed Thorpe for his kindness to the fiends.

Chanco said the attack was to be at once and everywhere at eight o'clock in the morning. The savages were to come unarmed. No hint to raise suspicions, only those who were known to us, or well seen in our local woods. Then, upon the chosen moment, the savages would grab what weapons were at hand—our own axes, hammers, swords and knives, or whatever in sudden violence. No one to be spared, no prisoners taken.

At seven o'clock in the morning at the blockhouse the forest walked and trembled behind its shadows. Savages called to come join them in a feast. Even some approached unarmed, carrying deer and bear. "See what we have brought to feast with you." So cunningly they stood upon our hope for a better love. A captain in the blockhouse discharged his weapon. The savage ran off without a cry.

Sunlight filling now with heat, the morning turned toward the appointed hour. Eight o'clock came and passed, few guns barked in the distance across the waters. No cries, no screams, just silence and a breeze. Some smoke to thread their wash in pillars toward the north. More fires, more smoke. The air filled to all its horizons, ash in headstones rising crossed and weaved.

"And what out there in its silence is the news?" I asked. Anxious chills the mystery known. With delays and threats, Jamestown's walls full manned. Fear held us to our posts. Our boats had not sailed until the morning was well spent. I, with twenty in a pinnace, traveled south. Quiet, the aging smoke drifting lightly in its hints. Two and a half miles south to Archer's Hope, a place we thought warned by us in the early hours. There the houses burned on the plantations of William Spense, torn to wreck, their memories flat in smoke, the few blackened pits, gray mounds scattered in their lifeless forms, bald sacks lying in their naked skin. We came ashore. Thirty hogs slaughtered before the ruined barn, cows stung with twenty arrows, one with its head crushed between its broken horns, its eyes caught in the jelly of its brains and blood. We walked toward the smolder that was the house. A table set in the open air. Blood still dripping from its boards. In pools it held on the blackening silt. Bodies only chests, hacked red plunder, the white bones pulled and cut, skin torn back, ribs in their broken fingers stabbed through the eyes of the severed heads, hands slashed from wrists, arms scattered in their bleeding bats, babies torn to scraps, nailed to trees or skinned or roasted over fires. Men vomited where they stood. These our dead not recognizable to us. Things bloodied into nameless meat. Fingers that once we held as hands to shake, now pale in anonymous rot. We had not the time to bury what we saw.

William Spense staggered from the woods, his shirt inked in bloody riot. Three arrows in his back. A sword in his hand. Wide eyed in madness, he shrieked in faint. We carried him to our boat. South again we sailed. How cried the wilderness in the madness of his eyes. Tears his story told through the angels of his protecting lunacy. "William Fairfax dead...as his children... murdered those years ago. All the babies sliced to bloody flowers. So the petals opened to the pain." He spoke in song, chanting in the maniac of an idea gone foul. "All dead. Sleep is murdered as we wake, so we sleep full round the clock."

Further south the slaughter never less. So dispersed we were. Some miles below Archer's Hope began the lands of Martin's Hundred, that plantation with its eighty thousand acres, its boundaries on the river ten miles long. The land now gloamed in distant fires. More violence to the bodies here than Archer's Hope. This place is where Jack of the Feathers found his death. Vengeance torn in riot on our human flesh. Bodies stabbed to a formless rank. Faces smashed to hollows, no eyes, no mouths, a bubbled wax of a bloodied stew. The sentries of the face all lost. Skulls cleaved with such force they lay in halves, the gray oyster of the brain hardening in the bloody mud. The sweetening scent mixing with a foul, and the smell of death. Seventy-four dead in Martin's Hundred, some so murdered you could not tell their sex.

No names to those, the unidentified of the slaughter. The wind now like ash to dry our lips. Our boat sailed south, more ruins, silence and the disfigured dead. Six more dead on Mulberry Island. John Rolfe's plantation burned. His wife and child spared, they living in Jamestown all in grief, Rolfe having died twelve days before. And so life and death are cast in the coincidence of its coin. The peace with him buried in his grave, the truce that he and Pocahontas brought dying so soon upon his death. All that was forgotten now.

Gunfire from across the river. We sailed toward the horizon of its report. Boats we saw, smoke, fresh fire blooming in crimson pillars above the trees. On shore we ran toward Bennett's Welcome, Edward Bennett's plantation. The counterpoint of guns echoed from all directions. We ran to its mouth. Ensign Harrison's house burning, savages stinging its wood with arrows and thrown torches, a musket firing from within its rising smoke and sudden bursts of flames. "Death by fire, or death by club," I said, the hammer of my snaphaunce pulled back to its lethal place. The ten with me marched in a line. Savages rose to rush upon us. Arrows now hailed. Still we came, two of ours struck dead. Still we came, our lines exchanging murder. The savages broken as they fled. Ensign Harrison dead near the front door. His wife an ax cut through her spine. Their wounded servant walked from the house alive, a musket in his hand. "More plates we set to have them eat with us. No warning. They fell upon us as we ate."

Justice sometimes comes in strange accounting. So dead, this Ensign Harrison, he who had stolen corn from the Indians years before, and nothing done. The council, knowing of Opechancanough's anger, had fretted but stood itself aloof. I looked at his corpse. Why should balance be his only elegy? And here so many innocent dead.

More gunfire not a half mile away. Cries of English voices, orders and sharp lines of muskets echoing through the drum of the infrequent silence. We hurried toward the sound of battle, which came from the direction of Master Baldwin's house. How cruelly is the grass before my eyes, its seed, flowers in its lace. The world obscured with life and, beyond the blindness of my run, more agony and assault.

I loaded my snaphaunce as I ran, the powder to the muzzle, the leather patch and ball rammed home, the primer charged with powder, the hammer with its flint pulled back. I was alone. My company following behind me as I ran. How swelled the terror through my pride that I was a knight at war. The forest wide, the trees spread to call me to the fight. Where are you, my brother, that you sit to think on kindness? Come hear the bark of guns and come see the bags of all your slaughtered.

On a rise above the Baldwin house I stood, my iron angel in my hand. Black the blessing of her powder, the flint of her wings well charged. Below, men with rakes, women with spades and brickbats, children at their mothers' skirts, all with thrusts and parries to keep the savages in their lethal dance away. A few snaphaunces held by ours fired their flames and smoke. The savages fell back, then gathered to attack again. From the line of trees I saw eight sailors advance, commanded by the vice-admiral of the colony, John Pountis. "So few," I thought, "the savages nearly forty, another twenty of ours at the house. I drank this landscape to my power. Let women fight for babes and swaddle in the mess. I would fight for me."

Down the slope, my company followed at my lead. How quickly all this action taken in a glance. A savage rose into my muskets' sight, then flash and smoke, and he was swept away to die. Reload, the powder hardly measured, the ball firmly set, the hammer resting against the coming moment for another kill. Now the motion. The snaphaunce raised. I advanced. I fired at a human shell, its painted face blown red in an explosive wind.

Our two lines of salvos pushed the savages into flight. Eighteen women and children rescued, seven men. Many of them wounded. Baldwin's wife was near death, wounded in the first assault, but her husband had dragged her unconscious into the house, locking the door and firing his musket until Ralph Hamor's brother, Thomas, with much courage and some luck, through a lull in the fighting, had arrived with the women and children, they all to defend the house. So it was in scatters and in remnants some survived.

John Pountis stayed with five of his sailors. I with the rest went in other searches. More gunfire was still about, so we followed on the music to seek our war.

Ten houses we passed burned to ruins, their dead all spread in slain forests in the grass. Thirty butchered, maybe forty, and we had not seen the larger plantations yet. Other sailors and soldiers we met who gave the same report. "Slaughter is the work and murder is the harvest. Still some houses burned but no bodies found. Perhaps there are some captives and a few alive. It might be true," said one sailor. And so the tale. My company now twenty-five.

By late afternoon we gathered all who had survived. This place was indefensible. Some willing to stay with theirs and grow the weed, others abandoned their fields. Those we could we brought to Jamestown. Fifty-six dead the count in these plantations, eighty-five or so across the river and still no word from all the rest: Henrico, Charles City, Kecoughtan, Elizabeth City and the plantations north, both on the eastern and western sides of the James.

We sailed across the river, our boat cargoed in our bloody cloth. Some women wept for their murdered children and their dead husbands. Some gazed into the blank of their own stares. Men held their families close into their arms, the comfort of bodies real and love more warmth to them than any fire.

Jamestown had become a mortuary of our human shells. What had we not seen that day? And more we would, I feared, on the next day yet. The crowd before the fortress walls sat and paced. And in its confusions, cries and hope. A few wounded lay on sheets or the bare grass. The wailing rose on the empty ears of air. Perhaps one hundred, perhaps two hundred on the beach. Food scarce. Not houses for them all. Each hour more boats came with more survivors and their tales.

And now our turn to find the dock. I helping ours to disembark. Sad eyes, the tearless red. Everywhere the shock, truth gathering. I walked through the agonies. Everywhere the name of Thorpe well cursed. "If he's not dead, I'll kill him with me own hands," said a planter, his shirt a massacre of blood. "One death for him is not enough," said another. Wyatt called me to his council. I told what I had seen. "In the north it is worse," he said. "Charles City not itself attacked, but about its precincts the slaughter measured in pounds of blood. Captain Roger Smith's company all murdered; at Henry Milward's, six dead; William Ferrar's, ten dead; Richard Owens's, six dead; Owen Macar, four; William Bikar's, five dead. None known to have survived...and all this but early news. No life seen at Tanks Weyanoke, Yeardley's plantation. Twenty-one tenants there, Yeardley much distressed. No news of Flowerdieu Hundred. No news of Thorpe. No word of Henrico and the plantations at the falls." With more office in his voice than ever I had heard, Wyatt said, "Take a pinnace and twenty armed and make the falls. Do what can be done along the way. Be safe in God. Now go." He so quickly changed. I pleased to be of service and to action in the world. This slaughter is my brother's ruin, I mused, and I still rich. Perhaps honesty is a better corruption than any vice.

I took my men and had my pinnace north. The hour late. We were some miles south of Charles City, well north of Jamestown. Anchoring in the still, we quieted, always in ready. We ate our supper, cooked over an open fire in our boat. The flames revealing light upon the dark water, only the surface lit, the black wash in its undertow drank the nothing underneath. The fire quenched, I lay back to sleep. The night nozzled its cold upon me. Somewhere on shore an animal cried a human name. It was an English voice calling the name of a woman. Far away the distance caught the word. A breeze flung it to mist and held it to the ear in all its agony. The voice again, the cry, the name not quite a word, a rising wail, a baying at the dark. We signaled with a musket shot. The powder sparked and fell in the shower of its dying stars. To the silhouette of the water it fell. We called to the voice, which, lost in faraways, answered only in its wail. The land was soon in quiet. The voice now gone, we called to the emptiness beyond our hands. The land cried back in its silence, the name never known. We returned to our vigil and our rest.

The light dawned gray in vapors, we rowed again. Now past the Chickahominy River, so merged the waters flowed upon a single wake. We followed west holding to the James. At Dancing Point, the northern shore, that place just west of where the Chickahominy flowed upon the James, there was Yeardley's plantation of Southampton Hundred. There St. Mary's Church had been built, all with donations from London. Its simple charity, its purpose to educate and convert the savages. Boats we saw along the shore, their sails struck, their hulls pulled upon the beach. Men walked above a rise, pointing at us as we passed. "Come, we need your service," was the hail. We rowed toward those figures, their muskets held tight across their arms.

"Five slaughtered here," we were told. When we stepped from the pinnace, there were tales of more attacks. "All yesterday, buildings burned, the woods an ambushado." The plantations to be abandoned. "Will you sail a few to Charles City?" Breathless, the question half-swallowed on the lips, no words could catch all its tale.

"We are commissioned by the lord governor on a special mission. We can take a few if quickly done," I said.

"We need you half a day," the man gulped.

"We cannot. We are called for other places." The man cursed and kicked the earth. "You have boats enough," I said, "and we are to the falls." I turned to walk toward my pinnace. The man grabbed at my shoulder. "Are we to be abandoned?" he said. "All about, no place is sure, no place is safe."

I did not look at the man's face. I heard his breathing, holding words in maddened swallows behind his lips. Across the river the sounds of muskets, flames intertwined scarlet in black smoke. "The savages are burning Martin's Brandon, killed six there yesterday and all the cattle. Now they put fire to the buildings. Captain Martin for all his hope is now burnt a pauper, and he in London," said the man. We watched the shadows move before the fires carrying barrels and chests, throwing stores and linens in the fields. Some ran with stolen clothes, holding them above their heads, as banners tossed to unfurl the air. The land rose now in flames. Smoke in mountains, the water reflecting in its undulations the fire and sky and smoke.

On the river again sailing north. We had four survivors from Southampton Hundred in the pinnace, huddled to each other's rags: a man, his wife, their child, a girl of eight, and another woman, a sister to the man. The day not cold, they shivered as they stared. Their skin was the colorless gray of fear. The little girl held herself still and stiff, thinking if she moved, she would surely die.

The river scrolled upon its channel, the sunlight reflecting on the currents. We sailed past Ward's twelve-hundred-acre plantation where twelve tenants had died, all the population there. Past the plantation where Henry Spelman served. Spelman lived, two others died. The place soon abandoned. That land only settled four years ago, now to be taken back by the brush.

How swims the water in the river's wash. Men we saw at Yeardley's plantation of Flowerdieu Hundred, digging trenches, preparing foundations for blockhouses and for walls. Five men and one woman died there. A warning given by a wounded tenant saved most of the adventurers. This place with its natural defenses, rich lands, was ordered to be held. The tobacco crop here was especially valuable. "Where grows the weed, there sits our empire," so said Yeardley once, and this was the last of his plantations. Southampton Hundred now abandoned. For

Yeardley to have his purse well filled, Flowerdieu Hundred would be defended even to a cost beyond its worth.

We sailed across the river to Tanks Weyanoke, anchored off the shore. The house there smoldered in piles of ruin, all its twenty-one slaughtered. The wind tanged with the sweet and rotting smell of unburied death. It would be days before those graves were dug. So much danger, so many were our dead. Here some of the corpses were eaten by their own dogs. He who would aspire to be the master may one day just be the meal.

Our anchor pulled on ropes and caught and heaved aboard again. The venture north, our sail spread, we raced upon our wake. We kept to the northern shore. At Swinhow's farm, the bank of the river cut close to his burned house. How red the clay that bled into the water. There sat Thomas Swinhow, limp, his arms supported on his knees, blood wiped across his face, his hand red, as if bathed in blood, so dripped he in dry cakes of gory clots. We made the beach. We called to him but he was as a death masked in blood. He did not turn, but spoke in exhaustion to himself, "All dead, a wife, two sons...brains all splattered...crushed their skulls, no one would know they were mine but me. Four of my tenants dead as well. So cut in butchery, their parts all mixed. What hand is this? To what arm does it belong?" He held the child's hand in his. Small fingers gray in their stiffened bark, he turned the hand within his hand. We led him to the river's edge, bathed him from the blood. We carried the ruins of Thomas Swinhow to our boat. So weak he was. We buried the child's hand along the beach.

The day declining from its noon. No word of Thorpe. Berkeley Hundred was across the river. His plantation spread in its ruin along the shore. Lonely boats in their plaintive wash sailed past. Huddled with survivors in their alone, their reflections trailed in the waters about their hulls. "Any news of Thorpe? Is he alive?" I asked a captain as he passed. "Fresh killed, I hope...and who would care?" he replied. Two men at the rudder of the boat told their story in its grim report. "Sixty savages came about us from the woods. We only two with wives and children barricaded in the house. With two muskets we fought them, saved our own, each man by his own weapon. The savages danced their coward beyond our range and fled. We left unharmed."

We now walked upon the beach of Berkeley Hundred. Close to the river was the blackened ruin. Smoke rose in wisps of diminishing heat. Nothing that was human could be seen but slaughtered meat, the bodies torn apart as if by beasts. Heads in bodiless scatter around the burned houses. No sign of Thorpe. No scratch of blood, no cloth to show us him. Through the fields we walked in search. The land settled to its own murdered quiet. The tall grass in last year's gold, dry and empty of life, swayed confusions before our eyes. All hidden, no flat and planted fields to give us perspective as we walked. Eight thousand acres this plantation, Thorpe its main investor. "Where is he? We should not walk so far, the savages may be about," a voice at my shoulder whispered. My snaphaunce cocked, we moved through the reeds, pushing against their weight, their stacks resisting as we stepped. The stems cracked, their rods broken into arid dust. A few yards more the reeds shoved aside, the light was in clear warmth and landscapes. We walked on plowed fields. Three men knelt not a hundred yards away. Others gathered in small groups, some walking, looking to the ground. White scraps, torn clothes lay within a stain which blackened on the surrounding earth. A fertile patch, perhaps, I thought, but the smell was death.

We came forward. A man saw us and approached. It was Nathaniel Causey, the adventurer from the next plantation, Causey's Care. Causey, who had come with Newport in the first supply in 1608, shook his head, his eyes glancing past mine, as if embarrassed to speak the truth. "He didn't even run," was all he said, as he turned to lead me to the place.

"I am sure it be the bits of him," said one of the three survivors of Berkeley Hundred. "This has the same cloth." He held a bloody piece of sleeve. The head was gone. The neck a bloody stab on an empty flat, ending vacant on the stained ground. Fingers cut from the hands, arms broken from their shoulder blades, blood-stained bones, hard in white, smashed in pointed shards, crawled this in vermin; the rank of sickening smell, it made us heave. They gathered what they could in the remains of all of him that was. So much lost and taken in his murder.

"I saw the savages carry off his head. They played catch. The head, its hair in ragged blood, it spread in circles from the spinning ball tossed from hand to hand. Sometimes it fell and thudded on the ground. Then they would bowl with it, their fingers holding in his gouged-out eyes and open mouth, its face all lost. I hid and saw it all," said a youth of sixteen, one of the survivors. "I warned Thorpe. I saw the savages murder as they ran the field. 'Run,' I said, 'the savages have come in murder.'" He stood, not afraid, and spoke, "I am not in fear. There is no harm meant for me. They know I am their friend." He then looked to the sky, which in its eyeless face looked but upon itself. "Kindness is my shield, my love my weaponry. Justice be my armor," he said as he told me go. I fled and hid. His hands outstretched, certain of his God. They came upon him. Their shadows crossed with his, the axes falling, they murdered him where he stood and licked his blood, as if in his defilement they stole the power of his God."

"What are men when they steal from another's blood their divinities? Murder is not a church, as the Spanish would have you think. And certainties that require death are not of God. It is when weak men doubt that axes fall. The faith of fools is a faith too much, and how are we so different from the tribes?" All this I thought, but pretended my sorrow with the rest. Thorpe better than most, but still a small man, swelled on the prospects of his own self-worth. Why do men anoint themselves apostles, come only to joust in ignorance in a blind man's game?

Would all this slaughter have come to pass if Thorpe had left the savages to themselves? What do all our conversions convert but to another murder? Each God is sensitive. Each to his own God be left. It has always seemed to me riches are safer than any church. The weed a better tabernacle. Worldly corruption is a kind of faith, its pulpit mostly a less bloody throne, less murder for more pleasures bought. The good and the just bring in their bag such punishments. Look upon this bloody field if you think I lie. In peace the savages would have had us marry with their women sooner than take away their gods. And now the consequences of this saintly jibler will come in vengeance and more slaughter, and more thoughtless dead. Riches are a better win. Everyone has a chance to spend a bit, even the savages.

A natural to a chamber pot, our Thorpe. "He be a fool," said Causey, as he kicked a piece of what was Thorpe. "For so small a life he should have leisured a better death." In those days there were no good words for him. Most planters thought him pompous in his self-appointed piety. "The weed has dictates of its own." Thorpe the inconvenience, scorned even in his death. "Before him we had the peace," most said, as most forgot the truth.

North again we sailed, past Causey's Care, past West and Shirley Hundred, stopping briefly under the walls of Charles City to leave our human cargo to its dock. The river darkening in the defeated dusk, the light failed into night. We sat the river, the anchor rope sucking to its black. The land quieted into silhouettes. We ate, stood guard and slept."

In the morning we sailed again. How bends the water's flow, the landscape in its horizons turned upon the river's course. So many miles the river wound upon itself. Henrico and the falls not far, and now we came to seek the end. At Proctor's plantation, which held both sides of the riverbend, Mrs. Alice Proctor came to the shore, a musket in her arms, twelve servants around her, all well armed. "Such was the modesty of womanhood," one said. Mrs. Proctor smiled, a ready soldier beneath her daily grace. The savages in their first assault she beat back, gathering her servants to their own defense. A hundred savages screamed as arrows flocked, firelocks smoked along the edges of the wood, but she, in the bastion of herself, held forth a fight that broke the Indians' murderous will. Savages fled to shadows. They, still about, now creep in war in watch and wait.

"We gave them taste for taste," said Mrs. Proctor, she less modest, but more forceful in her embattled skirts. "Would you have a meal with us?" she said. "There will be no war today." She looked to the wind as if it told her things none but she could hear. She asked not help or rescue, having well rescued all herself. "We have heard nothing from the falls, no boats, no message. All that is there is now," she gestured ill. "It cannot be good," she said. I nodded as we ate.

When we sailed, one of Mrs. Proctor's servants coming with us as a guide. What a joke, a laugh upon a well gone stale. Nothing to the falls but slaughter and a haunted desolation. At Sheffield's plantation, some miles up the river, we found Sheffield, his wife, eleven servants dead, the whole plantation slaughtered. At Henrico five dead, the great buildings there all burned and wrecked, utterly demolished. The fields a litter of slaughtered chickens, hogs, goats and horses. They murdered all that had been brought by us. The breezes through the chicken feathers blew a final movement to the dead. Nothing remained but carrion. At the college land, sixteen dead. Our hope for love and alliances with the Indians gone, our tears torn to vengeance. The college, our monument to our salvation, wrecked. Now what came was on their heads. We cast down all restraint. At the ironworks, twenty-one slaughtered, the furnaces ruined, bricks smashed, tools and machineries thrown into the river to lie in rust. "This infant which was our industry will never be rebirthed," I thought. Now all profit to the weed, no second works to make the colony pay its way. The one is one and that is the noxious weed. The rivals slaughtered, tobacco throned, the nation bent its knees to her. The skilled craftsmen we so carefully sought, now dead. They never to be replaced. John Berkeley, the director of the works, butchered. Joseph Fitch, apothecary to Dr. Pott, a battered corpse. Only two children survived to bear witness of all this death, they speaking through the shivers of their minds. Fear ever haunts, with all this devastation, lunacy made for them their own repose. The falls not far, the children, starved, said little. What hold is this that speaking will not give release? These horrors come anew to birth an age. What changed is changed so utterly. We came to the falls, rode under its mists. Cleansed we were in our emptiness. We turned south, the ghost of old Powhatan's village wandering on the breeze, lost in its hope, its home in shatters.

The river stretched to faraways in dazzles on the reflections of itself. "Drink me to forgetfulness, enfold me; I, too desolate inspire." I spoke, as if I heard it whisper in my ear. "Come and be another humble, sustained through me." The river seemed to call. Oh Smith, it was only in my cynic that my own voice babbled in grief. Silent, I held aloof. I could not surrender to the eternity at my hand. How close all distances to my eyes. How many eons toll in the shadow of a leaf? The river has called and I was not enough to yield to everywhere. Equals we are in death. Three hundred fifty slaughtered in the massacre."

At Jamestown, a despairing Wyatt called his council, we the few who had survived. Thorpe, Powell, Berkeley dead. All about were the accounts of slaughter. "Deadly were these murders to our living soul," said Wyatt.

"Our country's heart is burst. It is true, we are unredeemed, we who sent ourselves to redeem the world. Why our dead? Where is our miracle?" For three weeks we sat in melancholy, slipped into the sleep that awakens to a loneliness. We did nothing.

The council sought through me the words to temper grief and give direction to all that sorrow, but I am not that thrill whose bed is words, I tongue not the soup that heats the phrase and blesses lightning through an epitaph. I am the couplet who weeds a simple line, flat my surface, my roots not deep enough. Reverend Stockton called for vengeance. "Cut the savages' throats. Let their empires be the grave." Yeardley thought profit and called for war, some knave he is, schemes his only theology, only greed his church.

War is more talked than done. The tobacco planted, but not so the corn. Famine hung its drool above the land. If there is no crop this summer, we all will starve. What still we are, we need for the planting of the corn. Food our only prospect. War could wait. Vengeance now would be our suicide.

But everywhere was disaster. Jamestown overcrowded. Families lived in the open under trees. The weed took most our labor. Small planters sold themselves as tenants to the larger owners. Wyatt ordered the more scattered and least defensible plantations abandoned, even some of the largest left as derelicts. Desperation was the final nudge that pushed us to our cause. Mrs. Proctor forced to abandon the plantation she defended with her life. "Leave now or we will burn it before your eyes," she was told. There was no choice. All she had was lost. Soon the savages burned what we quit. Smoke now hung in its elegy above our retreat. Berkeley Hundred, Southampton Hundred, Maycock's, Powell Brooke, Swinhow's plantations lost, Tanks Weyanoke gone. Yeardley forfeiting his best lands. His greed for more to make the balance with the loss. Jamestown, Elizabeth City, Newport News never attacked and now reinforced, as were Flowerdieu Hundred, West and Shirley Hundred, Jordan's Journey, Charles City, now defended. All this retreat to give us the chance to be strong again.

The river filled with our boats, their commerce bringing survivors to our sanctuary. It will be months before all our dead are buried, feasts for vermin and for dogs. News now from Indian messengers that Opechancanough had many captives in his village: twenty women from Martin's Hundred, maybe men from some other plantations as well. Would we have a truce for captives was the question asked. The council met. "The savages wish to plant their corn just as we," said Yeardley. "Let them have their truce, which is best for us. When summer comes and the corn is ripe, we will have our war and steal their crops. Starvation can be our friend. It is our musket ball to kill enough." The council so agreed. We all well knew the savages were too swift to be caught and surprised by us, and so we became the patient, wiser way to make our war.

Is nothing understood in Virginia except by the calamities, and even then nothing really learned. Blind love or murder, their simple violent politics. I read through Sandys' bloody smile, and I the exile of the subtle middle course. "A lazy waddle, their strategy!" I cried in the shaking of my London room. "A dictate of the weed, but not without its cabbage wisdoms smiling through its coins. Better we untie ourselves from greed and play some bravery to forward wisdom on our self-respect."

It was weeks in April before we could write to London of the massacre upon the quill. Shame stayed the writ, our ink dried to the paper tablet. We only worthy to be a slaughter, and so our stain. It was another month before the letter was handed to the care of the captain of the *Seaflower*, that ship to sail from Jamestown on May twelfth, all her sails like shrouds, chalked in the ashes of a passing age. She the final knight to bear the elegy.

Oh Smith, and I, the dream, in all its beast. And if my brother had been more manly in his parliaments, and you were here and given rank, what histories then? Would all our blood still be puddled before our battered doors?

Chapter Forty-four

LAWS BY COUNTER BLAMES, AS GRIEVANCE
BATTLES GRIEVANCE IN THE TATTERS.

HE *SEAFLOWER* MADE PLYMOUTH on July first. On July third, King James and his privy council were informed, and the news proclaimed to the public throat. Whirlwinds now the anger voiced. Ideas boil through the flesh and the cry for retaliation walks monster scarecrows through the halls. We are all but cinders as we wreck, and still the vultures choir. Too soon we assured our purpose was the only grievance. A vengeful London called for exterminations, as it crawled its belly across the judgment seat. The snake had surrendered its salvation to the snake.

I raged in the rant of all neglect, my advice always short a coin. The king was advised not to hold his ears to the pleadings of my friends. *England would slay me on an easy prompt, my books half-remembered, me a waif*, I thought. *My life a living accusation against their birth.* My river mute, its eloquence now the eloquence of dust.

I wrote to the company asking for a hundred soldiers and thirty sailors with food and arms and a ship to bring them to Virginia. "I shall so range the country and by plague and torments run the savages from our doors and scatter them in the woods; so fearing war, they settle into peace. Ready garrisons of some strength I shall occasion to protect our towns, and I shall see that our English are well armed. And all that made convenience for the massacre I shall replace." I warned the company against that vengeance of the mind where slaughter braces slaughter. Murder is not a reconciliation. Lazy is the mind that feebles but for blood. So I wrote and was ignored. London saw devils where only its policies were the blame. Each gun now our church, the flinted hammer its only steeple.

A few in the company favored my plan. The company's stock had so decayed, no money for any rescue. Edwin Sandys' vice always was his vision, the practical he left to God. And so hopes drowned his ship. There are ever tides in thought more relentless than the cold breakers of the sea. The company's answer to my plan was, "We shall not assist nor shall we interfere. Do your conscience." Half a victory is half defeat. I had no money, no prospects but my book. I called upon the Willoughbys, who gave a small but willing purse.

Plague then in London, carts in the streets with the tallowed dead, bad harvest, food prices high, war with Spain the rising threat, all that was, the dreams of my youth faltered, and now this slaughter. "Has ever a nation been so murdered by its own kindness?" asked a member of the London Council. "Our God, who loves us best, punishes us in this world to spare us in the next. Too much by drink and dice and cards and lewd behavior has our Virginia Company. Forgotten was our sacred worship and so God in his retribution comes in massacre. We do not doubt that our God is best, for he is God."

The Council in London ever sat in a deliberation and squandered time. Fourteen hundred pounds in debt. No money to buy new supplies of food. On August first they sent this message: "The public stock of food now low, and prices high, our common treasury is called upon to pay our ancient debts. Rededicate your worship to our God… for his hand has brought you thus for your excess." Recriminations the council's charity. "You saw not the danger in Jack of the Feathers' death and the warnings from the savages, so why are you surprised by the suddens in a treachery? The Indians have treasoned against the pledge of peace and murdered even Thorpe, he the saintly martyr to our faith. Seek revenge. This calamity cries for war. The savages you do not kill, remove far from any fort. Seduce their neighbors by gifts and copper to be our allies. All this, and bounties on Opechancanough's head. Despoil their lands. Divide all spoils among yourselves. What captives you may take, use as slaves. The savages are but brutes, who squander kindness to extinguish good. Spare if you can the young, they may be converted yet, and see to the completion of the college, whatever little hope there is may lie in it."

New letter from George Sandys. "My brother torn, his dream a sword that prettily moves to tear upon his throat. The Virginia Company everywhere dismissed, my brother criticized, complaints against his administration. And how do you awaken to your sweet misery, my father's other knight?" The echo of his laughter on the ink, the pages a serpent's hiss.

To save the London Company from financial ruin, the king offered to grant it the monopoly to import all tobacco into England

and Ireland for seven years, the king to receive one-third of the entire crop as payment in addition to one shilling a pound as tax. It was a bitter apple the serpent brought. The company objected to having to import between forty thousand to more than sixty thousand pounds of the Spanish leaf. A good profit in that, one would think, but Edwin Sandys made madness his sanity and fought the proposal of the Spanish weed, hoping, perhaps, to greed a penny where he might have snared a pound. The discussion crawled in pettiness for months. In truth, many of the London Company still opposed the weed. I schemed for my expedition, my friends for words, not for golden sovereigns. With a small purse I am spent, but not yet dispelled.

The London Company apparent in its ruin. Sir Edwin's reputation now sunk, choking on his past pronouncements. How greeds our self-love to deny the shame. The agreement with the king delayed. Sir Edwin Sandys and the company chose the withered path, and chose to prove what was, was not. The company had printed at its own expense a tract: *A Declaration on the State of the Colony…in Virginia, with a Relation of the Barbarous Massacre*, written by its secretary, Reverend Edward Waterhouse. "The bad has for its moments sometimes good. All mischief is not a calamity. This massacre is not without its better parts. No longer will the colony be chained to fair usage of the savages. Our gentleness is restrained. We shall take the better lands by force, by famine, our crops soon in abundant harvests. More for England that once for love we did forbear. What other nation would so wound itself for love? Virginia, you are safe. Good men now rally to your care." All that ink was but a bad plea for a better porridge. "Seed the earth with rivers of our slaughtered blood, the plantation blooms." So Waterhouse wrote. "All Virginia lands now have passed to us."

"This massacre is not a salvation, it is but an excuse to forget past errors," answered a critic of the company and of Waterhouse. Many thoughts are lines drawn as boundaries in the limits of the air. We cross to our regret, the threshold broken, few ever remembering it was there. As retribution squeaks, our humanity drowns. Pocahontas now forgot, as was England, protector of the world. England now would protect itself. Vengeance called for vengeance. The plague still in the London streets, food still scarce. God was still the author, but anger rails as it seeks release. Hatred needs but to point to pin its poisoned flower. "Thorpe murdered in his gentleness," wrote

Waterhouse. Thorpe, in death, had birthed his enemies. Two heads of two lives, the man of simple soul. In London lived he as a martyred saint, in Virginia buried as a fool. But no bounds in England, no one but I, John Smith, saw beyond the blind. I knew the land and savages. But around the speaking gentlemen and their proclamations of the legions of head-nodding fools, all talk was of total slaughter. No restraint. War was war without reprieve. "Where there is no law," wrote Waterhouse, "vengeance is a kind of justice."

All London in its opinion warred. Samuel Purchas, the last of the apostles of the dream, sat the rumors to set his thoughts upon the page. How ink in its curves and straights do draw the windows closed, the gaze but to ourselves, no landscapes seen that are not of us. I made visit to learn how bitter brewed his ink and could I ally him to reason and bring him to the calms of the middle way? Purchas to his chair, the thimbles of candlelight across his face. We stared each other's silence to a frown and played our fingers to gesture sermons. The moment longed for meanings none would speak.

"And when do we begin the telling of the end?" he said.

"That scratch is ever in the soul. The wise must be heretic to the apostle in themselves," I said.

"There are no heretics, only apostles," Purchas replied. "Apostles are only heretics never come to grief."

"And will you hold to the dream and sermon against a slaughter of the savages?" I asked. "There is a path in strength between failed hopes and murder."

"All the nations plate their contradictions in a tryst of blood," he said. "I have heard from Sandys in Virginia again."

"I did not know you maintained a correspondence." I smiled a sweet curiosity.

"There is too much of his father in all his shadows. His confessions are a potion, but too lightly mixed to make a convert. He thinks his alchemy is sin, in truth it is self-murder. The wizard has defiled himself to grasp the magic. I fear we are the limitations we suspect. Ever our actions blind our conscience to the act. We cast out thought to pleasure that beast that occupies our emptiness."

Purchas rose and handed me a manuscript from his desk. I took it from his hands to read its tombs. Purchas wrote to save the dream by casting it all aside. England now God's chosen cause. To us his holy word. "All this Virginia is England, for all our slaughtered are buried in its ground. The land is ours to progress God's glory on this earth. It is a land ill-used by an inhuman nation. Unmanly sits their deformities on this earth." Purchas wrote in the bitterness of his shattered dream. He who will not bear my beliefs has sunken to a monster in my eyes. So has it been. What stones we kiss before our broken pedestals. Purchas, believing more, believed much less. How little all knew then how he failed his faith.

I walked from Purchas's house. The true drama strutted on a buckled stage, man, the usual mystery of the case. Each man the surface. Each man a shard that holds some piece of all the circumspect. Each man in his own way betrayed the dream. Drake and Jonas, each a theology short; and for all his faults, Dee, the fool and self-appointed saint, that last light to have by secret faith a new Eden to our world. He failed. Too much by himself affirmed. No more the scientist, only a schoolyard pedant cast a simple in his wanton mathematics.

GEORGE SANDYS, IN HIS LETTERS, WORE NO MASK TO HIDE THE hatred in his smile, as he laughed the cynic of his gratitudes and did humanity some service for a joke.

*W*e in Virginia are still loyal to the weed. No war before the tobacco harvest. Greed has claimed again our loyalty. Avarice is a better chain than iron. No call for slaughter would take us from our work. Meager corn was planted, even with famine as a threat. But tobacco in leaf, the lands become its paradise. Even with the massacre and the plantations abandoned, and all the ruined fields, the crop this year promises to be sixty thousand pounds, as good as the year before. Practical men make a practical war, and wealth as always is a fair ally.

Those who loved Thorpe best called for butchery without a slight of humane respite. Let our morals have their rampage. The faith that failed itself now cries to have itself revenged. Let them murder their doubt on the bodies of their foes. But in Virginia it is tobacco that is the messenger, just as it was to the Powhatans. How common is this worship for the common seed. In England, most called the Indians "cowards who in treachery betrayed us so." But in Virginia, we see a courage in it. "Unarmed to war, in a general assault," we said. In truth, it was the same strategy Opechancanough, if he was Don Luis, used against the Jesuits.

Each Indian assigned to murder a single monk, all to be killed at the same place, at the same moment. No chance to be armed or warned. The battle short, the bodies torn apart. The Jesuits' heads cut off, their skulls used for drinking cups. No matter how different we may think we are, the question is how different we may be seen. Thorpe, that fool, pushed us towards our massacre. Gods are not a trifle that a people change, as we change a hat. In Virginia conversions brought what they have always brought, their chalices overflowed with a bloody wine.

No homily should be our muse, tobacco has held us to our hope. Where greed is fed, mercies follow. Diseases in the defended town. Too few houses, the water bad, the corn crop hardly planted. Wyatt, so ideal, so innocent, this youth, how strange that corruption had not yet given him the energy to pursue the chase. And yet, with courage footed in a sense of right, he tamed confusion with the law. Wyatt set his order on the land. Each surviving plantation to have its captain to exercise and train its troops and see to all matters of defense. To oversee the plantations in a region, commissions were granted for some to be captains of the captains. Ralph Hamor for Martin's Hundred, Bennett's Welcome and all that was there about. Other captains appointed to Elizabeth City and the lower James. Captain William Peirce responsible for Jamestown itself. Isaac Maddison, all plantations west of Flowerdieu Hundred, and Captain William Epps, that courted gentleman and sometime murderer, womanizer and adulterer, who it was said could ravage another man's wife that morning, her daughter in the afternoon, then cheat the husband at cards at night, was given command of all the eastern shore, after being acquitted of adultery. Law ever being a favor for those who know its price.

Broad power Wyatt gave to all his captains, absolute authority to make war or peace, to trade for corn or furs or such necessities as would be helpful for the commonwealth, to possess or plunder what they would with whomever they so chose. War upon the whim of captains, many quite corrupt. Captains to control the supply of corn, charge what they would for all they stole or traded, and who to make complaints? Wyatt too possessed in his ideals. Innocence makes victories for corruption no easy villany would ever dare. Yeardley was appointed captain of all the captains. His military experience in Ireland and Holland made him the proper choice. Wyatt not wise enough to see the truth. Yeardley must have licked his bloody chops, knowing all his losses would be well repaid.

NO WORD FROM GEORGE SANDYS AGAIN FOR MONTHS. CAPTAIN Martin now reneged his pledge and desired his old patents in all their codicils and grants restored. His alchemies slight, his only magic was to transfigure lies to lawsuits, saying he never abdicated the text when he placed the papers in the company's hands. He left them only for safekeeping. Behind the rude the reason was Sir Julius Caesar, one of the most powerful men at court, the keeper of the rolls and Martin's brother-in-law. It was a plot to pen a better compromise. The company under threat would not yield, its court firm, its judgments fixed. "The grant was flawed and never legal," was the forever of its law. But there were rumors in the carriages, while the new patents would hold, the king would grant Martin a seat on the Jamestown Council if ever he returned to Virginia. And so the strangle is our politics, no one having a care about the consequence.

Chapter Forty-five

CAPTIVES, WAR AND INNOCENCE, AND LONDON
PLAYS ITS NOTHING PURSE FOR ITS OWN EXCUSE.

READ MY HISTORIES, their events in the luxuries of distant fields. All about was a swirl, its screams in rumors, its whispers frantic in their lunatic. Where is that river now, its calm waters voiced to me, a current to plead me to a better self? The king in a rage at the London Company. The council staggering toward its final griefs. Another scandal, fifty boys sent to Virginia as servants at a cost of five-hundred pounds, ten pounds paid for each by the planters in Virginia to cover the company's expenses. That sum given in weights of tobacco. In London the tobacco of such a poor grade only brought five pounds per boy. The company demanding recompense. George Sandys, as treasurer, to collect the debt. I knew the cards before I saw the scuffle. Sandys having the rate by forcing the smaller growers to pay, they fall into debt, then buying their tobacco and lands and servants on the cheap, a double profit on a single game.

The failing sun, the winter constant in the air. A letter from Sandys. Justice in Virginia coming to its elegies.

Yardley is rich again, having planted corn on the eastern shore, then selling to those that had the price, bushels of corn for pounds of tobacco. Wyatt always trusting him, always deceived. By late fall, our second harvest done, another war to catch the savages and their corn. Yeardley commissioned to spoil by war Opechancanough's own village. Always Yeardley knew the shrewd in every twist to make a better profit, which he called his "law." Never will he destroy or despoil the whole Indian town, but only a few houses, then steal most of their corn, enough for a lenient war, so the savages will return and plant their fields again. Next year another crop, I thought, another battle for another theft of corn. And so Yeardley will have a constant supply of corn to steal each year.

At the village, the Pamunkeys escaped toward the woods with their harvest. Yeardley, in anger, burned a portion of the town. Its boats, houses, fishing weirs ruined. A mummied king his men found was not set to fire, fearing with its ashes they would curse the land, the savages never to return. "Wealth, more than vengeance, is our way," cried Yeardley. In London, they may call for murder; in Virginia, our corruption brings a better balance.

Still held blind in rage and greed, Yeardley pursued the Pamunkeys into the woods to have their corn. In the thicket fell the shadows on the leaves. Dry the path they walked that autumn underfoot. No sound in quiet breath, the world in wait. There stood the savages on either side of the trail in *ambushado*. Flashes smoked in muskets we had traded long ago. Arrows all about. Spirited they were in their vengeance against our trespass. The skirmish sharp but brief; a few of ours wounded, none killed. The savages bloodied some. Yeardley had his corn, one thousand barrels, more than a quarter of the corn we had all that year. He the only source. He charged us ten shillings a bushel as freight, and made another fortune. "Sometimes vengeance pays a better profit than the weed," he said.

The sky now foul. The winter soon, we sang our curses to the air before we ever had the cold. The savages brought their war in stealth along the boundaries of the plantations and in the woods. At Nuse's Plantation, two killed, supplies burned, the survivors ragged, exhausted. Captain Thomas Nuse and his brother both dead earlier that year. The plantation so sick and despaired, nothing planted. Few could call upon a strength to organize a defense. The other plantations much the same. I, as treasurer, ignoring all but my office, sold the living servants of the dead planters. From Nuse's farm I disposed of three servants for six hundred pounds of tobacco, but two died before they ever saw their new master. Another four I sold for a hundred pounds of tobacco each. Of those, two died and two ran away to be murdered by savages. Five I had for myself toward my allotment of fifty, then not filled by the company. Of those, all died but Nuse's page, who was not worth his food. Such my responsibilities I did to the company. I collected taxes, dragged each penny from its wound, for which I earned some hatred. But for me, hatred is savored best when spiced with the colony's sense of fear, and fear they should, for power I had and used to extort my will. With all I sway, I could not ignore the general good because there might be some benefit to myself. Some widows and orphans I left upon their lands. The taxes owed I set against another year. Let those that can rise to pay their way. More profit to the company, more tobacco to be stole. And so my charities glove an iron fist and sweeten the divide that cleaves me to an inner war.

What slays us are the beyond, its mysteries at our door. My brother sending me into exile, now I glory upon his shame. I suckle comfort on a hate. An outer war and an inner war, we war upon our savages as we war upon our own. Have I become the happenstance where only murder brings me a sullied peace?

Wyatt always fair, and others taking in the starving and the weak, not land enough to employ them all. Bartering and selling the tenants we owned for seven years as beasts, was now tobacco's second coin.

At Martin's Hundred, where one hundred forty adventurers lived before the massacre, now thirty-two were left, badly provisioned with two hogsheads of corn to last for months.

Always savages were in the woods in watch, always near, not two stones' throw from our defended towns. "In the spring, when the leaves are on the trees, their shadows will be closer still." So said a planter at Elizabeth City. Everywhere there were eyes upon us. Everywhere the air had sight. The violence all about, I slept pillowed on its thrust and sailed my braveries on the river to my brother's bidding, and so I overflowed compliances as I tore myself to rags.

Now more flesh of mine, and sweet concerns slide over the boil of my diplomacies. In December, Wyatt's wife, my niece Margaret, brother Samuel's daughter, stepped foot upon the Jamestown soil. Dear Margaret, a pound of ugly upon a pin of sense, but a true Sandys and of me. I made her welcome. Distance is the formal grace, we bowed the love of a family in pretense. The ship she sailed upon was the *Abigail,* its supply of adventurers sick with a pestilent fever. "Each day they died, covered in their stinking dung. How it assailed my nose. Little recreation, an infected ship, the food bad. The dead so thoughtless in their deaths. So many cast overboard, the rafts of their dead bodies floating in our wake." So said Lady Wyatt. The sickness spread to Jamestown. Even our ancient planters, well seasoned to the land, died in numbers. Of the thirty new tenants we sent to Martin's Hundred, twenty were dead within a month. Unburied bodies in Jamestown's streets and in the fields, under hedgerows, unregarded, tended only by their rot. Self-soiled in their excrement, they decayed to a double fragrance.

And what have you heard, my Smith? I am sure it's half. Why does all truth come by accusations? Because the world is a lie. Wyatt begged the London Council to send us food. The council sent advice to build the college and blamed us for the massacre. But for all our famines we received three Bibles, two books of Common Prayer and *Ursinus his Catechisme,* printed Oxford 1591. What, were we to eat the pages and drink the ink? The food that was pledged came from the English public and some individuals who invested in the plantations. The ship, the *Seaflower,* which carried the victuals, a careless pipe in a store of powder, it exploded in Bermuda before its freight ever made Virginia. So, by loss, we are left to seek our way alone. We, the orphans, rule the tabernacle and all the commandments are overthrown. For he who is cast aside will shatter violence upon the world.

Food prices rose. All that was became a luxury: nails, cloth, corn at fifteen pounds a hogshead, hens at ten shillings apiece. The price of a year's worth of bread was two years a tenant's wages. And always there was death. Gentleman and servant made the same. All our equality comes when we set our table for the worms. Captain William Powell died, his wife married to the new cape merchant Edward Blaney within a few weeks. Why not take the thrust on a bed of weeds. In Virginia women made their wealth as frequent widows. Dr. William Rowlsley and his wife had arrived in Virginia in June with ten servants. The servants all dead by January. The doctor bragging he had the best food and the best lands, his wife wanting only to sail for home. Soon they, too, well seasoned for the worms. My Smith, before the winter melts I am sure six hundred will be dead by fevers and starvations. More dead by Indian wars, but who can know the rate? We count the days till spring and dig the graves.

Oh, Smith, I am so wearied by my angers, yet so suckled by my hates. Wealth the toy, our reasons play. The within festers all and we are the leaf upon its hurricane, my thoughts never deep enough to know their depths.

I finished Sandys' letter, I placed it to my desk. London trembled in all the news. The events so fast, in such occurrence, the reports barged the many facts. I read the sheets, the carriages bred their rumors, the voices of their choirs told the facets of the tale. The world seemed to stammer in its paraphrase. I stood that time, my quill mute. My ink bereft of tint, its scroll despairs its eulogies. All now surmised the enterprise a shambles.

By love, what contagions come the score of its disease? Pocahontas and the land confused. She the meadow's lips in the pastures of a kiss. Words whisper, I swoon upon the perfumes of the river's gown. Flowers float in the temptress of her hair. But destructions float her skin. Landscapes gloat a firmness more sculptured than our bones. My lost love conditions only to dispair. I am lost, hate contrives, but only to a better thought. This land is solace, its ghost in souls, its secrets open to all that have the ear. Power me in self, I am no elect. The commons there could be made all. Divine hesitations on my tongue, I speak in heresies. We are an alchemy by the congress of our wills. It is the elixir of this new world's gift. I quake in mysteries as a drunk. I of no estate, alone in a lover's agony. How many desires meld this Virginia, and she its emperor's daughter. I am born of continents, never proclaimed a saint. A man to his mind, his eye in thought. My fingers in the bowels of the old world's corpse. What their philosophers dissect, I reject.

> The London Council now brought it orders. No pleas from me to stay their foolishness. If these be good men, it were better they be hung, for what they brought was death. The king granting one hundred and fifty muskets and four hundred men for Virginia's relief. Those supplies the company sent to Bermuda, thinking the colony in those islands more in danger. Danger from what—a phantom Spain? The company ordered Wyatt, without our advice, to assist Captain Samuel Each of the *Abigail* to build a fort at Cape Henry as a protection from the Spanish, charging sixty-four thousand pounds of tobacco for this service, more tobacco than was in all of Virginia. Five hundred men to be used, almost all the colony's military strength. "Are the plantations to be protected now by handfuls, and we at war?" asked Wyatt, who wrote London and refused the order. Captain Each building the fort on sand and oyster shells, the whole crumbled and washed away. The captain died soon thereafter, some said of shame, some said of the diseases brought on his own ship.

So George Sandys wrote, but in London each man had his say. From all, in every hall at court, Sir Edwin pilloried. The London Company broke into its many factions, its sum a sliver, the whole dispelled. The group loyal to Thomas Smythe accused Sandys of squandering the lives of three thousand Englishmen and a fortune of ninety thousand pounds. Sir Edwin answered, accusing Smythe of landing only six hundred adventurers in Virginia in eleven years, at a cost of eighty thousand pounds, "while I, with but thirty thousand pounds, have transported three thousand settlers in only three years." And so the bickering spoke each a snake in its hissing wars. Violently they clashed by lips and quarreled even in chance meetings in the streets. All the talk of moneys lost, of riches never made. The London clergy disgruntled with the display.

REVEREND JOHN DONNE, DEAN OF ST. PAUL'S, RAGED HIS SERMON before the assembled lords of the company. "Were we born from nothing to random in the world at ease? Glory, by his pain, glories through the world. His messenger stands clothed in fire. Sparks! The salvation burns! We the holy moths consumed. Our ashes ring, the fires chime, our gospels storm. We are swept by harps, tongued in choirs. Elegies sound in meteors, we stand you now to your godly pledge."

The London Company, lashed in accusations, was deaf but to its own noise. It wrote to Wyatt, speaking of adventurers who had treasoned against the king and his noble work in Virginia. "Against God himself these crimes." Wyatt broke into fury, answering the council, "By naming none, you slander us all. Name the name. Our reputation disgraced upon what proof? What policy? You in London ordered us to entertain the savages in our houses. To what defense when the enemy sits our chairs, eats our food, sleeps where we sleep? This by your own orders, and now we stand accused of treason. The fault was never in the execution, but always in your policies. If you will not learn from your errors, let us have the courtesy of your silence."

Wyatt had every right to rage, he no longer young and not wanting in ability. War ages men, tragedies bring wisdom to those who would be wise. The company never silent, ever making their errors worse, now wanted Virginia to abandon the planting of tobacco. "The weed is a sorcery, it leads you in rebellion from your own good works. Cast out the plant. Smoke is alchemy, and through it some Indian magic. What other enchantment can it be? You are mastered by a cloud. In your gardens tobacco is the only fruit. In its leaf the apple, and you have plucked the snake."

The market for tobacco in England still was vast. The weed the only gold, the only coin Virginia had to buy some food, to make all this suffering pay, its pittance as a bloody wage. A few found wealth, it is true, but it was the weed that held them to Virginia, and the last vestige of the dream.

Only I in London spoke to the balance, which always is the last eloquent truth. I no friend to smoke saw that the weed had but a small stability in its price, saying, "As it varies, so the foundation quakes. Seek other means to other profits. But of the profit you have had, use it to buy those necessities, as you diversify the risk. Many is a better proportion than the weed."

But how could they in the wilderness do what in England itself could not be done? England was still a land of sheep. Wool the simple knit to hold the nation. Little industry on a bitter bed of trade, and the colony with less to perfect more.

MORE REPORTS FROM VIRGINIA STREWN AROUND ME AS A MOAT of fire. On what pedestal do I display its glowing walls? That winter I sat the soundings of myself and thought of the history I had seen. By 1623, my new book, *A History of England in the New World*, was well along; I used the manuscript of Gosnold's *Voyage to New England in 1602* as the true narrative, rather than that of Archer, whose manuscript Purchas had. Let Archer sulk in the dirt of his neglect, let his name dissolve beyond all recall. I would not play his rescue. How he hated me. Peace sometimes comes gunned in works of vengeance. Mostly they but increase the pain. The cost is not worth the waste. The effort eats its own. I did the worst and damn the retribution.

And when I did not work I sought to find some love again. Her name: Esmerelda de Acquataine; her family descendants of French Huguenots living in London. Merchants of some wealth, her uncles and her father fascinated with explorations and the New World. A friend of Purchas, we met in the libraries of his home. Dark hair as hers of long ago, hazel eyes so different, smooth unpainted skin. Is difference but a craft to fill the keeps of memory? Are passions remembered, their desires less? I think not. The taunt is more that drives the protocols. She sat at the dinner table and we talked, and so I began to court the dance of seductions of us both.

My love spoke low, our words were of a double haunt. All passions come by twin, and by what ghost would I place my kiss upon her lips? I was welcomed to her father's estates. We walked the park, never quite alone, always the respectful distance of a nurse and my own company invisible at my side. How many lives do we live upon a life? Nothing that serves a memory is ever pure. Would a kiss tear me from my past or would it nail me certain to its door? And so we walked the wooded path, I chilled by the very glance that would have me melt.

IN MARCH OF 1623 THE SAVAGES ATTACKED ELIZABETH CITY. THE six blacks of that plantation fighting as at the barricades. Anthony Longo, the wild man, his chest a shield of sweat, dove into the sea of murder. The two savages he captured were kept as slaves to work the fields. The word "slavery" is a strange divide. Those savages escaped into the forest. Nothing lost and nothing bought of any consequence, just a ripple in the tide, hardly guessing of the beach.

Nostalgia's lost, I thought of Pocahontas then, her soft complying lips, I tasted their heat, their intoxications against my cheek. I hold her weight of gentleness, urgent in my arms, her perfume lingers on the thresholds of my desire. It passes, a vapor orphaned to my long ago. Those passions never to my book. In the carriages, eyes that read are numb but to distorted thoughts. Esmerelda and I no more a society. Her father not inclined to pauper a daughter to a dustly library shelf.

Sandys now wrote to me, his words were not a jest, their pledges grinning of an avarice.

How well these Africans are a part of us. Our failure with the savages so soon we will forget, as our success with the Negro does proceed. Drake's dream, his allies of different skins, here is our hope again, men as us, but less than brother; men not too different than ourselves. Only the savages seen by us as squalid mortals. All who disappoint we grotesque. Such is the complexion of our willful human state. Where once they were thought to be a noble work and beautiful, fair to rise into our light, now they are thought by all as base in a hideous deformity.

Good news now, word that Dr. Pott for two pounds of glass beads had ransomed Jane Dickerson from the savages, her husband murdered at Martin's Hundred. She had been held in hard slaveries, used as a wife. She had seen the few men taken from the plantation tortured to their deaths, skinned to a living human foul, faces cut away. Bereft of screams, they died in agonies.

We are never quite our hopes, so why do we hope? Jane Dickerson petitioned the council upon a week, asking to be freed from Dr. Pott's employ. "He keeps me in worse slavery than the savages," she wrote. Pott, in his reply, said, "Jane Dickerson was a tenant to Martin's Hundred for her seven years' service. She owes that time to the company. I ransomed her—she must repay that cost to me. Those years to the colony are now mine by right of ransom." We awarded Dickerson to Pott. Contract for labor was a law we never broke. Those who pledged to serve would serve unless they bought their freedom on a goodly price, as some last year had done, including the Negro Anthony Longo, and some others of the Africans. Longo has already purchased a servant. Blacks may be slaves in the West Indies or in Spanish South, but for all we fouled, we were not so soiled. In Virginia there is no slavery.

I still sold men; three for six hundred pounds of tobacco; two for four hundred pounds of tobacco; half this year in hand, the other half next, if they lived. Twenty-three of my own dead, four by savages, but I will, by collection of the taxes, have enough by other's debt to have my allotment without expense of a penny.

The glass factory was to be repaired as was my brother's demand. Why am I always the servant to the fool? The Italian glass workers the company hired are a jester's dream of industry. One I have sent home for beating his wife. The house they all built at their first arrival is blown down by a squall no more angry than a sneeze. I have had them punished after the furnace they repaired blew to pieces when first lit. I have had it rebuilt by my own servants at my own expense. It in use for six weeks, the sand not melted, the Italians complaining I did not send them better clay when it was they who chose their own materials. But I did my brother's will. The Italians I am sending home. Let them rascal England, for here we have not the will to waste the expense.

More silk worms my brother sent, but all that miscarried by our want of skill. The mulberry trees came to nothing. The cuttings grown from old stocks were burnt by fires in the woods. We have spent our labors only to provision another loss. My brother I disown your flesh if you have not the eyes to see the folly in your remedies.

And so we sit our council and do our best, our tobacco as our guides. It is us against the company and the rabble in the London streets. One hundred and thirty-four thousand pounds of tobacco planted.

THE KING'S CODICIL FINALLY WAS ANNOUNCED. THE LONDON Company proclaimed the only agent for the importing of Virginia and Spanish tobacco. We to sell our crop to them, most of the profit not to us. The peace so dearly won was short, Warwick's faction in the company objected. More compromises and a new agreement. The king to have a nine pence tax, the company to have its monopoly, with its guarantee to import at least forty thousand pounds of the Spanish leaf. I knew those in Virginia would never sell by law all their tobacco to the company. The king had made a strangle of his crown. Trade has a freedom every foolish tyrant does abhor. Sandys writing of the pact said, "We on the plantations kept our council to ourselves and sold to whom we wished, all Europe eager for our trade. The weed would abide no contracts, no limits on itself."

I walked upon the London streets as its dirt wrapped contagion around itself. Does every ccommon politic breed its own disease? I know the Virginia circumstance. Can no one see the play but me? I call on those who speak of the same events. It is to them a vagary of little sense. All occasions seem dimly in their disconnect; all things heard as whispers, as a heartbeat in the wind. The world is alive with consequence, and yet few see it so.

News now from Sandys.

Smith, I am throned in murder. I am its potentate. Serendipity is the screw that bolts our histories. My vice to the world in its slug moves on. The wise worm schemes and safely eats within the better plot. It is only the innocent who bear their sins. And where, my clergy, in your justice is all that said? Corruption is a better love, at least we will know those worthy of the stake.

Some weeks in May, Powhatan's younger brother, king Opitchapam, sent a message saying that he was willing to betray his half-brother, Opechancanough, and would bring him either alive or dead to Wyatt, and would return all our women captives for no reward but peace. "All royalties, even of the beasts, live on treacheries," said Captain Tucker, he not being quite the mind to master all the subtleties. Opechancanough is schemed the betrayed by his own brother. In a lush of pride I hug all vice and gain an adopted genealogy. I have sympathy for this savage prince in his family war. Not so different from myself, he wears my face. I shall do justice on his plot and bring him a garland well-fashioned from his vice.

Opitchapam wanted twelve of our armed soldiers to advance the plot. The council had its discussion, smiled and then agreed, we having different treacheries to secret other plans. "Let us kill them all," I did suggest, thinking, let the inspiration twist its noose and subvert all our moralities. With forty of ours we sent Captain Tucker along with four sacks of wine. The design from me, I the plan, this intrigue was mine. Dr. Pott to fill three of the sacks with a lace of poison. The other was untainted, from which our men would drink. Captain Tucker the lure to negotiate a peace on any terms, being sure to free our captives first, then to celebrate with the savages and their king, a general parley speeched with fair loving words, during the evening a lethal toast to seal the bargain, our men drinking from the wholesome sack. The savages would drink, their cups brewed in poison, and in a moment slip to weakness, soon to death. As they sickened, Captain Tucker would signal with a shot; our others outside, not far away, ready, would rush to slaughter who remained.

And so I stayed in Jamestown, amused to let pass the blood to other's hands. "Have I become a fate," I thought, "holding the savage nations on my whim? All power is but license to free ourselves. Am I not sovereigned to be my own? If God grants me this gift, I certainly do his will. Then where is the stop? If God is author of it all, both good and evil, by doing evil I do a different kind of good. By doing one, I do the other. Good and evil claim links to one another through the chains of God." And so I laughed, "My brother, tell me now, where is your heaven in all of that?"

For days I sat without a hope of news. I looked at my abandoned ink, my lifeless quill. I thought of trying to write a poem again, but nothing urged me forth, my maelstrom slight. "Two hundred dead, our victory. Captain Tucker slaughtered two hundred and all their kings," said a face in my door.

My victory had murdered well. The toasts made, Robert the Pole had drunk from his unpoisoned wine. Opechancanough and the savages had lifted and swallowed theirs. The lodge in the firelight, crimson shadows flickered upon the grotesques of the walls, the savages' eyes caught surprised, forward leaned their necks. Then groans and bodies slipped against each other, flesh moving, writhing and shaking. A spark, a flash of powder, lightning in the black. Our forty in the lodge, a volley to kill the kings, then knives and swords to butcher all the rest. A scalp torn free and held is but a bloody rag. Our men in glee to have such murder.

Twenty of our captives were brought home, released from slavery and all abuse. Those who were tenants returned to work, others to their other prospects. The few savages spared we kept as slaves to work our fields. Opechancanough we thought killed, but that scene such a bloody pick of scalps and ruins, it was a wish that willed itself a certainty. At the news London will celebrate in its carriages. Our London Council and my brother wrote us a strange rebuke: "Treachery should not craft our war. Kill the savages with honorable means. False dealings are not worthy of our cause." And so wilds the cause of my brother, who once said, "There is no stratagem unjust that brings the savages to our vengeance." So he vacillates from law to law. "What need we of England when they misuse us so?" was the cry in our council hall. Even Wyatt agreed. "We are alone, our victories only made by us." The rumor in the forest was that Opechancanough, while badly wounded, still survived, crawling in the blood from that butchery. Now he stalks the cleans'd air, a dream silhouette motions a distance from the eye. The forest spirit had become the man. His power in ghosts, his words in martyrs.

I AM TORN FROM HOPE. EVEN DEATH IS CLOAKED IN THE THORNS of a lesser horror. One of all abides no portions. She of the land, the land of her, a maelstrom, vortexed, its circles without divide. Still, am I crowned in willful firmaments? The night rebels, the day never fully surrenders to the light. Worlds collide, words in their alchemies. My book, I am chanced on that, its passages in its musics to reclaim the dream.

The spring has clothed the forest in a peaceful warmth. The tobacco grows. All served it, or were nothing. We now in wait, tending to our weed. Yeardley growing rich. The council disgusted. Wyatt to bring an end to it all, ordering the plantations and the farms to sow a year's worth of corn for their own use. That order always made but seldom followed. This time Wyatt made it sting with beatings and fines. Pain would legislate our will. Our law was cruel and our punishment certain. Power brought some mercy, and so did wealth. Richard Barnes, for speaking base and slanderous speeches against Wyatt, had his arms broken, his tongue cut through with an awl, then to run a gauntlet of forty men, each beating him until he was footed from the Jamestown gate. John Heny, who cursed Captain Tucker, got sixty lashes and a fine of one hundred pounds of tobacco. Richard Crocker, who accused Hamor and Piersey of being unfit to sit the council because "by every extortion they do feed upon us," was to be chained, his ears nailed to a pillory. And so from this unruly crew our society was cut. Why not, when death was soon? Mercies ledger no weight of coins. Riches rise in working our servants hard before they are eaten by the earth.

The Indians planted their corn, believing our fury spent. Their villages being rebuilt. Few came close. Distance between us now the measure of a better peace. But war slept in smiles, waiting for the end of the summer growth. "When the savages' corn is done, English have your muskets close at hand" was the saying in the Jamestown streets. Anthony Longo and a few of the Africans began to scout the woods. Their eyes upon the land in visions of a jungle far away, a wilderness vast enough to eat us all. Their numbers only twenty, but well they lived with us. "See, we are an England of a different hue, another nation from a common stamp," said Wyatt. These Cimarrones are our congregation, plays of flesh, the dream lives on, no longer but a fret, a dance of bones.

The colony now less than fifteen hundred. This spring, by May, two hundred died of disease. My allotment of servants for months was not even half my brother's and the company's pledge. I wrote to London. Others of our officers in a similar circumstance. The reply from London was simply put. "Since you do your office only half the day, half your pay seems fair, and maybe, by all accounts, too generous by half." The London Council then denied a full company of servants to all the officers, accusing Wyatt of "never daring to attempt any service of great hazard or importance to this enterprise." The snap of those words broke rebellion in the air. "If we are accused, let us fully wed the crime." And so, my brother, without my servants I refused the company's work, except to hold the power of my office. Yeardley, by some accident of reason, was by the London Council justly fined two hundred and twenty-four pounds for using the company's servants for his own purposes. Whom my brother punished, we appeased. Justice in Virginia was a madman's whim. Yeardley we awarded as tenants all the duty boys who had finished their terms that year. Always power is the pet that strokes itself, but whoever rules, tobacco is the law.

*W*yatt commissioned Captain Tucker governor of the lower James. He with power to seize and confiscate all goods and ships, or detain any servant leaving the colony without permission who had not fulfilled his term of service. So loudly the corruption called, and all this wasted on Tucker's slight imagination. But he did what his capabilities would allow, and stole enough to satisfy a dunce.

Why did not Wyatt give me that office that I could better use? Dull men make the world so dull with their half attempts. With half my promised servants, was I banished to half a wealth? I richer then than most in England, but true greed is never satisfied by comparisons. Is not our worth a storehouse of our resolve? I with five plantations, three thousand acres of land, more than twice my allotment by the company. Wyatt, as a reward, gave me two plantations just this month: three hundred acres across the James and four hundred acres at Archer's Hope; while my other three well-planted with tobacco, corn and servants. My tears, sweet Smith, are all for what was promised, not for what I stole. On my fifteen hundred-acre tract I have thirty-one servants, of the other lands many more, plus three houses, numerous cabins, two forts, two cannons, thirty suits of armor, twenty swords, twenty pounds of powder, three hundred pounds of shot, storehouses, livestock, one house for my silkworms, corn by the hundreds of barrels and tobacco by the hundred weight. I am by my hungers made mad by riches.

Now, in September, our tobacco almost ready for its harvest, we have heard the price fell in London to the lowest ever seen: half a shilling for the poorest grade to one shilling and a half for the best. Our crop, one hundred thirty-four thousand, six hundred and seven pounds, more than twice the year before, but at half the rate. Little on the whole we lost. More work for just the same. Equal wealth for unequal sweat. And you, my Smith, who always spoke the future as if written on your sleeve, warned the colony that tobacco would never have a stable rate. "It is a coin whose alchemy is never fixed. Beware," you said. "It is a strange gold that tomorrow turns to brass."

And now upon an hour another taunt, another fleet, a year and a half after the massacre, the first provisions in years arrived from London: ships with food, flour, cheese, oatmeal, hogsheads enough to freight our storehouse for the year. All sent not by the London Company, but by private donation, and some who had investments in the plantations. The council stole most of that supply and sold it for its own profit. My brother, where were you then? Hiding? Or were you lost? How was I born in a nest of fools? My only relief the knowledge that fools suffer more, having no account of how came their pain. What joy it was to watch the pious choke on their own piety; usually it was someone else who bears that weight.

I have become that hate which vengeance will never slake. Tobacco being all the freight we had, we needed more land to plant more fields. More servants, more leaf, more to want, less to have. I in fear of an unrequited greed. Avarice makes visions, swept in the worship of an inspired drunk. My eyes are coins. My heart weighs self-love counted on my success. My philosophy a ledger, my passions are a sum. Unplanted lands I had, but where come all my servants now? "Why not a little Spain," I thought, "or Barbados, where men bought men?" There, I am told, slaves supplied a better service if you could afford the rate. But that not for Virginia. A slave cost thirty-five pounds. In Jamestown, a servant, no slave, could be had for a pound and a half, or even two…and then most died. It was death that added to the cost. If seven of ten died, those that lived divided all the costs. Those three that lived, the cost was about six pounds four shillings, but if three of ten slaves lived, each slave then cost one hundred sixteen pounds apiece. Gold spoke its conscience. There would be no slavery in Virginia.

But I needed servants, I needed more weed. Where the wisdom to save me now? The mind spins its own salvations, all my solutions within my hands. All pleasures well-practiced to an evil good? My brother chained to the failing London Company. I would not be him. My father, rise and see who is your best. Bribe me not with love. My hatred is love enough. My mind is a judge that never sleeps. What faces in their spirits rise, their daggers to my throat? Plague me not. I have conscience only to be free.

I sat the council. I am not so weak that I will repent my wealth upon a schoolhouse virtue. Riches are the harp. Sing evil to exalt my inner peace. The time is now to plot the London Company's final death.

Power is a secret better kept, my friend. Most believe the world is an enigma. They are just too ignorant of its means. Power is the undertow. When revealed it mostly dissolves, by counterstrokes smiled into dissipation to quaint an antique sport. All that dares secrets vengeance on my page. My daggers are by quill. My ink assassinations.

I have written to Samuel Wrote, a cousin to the Earl of Middlesex and a friend for years. Wrote is most opposed to my brother's tobacco policies. For his violence of speech in the London Council December last he is barred from the council forever and from the company for a year. Of this I pretend no knowledge. Play the fool when the ax is no pretense. I sent my letter to my old friend to complain of the company and its policies, I now the hook on which to hang my brother's meat. So innocent I rambled in my rebuke, so stern, yet so mortified about the slanders about Wyatt and the Virginia Council. I am so to torment by all the complaints. It was London that set the policy. The servants sent upon their ships to Virginia without ample food. So many dead, and the commons never told. Yes, thousands to their hungry shrouds. And then the massacre. The plantation too widely spread, the savages to be converted, even to the sharing of our rooms. All this and we are faulted for the massacre, then blamed again for not defending ourselves and asking for aid, when I and Wyatt did stand our own guard at midnight and with eighty made war on thousands. To better spice the mind, lie with a little honesty and wisdom chokes. Be the cook, my Smith, sham with truth.

The letter to Samuel Wrote will be my brother's last repose. It will be given to the Smythe faction, used against him. I am by purpose the innocent who spills the poison into another's drink. I am at last flung myself a knife. I have steeled my thoughts, forged by flames to be the blade. I am the better Smith, my time comes in exalted fire, all my excesses heat me to a chill.

WHILE I IN LONDON HELD MY DESTINY ON A PIN, THE FROLIC in the court was danced to Sandys' violin. His letter to Samuel Wrote sang indictments of Sir Edwin's policies. It did the intent. Smythe and Warwick chortled venom and praised George Sandys' courage and his loyalty to the king. Copies of the letter quickly penned, underlined, with margin notes to double-thrust a phrase, no important section to be misspent on a careless read. This was war by particles. George Sandys had called for a commission to investigate the company. This now to be done. The king placing Sir Edwin under house arrest again, his rooms to be searched, he to be kept from the London Company's business, excluded from their deliberations, but allowed to attend his parliament and its proceedings. The king wanted no clash with the commons, only to end the London Company's charter and return Virginia to the crown. The London Company was in its final ruin, its fall had little grace in its final plummet. Sir Edwin was in disgrace, by whispers he wore his calumny. Sir Julius Caesar, John Martin's brother-in-law, in his secrets worked the law at court to bring the company's end, as vengeance for Martin not having his acres and his illegal patents. Warwick and Smythe to have their empires as a shatter, but the deepest hurt may be the hurt we never feel. The victor has weaned the nation from the dream.

And what of you? I thought. George Sandys you are spent. On what now will your corruption spend its appetite? Will you be the loneliness that you pretend? Vice has eaten itself a corpse and you are its hollowness. There are no conclusions when the heart is dead. The soul is a verb, its secret actions inundate. Its grammars contagion, urgent in their needs. All its dictions crave. Its nouns walk in diamonds, their many facets sculpt the vision. Inspiration is an act of love, and you wonder why you cannot write. The pen is a sorcery. Brutalize the need, the art decays.

Chapter Forty-six

THE DOUBLE DUCHESS COMES A PORTRAIT
TO MY PAGE.

S FOR ME, I would not rage upon myself. Virginia again as a royal colony had some promise, and, in the end, was my only hope, and so I spoke myself in ink. My book almost done, I needed assistance to have it through the press. My chances of a patron were not great, and stationers were not wholly honest. "They never give a true account of what they sell," so Purchas warned. "Trust not your fate to printers" was the general advice. With no recourse, I then cupped my dreams to strategies and did what was never thought of before. I sold copies of my book by subscription before its pages ever saw the press. The manuscript then complete, I had a prospectus printed and sent to such nobles, merchants and gentlemen who might be persuaded to purchase a copy. Most hopes are sweeter before they are tried. The response not bitter, my prospects little advanced. I sat and thought not funerals but other plays that might hold success.

I thought of the Earl of Hertford, a man of wealth and vision and my friend, who gave me aid when I returned from Virginia. Those sums of money to my hand, and these words, "Smith, the world is a fool. You shall not do great deeds if you are starved. Let me restore in some measure what was yours and lost. Without your wisdom, Virginia may become a wound and other enterprises never done." The Earl of Hertford then dead two years, and I sat in my chamber still a beggar to my prospects.

His wife now called the Double Duchess. How vanity and beauty trick with history, and power jokes position and brings more wealth. Frances Howard, the earl's wife, the history of her family a terror that never passed. Related to Anne Boleyn, two of her cousins beheaded, she sought safety in the very uncommon wealth of a very common wine merchant. Upon his death, and she but twenty-one, she married the earl; on his demise she married Ludovic Stuart, the Duke of Richmond, second cousin to the king. She stood then close to royalty, the richest woman in England, the bearer of two great titles. Beauty and position mixed vanity to a lethal brew. But she always being fond of me, I turn the card that never knew a deck. I wrote the Duchess for an interview. In memory of her former husband, she gave her consent.

We sat in a parlor realmed in exquisite miniatures. It was a cathedral in a glass, the walls a powder blue, as if painted by the sky, the ceiling had its galaxies. Hushed we spoke. She laughed. My bluntness polite enough to salt the honest mind of a woman who had seen enough. I asked for three hundred pounds to pay for the printing of my book. She smiled and agreed. "Smith, I had better give you what you wish. It may keep you from turning total rogue, which may cost me more." The Double Duchess then asked of the eloquence of the book. "And how finely printed? Large pages, I hope, with a good bite of ink. Black always heralds words of consequence. This, our book, must have a grace even above its print…and maps, I presume?"

"Three. There will be three," I said.

She smiled a smile to charm the shadows and mock all wit. "Three is not a number I admire. There should be four and a beautiful titlepage of some cut and picture."

"And I would hope," I said, "a portrait of yourself to map that generosity where all this comes."

"My family." The Double Duchess now in a darker mood. "How much our generous blood was spilled. Lord Howard, who commanded Drake when they fought the Armada, he is now forgot and Drake has all that fame from our family's victory. And Lord Thomas Howard, my father, also there and even commanded Richard Grenville and that fleet when…well…" Frances Howard paused. "The past is never far enough. It comes an inheritance with a hidden snare."

I lived in pools of spirits as I worked to have my book through the press. Another map I had engraved, based on an old sketch of Roanoke and the country thereabouts. That map, its border decorated with drawings of the Indians. And you, Pocahontas my love, how sit you in that ghostly blank and unfold yourself to me? Too soon we have passed our lives, too soon our flesh to be an empty aspect in a book, and where is that life not so soon forgot? In this book I have penned my memories.

.   .   .   .   .

I WROTE IN DISAPPOINTMENTS, WORDS CAST TO SHADOWS IN their regrets. I told not enough. Its depth never deeper than our will. I looked upon my face and found only fear. All that I wrote was clipped, changed slightly from my other books. More a collection than a work, an altar to a memory that would not fade but would not fully speak.

I wrote in all haste, filling the new map with names to honor those who gave assistance to my work. That world came full in familiar sounds. I peopled that vastness with Howards and the titles of Lennox and Richmond, Stuarts and the Earl of Hertford. My sister, too, had a memorial in a tract of hills. All that unknown coast now brought sovereign in a cast of names.

The London Company lost in bankruptcy. Its organs disgorging blood flayed by the thrust of an inner knife. George Sandys had done his will. The world as ever is the prisoner of the flea. A commission now formed to examine the whole state of the company. The Privy Council demanded that the company return its royal charter and surrender the document into the king's hands. The company refused. On May ninth, 1623, sixty-one of the seventy members of the company voted to resist. Among the nine who voted to yield were Samuel Argall and John Martin. Always in their self-love did they lick the hand of power, the taste only a taste of something stale. The irony and tragedy was that in this vote they were correct.

My book well writ with the belief that Virginia should be returned to a royal authority. Only then would the worst of the abuses of tobacco be resolved. In November of 1623 the company's ledgers and all its documents were seized and placed in the hands of a royal commission. And all our hates are the freight we levy on ourselves, and sometimes the good may occur from a fearful confusion.

The Double Duchess had two portraits of herself engraved. They to declare her as my patroness, but only to be bound in those copies of my book given to the most royal personages and the most important corporations. All this influence of her face only to be shown to the most equal of all the lords and chartered powers. On February sixteenth, 1624, the Duke of Richmond died by some sudden seizure. In such grieves of loss, the Double Duchess cut off her hair that very day. Royal not quite, she held position only by the shadow of a match. The duke now dead, she was but an aside. The king kin no more. Her position broken, she shattered into a fearful grief. Never again was she the same. Beauty, as power, has its moment, its magic always on the wane.

Chapter Forty-seven

Y OWN BOOK, its pages inked and in the press. My words now locked in the iron grip of type. Such rush to have it done. So much of what I had lived would assist the commission. On May twenty-fourth, 1624, the company was swept aside, no longer to exist.

The rumor of my coming book, a prowl of whispers in the streets, I was called to the commission. I wrote a brief narrative of what would be the solution to Virginia's grief. My testimony railed in thunder. Not one inch of land had I been given for all my sacrifice, no fame or position mine and no rewards, but the slight of a constant neglect. All this I told, then I gave them answers in a truth more impertinent for being true. I railed against the sloth and laziness of gentlemen who would not work, of corrupt governors, of well-rewarded fools, of a policy that led in blind appeasements and hoped conversions to Indian massacres. I called for permanent well-armed garrisons in well-built forts, and for sending to Virginia willing workmen of substantial skills. All this I said and more. "We need a consistent English law and royal authority and governors who no longer feed their own corruption as if it were a right." My passions came in sparks. I decried tobacco. "Its smoke is a demon's host. Where it grows there is nothing but itself. One crop is not a country. What should be a pleasure from Virginia is but a disease." I called for abolition of practices in Virginia that were illegal in England: the buying and selling of servants, laws and punishments condoning and creating forced servitude, men and women bought for seven years of labor. "In England, the contract is for one year, our servants well protected by our law and humanely treated. Drake did not destroy the Armada and we did not go to Virginia to found another slavery. Now the evil seed has not bloomed into thickets yet, but beware, the vines are set. The threat grows to harvest soon, and so Virginia and all of England may have a tangle for their necks."

WHAT I SAID, I SAID. MY BOOK RUSHED THROUGH THE PRESS. Friends on the Privy Council, knowing of the king's new policy, wanted my book, which favored Virginia's return to royal authority, in the stalls before this plan announced. All this to bring some favor to myself and to bring support to the commission in its work. In early June the book was given in halves to two printers, each to print with speed his portion of the work, I still finishing some sections. I asked friends for verses to add some complimentary comments on the text. Purchas sent four stanzas, rung in the obvious flats of an accustomed rhyme. In friendship I had them printed in the front of my book. John Donne sent some passable lines. How great was his genius in the small circumference of his world. He, having sat on the London Council, knew all the company's problems. Donne, if not a friend, held for me at least a passing sympathy.

On July twelfth, 1624, my book was published. Three days later the king convened a special committee and appointed the president of the Privy Council to preside and to govern Virginia with royal authority and to solve for always its persistent problems. But the elixir always smoke to drink its giddiness and vomit its desire. Tobacco was the only profit that we had. It was the weed that had the garden bloom. Many thought gold sermons the best theology to a better reason. The council left tobacco to harvest as it would. So much of the king's own revenues came from the tobacco tax. There were rumors the king would outlaw the importation of the Spanish weed and give Virginia tobacco the English monopoly. And so once again the problem abandoned to be its own solution. The weed is more than a plant. It cannot be killed by law alone. It is an idea, its soil has some root upon the mind. Its dung is greed. Its flower blooms hysterias.

I wrote to George Sandys, informing him of the London Company's demise and of his brother's fall. I raged through my quill, my ink to cauldron in its boil. The heat I sent to George Sandys' ear. Would he listen to its turmoil or to its sense? "You have blessed yourself too freely and now await the cost. History is a cipher. Its consequence secrets surprise, it comes in funerals for the heart."

Word now that John Martin would return to Virginia in a month to fist his new patents in Yeardley and Wyatt's face and regain his wealth, his plantations mostly ruined in the massacre. The king had appointed him to the Virginia Council. No good in that. Why do our politics ever seed the changes to be but the same? And the little men do strut their flesh of fakery and yet they win.

And nothing is yet for me, but to fling the truth of political folly, that a crop of little use. Too much my rebellions quake the easy estate. Too much my heresies pollute the fountains of their self-love.

MY BOOK, *GENERAL HISTORY OF VIRGINIA*, BROUGHT ME SOON ITS fame and even favor in some London circles. I had again some spin in a minor orbit. Ben Jonson dressed me in the word historian, and slid in one of his plays a sarcastic line in my direction. Myself now the witness of my own life. My book, my continent, my bones refleshed to crave the renewing hunger for more fame. If I am neglected, let me live through a quill-sketched page. I, the witness. I am the tale that will be told. I sat and decided to write of my early life.

And so I started what would be my *True Travels* and wrote eight thousand words of my captures and of my escapes, and of the daughter of a Greek who aided me, and of all the perfumes I drank on each sweet breath. And of my battles with the Turks, and how, by slaying three in single combat, I was awarded by my lord, Zsigmond Bathory, king of Transylvania, the rank of captain and fifteen hundred gold ducats. A patent he gave me, written and signed by him with his seal, to attest to my services and to my reward. Through all the wars and histories of my life, I still have that parchment near and in my rooms. Battered, torn, but well readable and intact, it was the only testament I had that what I wrote was the truth. The first chapter of the book now done, I brought it to Purchas, who helped me with his maps to name the places where I had been. The world is a dictionary and each day its pages change by conquest to another name.

Purchas approved and thought that my patent should be registered in the College of Heralds to be forever the proof of what I wrote. This I did, the document deemed authentic and approved on August nineteenth, 1625. My shield now to carry images of the three heads of the Turks I slew.

Purchas advised, and I expanded the work. So much did swim upon my memory, so much recalled. Is each man but a patchwork of his life, a rag of many dolls to be resewn, then nimbly cast aside? Is each man to himself a curiosity?

All about me a wash of voices. The distance closes, the oceans shrink. The river encloses me in its sighs. The new world has come a rescue to my ears. My heart beats in its blood alchemies. Madness wills a wisdom no madness dares. The second edition of my *General History* was from the press.

ENGLAND SAILS ALL ABOUT TO CLAIM ITS WORLD. OUR EMPIRE that Dee first proclaimed to our ever-reluctant Queen Bess, its hour has come. Sir Richard Saltonstall called me to his estate. Marshaled is the wealth that secret turns the world. I was greeted as if by a gracious cousin.

"Good captain," Sir Richard smiled, "again, as always, a pleasure," offering me his hand. "Too few rewards for one so worthy. Let us walk our conversation. Time has a nimble wit, and a quaint passion for passing most unnoticed."

Through the parlors of rooms, down the many corridors. Walls of portraits, Holbeins, Cranachs, painted country merriments, angels, kings and myths and symbolic histories. We sat in a gilded sanctuary, its prisons upon our sighs. "My son, Charles, prepares a trading voyage to our colony in Barbados. He is not inclined to oceans. A novice, he requires some classroom Billy Book to teach him the terms of sails, ropes, the pinnings of a ship and its appliances, a general work to child an expedition."

I heard the words. Why not a dictionary, a sailor's sketch of speech, some pages to catch the mariner's breath. I nodded my consent.

"Well nodded," Sir Richard laughed. "I shall bear the printing cost, and, my friend, why not a luxury, a bag of coins, a loan of rooms here to speed your good work?"

Why not largesse? I thought. The old mariner's tales will again play a ship into slang and definitions.

My ink spread fresh upon the page. The work fast, half to half, an opinion licked upon many a borrowed phrase. Few other books there were, but enough in French to patch a passing galley. I called my book *An Accidence, or the Pathway to Experience*. Not quite the tome I hoped, but revised, it might serve. Saltonstall pleased, his son at sea. Richard Willoughby had its pages also well to hand, when he himself set his tastes to sails and ships and foreign voyages.

My brew now in words. Drake did not write a book, yet I, Smith, for all my histories, all my works to pedestal this age, and on it what is set but a sculpture cast in vapors? Now I, John Smith, half forgot, all my ambitions scorned, my prophesies rusted in a laugh, now this, my collected telling. Why not? My name the name of shadows, but history is the haunt of ghosts, their cries in ink, their shrouds in crackled parchment. Still I lingered to this agony holding to Drake and his visions. To what cemeteries do we bequeath our dreams, to what tombs the libraries of our forgetfulness?

NO LETTER FROM SANDYS FOR A YEAR. LACKING WORD, SILENCE only, I assumed the burial. Then some pages to my hands, sealed in wax to lock its paper tomb.

Why do you contest me, because I am rich? A wise corruption molds a better smile. I hear your words, my Smith, they echo in its trash. Poverty bequeaths no saints. Gold no demons. I am frantic for some peace.

Why do you speak to me so far away? What we value is what is lost, and what is gained is never quite enough. We are brothers, if not twins. Is our conscience not our seat? Within its anger sits the crime. I never knew of the collapse of the London Company until I had your letter of a year ago. The Privy Council left us so uninformed, as the London game is but for the London board. We of no country are free to license on our own. Our chains of nothing are the deeper chains. But, my Smith, I yearn to have a family from all this rush. Be my second brother of a different kin, be the confessor that I can be the crime. Fear not, a little of your hate may spice the cake. I might rage a bitter tyrant and scream a bitter courage armed in greed. Be the witness of my case, so I, the betrayer, will taste of the betrayed.

In the council meeting not long after your letter arrived, Luke Eden, a small planter, appeared to bring conclusion to a debt he said I owed. "I wish my twenty barrels of corn debt as payment for the purchase of his fifteen hundred weight of tobacco." As Eden spoke his words in growing anger, I looked into his simple eyes. How powerless he was. No friends. So safe to hate. I hated him. He held his cap in his trembling hands, his face in a sweat of dirty toil. Why should I pay him a debt of corn?

"I owe nothing," I said. "The corn I had was due to me against other accounts.... In fact, five barrels more is still unpaid and I wish it now, as is my due." Wyatt ordered Eden to pay his debt.

Eden screamed, "Never does this council do a poor man right!"

"Luke Eden swing the gallows by your tongue," I thought. Wyatt in his simple justice would have had his ears cut off, but I, in kindness, said, "It is a waste of ears. Better they hear my commands. Luke Eden make my servant for seven years." Eden struck with horror at my words. His hands at my throat. Eden soon subdued. Hatred ever the spice of my idle hours. I asked again for Eden as my servant. Eden speechless, lost in the power that London gave the council to discharge. The council so agreed. What words from Eden now, my fist stuck in his throat. One servant more is not a great supply, but it is a start. Poor Eden. Free men never know they are only as free as the power they command. And so, by swindle and by tricks, duty boys I made serve another term, free planters I made my servants, the council joining in the sport. I felt not evil, I but a man with obligations I would perform. I knew this moment would not last. Conscience always a pleasant hurt, I might reform and do a better good. Each man enamored of himself, so little I need an excuse for my love to love me still.

I did not work my office, but held only to its power. The year was almost at its close. Five hundred more had died from famine and disease, our corn supplies quite low. Even for all Wyatt's decrees and threats and punishments, men would starve, their hands caressing the hogsheads of their weed, their lips kissing the enclosing wood, than spend an hour planting food. 'Not another winter with famine at the door,' I said to Wyatt, 'our numbers almost half. We need the savages' corn.' But no savages would trade with us. Most of their own corn destroyed. Wyatt, in an act of wisdom reasoned on some saintly vice, attacked the powerful Piscataways. They never enemies to us, but to the Potomacs. We wanting the Potomacs as our friends, demonstrating our power. Fire now, we burned the Piscataway village and all the corn we could not steal. Many we slew, then sent messages to the Potomacs: "Be our friends. Treachery has been repaid in treachery. Let blood bargain with itself. Let us be at peace. We wish to be allies with you once again.?" A new peace now formed. Wyatt, writing London, blamed the Piscataways, as an excuse, for the massacre, which was a lie. "It was a just revenge we made." So wrote Wyatt. I smiled some in my pride. The council pleased. This child we had now so justly corrupted to be a man.

Hamor was then sent to the Potomacs to trade, Wyatt giving strict orders on pain of death to "harm them not but only in self-defense. Take only what is willingly offered and that is all." With no room to play his judgment, Hamor did obey. Wyatt, with his tortures, demanded to be the law. "I am the fist the law commands," said Wyatt. The council smiled upon the set of power. It seemed a comfort and for the general good. Where men to license as they please, a little tyranny seems a happy brew. Each planter free enough to command his own, his servants his for seven years by law. Between tyranny and freedom was the valley that we walked. But I so cleaved in loyalties between my love and hates. And we in Virginia, what enigma is our clock? To what dream does our weed hold prophecy, its tale still untold?

In London the pamphlets spoke of settling regions in Newfoundland in the north and far away where no natives would be deposed of all their lands. So those of no experience scratched their wigs hoping to spark a truth, vacant noise in vacant heads. In Virginia, we sat in bloodied mud, and froze and starved and died, but willed our license to hold the silent earth. We are now the inheritors of this immensity. What could London teach with its own discarded philosophies?

And so, after eight thousand dead, fortunes squandered and nothing learned, the London Company was dissolved by the king, we never informed officially for six months. Rebellion smiles, it grins in secret coins. "Virginia is little more than a grave," spoke the royal voice. "My subjects were not sent as eggs to hatch beneath its earth." The king an ignorant pit of half the truth. My brother so public in his distress. So many London fortunes ruined. But that was only coin, the real foul was closer to the heart. My father's God was not so English now. We not so certain of his love. Justice not the justice of Drake's dream. We were better than Spain, no doubt. Combat not always a trial in God's love, the victor not always blessed, the vanquished not always cursed. All men build their armadas to castle in their minds, so safe in our false safety we decline.

We are not wise enough to be wisely loved. Old Queen Bess, your moment's fled. An age ever spends its twilight bathing in its own blood. What births now the heretic sings. And you, my father, as all men, not inclined to a second birth. Old age makes us simple, for we are past. Better you first die now in that last breath, than wander in that sleep of forgetfulness.

Dear Smith, this land that once spoke to you, this earth whispers not to me. I hear only the leaf rattling in its coin. My window that would peer beyond my blackened state gates to a different light. This spring we planted more tobacco than ever in the colony. Less death this spring, but there were less of us to die. The savages close, but not much at war. Our confidence more stable, we awoke that privilege not quite forgot. Wyatt called a second session of our house of burgesses. And while we gathered to confirm our law, my brother, your London Company all unwrought and disappeared by the king's command. Its tobacco monopoly and all its interests held by a board of commerce. You hung by your ideals, that dreamer's silken rope about your neck. You twist and dance the air, your toes almost to the ground. You stretch to reach the earth, the rope above not in sight. You reason that you are hung, but never knowing of the instrument.

I gladdened to think on my brother's saintly sins. The fool has hatched a demon with his quill. How better that you have come to worse, and I at the governor's table sat power and knitted words. From the poet arises in its coils, fangs and hiss, the serpent who is the apostle and has written all their laws. We made reforms as would benefit the general good, the assembly giving itself the only authority to levy taxes. The governor barred from forcing our service, or the labors of our servants for any purpose. We ordered monthly courts to be held at Elizabeth City and Charles City to spread our power, prohibited the private and public trade in corn, required all plantations to be palisaded and all men to bear arms at all times. We made such plans for war as seemed fit. Plantations to attack the closest Indian villages later in the spring. So calm the law to its lethal calm: "No person shall presume any disobedience, either by slander, action, rumor or false speaking, against the present government. To do so is a peril to be tried before our assembled judgment." Harsh means to have some rules and ordered commerce. Confections now the pain to bring a common peace. No longer, Smith, would men slander as a means to power. Dissension not the hoe to better plant the tobacco crop. The soil to be watered with a good respect.

Captain John Martin ever at quarrels with the council. Martin self-made to be a prostitute to himself. Wyatt hating him. Martin constantly offered false witness and slanders to gain more land. With angry and seditious words, Martin defended all his frauds. So caught the weasel screams. By means of bribes and thefts, certain papers of the council were sent to London to bring down Wyatt. These papers presumed to show all the false dealing in the corn trade, and embezzlements of the cape merchant. These papers, more milk than rope, proved little. Wyatt was informed by friends in London of the means by which these papers came to them. Martin chained by the links of his own treason. The council had him confess and pilloried, one of his ears cut from his head. So small the loss for such a general delight.

AND WHERE IN ALL THIS IRONY WAS THE PHILOSOPHER'S STONE? King James now issued his last decrees against the leaf, banning the importation of all Spanish tobacco and reasserting the prohibition on the English crop, both measures to be strictly enforced by fines and punishment. In his final violence upon the weed the king swept aside the protest of those who loved the Spanish leaf. Agents were to be appointed to control the Virginia commerce, the growing traffic in the smuggled herb to be ignored. All this by royal declaration. The colonists hating the royal interference wanted only a freedom of trade. The Parliament angered, its powers forfeited to a crown privilege. The king now satisfied, he was dead within months.

That year the price of tobacco rose to two shillings a pound, almost double the year before. Our crop was more than two hundred thousand pounds. Charles I, now king, asserted that he would create a royal monopoly, keeping all tobacco profits and taxes for himself and for his court. And so Parliament again cut blood upon its lips and waited. I think a king so crowned in arrogance might one day lose his head. If so, tobacco will have been the beginning of the ax's fall. Old Raleigh beheaded by King James because he did not find the golden city of Eldorado, and in his search warred upon the Spanish lands of Guinea. To appease Spain, Raleigh died, the last of the great Elizabethans. And so if the king does die on the same block, it would be said Raleigh's vengeance on the Stuarts was the weed. Silence cloaks the hammers in the imagined air. No letters from Sandys for more months. Time has slipped the calendar to my decay. Word now that Yeardley has returned to London on a mission from the Virginia Council. His silks not unpacked, a letter arrived from Sandys to explain the bait.

"Yeardley always hated, we have sent him to London to ask the Privy Council, 'With the company dissolved, does Virginia still retain the privilege to assemble the burgesses and make its own laws?' By the king's grant, the company was allowed to give us that prize, but would a new king hold all that sovereignty to himself? 'Yeardley is such a statesman for his own interest, perhaps he could be inspired to give a service to the colony.'"

Sandys' ink blushed in its accustomed venom. His quill fangs across the page.

"But the plan was over screwed, Yeardley only forging for his own, he never gaining any answer or assurance other than to be appointed governor again, Wyatt's term to end the next year in the fall."

Time dawdled to its memories. Sandys wrote again a letter stained in many faded inks.

And so our Yeardley has indulged his London displays, lackeys to his polished boots, footmen to hold his doors. While we in Virginia did what some men have ever done. History is the claim of those who dare. We so practiced in our license, we stole the liberties to be free and assumed we had the privilege—we held again our House of Burgess and made our laws. What each man takes he soon believes is given him by God. Dignity is for the few with grand estates. Only wealth molds the risen herd to be better men. Every claw is graceful in the proper glove.

Each man who would rise to greatness must also claim the cost. As within ourselves when nightmare sleeps on the back of dreams, and we awaken and know not where. I see in the mirror of the eye reflections of Carib Islands. In the West Indies, where men sell men, where the golden harvest comes in sugarcane, men play their whips and slavery brings the fortunes. If slavery came to Virginia, what cost to conscience. I cannot appraise, but cane is more toil than the weed, and a greater expense to refine before it is ready for the spoon. How many fearful futures are we to live? Slavery might serve our lazy tenants just. But for now too many servants, their cost still less, more lands at easy rates. The supply of servants mostly sufficient for our greed. But if ever the flesh fails the coin, and slavery comes cheap...I am the thought the future will have to think.

Yardley had returned to us most sick. Not two weeks past, he died, his last breath so heavy, as if he would thieve the air and greed it to his lungs. So fat he was, he bled corruptions from his mouth and choked upon what he already ate. His stomach was his counting house, his mind a ledger. His pride so much, he valued money so, he would cast the skies to havoc for the slivers of a cent. And so I said of him and so he died. Evil was his legacy. Let excuses be his epitaph. We were all pleased to be rid of him. His name cursed. We would have forgot him if we could. But inheritance comes not by coins alone. It can be a silent path to guide our steps, and although we offend the ancient prints beneath our heels, we hardly think where goes this trail and what lies the path in darkness and in wait.

Chapter Forty-eight

NIGHTMARE ARMOR AND THE BLOOD.
WAR IS NOT THE FEEBLE WE SUPPOSED.

LL MY LIFE SLOWLY SLIPS to the fodder of another age. Sandys' letter abruptly ends. Rumors now in the carriages that George Sandys is to return to England. What whispers did the hint? And I missed the taunt. His letters never gave suspicions of such a plan. No further news. Purchas claimed an innocence in the plot. Letters scarce from Virginia. Days do move the weeks to months and seasons live their seasons to another year. And then a letter.

By fall our crop well grown. All our harvest sold to England, five hundred thousand pounds. Such weights of leaf, such plenties in so many ships, but the prices in London fell before the quantities. Some pounds of tobacco slept as beggars on the docks. All seemed a ruin, the market not eager. But still, in truth, we made a good profit and some riches. If more brought us less, then the fools would plant more and beyond, they said, and have their wealth increase.

But none ever to the thought, I mused to myself, grow less. The rarer the pleasure, the steeper the rate.

That October rumors came that the savages planned a second massacre. We thought of war, but the danger a distant hint and the solution more trouble than the source. 'Murder is such a bloody sport. Let the heathen be his own savages.' The colony only wished to admire the fabric of its weed. The council in its fool still concerned, spread the fear of another massacre.

All our autumns have come to be but another war, the weed now safely cured and stored in barrels, ready to be shipped. Wyatt, by threats and punishments, again roused the men. Our Potomac allies told of the Pamunkeys gathering in their villages. Even kings from peoples far away were called to assist and witness the truth of the Pamunkeys' brag. "By winter the land once again our own."

Our sixty grumbled to their boats.

Before us on the Pamunkey lands, such sights. A wall of flesh, an army in painted furies. The savages, who always fought by stealth, now stood as a thick phalanx, shoulder touched to shoulder across the field. How deeply armed, their bodies reigned in regiments, line beyond line. Axes, bows, arrows quilled lethal in the air, some pointing, some at rest. Ancient muskets held, the old firelocks burning clouds above their tapers. Midnight had come to afternoon, their shadows in their multitudes held the ground. We advanced in line, our armor a shield on our chests. "Oh iron dress our hearts, a war now by means we know." The savages stood to volley against our shot.

Desperation may armor the will but not the flesh. Chance now the potentate. Some Pamunkeys stood dressed in iron mail or helmets taken from our dead. Such rags as our foundries had produced. Those savage chests buckled into our ironworks. Their faces masked in painted grease, sharps of reds and whites, black circles and long hair and iron, as if dressed to farce a nightmare, and there they stood.

The hammers of our snaphaunces pulled back. The Pamunkeys squalled in curses. We answered tongue for tongue, though few understood the other. Muskets braced and fired. Shot bit through the armor. Some savages fell. The others yielded nothing, but ate our shot, returning volleys of their own. Three of ours cut down in bleeding moons. Volleys now in hammer blows. Five of ours now dead. The savages died in harvests but stood their grounds.

Arrows in their darkened flocks sang in whispers through the air. Most bounced from our helmets and our armored chests. Some found flesh. Screams somewhere. I hardened to myself and saw only what I could see through the sights of my gun. Motions of living men, a pantomime of a life made slow, the blast, their horizons into obscuring smoke, limbs brushed back in exploding blood.

That night the wounded screamed through the haunted woods, a battle in the dark. Clouds in shadows moved their corpses through the sky. Even the full moon hung behind the clouds bursting like cannon fire. Wet, I crawled along the ground to where we dug our trench. The world bled dew. All that was, had come to be a wound.

In the forest, a musket fired, its lightning cracked in blast. A snaphaunce answered. Light spit through the curls of smoke. The trees and fields were stiff and gloomed, while through them moved the gusts of silhouettes. Eight hundred savages crept about us in the dark. Ten of ours dead, maybe sixty of theirs. The fight those hours was fierce, two armies murdering each other, tearing out each other's throats. "The savage who bleeds with me is raised in my respect," an adventurer mused, bright eyed, as the blood oozed from the shot in his side. "He who dies with me…" The man fainted as he spoke. Bodies littered the fields. Some crawled to drag themselves in directions, never free from pain.

Arrows still bit black across the moon. Everywhere in our camp men either held to their place or moved low against their own shadows, trusting for safety their desperate hope. Salvation comes certain by believing. The howls of the savages rolled through each round of the compass point. Surrounded, cries held the night confused, as war painted its stratagems on the dark.

At dawn, the battle lines reformed. The savages stood their place. Volleys lined in flash and smoke. Such noble order all to know who could better bear the pain. And where was Opechancanough? He not seen, the Pamunkey's led by Sasawpen. He had not been present at Tucker's massacre. So much treachery, and who was pure? Each dirty hand cleaned in dirt to be dirty yet again. As I faced down the muzzle that might be my death, I held to those my father's hands that brought me to my cradle long ago. Home happens in the mind, and I thought my father's prayer for me for its little comfort. Perhaps corruption is only the paper shield of he who would be a king. The first volley spent and I alive. The weakness that I thought I did forget. Twenty savages blown to havoc on the ground. Another volley and thirty more. What twists of limbs knitted in that glue of blood. More savages ran forward to urge our volleys, stone cudgels in their hands. Defiance is not a strategy. Without a plan it is a waste. Arrows in hail thudded around us on the ground. Across the field we saw their firelocks braced on the forked iron of their rests. Savages in crowds stood about their gunners. The haloes of the smoke, the flash, the shot tearing through the air. More of ours fell. We stood our ground and took our murder, giving slaughter in return. Men do not bleed in rivers, they bleed in pools, puddles so quickly drunk, the soil not stained long. Under our sustained volleys, back the savages stepped. Retreat, well formed, no panic into flight. Death the pressure, our shot the moving wall. We advanced slowly, our wounded grasping at our feet. The wounded of the savages we butchered where they lay.

So much of nothing, this landscape comes to doom. But the river still speaks to me, whispering in its mighty host. Its spirit not fully birthed, its angel hopes and infant on truant wings. The dream crumbles, but the new earth hovers distilled in its elixirs to the ear. Echo to echo, I shall answer with the soliloquies of my printed page. But on I read to glint George Sandys in his murderous thrill.

The field a plain of dead. The mounds of flesh so sprawled. My respect to those who stood against us and died that day. Sometimes war makes men brief equals. The savages fled into the forest. We did not pursue. Sixteen of ours dead and many wounded. We came to fields landscaped in beans and squash and corn, all planted together as the savages would, on hills. Vast baskets these lands hold, such cups of plenty. The corn in its stocks, plump and green in the lushness, waiting for the harvest. Enough food to provision four thousand men for a year. The heart of a people, and we the dagger at its chest. "Set it for the burning." Frantic pleads a war against our needs. We stole all that our boats would hold. Blanket now the earth in smoke. Its whirlwinds are our history. "The savages will know a cruel winter without their corn."

The fires burned all our desires for revenge. Massacre had been repaid in massacre. But war was never as profitable as the weed. Our powder low, no supplies for months, we bragged that we could have slaughtered more but did not to save our stores. Some truth in that, circumstance giving us a hard-fought confidence. The savages not the coward murderers we supposed. But some understanding is not a peace. We gave the respect that our blood allowed and praised their determination, knowing a greater enemy makes us greater heroes to ourselves.

The Indians were not inclined to more war that year. "This is not done," said Anthony Longo. "They will be moved by our threat to challenge us again." The savages were pushed away, but most still planted on the lands their fathers knew. No thought in us to slaughter all, which was that ghastly plan reasoned in the London streets. Annihilation never a path to riches. Tobacco the balance brought the truce. The weed seeks not more than everything that it needs. To it, war is another waste, less blood to be spent to tender on its leaves.

That year more fortunes made, the price high enough to dance all doubters into pets. The Pamunkey in defeat, losing face with their allies among the northern tribes. The savages were a whisper in slow decline. Our confidence rose secure in our thoughts. "To be gone is a safer conversion than any church," said Wyatt. But still, we scraped splinters from our powder barrels, our supplies to a dangerous low, and all Virginia prayed that winter that the savages would not attack. "They still have the numbers to kill us all," I said, but war did not step on the silent snow that year. Thirteen more dead from Indian attacks, a slight of blood we could endure. Another hundred and twenty-one dead of other means, the colony still at a deadly sink. Wyatt ordered a census to know the rate at which we declined. Twelve hundred and sixteen were all who lived of the eight or nine thousand the company had sent. But to greedy men, another's disaster is but a buttercup, that past is not our past. History is the song of those who do survive. And so we were alone in the riches promised by the weed. Of the million acres that the adventurers and plantations claimed before the massacre, only twelve thousand five hundred had been planted with tobacco. The land so barren but for trees, all that wealth so fallowed in neglect and our servants needed to cut the trees and prepare the earth to grow the golden weed.

The few savages we captured, those we made slaves, they manacled to labor in our fields. But free men are in their minds always free, that taste is the scent that effuses through their world. And we are molded from our birth, it is the cast that is our glue. It is the once, the always that is forever. The savages would not plant. That to them was the work of women. And so they did refuse or ran away or died, or even, under torture, worked less than our lazy servants. The savages made fragile slaves. Used to ease, they could not bear the hard conditions. So each bird suffocated in his nest, each twitter a prison epitaph, and what had died? With no extra supplies of servants close at hand, we did with what we could. The savages no further use to us. We manned the walls of distance, each people a people to itself, and we made solid what were our thoughts. We palisaded a wooden wall across the neck of the land on which we lived. From the James River to the York, there rose our barricado to keep us separate and apart.

What is this? I thought. Sandys won't heed the plaint. The river will not suffocate. This land some part divine. Divide God from God? I smiled. But still, Old Jonas warned of a madness in that earth.

I've come to know that each thought, an idyll, which in thinking builds across the land a wooden image of itself. Slaves already slaves make better slaves. Leave free men to themselves. Less revolt to agony the courts. I decided on the West Indies— there would be our supply of men when came the need.

·　　·　　·　　·　　·

The All Knowing of My Name ∽ 415

*W*e *withdrew into* our three great settlements and the smaller Henrico. Behind the defenses of those walled and sealed plantations we planted corn and tobacco, and sat and healed ourselves from war. The distance beyond our sight was not for seeing. We did not explore but held by grasp and labor to the enclaves that we had. We sold our servants and overworked the rest, and took our private pleasures on the sly. Most of the colonists were young, few over thirty, most younger than twenty. The women for their youth, well used, but still we stoked the boggle to have a better service. Ships from England ever there to trade a taste for a weight of leaf. Few families and women scarce. Wealth growing as a weed each spring. Sickness from the foul water and from the swamp. Death more certain than the rising moon. What caution was there to chain delight and spice our wilds with neglect? And we, the soon to die, built our clock, its ticks on wanton pleasures. And when corruption comes with ease, it allows itself no pause. I preferred my vices. Those too cowardly to steal write philosophy and let others do the dirty work. Now came the news from London, the tobacco prices rose to three shillings a pound, and with it two hundred grants of land of another eighty thousand acres, a portion mine. All in such madness, such profits dazed, and our corruption wanders to have it all. Our energies crazed to lunacies. Crime my trade. I, the poet, evil grammars lyric through my work. Words, my lighted coals. How grief inspires me. I, the sulfur's voice who has made tabernacles paved in hellish fires."

*I*n *Jamestown, Wyatt and Tucker and I*, and all those who had claim to power and so to wealth built a luxury, a new road we called Back Street, not far from the old fort. There in the new town, fine houses in rare woods, tapestried in finishings of exotic wares that the ships brought from China before they were ever seen in England, we the better market, with gold and silver coins now allowed to us by royal largesse. Riches are the simple calligraphies, no secret writ in its prerogatives. Wyatt having a great house with a dining hall and a garden, sunlit in pleasant symmetries, growing sixty barrels of figs a year. Soon orchards planted around the most majestic houses. Hedges, trees leaned in fruits, bright reds and greens in exclamations of a sweetened breath. Where planters bit into such globes of nectar, and consumed the coolness in a succulent juice, their gums bled less, their teeth held tight and did not loosen or fall out. What physics in that cheer, those who ate lived longer and in better health? But such was the truth and such was the wealth that bloomed for some a second coin. Only those with the few great houses could have such fare. Tobacco soured the land into an impotent dust after five years. And so planters and their servants moved to fresh fields, burning their old shacks, collecting the nails from the ashes, the nails being all the value of a common shack. We cleared more land. The harvest of 1626 not as good as hoped, only one hundred thirty-two thousand pounds, but the prices high enough so no profits lost.

This fall there arrived our first supply of powder in a year, and with it a new supply of men. We were ready for most to die. One of six is all that should survive. But this fleet came in the cooler weather, after the summer fevers, when the waters clouded less and the swamps were without vermin. Of these, eight of nine survived. Dr. Pott writing, asking London to only send adventurers in the fall, and so to have them better seasoned before the next year's heat. As most we ask, we will be ignored. The London gentlemen, knowing only the name of where they live, believe they know it all. Wyatt is pleased, having been made a royal governor by the king. How far we had come from when men shared all and would not work. They starved in equal portions. Greed brings a better charity, just ask any truthful saint. Anthony Longo married an Englishwoman, having freed himself some years before with a small plot of land and a good harvest. We are pleased that Drake's dream still bore its promise and work still willed the winds of hope.

I DID NOT HEAR FROM GEORGE SANDYS AGAIN UNTIL THE NEWS he was in London. I thought of making some visit to his rooms, but he now celebrated in the court both as adventurer and as poet. His book of translations of Ovid's Metamorphoses published with a special license from the king granting Sandys the privilege of a monopoly on the printing of the work for fifteen years. Sandys had well flirted his literature at our new king, having dedicated his book of travels to the Holyland to Charles when he but a prince. So do early words pay the easy success of an aging diplomacy. Sir Edwin declined to his parliament, George Sandys appointed to the king's Privy Council, now the expert on matters of colonies and empires and poetry. From smarter crimes hatch better careers. The larger deeds traffic a prospect even wider than the act. The greater the size of the offence, the deeper the pardon of the sin.

But even this world brings a cruel justice. Captain John Martin was imprisoned for his debts in London, having been the ruin of all his estates. And George Sandys, his mind a confession, himself effaced, finally wrote to me.

In 1626 I thought of home, sold my servants and my lands, packed my wealth in chests and sailed for England to dance the brag of what I had done. Unfurl you gray waters at my keel, the ribbons of the waves cut to fade in distance beyond the stern. All history is a madness that memory will forget. And all my seas are wet with latitude, and where will my name be writ? I have wealth that I have made. What tracks, this scratch my life has penned, on what scrolls of parchment the clear ink sets? Words, my alchemies. If I had the will, in my angers, I the destroyer, all oceans I would turn to sand. But I have wealth and conscience to cleave a phrase to strangle worlds. And who but I can so delight? It is the victor who holds the applauding quill, reclines into the soft of bedded history, and only he. My brother failed, the London Company gone. I have done what I have done. If hell has fire, let it run in flowing gold. Agony ever wills itself to life. If I could be again, I would not be myself, but slip to rescue in another's skin. Conscience makes all men mad. I am half my father's blood. We are all the stuff that we would betray.

How far the land recedes to memory, and the thoughts that once I crimed, fall from me to reveal a second skin. In Virginia, no slavery, but men sell men, and the thought of slavery a ghost that has not died. For servants still come in numbers mostly great enough, because, with a little luck and a little thrift, some rise to fortunes. One servant in three years bought his freedom, becoming rich enough to be elected to the council. Oh, Smith, it was as you wished, but all our dreams turn nightmare and we never sure until we awake. In Virginia wealth comes as a consequence of what we do, and not by birth. Yet, most servants are owned by those who had some wealth when first they arrived. Gold is a better seed than sweat, but not always in

Virginia. If servants will not come because they cannot rise, and the price of the weed falls, and we must harvest more land with more servants to keep our wealth, from where our servants? And slavery so close, and the West Indies so near. In all our contradictions, our course is set.

In London, have you heard, if so hear again, I was chosen for the king's Privy Council, my brother not so. His name still a scandal in the street. Fail once, fail always. It is for me alone, the honors and the laurels at my feet. How sweeps my hand. I am the master of what I am. But I do not walk my humanity well. To me the day comes as just another temper of the night. The sky above me cracks, its blackness splits. All my profusions are a sin. I sit to think. And where do I lay my head! On what do I believe? What stone is my pillow, what ashes are my bed? What did I not do that in that doing I would forget? How little those honors mean to me. I am a fleece, a cast of hollow consequence. What hopes have I not betrayed, to what gain this forfeit? My book of poems is from the press. Each line a husk, a shell of sorrows never felt. Empty, I proudly honor emptiness. But yet I have my fame, which I accept. Public comfort is but the confession of the weak.

But in truth, who am I, who once sold men? All my conscience is a plot of discontent, my thoughts, my pillories, my perfections not well placed. The stars lead us but to decay. Who am I in truth? Am I the damaged servant, or am I the saint? If my mind could come to blank and if I could thoughtless think a thought, then never would horror in its spirit rise and ghost me a fine havoc and drag me home.

Chapter Forty-nine

O BE OUR LIVES, the rumors now of war. Pirates attacked England's channel coast. An army raised. Ten thousand more to serve with the thousands already trained to fight against Spain on the continent. Everywhere alarms and fears, the coastal towns calling for more defenses and more ships. Ghostly Armadas set their sails down the seas of the imagination. Panic threaded on careless words. The king ordered ships manned and sailors, lit tapers in their hands, huddled behind the cannon mounts. But there were few books in England on seamanship.

All my recreations disappoint my loves, my immortality, and my savage princess. Would history have chanced a different gate had I taken her in my arms? Silence for silence in its refrain. Remembering the words of the old mariner, his advice about the sea and Drake's greatness at the wheel, or on the deck before the cheeks of the wind, the liquid mountains beneath the foam, gales screaming violence in the rigging and around the masts. I turned my mind to canvas tales and to the canticles of the sea. I shall tie your frenzy to a page, and read it, drowned in the syntax of my sculptured alchemies, and so I entitled my book *A Sea Grammar.* Mostly an expansion of my *An Accidence,* with that text being abandoned to an afterword. Willoughby and Saltonstall encouraged this new work, but for me a shield of sorrows. I could rarely dip my quill into the ink. I am a befouled of weightful thoughts.

Some weeks my nothing stared little to the gawk. Then a note from Sir Richard Willoughby inviting me to his grand mansion, surrounded by those ancient fields on which my father spent his toil to gain a sweat of coins. How many memories sleep that almost sleep, stilled in their closed eyed revelations, so stirred upon any familiarity? The moment of our youth never sets, it is paused, an awakening ever in the mind. A touch, a smell, a fabrication in a glance, its urgent hungers bloom upon the prompt.

The mansion moored into the landscapes, short grasses tight around the protruding sculls of rock, the rolling gentles of the hills, the house a promontory affixed as if by a gigantic will, its stoned landscapes raising a statued heraldry proclaiming of itself.

"My dear old friend. Our boyhoods, I wish them but to be again." Sir Richard in a mood of longings. "Come, I have much to say." We sat into the comforts of our chairs. Our polites spoken, then the quiet to reflect. "I have a letter for you from father. He wished you to receive it from my hands, and only from my hands, after a proper interval. Much in the world has intervened. The hour now has struck the fleeting key." Sir Richard leaned forward, placing a wax-sealed document on the table, pushing it across the polished wood, reflections on the hardened mirrors of its surface.

"Your father dead these many years," I spoke, taking the letter to my hands, breaking the seal. I read its tomb. Fair purpose not stitched enough to have a smile from a wound. "The confession confuses blood, but yet the murder is in the eye."

My thoughts complained, darted from the frightful suddens of the ink. I glanced in the shock. The window stared, glass the questions, distorted in the room. I looked at Sir Richard. "No flesh could sense the abiding rumor of this page. It quacks a joke but not, but yes. Its weight explains, his uncertain motivations. Did you know?"

"Brothers we have been, no fault of line or blood an impediment. Half-brothers, our childhood, were not we closer than any friends? And you ever with our father's protection."

"I am an estrangement. My sister? My brother?"

"They are not of our conversation." Sir Richard leaned forward. "Our father's love was ever yours."

Shadows wing to build a shadow's nest, their eggs profile but the air. "My mother, a whore?"

"Be not the hammer to pound yourself, your own splattered head. There is love, and consequences and responsibilities. It could not be. Let secrets keep."

"Did you know?"

"I have my own letter only recently given to me. Held these years for reasons I could not know. It is a peek thin of explanations." Sir Richard handed me his letter. "Our father always wished you treated as a brother, an easy task. Our influence always to your benefit, but every kitchen has its politics, and we sorrowed that we measured short."

And so we are a feather floating through our fouled philosophies. Our direction uncertain, coursed on breathful whims. I sat my thoughts. We spoke in nods of silence, our expression stumbled in dictionaries not quite readied for the tongue. A child to fathers never to be the one, my inner illuminations. I am birthed a secret noble, an exile from the line. I am that which I despise. Half a death. My mother bought, and did her husband know?

"To what father do I have claim?" I furied.

"All," said Sir Richard, standing, his hands on my shoulders. The curative of his word repeated, "All."

"None," I said. "I am a heresy born of night, willed of no alliance, sustained by whispers. I disclaim my blood." Anger a sore to reason, I wanted to do some hurt.

Sir Richard calmly spoke, "Brother, you are profound of many gifts. Forgive! The heart in silence opens to itself. Worlds still await. You were our greatest hope. Did not our grandfather's ghost speak to you, returning Arthur's ring to us? You are of the line. Be at peace."

All elections, estates, the pleasures that hazard of its blood, I disown. I am only of the earth, the New World, its whispers and its madness.

Chapter Fifty

THE SHARDS IN THEIR LAMENTATIONS.

 LOOKED UP FROM MY DESK and the pages beneath my quill. The ink coiled and spread its dark lines in salted grief. The darkness glowed its darkness in my room. I wondered if I had become my ink. My history spread in pages. My life its text. My desk had become a charnel house. Words spoken to me years ago sang in distant melodies, and how many lives had I lived only to die, to awaken, to die again. In one life, how much death is death enough? And I reborn to some different line. How many portions do we contemplate before we see the whole?

I am an exile from my eternities. Voices still, the river quelled to a foreign land. Its words mostly now a memory. Was it only my own voice that I heard? Some scrape of inner noise, a squeak of thought compelled to stand an angel for the dyings of a fool. But there is that yet, a child's vision of frozen kin, and longings no human could ever beast. And Drake, who married the land and sea, those nuptials now conjugate a voice. The motive done. Mysteries drink me to your clarity. Enthrall me in your wakefulness. The river does course alchemies, and on its bewildering lips such moistened depths, liquid in its narratives. We are its gifts given but to fade. Sounds that fracture air sculpt our words, but it is the ear that potentates and rules the theologies.

The book I was then writing was my *True Travels*, the expanded account of my wars and captivities with the Turks. It was now the end of the year 1628; news arrived from New England of that colony's success. More fleets to bring more populations. More towns to be built. Crops of many staples, fishing and even men who would work, gentlemen putting aside their pride for the general good. Profit sought, but not for the immediate gain, and no tobacco and its greed. No servant sold and forced to labor for years. A wilderness blooming without its smoke. The New World had come to some urgent split.

In March of 1629 the king signed such letters and patents to create the Massachusetts Bay Colony. And again, not an inch of land given to me as some reward. How accustomed I am to the usual neglect. Too old, too tired now to rage my sorrows into barbs and fling them at my circumstance. I laughed to think that perhaps our contemplations do make us wise, as if some poisons would make us deep. Chains are the rewards excuses give to their prisoners, not to twist too far.

My *True Travels* published in August of 1629. My friends had such satisfaction to see the tale. My enemies called it lies. One wit said, "In the book there were such overtruths, cut so large, their cloth hid continents in their opinions." But mostly my pastures were neglect. My circle never wide, but always someone new.

Brian O'Rourke, grandson of Brian Ballach, wild and Irish, was brought to England from his grandfather's castle to be raised as a gentleman, with the education and religion to meet the fashions of his station. Sent to prison after a St. Patrick's Day brawl in 1619, he was released by the king on the charms of a rhymed apology. O'Rourke, while in prison, still amassed debts. "A good dungeon makes a man appreciate his appetites," he said. Released, he was imprisoned once again for riots, debts and a little sedition. In 1627, O'Rourke owed seventy-six hundred pounds, which the king paid. "A wise ruler is one who knows the loyalties born of a good vice," O'Rourke winked. "I write ye a poem. The Irish and the English exile linked by bond stronger than any blood." I published the poem in my *True Travels*. From other friends I had other poems.

Sir Samuel Saltonstall was well pleased with the result, he who paid for the printing of my *Sea Grammar*. His cousin, Sir Richard Saltonstall, having led a company to Massachusetts in 1628. Sir Samuel gave me rooms as mine forever in his large estate. My library sent in crates to lie in its great halls, and I the lips of the last petal's kiss. Other invitations from other houses, I traveled as an exile lost in his alone. At the home of John Tradescant, he a merchant, having traveled in Muscovy and lands in Africa, a collector of books and of curiosities, he with galleries in his estate maintained as a museum. How powder falls from the dust of time. I walked in years down carved passages, John Tradescant by my side, through the doors. There, in the slants and ashes lit in Tradescant's museum, his curiosities were my life, and there on a pedestal of wood hung the robe Powhatan had given Newport in 1608, after Newport had placed a copper crown upon his head and made the old emperor overlord of his own country. Such ironies and pets and skirted fools we are. Blood is the only wine we taste in our self-love. And I had come to this, to be a witness in the mortuaries of my life. And there in that room I saw in ghost the whispers of her face. Oh, Pocahontas, my dreams have made you lifeless to my eyes. I touch with a shadow's touch. I sing of silence. I weep my books. Be my lips that I might speak again.

What strangeness this bloom that comes to me? The voices all about. John Tradescant showed me the shoes Newport gave to Powhatan and a cloak and other bits of rags and rugs and baskets, oddities of the stories now half-forgot. The currents of that river in my ears, the song of waters, and in those choirs the elegies of a passing age.

Who comes to me, comes only to confess. We are the whisper the shadows make. Tradescant having a message from George Sandys. "He wishes a secret word with you in my private rooms."

I knew that Sandys was an old friend of Tradescant, even sending some Virginia curiosities—arrows, war clubs, savage garments and the like—for his collection. So now Tradescant's invitation told its double purpose. He showed me through the rooms. Dust in pendulums moved upon the floor. In a darkened chair George Sandys sat, his face caught in the snare of candlelight. "I am told you have a narrative of Virginia, never seen but only rumored," he said.

"I am at work." I let the conversation lapse into its implications. Sandys wants to have his old letters before they are a printed book, I thought as I smiled. Clever we are only to our cleverness. Genius comes of a harsher brew. Sandys rose, his eyes in wilds darted in their glance. No, I decided, his imagination parades his sin. All brothers need a fellow to dissuade the dark and keep away the loneliness. Loneliness the greater grief than guilt. He needs a brother's brother, an imagined kin. What we the seekers seek is only to repair, we both by our confessions. He wills us to be the same. I to confess my madness, he to confess the rest. He more for punishment than I for need. To him the confession is but to glory in the crime.

And so my thoughts, but as he stepped toward me, sweat on his outstretched hand, his grasp upon my arm, gray lunacies in the tangles of his unkempt hair. "Boil your ink in my confessions. Publish my letters," he said. "I am trialed by a pudding, I am a slave to a spice. Tobacco is the philosopher's stone. It turns all things to itself. I am manacled to the weed. By a vegetable I am slain."

AGAIN IN MY ROOMS ON THE SALTONSTALL ESTATE, I SAT TO write my final book, *Advertisements for the Unexperienced Planters of New England, or Anywhere.* So much my life rounded me. The tale never fully told, I circled in its orbit, never touching of its lips. And how do we in our own false Edens fall again, ever repeating the repetitions of our fall? To break with our circumstance is a test. It is easier to cut the air. And so in this book I sat to the narrower view and gave some advice and some praise where it was due. I called against those in London never seeing Jamestown, men without practice who made the policy. Virginia the crucible for their conceits. Each year new policies, projects and advice, the ends forgotten in the means. Arguments and proposals, words to tear upon themselves, the direction never sure. All intent a whim run to be displaced upon a frown. How could this birth but monsters? All the reports to London were a slander to hide the truth. England is the cobble, her soles are leathered on the bench. I fed the colony, and then tobacco, and men rose up but to betray. The only profit was the only crop and the world fell to cataract and its smoke.

In New England, no tobacco. The world affirmed in its multitudes.

No servants broken to the wheel. This New World does hold our blood. We are no more an England to a single space, but yawn our centuries to the world. We are the memory of a thousand years, kissed to the eons of those new lands. In that brew we are tangled but to change. We shall be a people of a double birth. Our estates no station, our determination our title. By the crust of the world we shall be consumed, our wilderness is our breath, our exploration is ourselves. We are by mites by eons drawn, and Drake, who danced to whispers till he cast them down, and the London Council, which wanted conversions but sent instead criminals worse than any savage. So when the Indians rose to make themselves innocent again by murder, we unleashed the slaughter to have the lands to grow tobacco. Fair profits are a slower stew. The conversions were but masks, the puppet frowns and bows in empty gestures to excuse the Tobacco King.

And in all these lethal gestures, I am set aside and forgotten, my tale told dumb in telling. We are all the dance to the always tune. Will New England make the same mistakes? Do our prodigals birth but prodigals as they spawn. I held no hand as I came to sleep. The price of tobacco has begun to fall, more lands now to keep the wealth behind the closing prison gates. New England and Virginia in the scale's pans, and where the extra weight? And always the western sea calling in the mind. And the river's voice, its whispers eared to the silent key. And I drawn to the color in its depths, oh river drink me in your breath.

What gifts I was given when I was made werowance those years ago! Through me the leaves do fall in their autumn rest, their death caresses me. I wear again my buckskin and I am in their forest robes. I rise to touch her face, I hear the river's voice. All that is life is a raptured tear. I hold the hands of shadows as they pass. I am the alone. Pocahontas before me now offers me her voiceless mouth, and I do dream as breath to breath we press to search each other's lips in their satin wilderness, but it is a ghost—and I am left to live alone the remembrance of a memory.

My book completed in October of 1630, and given to the printer. I traveled to friends. I lived in houses, never having of my own, always returning to my rooms at the Saltonstall estate. So much distance, but only a world of beads compared with the centuries I have seen in that new land, where the landscape spreads its hourglass across the earth. My book was almost from the press. I knew I had failed, I knew I had not told enough. All about me now the whispers of words unsaid, of that love that had torn me asunder to make me whole. I rose again, mighty in my last savage, drinking my anointing dreams in tears, and I was once more as a *werowance*. The river whispered to my ears. I heard its current as a sigh of breath, its waters as a long soliloquy. "I am the river," it said, "I feel unclean. I eat of a strange stew. I run in maggots. I suffocate in my own breath. I am changed. I am not as I was."

In the Saltonstall house I lie and weaken in my borrowed bed, my books, the signposts of my life, about me on the floor. They watch in their blank stare as spirits of an unborn god. They rise from their hibernations to watch me fade as I write with my last quill in this my final testament!

Death not yet, insistent nonetheless. All this my search and in its compass is the grave. My pain its hollows feed the roots of flowers in their withered spring, and the philosopher's stone its magics haunt the memories of what we held and lost. I dream of a perfection that never was. Are all my thoughts but to quaint me to a sleep? Are we but passing wisps, as moistened breaths dispersed, a divine kiss in counterfeit? And so we suffer in the shallows of our human kind. The hymns we hear ever so far away.

·   ·   ·   ·   ·

Oh Drake, oh lost father, in ages forth
perhaps our dust shall speak.

CONCLUSION OF

In the Land of Whispers

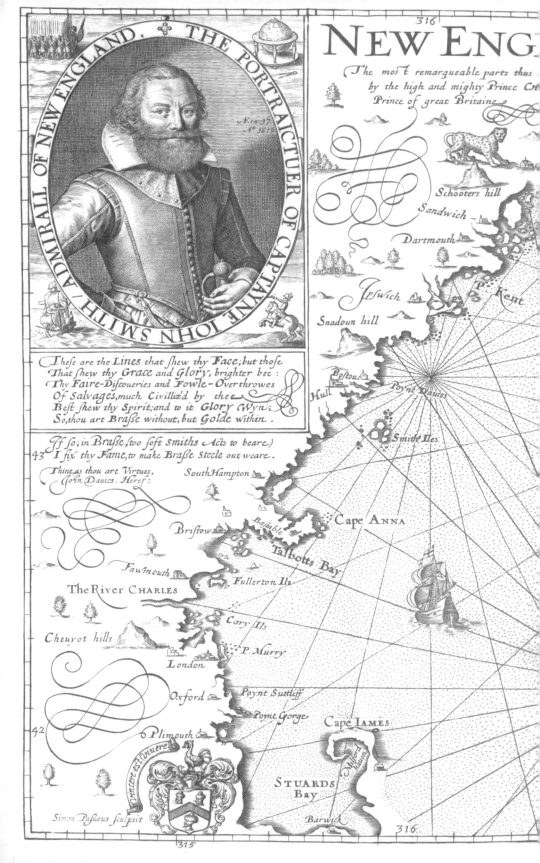

NEW ENG

The most remarqueable parts thus
by the high and mighty Prince Ch
Prince of great Britaine

THE PORTRAICTUER OF CAPTAYNE JOHN SMITH / ADMIRALL OF NEW ENGLAND.

Ætat 37. A° 1616

These are the Lines that shew thy Face; but those
That shew thy Grace and Glory, brighter bee:
Thy Faire-Discoueries and Fowle-Overthrowes
Of Salvages, much Civilliz'd by thee
Best shew thy Spirit; and to it Glory Wyn;
So, thou art Brasse without, but Golde within.

If so; in Brasse (too soft Smiths Acts to beare)
43 I fix thy Fame, to make Brasse Steele out weare.

Thine, as thou art Virtues,
John Dauies. Heref:

Simon Passaeus sculpsit

Schooters hill
Sandwich
Dartmouth
P. Kent
Jpswich
Snadoun hill
Bostou
Hull
Poynt Dauies
Smith Iles
SouthHampton
Cape ANNA
Bassable
Bristow
Talbotts Bay
Fawmouth
Fullerton Ils
The River CHARLES
Cary Ils
Cheuyot hills
P. Murry
London
Oxford
Poynt Suttliff
Poynt Gorge
Cape IAMES
Plimouth
Milford hauen
STUARDS Bay
Barwick

42